"Why did he come after us?" she asked. "I thought you shot him back at the camp."

"Obviously it wasn't enough to stop him."

"But he won't stop us."

"No, he won't." He started out of the culvert, but she took hold of his arm, turning him toward her.

"What—" She cut off the question, her lips on his, her body pressed against him. All the fear and anxiety and the giddy relief of being alive at this moment coalesced in that kiss.

He wrapped his arms around her, crushing her to him. Every kiss touched some vulnerable part of her, coaxing her to let go a little bit more, to surrender. To trust.

He rested his forehead against hers. "This isn't the best time for this," he said.

"I know. We have to go. I just... I wanted you to know how I felt."

"I got the message, loud and clear." He wrapped both hands around her wrists and kissed the tips of her fingers, a gesture which set her heart to fluttering

UNDERCOVER HUSBAND

BY
CINDI MYERS

First Published in Great Britain 2017
By Mills & Boon, an imprint of HarperCollins*Publishers*
1 London Bridge Street, London, SE1 9GF

© 2017 Cynthia Myers

ISBN: 978-0-263-92900-3

46-0717

Our policy is to use papers that are natural, renewable and recyclable products and made from wood grown in sustainable forests. The logging and manufacturing processes conform to the legal environmental regulations of the country of origin.

Printed and bound in Spain
by CPI, Barcelona

Cindi Myers is the author of more than fifty novels. When she's not crafting new romance plots, she enjoys skiing, gardening, cooking, crafting and daydreaming. A lover of small-town life, she lives with her husband and two spoiled dogs in the Colorado mountains.

Chapter One

"I was told you're the ones who can help me."

The soft, cultured voice as much as the words caught the attention of Bureau of Land Management special agent Walt Riley. The Ranger Brigade headquarters in Black Canyon of the Gunnison National Park didn't get many visitors, and certainly not many women as beautiful as the one standing on the opposite side of his desk now. Slender, with blond hair worn piled on top of her head, she spoke with an air of command, as if she was used to overseeing a corporation or running board meetings. Everything about her—from the designer sunglasses to the diamonds glinting at her earlobes to the toes of her high heels—looked expensive, and out of place in this part of rural Colorado, where jeans and boots were the most common attire for men and women alike.

Walt stood. "What do you need help with?" he asked. He selfishly hoped she wasn't merely a lost tourist or someone who needed a camping permit or something that was better handled by the park rangers in the office next door.

She opened the sleek leather satchel she had slung over one shoulder and pulled out a sheaf of papers and handed it to him. At first glance, it appeared to be some kind of legal document. "What is this?" he asked.

"It's a court order awarding me custody of my niece, Joy Dietrich." She removed the sunglasses and he found himself staring into a pair of intensely blue eyes, their beauty undimmed by the red rims and puffy lids, evidence that Miss Cool and Collected had, very recently, been crying. "I need your help getting her back from the people who have kidnapped her," she said.

This definitely was more serious than a camping permit. Walt dragged a chair over to his desk. "Why don't you sit down, Ms.—?"

"Dietrich. Hannah Dietrich." She sat, crossing her long legs neatly at the ankles. There was nothing particularly revealing about the gray slacks and matching jacket she wore, but she still managed to look sexy wearing them. Or maybe it was only that Walt had always had a thing for blue-eyed blondes.

"Wait here, Ms. Dietrich," he said. "I'm going to get my commanding officer and you can tell us your story."

He strode to the back of the building and poked his head around the open door of Commander Graham Ellison's office. The FBI agent, who still carried himself like the marine he had once been, broke off his conversation with DEA agent Marco Cruz. Elsewhere in the office or out in the field, officers from Immigration and Customs Enforcement, Customs and Border Protection, and Colorado State Patrol worked together to fight crime on thousands of acres of public land in the southwest corner of Colorado. Walt, one of the newest members of the Ranger team, had jumped at the opportunity to be involved in the kind of high-profile cases the Rangers were becoming known for. A kidnapping would definitely qualify as high-profile. "Something up, Walt?" Graham asked.

"There's a woman out here who says she needs our help recovering her kidnapped niece," Walt said. "Before I had her run through the whole story, I thought you might like to hear it."

"Who does she say kidnapped her niece?" Marco, one of the senior members of the Ranger Brigade, had a reputation as an expert tracker and a cool head in even the tensest situations. Walt hadn't had a chance to work with him yet, but he had heard plenty of stories from others on the team.

"We haven't gotten that far yet," Walt said.

"Let's hear what she has to say." Graham led the way back to Walt's desk, where Hannah Dietrich waited. If the prospect of being confronted by three lawmen unsettled her, she didn't show it. "Ms. Dietrich, this is Commander Graham Ellison and Agent Marco Cruz."

"Hello." She nodded, polite but reserved. "I hope you'll be able to help me."

"Why don't you tell us more about your situation?" Graham pulled up a second chair, while Marco stood behind him. Walt perched on the corner of the desk. "You say your niece was kidnapped?"

"In a manner of speaking."

"What manner would that be?" Marco crossed his arms over his chest.

"I think it would be best if I began at the beginning." She smoothed her hands down her thighs and took a deep breath. "I have—had—a sister, Emily. She's six years younger than me, and though we have always been close, in temperament we're very different. She was always carefree, impulsive and restless."

Nothing about Hannah Dietrich looked restless or impulsive, Walt thought. Even obviously distressed as she was, the word she brought to mind was *control*. She controlled her feelings and she was used to being in control of her life.

"About a year ago, Emily met a man, Raynor Gilbert," Hannah continued. "He was working as a bouncer at a club in Denver that she used to frequent, and they became lovers. She found out she was pregnant, and they had plans to marry, but he was killed in a motorcycle accident only a week after Emily learned she was expecting." She paused a moment, clearly fighting for composure, then continued.

"My sister was devastated, and acted out her grief with even more impulsive behavior. I wanted her to come live with me, but she refused. She said she wanted a different life for herself and her child. She attended a rally by a group that calls themselves the Family. Their leader is a very handsome, charismatic man named Daniel Metwater."

"We know about Metwater." Graham's expression was grim. Metwater and his "family" had a permit to camp in the Curecanti National Recreation Area, adjacent to the national park and part of the Rangers' territory. Though Metwater had recently been eliminated as the chief suspect in a murder investigation, the Rangers continued to keep a close watch on him and his followers.

"Then you are probably aware that he recruits young people to join his group, promising them peace and harmony and living close to nature," Hannah said. "His message appealed to my sister, who I believe was looking for an excuse to run away from her life for a while."

"When was the baby—Joy—born?" Walt asked.

Her eyes met his, softening a little—because he had remembered the child's name? "She was born a little over three months ago. Emily sent me a letter with a photograph. She said the baby was healthy, but I know my sister well enough to read between the lines. I sensed she wasn't happy. She said things had been hard, though she didn't provide any details, and she said she wanted to come home for a visit but didn't know if the Prophet—that's what this Metwater person calls himself—would allow it. I would have gone to her right away, but her letter gave no clue as to where she was located. She said the Family was moving soon and she would write me again when they were settled."

"Did she usually contact you via letter instead of calling or texting or emailing?" Walt asked.

"Apparently, one condition of being a part of this group is giving up electronic devices like computers and cell phones," Hannah said. "I don't know if all the members comply with that restriction, but Hannah was very serious about it. Shortly after she joined the group, she wrote and told me we could only communicate through letters."

"Did that alarm you?" Graham asked.

"Of course it did." A hint of annoyance sharpened Hannah's voice. "I wrote back immediately and tried to persuade her that a group that wanted its members to cut off contact with family and friends had to be dangerous—but that letter came back marked Return to Sender. It was months before I heard anything else from Emily, and that was the letter informing me of Joy's birth. In the interim, I was worried sick."

She opened the satchel once more and withdrew an

envelope. "Then, only two weeks after the letter announcing Joy's birth came, I received this." She handed the envelope to Walt. He pulled out two sheets of lined paper, the left edge ragged where the pages had been torn out of a notebook.

"'I'm very afraid. I don't think anyone can help me,'" Walt read out loud. "'If anything happens to me, promise you will take care of Joy.'" He looked at Hannah. "What did you do when you received this?"

"I was frantic to find her. I hired a private detective, and he was able to track down Metwater and his followers, but they told him there was no one in the group who fit my sister's description and they knew nothing. Look at the other paper, please."

Walt handed the first sheet to Graham and scanned the second sheet. "Is this a will?" he asked.

"Yes. It names me as Joy's guardian in the event of Emily's death. I was able to have a court certify it as legal and grant me custody."

"How did you do that?" Graham asked. "Without proof of your sister's death?"

"I was able to find proof." She brought out another envelope and handed it to the commander. "Here are copies of my sister's death certificate, as well as a birth certificate for her daughter."

Graham read the documents. "This says she died in Denver, of respiratory failure." He frowned. "Did your sister have a history of respiratory problems?"

"She had suffered from asthma off and on for most of her life, but it was well controlled with medication. She never had to be hospitalized for it."

"Do you have any idea what she was afraid of?"

Walt asked. "Did she specifically say that Metwater or anyone else threatened her?"

Hannah shook her head. "She didn't. But I know my sister. Emily was a lot of things, but she wasn't the nervous type and she wasn't a drama queen. She was truly terrified of something, and I think it had to do with Metwater and his cult."

Walt scanned the will again. His attention rested on the signatures at the bottom of the page. "This says the will was witnessed by Anna Ingels and Marsha Caldwell."

"Marsha Caldwell was a nurse at the hospital where Joy was born," Hannah said. "She left when her husband was transferred overseas, so I haven't been able to talk to her. And I wasn't able to determine who Anna Ingels is."

"Maybe she's one of Metwater's followers," Walt said.

"Except that most of them don't use their real names," Marco said. "It makes tracking them down more difficult."

"But not impossible," Graham said. He shuffled the papers in his hand. "This birth certificate says your niece was born in Denver. Have you talked with anyone there?"

"The hospital wouldn't give me any information, and the PI wasn't able to find out anything, either." She shifted in her chair, as if impatient. "When I talked to the local sheriff's office, they said the area where Metwater is camping is your jurisdiction," she said. "All I need is for you to go with me to get Joy."

"You haven't tried to make contact with them on your own?" Graham asked.

She shook her head. "The private detective I hired paid them a visit. That's when they refused to admit they had ever known Emily or that Joy even existed. He told me the conditions in their camp are pretty rough—that it isn't the place for an infant." She pressed her lips together, clearly fighting to maintain her composure. "I don't want to waste any more time. I thought it would be better to show up with law enforcement backing. I know this Metwater preaches nonviolence, but my sister was genuinely afraid for her life. Why else would she have made a will at her age?"

"It doesn't seem out of line for a new parent to want to appoint a guardian for her child," Marco said. "Maybe she was merely being prudent."

"One thing my sister was not was prudent," Hannah said.

Unlike Hannah herself, Walt thought. He certainly knew how different siblings could be. "May I see the birth certificate?" he asked.

Graham passed it to him, then addressed Hannah. "Do you have a picture of your niece?"

"Only the newborn photo my sister sent." She slipped it from the satchel and handed it to him. Graham and Marco looked at it, then passed it to Walt.

He studied the infant's wrinkled red face in the oversize pink bonnet. "I don't think this is going to be much help in identifying a three-month-old," he said.

"We can go to Metwater and demand he hand over the child," Graham said. "But if he refuses to admit she even exists, it could be tougher."

"You can't hide an infant for very long," Hannah said. "Someone in the camp—some other mother, perhaps—knows she exists."

"What makes you think Metwater's group has her?" Marco asked. "It's possible she ended up with Child Welfare and Protection in Denver after your sister's death."

"I checked with them. They have no record of her. I'm sure she's still with Metwater and his group."

"Why are you so sure?" Walt asked.

Her expression grew pinched. "Take another look at her birth certificate."

Walt studied the certificate, frowning.

"What is it?" Marco asked.

Walt looked up from the paper, not at his fellow officers, but at Hannah. "This says the child's father is Daniel Metwater."

HANNAH HELD HERSELF very still, willing herself not to flinch at the awful words. "That's a lie," she said. "Emily was pregnant long before she ever met Daniel Metwater, and I know she was in a relationship with Raynor Gilbert. I have pictures of them together, and I talked to people at the club where he worked." The conversations had been excruciating, having to relive her sister's happiness over the baby and being in love, and then the grief when her dream of a storybook future was destroyed by Raynor's death. "They all say he and Emily were together—that he was the father of her baby. A simple DNA test will prove that."

"Yet the court was willing to grant you custody of the child?" Graham asked.

"Temporary custody," she said. "Pending outcome of the DNA test. Believe me, Commander, Daniel Metwater is not Joy's father. Her father was Raynor Gilbert and he's dead."

"Let us do some investigating and see what we can find out," Graham said. "But even if we locate an infant of the appropriate sex and age in the camp, unless Metwater and his followers admit it's your sister's child, we won't be able to do anything. If some other woman is claiming to be the infant's mother, you may have to go back to court to request the DNA testing before we can seize the child."

She stood, so abruptly her chair slid back with a harsh protest, and her voice shook in spite of her willing it not to. "If you won't help me, I'll get the child on my own."

"How will you do that?" Walt asked.

"I'll pretend I want to join the group. Once I'm living with them, I can find Joy and I'll leave with her."

She braced herself for them to tell her she couldn't do that. Their expressions told her plainly enough that's what they were thinking—at least what the commander and Agent Cruz thought. Agent Riley looked a little less stern. "You've obviously given this some thought," he said.

"I will do anything to save my niece," she said. "I had hoped to do this with law enforcement backing, but if necessary, I will go into that camp and steal her back. And I dare you and anyone else to try to stop me."

Chapter Two

Daniel Metwater and his followers had definitely chosen a spot well off the beaten path for their encampment. After an hour's drive over washboard dirt roads, Walt followed Marco down a narrow footpath, across a plank bridge over a dry arroyo, to a homemade wooden archway that proclaimed Peace in crooked painted lettering. "Looks like they've made themselves at home," Walt observed.

"They picked a better spot this time." Marco glanced back at Walt. "You didn't see the first camp, did you?"

Walt shook his head. While several members of the team had visited Metwater's original camp as part of the murder investigation, he had been assigned to other duties.

"It was over in Dead Horse Canyon," Marco said. "No water, not many trees and near a fairly popular hiking trail." He looked around the heavily wooded spot alongside a shallow creek. "This is less exposed, with access to water and wood."

"Their permit is still only for two weeks," Walt said.

"There's plenty of room in the park for them to move around," Marco said. "And Metwater has some kind of influence with the people who issue the permits. They appear happy to keep handing them out to him."

A bearded young man, barefoot and dressed only in a pair of khaki shorts, approached. "Hello, Officers," he said, his expression wary. "Is something wrong?"

"We're here to see Mr. Metwater," Marco said.

"I'll see if the Prophet is free to speak with you," the man said.

"I think he understands by now it's in his best interest to speak with us," Marco said.

He didn't wait for the young man to answer, but pushed past him and continued down the trail.

The camp itself was spread out in a clearing some fifty yards from the creek—a motley collection of tents and trailers and homemade shelters scattered among the trees. A large motor home with an array of solar panels on the roof stood at one end of the collection. "That's Metwater's RV," Marco said, and led the way toward it.

Walt followed, taking the opportunity to study the men and women, and more than a few children, who emerged from the campers and tents and trailers to stare at the two lawmen. More than half the people he saw were young women, several with babies or toddlers in their arms or clinging to their skirts. The men he saw were young also, many with beards and longer hair, and all of them regarded him and Marco with expressions ranging from openly angry to guarded.

Marco rapped on the door to the large motor home. After a few seconds, the door eased open, and a strikingly beautiful, and obviously pregnant, blonde peered out at them. "Hello, Ms. Matheson." Marco touched the brim of his Stetson. "We'd like to speak to Mr. Metwater."

Frowning at the pair of officers, she opened the door wider. "I don't know why you people can't leave him alone," she said.

Walt had heard plenty about Andi Matheson, though he hadn't met her before. Her lover was the man murdered outside the Family's camp, and her father, a US senator, had been involved in the crime. She was perhaps the most famous of Metwater's followers, and apparently among those closest to him.

"We need to ask him some questions." Marco moved past her. Walt followed, nodding to Andi as he passed, but she had already looked away, toward the man who was entering from the back of the motor home.

Daniel Metwater had the kind of presence that focused the attention of everyone in the room on him. A useful quality for someone who called himself a prophet, Walt thought. Metwater was in his late twenties or early thirties, about five-ten or five-eleven, with shaggy dark hair and piercing dark eyes, and pale skin that showed a shadow of beard even in early afternoon. He wore loose linen trousers and a white cotton shirt unbuttoned to show defined abs and a muscular chest. He might have been a male model or a pop singer instead of an itinerant evangelist. "Officers." He nodded in greeting. "To what do I owe this pleasure?"

"We're looking for an infant," Marco said. "A little girl, about three months old."

"And what—you think this child wandered in here on her own?" Metwater smirked.

"Her mother was a follower of yours—Emily Dietrich," Marco said.

Metwater frowned, as if in thought, though Walt suspected the expression was more for show. "I don't recall a disciple of mine by that name," he said.

Walt turned to Andi. "Did you know Emily?" he asked.

She shook her head.

"What about Anna Ingels?" Walt asked.

Something flickered in her eyes, but she quickly looked away, at Metwater. "We don't have anyone here by that name, either," Metwater said.

"I asked Miss Matheson if she knows—or knew—of an Anna Ingels." Walt kept his gaze fixed on Andi.

"No," she said.

"Asteria, you may leave us now," Metwater said.

Andi—whose Family name was apparently Asteria—ducked her head and hurried out of the room. Metwater turned back to the Rangers. "What does any of this have to do with your missing infant?" he asked.

"Her aunt, Hannah Dietrich, came to us. She thinks her sister's child is here in this camp," Marco said. "She has legal custody of the baby and would like to assume that custody."

"If she believes this child is here, she's been misinformed," Metwater said.

"Then you won't mind if we look around," Walt said.

"We have a number of children here in the camp," Metwater said. "But none of them are the one you seek. I can't allow you to disrupt and upset my followers this way. If you want to search the camp, you'll have to get a warrant."

"This child's birth certificate lists you as the father," Marco said.

Metwater smiled, a cold look that didn't reach his

eyes. "A woman can put anything she likes on a birth certificate," he said. "That doesn't make it true."

"Are you the father of any of the children in the camp?" Walt asked.

"I am father to all my followers," Metwater said.

"Is that how your followers—all these young women—see you?" Marco asked.

"My relationship to my disciples is a spiritual one," Metwater said. He half turned away. "You must excuse me now. I hope you find this child, wherever she is."

Walt's eyes met Marco's. The DEA agent jerked his head toward the door. "What do you think the odds are that his relationship with all these women is merely spiritual?" Walt asked once they were outside.

"About the same as the odds no one in this camp has a record or something they'd like to hide," Marco said.

"It does seem like the kind of group that would attract people who are running away from something," Walt said.

"Yeah. And everything Metwater says sounds like a lie to me," Marco said. He turned to leave, but Walt put out a hand to stop him.

"Let's talk to those women over there." He nodded toward a group of women who stood outside a grouping of tents across the compound. One of them stirred a pot over an open fire, while several others tended small children.

"Good idea," Marco said.

The women watched the Rangers' approach with wary expressions. Walt zeroed in on an auburn-haired woman who cradled an infant. "Hi," he said. "What's your baby's name?"

"Adore." She stroked a wisp of hair back from the baby's forehead.

"I think my niece is about that age," Walt said. "How old is she? About three months, right?"

"*He* is five months old," the woman said frostily, and turned away.

The other women silently gathered the children and went inside the tent, leaving Marco and Walt alone. "I guess she schooled you," Marco said.

"Hey, it was worth a try." He glanced around the camp, which was now empty. "What do we do now?"

"Let's get out of here." Marco led the way down the path back toward the parking area. They met no one on the trail, and the woods around them were eerily silent, with no birdsong or chattering of squirrels, or even wind stirring the branches of trees.

"Do you get the feeling we're being watched?" Walt asked.

"I'm sure we are," Marco said. "Metwater almost always has a guard or two watching the entrance to the camp."

"For a supposedly peaceful, innocent bunch, they sure are paranoid," Walt said. What did they have to fear in this remote location, and what did they have to protect?

Their FJ Cruiser with the Ranger Brigade emblem sat alone in the parking lot. Before they had taken more than a few steps toward it, Walt froze. "What's that on the windshield?" he asked.

"It looks like a note." Marco pulled out his phone and snapped a few pictures, then they approached slowly, making a wide circle of the vehicle first.

Walt examined the ground for footprints, but the

hard, dry soil showed no impressions. Marco took a few more close-up shots, and plucked the paper—which looked like a sheet torn from a spiral notebook—carefully by the edges. He read it, then showed it to Walt. The handwriting was an almost childish scrawl, the letters rounded and uneven, a mix of printing and cursive. "'All the children here are well cared for and loved,'" he read. "'No one needs to worry. Don't cause us any trouble. You don't know what you're doing.'"

He looked at Marco. "What do you think?"

"I'm wondering if the same person who left the note also left that." He gestured toward the driver's door of the cruiser, from which hung a pink baby bonnet, ribbons hanging loose in the still air.

"I'M SURE THIS is the same bonnet that's in the picture Emily sent me." Hannah fingered the delicate pink ribbons, the tears she was fighting to hold back making her throat ache. "Whoever left this must have wanted to let us know that Joy is there and that she's all right." She looked into Walt Riley's eyes, silently pleading for confirmation. The idea that anything might have happened to her niece was unbearable.

"We don't know why the bonnet was left," he said, his voice and his expression gentle. "But I agree that it looks very like the one in the picture you supplied us."

"What will you do now?" She looked at the trio of concerned faces. Agent Cruz and their commander had once again joined Walt to interview her at Ranger headquarters. She had broken the speed limit on the drive from her hotel when Walt had called and asked her to stop by whenever it was convenient.

"We're attempting to obtain a warrant to search the

camp for your niece," the commander said. "We've also contacted Child Welfare and Protection to see if they've had any calls about the camp and might know anything."

That was it? When she had come to the Ranger office for help, she had expected them to immediately go with her to the Family's camp and take the child. When they had insisted on visiting the camp alone, she had held on to the hope that they would return with Joy. But they had done nothing but talk and ask questions. They seemed more interested in paperwork than in making sure Joy was safely where she belonged. "What am I supposed to do in the meantime?" she asked. "Just sit and wait?" And worry.

"I'm sorry to say that's all you can do right now," Agent Riley said. "Rushing in there on your own won't do anything but put Metwater and his people on the defensive. They might even leave the area."

"Then you could stop them," she said.

"On what grounds?" the commander asked. "So far we have no proof they've committed any crime."

"They have a child who doesn't belong to them, who isn't related to them in any way. A helpless infant." A child who was all she had left of her beloved sister.

"If they do have your niece, we don't have any reason to think they've harmed her or intend to harm her." Agent Riley reclaimed her attention with his calm voice and concerned expression. "The children we've seen in camp look well cared for, though we'll verify that with CWP."

"You're right." She clenched her hands in her lap and forced herself to take a deep breath. "Patience isn't one of my strong suits." Especially when it came to a baby.

So much could go wrong, and could anyone who wasn't family watch over her as carefully as Hannah would?

"Go back to your hotel now," the commander said. "We'll be in touch." He and Agent Cruz left, leaving her alone with Agent Riley.

"I'll walk you to your car," he said.

"You didn't have to walk with me," she said, after they had crossed the gravel lot to the compact car she had rented at the Montrose airport. A brisk wind sent dry leaves skittering over the gravel and tugged strands of hair from her updo. She brushed the hair from her eyes and studied him, trying to read the expression behind his dark sunglasses.

"I wanted to talk to you a little more. Away from the office." He glanced back toward the low beige building that was Ranger headquarters. "Having to talk to a bunch of cops makes some people nervous."

"As opposed to talking to only one cop."

"Try to think of me as a guy who's trying to help."

"All right." She crossed her arms over her stomach. "What do you want to know?"

"I'm trying to figure out what Daniel Metwater stands to gain by claiming your niece is his daughter," he said. "Understanding people's motives is often helpful in untangling a crime."

"I imagine you know more about the man than I do. He's been living in this area for what, almost a month now?"

"About that. Is it possible your sister listed him as Joy's father without his knowledge?"

"Why would she do that?"

"You said she was one of his followers. He refers

to himself as a father to his disciples. Maybe she was trying to honor that."

She studied the ground at her feet, the rough aggregate of rocks and dirt in half a dozen shades of red and brown. She might have been standing on Mars, for all she felt so out of her depth. "I don't know what my sister was thinking. As much as I loved her, I didn't understand her. She lived a very different life."

"Where do you live? I haven't even asked."

"Dallas. I'm a chemist." The expression on his face almost made her laugh. "Never play poker, Agent Riley."

"All right, I'll admit I'm surprised," he said. "I've never met a female chemist before. Come to think of it, I may never have met a chemist before."

His grin, so boyish and almost bashful, made her heart skip a beat. She put her hand to her chest, as if to calm the irregular rhythm. "My job doesn't put me in contact with very many law enforcement officers, either." Impulsively, she reached out and touched his arm. "You'll let me know the minute you know anything about Joy? Call me anytime—even if it's the middle of the night."

He covered her hand with his own. The warmth and weight of that touch seeped into her, steadying her even as it made her feel a little off balance. "I will," he said. "And try not to worry. It may not seem like it, but we are doing everything we can to help you."

"I want to believe that." She pulled her hand away, pretending to fuss with the clasp of her handbag. "I'm used to being in charge, so it's not always easy to let someone else take over."

"Let us know if you think of anything that might be helpful."

"I will." They said goodbye and she got into her car and drove away. For the first time since coming to Colorado, she wasn't obsessing over Joy and Emily and the agonizing uncertainty of her situation. Instead, she was remembering the way it felt when Agent Walt Riley put his hand on hers. They had connected, something that didn't happen too often for her. She had come into this situation thinking she was the only one who could save her niece. Maybe she wasn't quite so alone after all.

WALT SPENT EVERY spare moment over the next twenty-four hours working on Hannah's case. Though he prided himself on being a hard worker, the memory of Hannah's stricken face when he had last seen her drove him on. The afternoon of the second day, the Ranger team met to report on their various activities. Everyone was present except Montrose County sheriff's deputy Lance Carpenter, who was on his honeymoon but expected back later in the week, and Customs and Border Protection agent Michael Dance, who was following up a lead in Denver. After listening to a presentation by veteran Ranger Randall Knightbridge on a joint effort with Colorado Parks and Wildlife to catch poachers operating in the park, and a report from Colorado Bureau of Investigation officer Carmen Redhorse on an unattended death in the park that was ruled a suicide, Walt stood to address his fellow team members.

After a brief recap of Hannah's visit and his and Marco's foray into Metwater's camp, he consulted his notes. "I've gone over the documents Ms. Dietrich supplied us. We couldn't lift any useful prints from the letter or the will. Nothing on the note that was left at the camp, or the bonnet, either. I contacted the Denver hospital where the baby was born—the hat isn't one of theirs. They think the mother probably brought it with her, and they can't give out any information on patients. We're trying to reach the nurse who was one of the witnesses on Emily Dietrich's will, Marsha Caldwell. She is reportedly living in Amsterdam now, where her husband recently transferred for work, but I haven't gotten a response yet. We haven't had any luck locating the other witness, Anna Ingels."

"I talked to a contact at Child Welfare and Protection and she had nothing for me," Carmen said. "They did send a social worker to visit the camp a couple of weeks after Metwater and his group arrived here, but they found no violations. They said all the children appeared to be well cared for."

"And I don't guess they noted any baby crawling around with no mother to claim her," Ethan Reynolds, another of the new recruits to the Ranger Brigade, quipped.

"We got word a few minutes ago that the judge is denying our request for a warrant to search the camp," Graham said.

The news rocked Walt back on his heels, as if he'd been punched. "What was their reasoning?" he asked.

"We didn't present enough evidence to justify the search," the captain said. "At least in their eyes. The judge feels—and this isn't the first time I've heard this—that the Ranger Brigade's continued focus on Metwater and his followers is tantamount to harassment."

"This doesn't come from us," Randall said. "Ms.

Dietrich came to us. She's the one who made the accusations against Metwater. We weren't harassing him. We were following up on her claim."

"And we found nothing," Graham said. He looked across the table and met Walt's steady gaze. "As long as Metwater and his people deny the baby exists, our hands are tied. There's nothing else we can do."

Chapter Three

Protests rose from all sides of the conference table after Graham's pronouncement. "We need to go back to the judge and try again," Michael Dance said.

"I can talk to Child Welfare and Protection," Carmen said. "Ask them to take another look."

"Unless we have CWP on our side, we're not going to get anywhere with this," Randall Knightbridge said.

Walt raised his voice to be heard over the clamor. "There's still something we can do, even without a warrant," he said.

Conversation died and everyone turned to look at him. "What do you have in mind?" Marco asked.

"I think we should do what Hannah suggested and infiltrate the group." Walt said.

"You mean, send someone in undercover to determine if the baby is really there?" Carmen asked.

"And maybe find out what really happened to the child's mother," Walt said. "Hannah said her sister was afraid for her life—maybe there's more to this story that we need to find out."

"It's not a bad idea," Graham said. "I've thought of it before, if only to get a better sense of what Metwater is up to."

"It could backfire, big time," said Simon Woolridge, tech expert and Immigration and Customs Enforcement agent. "If Metwater figures out what we're doing, he could take it to the press and gain a lot of traction with his claims that we're harassing him."

"He won't find out," Walt said. "Not if we do it right."

"By 'we' you mean who?" Graham asked.

Walt squared his shoulders. "I could go," he said. "I've done undercover work before."

"They'd recognize you," Marco said. "We were just at the camp this morning."

"I'd dye my hair and grown out my beard, and dress differently. They wouldn't recognize me as the lawman they saw one time."

"How are you going to know you found the right baby?" Carmen asked.

"Hannah Dietrich could come with me. I could say she's my sister."

"That won't work," Simon said. "You two don't look anything alike."

"Say she's your wife," Randall said. "From what we've seen, couples sometimes join Metwater's Family together."

"I could do that," Walt said. "If she agrees."

"You heard her," Marco said. "She'll do anything to save her niece."

"Talk to her," Graham said. "See what she says. But she has to agree to follow your lead and proceed with caution. And if you get in there and learn there's a real danger, you get out. No heroics."

"Yes, sir." He didn't want to be a hero. He only wanted to make things right for Hannah and her niece.

HANNAH HAD LOST the plot thread of the movie playing on the television in her hotel room an hour ago, but she left it on, grateful at least for the background noise that helped to make the room a little less forlorn. She glanced toward the porta-crib and the diaper bag in the corner of the room and felt a tight knot in her chest. Had she been naive to believe she would be bringing Joy back here last night, before heading back home to Dallas today? Now she was trapped in this awful limbo, not knowing when—or even if—she would see her niece.

A knock on the door startled her. She punched the remote to shut off the TV and moved to the door. A glimpse through the peephole showed Walt Riley, dressed not in his khaki uniform, but in jeans and a white Western-cut shirt. With trembling hands, she unfastened the security chain and opened the door. "Has something happened?" she asked. "Do you have news?"

"Hello, Ms. Dietrich," he said. "Can I come in? There are some things we need to talk about."

"All right." She stepped back and let him walk past her into the room. She caught the scent of him as he passed—not cologne, but a mixture of starch and leather that seemed imminently masculine.

He crossed the small room and sat in the only chair. She perched on the edge of the bed, her stomach doing nervous somersaults. "Were you able to get the warrant to search the camp?" she asked.

"No." He rested his hands on his knees. Large hands, bronzed from working in the sun, with short nails and no jewelry. "The judge didn't feel we had sufficient grounds to warrant a search. Metwater has complained we're harassing him, and the court is taking that complaint seriously."

"What about Child Welfare and Protection? Would they support you? Or go to the camp to look for Joy?"

He shook his head. "CWP says there aren't any problems at the camp. They would have no reason to be there."

She felt as if she had swallowed an anvil. The weight of it pressed her down on the bed. "What am I going to do now?" she asked.

"We've come up with a plan."

She leaned toward him. "What is it?"

"It's your plan, really. We'll send two people in, posing as a husband and wife who are interested in joining the Family. That will give us the opportunity to determine, first, if there is even an infant matching the description of your niece in the camp, and if her mother is there or not. We also hope to determine the circumstances surrounding your sister's death."

"I want to go. I want to be the woman."

"We're not talking a quick overnight visit," he said. "It could take weeks to gain their trust and learn anything of real value."

"I've taken a leave of absence from my job. I have however much time it takes."

"You said you're a chemist? Is your employer willing to let you off work indefinitely?"

"I'm very good at my job and I've been there a long time. I have savings and not many expenses. And when Joy comes to live with me, I intend to take family leave to spend time with her." She hoped that would give her enough time to adjust to being a mother—something she had never planned on being, but now wanted more desperately than she had wanted almost anything. "I want to do this, Agent Riley. I want to help find my niece."

"If you do this, you have to agree to follow the direction of the male agent who would be posing as your husband," he said. "You can't take any action without his knowledge and you have to agree to abide by his decisions."

She stiffened. "I'm not used to other people making decisions for me."

"Obviously not. But in this case it would be vital. As law enforcement officers, we're trained to put together a case against someone that will stand up in court. If Daniel Metwater and his followers have kidnapped your niece, or if they had anything to do with your sister's death, we want to be sure we can build a solid case against them that will lead to a conviction."

What he said made sense, and she had always been good at following rules, as long as she saw a good reason for them. "All right. I can respect that," she said. "Who is the male agent?"

"That would be me."

She sat back a little, letting the words sink in. Relief that she wouldn't have to work with a stranger warred with the definite attraction that shimmered between them. She didn't need to be distracted right now. She had to focus on Joy, and the future they were going to have together. But what choice did she have? If she refused to work with Walt Riley just because she could imagine sleeping with him, wasn't she being foolish, and maybe even a coward? They were two adults. Surely they could control themselves. In any case, he had given no indication that he felt the same attraction to her. "All right," she said. "What do we do next?"

"Why don't we start by going out to dinner?"

Yet again, this man had caught her off guard. "Are you asking me on a date?"

"If we're going to pass ourselves off as husband and wife, we need to know more about each other and get comfortable in each other's presence."

He was right, of course. "All right."

He stood and held out his hand. When she took it, he pulled her up beside him. "Why don't you start by calling me Walt?"

"All right. Walt." It wasn't so hard here, in the intimacy of her hotel room, to think of him by his first name. A simple and strong name, like the man himself. "You should call me Hannah."

"It's a nice name."

"I think so. I don't understand why so many of Metwater's followers feel compelled to take new names."

"It could be the symbolism of starting over, taking on a new identity," he said. "It's also a convenient way to make yourself harder to track down if you're wanted for a crime, or have something else in your past that you don't want to come out." He held the door as she walked through, then followed her outside. "Did your sister take a new name when she joined the group?"

"I don't know. She never mentioned it." She glanced over her shoulder at him. "I feel terrible that I don't know more about what my sister was doing in the last months of her life. A year ago, I would have said I knew her well, but so many times now, she feels like a stranger to me. It's depressing. You'd think if you could know anyone well, it would be a sibling."

"I think we're most surprised when family members behave in unexpected ways," he said. "It feels more personal, I guess. More like a betrayal."

"Yes." He opened the passenger-side door to his Cruiser and she climbed inside. He put a hand on her shoulder, as if making sure she was safely settled before he shut the door behind her. Again, she felt that current of connection with him. She hadn't felt anything like that—or rather, she hadn't allowed herself to feel it—for a very long time. Maybe losing Emily had made her more vulnerable. Or finding Joy. So many things in her life felt out of control these days, it shouldn't have surprised her that her emotions would betray her, too.

THERE WERE DEFINITELY worse ways to spend an evening than sitting across the table from a beautiful woman, Walt thought, once he and Hannah had settled into a booth at a local Italian place. More than one male head had turned to watch Hannah walk across the room, though maybe only Walt saw the fatigue and worry that lurked in her sapphire-blue eyes. He wished he had the power to take that worry and fatigue away from her.

"Tell me about yourself," he said, once they had placed their orders. "How long have you lived in Dallas?"

"Ten years. I took the job there after I got my master's at Rice University in Houston."

"So you're beautiful and brilliant. I'm already out of my league."

She sipped her iced tea and regarded him over the rim of the glass. "I don't know about that."

"Trust me, it's true," he said. "I have a bachelor's

degree from the University of New Mexico and was solidly in the middle of my class. And while I'm sure there are a few professions less glamorous than law enforcement, patrolling the backcountry of public lands is about as far away from a corporate suite as you can get."

"Your job doesn't sound boring, though."

"You might be surprised how boring it can be sometimes. But mostly, it is interesting."

"What drew you to the work?" She relaxed back against the padded booth, some of the tension easing from around her eyes.

"I like the independence, and I like solving puzzles. And maybe this sounds corny, but I like correcting at least some of the injustice in the world. It's a good feeling when you put away a smuggler or a poacher or a murderer." His eyes met hers. "Or a kidnapper."

She rearranged her silverware. "Do you think this will work? Our pretending to want to join up with them?"

"It's the best way I can think of to learn what really goes on in their camp. I figure you can get to know the women—especially the mothers with children. I can talk to the men. We might be able to find Anna Ingels—the woman who witnessed your sister's will. If your niece is there, someone will know it and eventually they'll let something slip."

The waiter delivered their food—ravioli for Walt, fish for her. They ate in silence for a moment, then she said, "Have you done anything like this before?"

"You mean undercover work?" He stabbed at a pillow of ravioli. "A couple of times. I posed as a big-game hunter to bring down a group of poachers. And I did a few drug buys, things like that."

"Did you ever have to pretend to be married to someone?"

"No. That's a new one. Does that worry you?"

"A little. Not you, I mean—well, I've never been married before."

"Me either." He laid down his fork and wiped his mouth with his napkin. "Before we get too far into this, are you engaged? Seriously involved with someone? Dating a mixed martial arts fighter who's insanely jealous?"

Her eyes widened. "No to all of the above. What about you?"

"I don't have a boyfriend either. Or a girlfriend."

She laughed. "Really? That surprises me."

"Does it?"

"You're good-looking, and friendly. I wouldn't think you'd have trouble getting a date."

"No, I don't have trouble getting dates." He took another bite of ravioli, delaying his answer. "I'm new to the area," he said. "I transferred from northern Colorado just last month."

"And?"

"And what?"

"And there's something you're not saying. I heard it in your voice."

Was he really so easy to read? He searched for some glib lie, but then again, why shouldn't he tell her? "The last woman I dated seriously is now married to my younger brother."

"Ouch!"

"Yeah, well, he's very charming and untroubled by

much of a conscience." The wound still ached a little—not the woman's betrayal so much as his brother's. He should have seen it coming, and the fact that he hadn't made him doubt himself a little.

"So that's what you meant when you said you understood about thinking you knew a family member well, and turning out to be wrong."

"Yep. Been there, done that, got the T-shirt."

"That must make for some awkward family dinners," she said.

"A little. There are four of us kids—two girls and two boys. For the sake of family harmony, I wished the newlyweds well and keep my distance."

"It was just Emily and me in my family," she said. "I think it took my mom a long time to get pregnant again after me." A smile ghosted across her lips. "I still remember how excited I was when she was born. It was as if I had a real live doll of my own to look after. After our parents were killed in a car crash when Emily was nineteen, all we had was each other. We were inseparable, right up until I went away to Dallas to work. And even after that—even though we lived very different lives—I always felt we were close." She laid down her fork and her eyes met his. "I blamed Daniel Metwater for taking her away from me. After she joined his cult, I seldom heard from her. What kind of person encourages someone to cut off ties with family that way?"

"We haven't been able to learn a great deal about him, other than that he's very charismatic and seems to be offering something that some people find attractive." He wanted to take her hand, to try to comfort her, but resisted the temptation. "There are probably experts in this kind of thing who could tell you more than I can."

"He calls his followers a family—as if that could substitute for their real families."

"Maybe this undercover assignment will give you some of the answers to your questions," he said. He picked up his fork again.

They ate in silence for a while longer, until she pushed her plate away, her dinner half-eaten. "I've been thinking about what you asked me," she said. "About what Daniel Metwater stood to gain from keeping Joy and claiming her as his own."

"Did you come up with something?"

"It's not much, but Emily had a trust from our mother. An annual stipend now, with the bulk coming to her when she turned thirty in two years. Under the terms of the trust, it automatically passes to any children she might have, and can be used to pay living and educational expenses in the event of her death."

He considered this information, then shook his head. "Metwater supposedly has money of his own."

"That's what I understood from the research I did." She took a sip of tea. "I told you it wasn't much."

"Still, having money doesn't mean he might not want more. And we don't have any idea what his financial picture is these days. Maybe he made some bad investments, or being a prophet in the wilderness is more expensive than he thought it would be."

"I keep coming back to her last letter," Hannah said. "Emily sounded so frightened—I thought maybe that so-called Family was holding her prisoner."

"The death certificate said her cause of death was respiratory failure."

"I know. She died in an emergency room. Someone dropped her off—they don't know who. And people do die of asthma, but I can't help thinking—what if they were withholding her medication, or the stress of traveling with this group brought on the attack?"

"It would be tough to prove murder in either case."

"I know." She sat back and laid her napkin beside her plate. "And none of it will bring Emily back. I have to focus on what I can do, which is to raise Joy and take the best care of her I know how."

A light came into her eyes when she spoke, and her expression changed to one of such tenderness it made Walt's chest ache. "You already love her, don't you?" he said.

"Yes." That fleeting smile again. "And that surprises me. I never thought of myself as particularly nurturing, but this baby—this infant I haven't even met yet—I already love her so much."

"If she's in Metwater's camp, we'll find her," he said.

She surprised him by reaching out and taking his hand. "I believe you," she said. "And if I have to pretend to be someone's wife temporarily, I'm glad it's you."

He gave her hand a squeeze, then let it go before he gave in to the temptation to pull her close and kiss her. As assignments went, this one was definitely going to be interesting, and a little dangerous—in more ways than one.

Chapter Four

Two days later, Hannah studied herself in the hotel mirror, frowning. She wished she had taken more of an interest in drama club in school—she might have learned something that would come in handy now. The only advice Walt had given her was "Stick as close to the truth as possible and only lie when absolutely necessary." So she was going into camp as Hannah Morgan—her mother's maiden name—and she was a corporate dropout looking for a more authentic life.

She had dressed as Walt had instructed her, in a gauzy summer skirt, tank top and sturdy sandals. She wore no makeup and had combed out her hair to hang straight past her shoulders. Silver bracelets and earrings completed the look—definitely not her normal style, which tended toward plain classics, but that was all part of playing a role, wasn't it...dressing the part?

A knock on the door interrupted her musing. She checked the peephole, but didn't recognize the rumpled-looking man who stood on the other side. Then he shifted so that the sun lit his face, and she sucked in a breath and jerked open the door. "I didn't recognize you at first," she said, staring at Walt. Several days' growth of beard darkened his jaw, giving him a rough—and definitely sexy—look. His hair was streaked blond and tousled and he wore jeans with a rip in one knee, hiking boots and a tight olive-green T-shirt that showed off a sculpted chest and defined biceps. A tribal tattoo encircled his upper right arm. Looking at him made her feel a little breathless.

"What do you think?" He held his arms out at his sides. "Will they still make me as a cop?"

Slowly, she shook her head. "No, I don't think so." *A biker or a bandit or an all-around bad boy, maybe, but not a cop.*

"You look great," he said. "I didn't realize your hair was so long."

She tucked a stray strand behind her ears. "I usually wear it up. It gets in the way otherwise."

"Are you ready to go? Marco just radioed that our contact is at the laundry."

She smoothed her sweating palms down her thighs and took a deep breath. "Yeah, I'm ready."

She collected the backpack into which she had stashed a few essentials and followed him across the parking lot. But instead of a car or truck, he stopped beside a motorcycle. The black-and-chrome monster looked large and dangerous. "We're going on that?" she asked.

He patted the leather seat. "I figured the Harley fit the image better. I've got a small tent and some other supplies in the saddlebags and trunk." He handed her a helmet. "Put this on."

She settled the helmet over her head. It was a lot heavier than she had expected. "Does this belong to the Rangers?" she asked, fumbling with the chin strap.

"No, it's my personal bike." He fastened the strap

for her, a tremor running through her as his fingertips brushed across her throat. But he gave no sign that he noticed. He straddled the bike, then looked over his shoulder at her. "Get on behind me. Put your feet on the foot pegs."

Feeling awkward, she did as he instructed. "I've never ridden a motorcycle before," she said.

"Don't worry. Just hang on." She started as the engine roared to life, the sound vibrating through her. The bike lurched forward and she wrapped her arms around him, her breasts pressed against the solid muscle of his back, his body shielding hers from the wind. She forced herself to relax her death grip on him, but didn't let go altogether. He felt like the only steady thing in her world right now.

She tried to focus on the task ahead. Apparently, several women from Metwater's group came into town once a week to do laundry. The plan was for Walt and Hannah to meet them and turn the talk to the Family. They would express a desire to join the group and ask for an introduction. Walt had explained that interviews with some former group members had revealed this was how new members were often acquired. And Metwater had bragged on his blog that he didn't have to recruit members—they came to him voluntarily after hearing his message.

The laundry occupied the end unit of a low-slung building in a strip center not far from the campus of the local college. Though Metwater's three followers were the same age as many of the students who lounged on chairs between the washers and dryers or gathered in the parking lot, they looked somehow different. Their bare faces were pink from exposure to the sun, and their long skirts and sleeveless tops were faded and worn. One of the women had a baby on her hip, and Hannah couldn't keep from staring at the child, who wore a stained blue sleeper and had a shock of wheat-colored hair and plump, rosy cheeks.

"That's a beautiful baby," she said, forgetting that they had agreed she would let Walt do most of the talking.

"Thanks." The woman, who wore her light brown hair in two long braids, hefted the child to her shoulder, her eyes wary.

"How old is he?" Hannah asked. "Or she?"

"He's almost seven months," she said.

Hannah realized she had been staring at the child too intently. She forced a smile to her face. "I'm Hannah," she said. "And this is my husband, Walt. A friend told me she had seen you all doing your laundry here sometimes, so we came here hoping to meet some members of the Family."

"We've been reading the Prophet's blog," Walt said. "His message really spoke to us. We were wondering how we could go about joining the group."

The baby's mother looked over her shoulder, toward where the other two women were filling a row of washers. "You should talk to Starfall," she said. "Starfall! Come talk to these people."

Starfall had curly brown hair and a slightly crooked nose, and the beginnings of lines along each side of her mouth, as if she frowned a lot. She was frowning now as she approached them. "What do you want?" she asked.

"We wanted to know how we could go about joining up with the Family," Walt said. He took Hannah's hand

and squeezed it. "We've been reading the Prophet's writing and we really like what he has to say."

"Is that so?" Starfall addressed her question not to Walt, but to Hannah.

She licked her too-dry lips and tried to remember something from Daniel Metwater's blog, which she had read repeatedly since Emily had announced she was joining his group. "We're tired of the shallow commercialism and focus on materialism so rampant in the modern world," she said. "We want to be a part of the community the Prophet is building—close to nature and working for the good of one another."

"It's not just a matter of camping in the wilderness for a few weeks," Starfall said. "You have to agree to contribute your resources for the good of all. And you have to work. Everyone in the Family has a job to do."

"We're not afraid of work," Walt said. "And we wouldn't expect the Prophet to take us in and provide for us without us contributing. We have money to contribute."

Starfall's unblinking gaze was starting to make Hannah nervous. She moved closer to Walt, her shoulder brushing his. "Can you arrange for us to meet the Prophet?" she asked.

Starfall's expression didn't soften, but she nodded. "You can follow us to camp when we get ready to leave here."

"Is there anything I can do to help?" Hannah asked. She turned to the first young woman. "I could hold the baby for you."

The woman put one arm protectively around the child. "He's happier with me."

"Wait for us over there or outside." Starfall pointed to the corner of the laundry.

"Come on, honey." Walt took her arm and led her to the grouping of chairs. "You need to rein it in a little," he said under his breath. "She thinks you want to kidnap her kid."

"I just wanted to verify it's really a boy. Don't you think he looks small for seven months?"

"I have no idea. I haven't spent a lot of time around babies."

She slumped into one of the molded plastic chairs grouped against the back wall. "I haven't either. Before I left to come here I read everything I could find on babies, but there's so much information out there it's impossible to absorb."

"Most new parents seem to manage fine." He patted her shoulder. "You will, too."

She studied the trio of women sorting laundry across the room. "What kind of a name is Starfall?"

"I'm not sure where Metwater's followers get their names," he said. "Maybe Metwater christens them."

"If Emily took a new name, maybe that's why no one recognized her when you asked about her."

"It's possible." He squeezed her hand. "We'll try to find out."

Odd that holding his hand felt so natural now. If he was really her husband, it was the kind of thing he would do, right? But it annoyed her that she was settling into this role so easily. She was a strong woman and she didn't need a man to make her feel safe. And she couldn't afford to lose focus on her real purpose here—to find and care for her niece.

She slid her fingers out of his grasp. "I think we

should come up with a list of reasons Metwater would want us as part of his group. It makes sense that he wouldn't want a bunch of freeloaders."

"From what little we've seen, men seem to leave the group more often than women," Walt said. "So he's always in need of extra muscle."

Her gaze slid to his chest and arms. He had muscle, all right. She shifted in her chair. "It doesn't look as if he has any shortage of young women followers. I should think of something to make me look like a better possible disciple. I supposed I could offer up my bank account."

"I'll admit that would probably be an inducement, but I doubt you'll need it."

"But I ought to have something to offer," she said. "Maybe I could say I was a teacher and I could teach the children. That would be a good way to get to know the mothers, too."

"It would. But babies don't really need school yet. I think Metwater will want you in his group because you're just his type."

"His type?"

"Beautiful."

She stared at him, a blush heating her face. Not that she was naive about her looks, but to hear him say it that way caught her off guard. She glanced at the women in front of the bank of washers, noting that they were all young, slender and, yes, quite attractive. "Are you saying Metwater favors beautiful women?"

"From what I've heard, he's got a regular harem around him all the time. The Rangers did a rough census of the group when they first moved onto park land, and there wasn't anyone out there over the age of forty, and most of them are a lot younger. Two-thirds of the group are women and a number of them are, well, stunning." He shrugged. "You should fit right in."

He probably meant that as a compliment, but his words made her uncomfortable. "I really don't like being judged by my looks—good or bad," she said. "It's something I've had to struggle against in the scientific community my whole career. There are plenty of people out there—plenty of men—who still think a pretty blonde can't possibly be smart."

"I don't think you're dumb—not by a long shot," he said. "I'm just telling you what I've observed about Metwater. If you know what you're getting into, maybe you can use his predilections to your advantage."

"You mean, pretend to be the dumb blonde so he'll be less likely to suspect me of being up to something?"

"That's one way to approach it."

She crossed her arms over her stomach. Playing down her intellect and playing up her looks went against everything she believed in. But if it would help her find Joy and bring her home safely... "I'll think about it," she said, and stood. "Right now, I'm going outside to get some fresh air."

WALT WATCHED HANNAH walk away. She nodded to the three Family members as she passed, but didn't stop to chat. He settled back in his chair, chin on his chest, pretending to nap, though he kept an eye on the three women. Hannah was ticked off about his comments about her looks. He was only stating fact, and trying to give her a hint at what she might be in for.

Not that he intended to let Daniel Metwater lay a finger on her. One more reason he was glad they had decided to pass themselves off as husband and wife instead of brother and sister. He couldn't count on the Prophet not to go after a married woman, but it might slow him down. Walt didn't intend for the two of them to be in the camp any longer than necessary. With luck, they would find Hannah's niece within a day or two and get out of Dodge.

"We're ready to leave now, if you want to follow us."

Starfall hefted a large garbage bag he presumed was full of clean laundry and started out the door. Walt hurried to catch up. "Let me take that," he said, and carried the laundry the rest of the way to the battered sedan she pointed out.

Hannah joined them beside the car. "Do you need help with anything else?" she asked.

"No." Starfall slid into the driver's seat and turned the key. "Just try to keep up."

She was already pulling out of the parking lot when Walt and Hannah reached his motorcycle. "I think she's purposely trying to lose us," Hannah said as she pulled on the helmet.

"No chance of that." He put on his own helmet and mounted the bike. "I already know where the camp is." She climbed on behind him and he started the engine. "It's going to be a rough and dusty ride once we reach the dirt roads. Nothing I can do about it."

"Despite what you might think, I'm not some delicate flower who withers if I have to deal with a little dirt," she said. "I'm tougher than I look."

He heard the steel in her voice and sensed it in her posture as she sat up straight behind him. Only her hands tightly gripping his sides gave any clue to her nervousness. He remembered the matter-of-fact way she had laid out her story in the Rangers' office, with no tears or pleadings. As much as he found himself wanting to look after her, she was a woman used to looking after herself, and she wasn't going to let him forget it.

Starfall obviously wasn't concerned about speed limits, as she drove fifteen and twenty miles over the posted speeds all the way into the park. Only when they turned onto the first dirt road did she slow down, in deference to the washboard surface of the two-track that cut across the wilderness.

The landscape that spread out around them was unlike what most people associated with Colorado. Though distant mountains showed snowcapped peaks against an expanse of turquoise sky, the land in the park and surrounding wilderness areas was high desert. Sagebrush and stunted pinyons dotted the rolling expanse of cracked brown earth, and boulders the size of cars lay scattered like thrown dice. Though the terrain looked dry and barren, it was home to vibrant life, from colorful lizards and swift rabbits to deer and black bear. Hidden springs formed lush oases, and the roaring cataract of the Gunnison River had cut the deep Black Canyon that gave the park its name, a place of wild beauty unlike any other in the United States.

Walt had to slow the Harley to a crawl to steer around the network of potholes and protruding rocks, and to avoid being choked by the sedan's dust. Even if he hadn't already known the location of Metwater's camp, the rooster tail of dust that fanned out behind the car hung in the air long after the vehicle passed, providing a clear guide to their destination.

By the time he and Hannah reached the small park-

ing area, the women had the car unloaded and were
preparing to carry the bundles of clean laundry over
the footbridge. Without asking, they left two bundles
behind. Walt and Hannah took these and fell into step
behind them.

The camp looked much as it had on his visit four
days before, people gathered in front of trailers and
tents, others working around picnic tables in a large
open-sided shelter with a roof made of logs and woven
branches. A group of men played cards in the shade of
a lean-to fashioned from a tarp, while a trio of children
ran along the creek, pausing every few steps to plunge
sticks into the water.

"There are a lot of people here," Hannah whispered.

"A couple dozen, best we can determine," Walt said.

A man stepped forward to take the bag of laundry
from Starfall. "Who are they?" he asked, jerking his
head toward Walt and Hannah.

"They want to join the Family," she said.

The man, who looked to be in his late twenties, wore
his sandy hair long and pulled back in a ponytail. He
had a hawk nose and a cleft in his chin, and the build
of a cage fighter or a bull rider—not tall, but all stringy
muscle and barely contained energy. He looked them
up and down, then spat to the side. "I guess that's up
to the Prophet," he said.

He and Starfall walked away, leaving Walt and Hannah standing alone on the edge of the camp. Hannah
moved closer and he put his arm around her. "What
do we do now?" she asked.

"Let's go talk to the Prophet."

"Where is he?" she asked.

"What's your best guess?" he asked.

She surveyed the camp, taking in the motley collection of dwellings, from a camper shell on the back of a pickup truck with one flat tire to a luxurious motor home with an array of solar panels on the roof. "My guess is the big RV," she said.

"You get an A." He took his arm from around her. "Come on. Let's see if the Prophet will grant us an interview."

No one said anything as they headed toward the motor home, but Walt could feel dozens of eyes on them. No one was rushing to welcome the new converts with open arms, that was for sure. Was it because they were waiting to take their cue from Metwater? Or had the Prophet instilled suspicion of all outsiders in his followers?

They mounted the steps to the RV and Walt rapped hard on the door. After a moment it opened and Andi Matheson answered. Andi—or Asteria, as she called herself now—had had more contact with the Rangers than anyone else in camp, but she showed no sign of recognition as she stared at Walt. "Yes?"

"We'd like to see the Prophet," he said. "We—my wife and I—" he indicated Hannah "—are big admirers of his and would like to join the group."

She nodded, as if this made perfect sense, and held the door open wider. "Come in."

The interior of the RV was dim and cool, the living room filled with a leather sofa and several upholstered chairs. Andi indicated they should sit, then disappeared through an archway into the back of the vehicle.

Walt sat on the sofa and Hannah settled next to him. She was breathing shallowly, and he could almost feel the nervousness rolling off her in waves. He gripped her hand and squeezed. "It's going to be okay," he said.

She nodded, and didn't pull away.

"The woman who let us in is Andi Matheson," Walt said, keeping his voice low.

Hannah nodded. "I read about her online. She's the daughter of someone famous, right?"

"Her father is Senator Pete Matheson—though right now he's serving time for murdering an FBI agent."

"She's obviously pregnant," Hannah said. "Is Metwater the father?"

"No," Walt said. "That would be the man the senator killed."

Hannah's face softened with sympathy. "How terrible for her."

"She seems to have settled in nicely with Metwater," Walt said.

There wasn't a clock in the room, so he had no idea how long they waited, though he thought it might have been as long as ten minutes. "What's taking so long?" Hannah whispered.

Just then, Andi reappeared from the back of the RV. "The Prophet will see you," she said.

Walt and Hannah stood and started toward Andi. She held up a hand. "He doesn't want to see you together," she said. She turned to Hannah. "He wants to interview you first. Alone."

Chapter Five

"I don't think—" Walt began, but Hannah interrupted him.

"I don't mind talking with him by myself." She assumed what she hoped was an eager expression. "It would be a privilege to meet the Prophet." Was that laying it on too thick? Probably not, for a man who had the nerve to refer to himself as the Prophet.

Andi turned to Walt. "You can wait outside," she said. "I'll call you when it's your turn."

Walt turned to Hannah. "If you're sure?"

"I'll be fine." After all, it wasn't as if Metwater was going to do anything with Andi right here and a bunch of other people around. And it wasn't as if she hadn't had experience fending off fresh men. Even if Metwater was the lecher Walt had made him out to be, Hannah could handle him.

Walt left, then Andi put on a broad-brimmed hat and headed for the door also. "Where are you going?" Hannah asked.

"The Prophet wants to speak with you alone," she said, and left, the door clicking shut behind her.

Hannah hugged her arms across her chest and walked to the window, but heavy shades blocked any view out—or in. She took a deep breath, fighting for calm. She shouldn't be afraid of Metwater. Walt was close by if she needed anything. She needed to keep her head and use this opportunity to learn as much as possible about the Prophet, and about Emily and Joy.

"Please, have a seat. I want you to be comfortable."

She turned and stared at the man who spoke. Metwater—and this had to be Metwater—was almost naked, wearing only a pair of low-slung, loose lounge pants in some sort of silky fabric. The kind of thing she'd seen Hugh Hefner wear in old photographs. At the thought, she had to stifle a laugh.

"Please share what you find so amusing." Barefoot, he moved into the room with the sensual grace of a panther, lamplight gleaming on the smooth muscles of his chest and arms and stomach. Curly dark hair framed a face like Michelangelo's *David*, the shadow of beard adding a masculine roughness.

All mirth deserted her as he moved closer still, stopping when he was almost touching her, so that she could feel the heat of his body, smell his musk and see the individual lashes that framed his dark eyes. He stared at her, crowding her personal space, stripping away her privacy. She found it impossible to look away from that gaze—the hypnotic stare of a predator.

"What amuses you?" he asked again, his voice deep and velvety, seductive.

"I laugh when I'm nervous," she said. "I never thought I'd get to meet you in person." This much was true. She had never really wanted to meet the man she blamed for her sister's death. Even if Metwater hadn't killed Emily, Hannah believed her sister wouldn't have died if she had stayed near her real family instead of joining up with this pretend one.

"There's no need to be nervous around me." He took her hand and led her toward the sofa. She forced herself not to pull away. Better to let him think she was under his spell. He had the kind of personality that would enchant many women. She could see how Emily, pregnant and feeling alone, mourning the loss of her fiancé and the future she had planned, might fall for someone like this. She would revel in the attention of someone so charismatic and seemingly powerful. She wouldn't have seen through his charm the way Hannah did.

She slid her hand out of his grasp and sat up straight, hoping her prim posture would put him off a little. The dimples on either side of his mouth deepened and he leaned toward her. "Tell me why you're interested in becoming a member of my family," he said.

His family. Not "our family" or "the family", but something that belonged to him. "My husband and I want to build a life that focuses on essentials—what's really important." That was a quote straight out of his blog.

"Why not do as so many others have done and set up a homestead on your own, or sell everything and take to the road?" he asked. "You could sign up for missionary work overseas or join a religious order. Why come to me?"

"While we believe in spirituality, we don't belong to any particular religion," she said. "And we want to work together with a like-minded group with an inspiring leader." Because, obviously, it was all about him.

"We don't have many married couples here," he said. "We discourage it, in fact."

"Why is that?" She knew he wanted her to ask the question.

"I see marriage as an outdated construct," he said. "And it's a distraction. How can you pledge loyalty to the Family as a whole when you've already pledged yourself to one other person? A single person is much freer to follow the dictates of her heart."

"So you require your followers to be single?" she asked.

"Not at all." He brushed his fingers across her shoulder. "I merely see it as a preferable state."

She shifted, putting a few more inches between them—the most she could manage.

"How did you learn about me?" he asked.

Walt had instructed her to say she had discovered the Prophet's blog online and that had led to the two of them reading everything they could find about him and his disciples. But she couldn't pass up the chance to learn more about his connection with her sister. "A friend told me about you," she said. "Before she left to join your group. I'm hoping she's still here. I would love to reconnect with her."

"What is your friend's name?"

"Emily Dietrich."

His expression didn't change, but something flickered in his eyes—a darkness he quickly masked. "Your friend told you she was going to join the Family?"

"Yes. I'm sure that's what she said. She attended a rally where you spoke and was convinced you offered exactly what she was looking for, for herself and her baby. Is she here? When can I see her?"

He took her hand again, holding on tightly when she

tried to pull free. "When was the last time you spoke to your friend?" he asked.

"About six months ago, right before she left to follow you." *Stick to the truth as much as possible*, Walt had told her.

"Your friend must have changed her mind," he said. "She never came to me. At least, no one using the name Emily Dietrich has ever been a member of my family."

He sounded sincere, but the flash of irritation she had seen at the first mention of Emily's name told her he was lying. He had recognized the name, and didn't like that she had brought it up. "How odd," she said. "I wonder what happened to her?"

"Does it change your mind about joining us, knowing your friend isn't here?" he asked.

"Of course not," she said. "You asked how I learned about you, and it was through her. I was hoping I'd get to see her again, but she isn't the main reason we're here. It's because we believe in everything you teach and we want that kind of life for ourselves."

"Do you know what it means to be a part of a family?" he asked.

"Well, I suppose…" She hesitated, trying to remember what he had said about this in his writings, but she was drawing a blank. "Family members look out for and support one another," she said. "You try to live in harmony and act in a way that's to the benefit of everyone, not simply yourself."

"True." He nodded. "As a part of my family, I would expect you to put the needs of the group ahead of yourself. We purposely separate ourselves from the outside world in order to focus on perfecting our union. While I would never forbid you to be in contact with relatives and friends from your old life, most people find as they immerse themselves in the day-to-day life of the Family, they are less and less inclined to want to be with others who don't share our sense of purpose and our views."

She tried to look thoughtful. "I can see that," she said.

He rubbed his thumb up and down the third finger of her left hand. "You said you were married. Where is your ring?"

She stared down at her empty fingers. She and Walt had spent hours going over all the details of coming here. Why hadn't they remembered a ring? "We don't hold with the trappings of society. We don't need a band of precious metal to seal our vows to one another."

He gave her hand a final squeeze—so hard she winced—then released his grip on her and sat back. He was no longer the seducing lover, but the practical businessman. "What resources do you bring to the group?" he said. "Everyone must contribute for the good of the whole."

"We have some money, from savings and from selling some things to pay for our trip here," she said. "And I enjoy working with children. I can teach the older ones and help care for younger ones."

"What about your husband? What does he do?"

They had rehearsed this. What had Walt said? "He was a carpenter. He's very good with his hands."

"Oh, is he?" Why did the words sound so sarcastic? "You'll have to provide your own shelter and clothing," he said. "Everyone here has to earn his or her keep. You'll be expected to embark on a course of study until you prove yourself ready to join us."

"What will we study?" she asked.

"Whatever I deem necessary." He rested his hand on her shoulder, a heavy, possessive touch that had her fighting her instinct to pull away. "I will personally instruct you on what you need to know to be a good disciple."

"Walt and I will look forward to learning more," she said.

"It's important for you to maintain your individuality, even though you are married," he said. "I consider you and your husband two separate candidates for inclusion in our group. Not everyone earns full acceptance as a member of the Family. You'll come to see the benefit of this as part of your teaching."

"Do you ever kick anyone out?" she asked. "I mean, if they do something that upsets the harmony of the group?" Had Emily done something to upset him? Is that why she had been so afraid?

"We punish when necessary. Our justice is not the justice of the world. We answer to a higher power."

"What does that mean?" It sounded as if he thought he was above the law, free to act in whatever way he wished. No wonder Emily had been afraid.

"You'll learn as part of your training." He took her hand and pulled her to her feet. "Come. It's time for you to meet your future sisters and brothers."

"What about Walt?"

"Don't worry about him. I'll see that he's taken care of."

She wasn't sure she liked the sound of that. He had made it clear he didn't think too much of marriage— and the implication was that he preferred to focus on her and leave Walt out in the cold. She definitely didn't like the possessive way he held her hand—she had al-

ways resented men who tried to take over and drag her
around like some pretty ornament who was supposed to
smile and look nice, but not express too many opinions.
She managed to pull her hand from his grasp. But she
hastened to soothe the affront that flashed in his eyes
with a smile and flattering words. "I'm thrilled you've
taken such an interest," she said. "I never dreamed I'd
be so privileged as to study with you personally."

He put one arm around her and pulled her close.
"You and I are going to be good friends," he said, and
pressed his lips to her cheek. "Very special friends."

WALT DIDN'T HAVE to spend very long in the Family's
camp to confirm a few things the other Rangers had
told him about Daniel Metwater. The Prophet had surrounded himself with mostly young people and mostly
women. Beautiful women. Every woman Walt en-
countered was strikingly attractive. Hannah would fit
in perfectly with the rest of Metwater's harem—the
thought made Walt's jaw tighten. He told himself if she
was a trained officer, instead of a civilian, he wouldn't
be so agitated about her being in that RV alone with
the self-proclaimed prophet. The sooner they learned
what they needed to know about Hannah's sister and
niece, the sooner they could get out of here.

He could feel the other Family members watching
him as he stood outside the RV, the sun beating down,
making him sweat. He wiped his brow, then strode
over to the card players. They looked up and watched
his approach, expressions wary. "Hey," he said, nodding in greeting. "My name's Walt. My wife and I are
hoping to join the Family."

The stocky, bearded man who had greeted Walt

and Marco when they had previously visited the camp looked him up and down, but gave no indication he recognized him. "I saw you ride in," he said. "Nice-looking bike."

"Nice-looking wife, too." A lanky blond laid his cards facedown on the blanket they were sitting around. "The Prophet will like her."

A couple of the other men snickered. Walt ignored them. "Good to meet you."

He offered his hand to the blond, who shook it. "I'm Jobie. This is Emerson." He indicated the man next to him, who wore black-rimmed glasses and a panama hat. "That's Kiram." He nodded to the bearded man.

Walt acknowledged each man in turn. Emerson offered his hand to shake, but Kiram only regarded him coolly.

"The camp looks pretty nice," Walt said. "It's a good location, you've got time to play cards, nobody hassling you."

"It's okay." Kiram laid aside his cards also and nodded to an empty space across from him. "Have a seat."

"Thanks." Walt lowered himself to the blanket. "How long have you been following the Prophet?" he asked.

"A while."

"Kiram's been with the Family practically from the beginning," Jobie said. "You got any cigs?"

"Sorry," Walt said. "I don't smoke."

"Smoking isn't allowed in camp," Kiram said.

Jobie scowled at him. "I didn't say I was going to smoke it in camp."

"I guess there are a lot of rules you have to follow," Walt said. "I know I read on the Prophet's blog that he doesn't allow guns in the camp or anything." An injunction Walt had ignored. He considered the pistol he wore in an ankle holster as one more way to protect himself and Hannah out here in the wilderness.

"There are rules," Kiram said. "It wouldn't say much about a group that preaches peace to have us all walking around armed."

"I can see that," Walt said.

"Was it your wife's idea to join up or yours?" Emerson asked.

"We decided together," Walt said.

"My girlfriend talked me into it," Emerson said. He nudged his hat farther back on his head. "We thought it would be cool living together with a bunch of people who thought the same way we did, communing with nature, hanging out in the woods and living off the land."

"And is it?" Walt asked. "Cool, I mean."

Emerson glanced toward Kiram, who was studying him, expressionless. "Sometimes," he said. "I guess no life is perfect. My girlfriend likes it well enough."

Jobie leaned toward Walt. "The thing you need to know about this place is that the women run the show. Well, the Prophet runs everything, but mostly, he runs the women."

"So you're telling me a woman can get away with anything around here," Walt said.

Jobie shook his head. "Even the women have lines they can't cross," he said. "If they displease the Prophet, then they're out of here. Doesn't happen often, but sometimes..." His voice trailed away and he picked up his hand of cards again.

Though the words weren't particularly ominous,

something in Jobie's tone sent a chill up Walt's spine. "A girl I went to school with used to talk about joining up with the Family," he said. "I wonder if she ever did. Her name was Emily Dietrich."

"A lot of people here take on a new name," Jobie said. "Or they just go by one name."

"This girl was blonde, with blue eyes. Really pretty." Which essentially described Hannah. The picture Hannah had shown him left little doubt that the two were sisters.

Jobie and Emerson looked at each other. "Was that the woman who was here in the spring for a while?" Jobie asked. "It kind of sounds like her."

"That wasn't her." Kiram didn't look up from his cards when he spoke, but Walt sensed the man was focused on the conversation.

Jobie shrugged. "Guess not, then. Maybe she changed her mind about joining up. I'd probably remember her if she had. There aren't that many of us, and I tend to remember the women, especially." He grinned.

"What happened to the woman who was here in the spring?" Walt directed his question to Kiram.

Still holding his cards, Kiram stood. "If you want to get along here, you need to learn not to ask so many questions," he said.

He walked away. Walt turned to the other two. "What's his problem?"

"He's got a point," Emerson said. "Asking questions is a good way to get into trouble around here."

"What kind of trouble?" Walt asked.

The two exchanged looks. "The Prophet punishes the disobedient."

"What kind of punishment?" Walt pressed.

"Just keep your mouth shut and you won't have to find out." Jobie nodded toward the motor home. "Here comes your wife."

Hannah exited the RV with Metwater at her side. The Prophet had one arm around her shoulders. She was smiling, but Walt sensed tension. "Everyone, I have an announcement to make," Metwater said.

Everyone around Walt put aside whatever they were doing and moved toward the RV. Even the children stopped playing and ran to their mothers' sides to stare up at Metwater. It was as if he had brainwashed them all into thinking he really was a prophet, Walt thought, as he pushed through the crowd to the bottom of the steps. Hannah met his gaze, but Metwater ignored him.

"I'd like you to meet a new candidate for membership into the Family," Metwater announced, in a deep, rich voice that carried easily over the crowd. He smiled at Hannah and squeezed her shoulder. "I think we'll call you Serenity."

"Oh." Her smile faded. "I really prefer my own name," she said.

"Serenity suits you," he said. He turned back to the crowd. "Say hello to Serenity, everyone."

"Hello, Serenity," they chorused.

Hannah frowned, but said nothing. Walt mounted the steps, brushing aside the one man who moved forward as if to stop him. He moved to Hannah's side and put his arm around her.

"This is Walter," Metwater said. "He came to us with Serenity."

"Hannah is my wife," he said. "And it's Walt, not

Walter." His grandmother was the only one who ever called him Walter.

The dreadlocked blond who had taken the laundry bag from Starfall ran toward them, a little out of breath. "The cops are back," he said.

Metwater looked over the crowd, to the path that led into camp. Sure enough, Rangers Michael Dance and Lance Carpenter were making their way down the trail. Obviously, Carpenter had made it back from his honeymoon and Dance had returned from Denver, but what were the two officers doing here?

Dance and Carpenter stopped at the edge of the clearing and looked the crowd over. Walt took Hannah's hand and tugged her toward the steps, planning to melt into the background. He figured his fellow officers were savvy enough not to give him away, but he didn't want to risk anyone—especially Metwater—picking up on any subtle cues that they knew each other.

"We've had a report of a young woman who went missing from Montrose a couple of days ago," Dance said. His voice didn't have the orator's tones of Metwater, but it carried well over the crowd. "A witness thought they saw her hitchhiking near here and we wondered if anyone here has seen her." He consulted his phone's screen. "She's described as five feet six inches tall, with short black hair, olive skin and brown eyes. Her name is Lucia Raton."

"We don't know anything about this missing girl," Metwater said. "Why would you assume we would?"

"She might have left her home intending to join your group," Lance said. "Or if she was lost, she might have wandered to your camp looking for help."

"These are the only people new to our camp," Metwater said. "And as you can see, neither of them fit your description of this girl."

Walt realized that Metwater was pointed to him and Hannah, and that everyone—including the two Rangers—had turned to look at them.

Lance frowned. "Hey, Walt," he said. "What are you doing here?"

Chapter Six

Hannah tightened her grip on Walt's hand. Nothing like having a cop call you out to arouse suspicion in a group of people you were lying to. Walt had tensed up and was all but glaring at the Ranger.

"I think these are the two who stopped me and gave me a ticket day before yesterday," he said. His glower looked real enough to Hannah—he was probably furious at his coworkers for blowing his cover.

The taller of the two Rangers nudged his partner. "Should have figured his type would show up with this bunch," he said.

Hannah saw the moment the first Ranger—his name badge said Carpenter—clicked to what was going on. He moved to stand in front of Walt. "Do you know anything about this missing woman?" he asked. "Maybe you gave her a ride on your bike?"

"I only have room for one woman on my bike," Walt said, and pulled Hannah closer. "You remember my wife, Hannah, don't you, Officer?"

If Carpenter was surprised to learn that Walt suddenly had a wife, his sunglasses helped hide his reaction. "She's not the kind of woman a man forgets," he said. He held up his cell phone, which showed a picture of a round-faced, dark-haired woman who couldn't be very far out of her teens. "Have either of you seen this girl?"

Hannah shook her head.

"Why do you people automatically assume we're responsible for anything that goes wrong?" Metwater moved in behind them. "We are a peaceful people and you've never found any evidence to contradict that, yet you continue to harass us."

"In this case, Lucia's parents found your blog bookmarked on her computer." The taller officer, Dance, joined them. He focused on Metwater, avoiding looking at Hannah or Walt.

"That doesn't make us guilty of anything," Metwater said.

"No, it doesn't," Dance agreed. "But we're talking about a missing woman. We have to check out every possible lead. We're questioning a lot of people, and you're one of them."

"So, you don't know anything about Lucia Raton?" Carpenter asked. "You haven't seen her or heard from her?"

"No, I haven't." Metwater spread his arms wide. "Look around you, officer. The camp isn't that large. It's not as if someone could sneak in here without my knowing about it."

"Do you get people stopping by often, wanting to join up?" Dance glanced at Hannah.

"Occasionally," Metwater said. "My message touches people. They want to be a part of what I'm building here."

"What exactly are you building?" Carpenter

frowned at the haphazard collection of tents, shanties and trailers.

"A community of peace and cooperation."

Were they really as peaceful as Metwater wanted everyone to believe? Hannah wondered. Metwater's charisma could only go so far in controlling his followers. Did he use other methods to keep everyone in line—methods that had frightened Emily, and maybe even led to her death?

"Let us know if you hear or see anything that might help us find this woman," Dance said. "Her family is very worried."

Metwater inclined his head, like a king deigning to notice a subject. Dance and Carpenter left. Walt took Hannah's hand. "Come on," he said. "We'd better find a place to set up our tent."

WALT HADN'T TAKEN a step when a strong hand gripped his shoulder. "What was that all about?" Metwater asked, his voice a low growl.

Walt played dumb. "What was what all about?"

"That officer recognized you. He greeted you by name."

"He was just giving me a hard time, the way he did when he gave us that ticket. You know how those cops are."

Metwater's eyes narrowed. "I would have thought the Rangers had better things to do than to give out speeding tickets."

"I guess he just wanted to hassle me—the way he did you."

Metwater nodded, though the suspicion didn't leave

his eyes. "Tomorrow you can begin your training," he said.

"Training?" Hannah didn't look happy about this prospect.

"I will instruct you in preparation for you being accepted as full members of the Family," Metwater said.

"Okay." Walt hid his annoyance at the prospect. All he wanted was to find Hannah's niece and leave. He couldn't say if Metwater was guilty of breaking any laws, but Walt disliked pretty much everything about him, from his snake-oil salesman charm to his glib new age pontificating.

"It's time to eat," Metwater said. He took Hannah's hand in his. "We'll share a meal and gather by the fire. You can begin to learn our ways."

Walt moved to Hannah's side and took her other hand. Now that they were embedded with Metwater and his group, he realized he would need to add another job to his list of duties. In addition to locating Hannah's niece and finding out more about her sister's death, he would need to keep a close eye on his pretend wife, to keep her out of the Prophet's clutches.

It was after ten before Walt and Hannah had the chance to break away from the group. Dinner had consisted of decent stew and bread. Afterward, everyone had gathered around a campfire to witness what Metwater explained was a spiritual dance but what looked to Walt like two scantily clad women performing for Metwater. The man himself stayed glued to Hannah's side until the evening's festivities ended. "You're welcome to stay in my RV," he told her as she and Walt prepared to leave. "You'll be much more comfortable there."

Walt bristled and was about to remind Metwater that Hannah was his wife and therefore her place was with him when she stepped between them. "Thank you," she said, with a sweet smile for Metwater. "That's so considerate of you, but I'll be fine in the tent with Walt." Then she took Walt's hand and led him away.

"He's got a lot of nerve," Walt fumed. "Propositioning you with me standing right there."

"It wasn't exactly a proposition," she said. "And there's no need for you to go all caveman. I know how to look after myself."

"Sorry." He winced inwardly, realizing how the words he had almost said would have sounded to her. It wasn't his place to tell her where she belonged— even if they had been truly married. "He just rubs me the wrong way."

"He knows that and he uses it to his advantage."

They retrieved the tent and two sleeping bags from the motorcycle. "We should set up away from everyone else," Walt said. "Less chance of being overheard or spied on."

"Do you think Metwater suspects something?" she asked.

"I think he's the type who suspects everyone. I'm no expert on groups like this, but I've done a little reading. The best way for one man to control a group of diverse people is to have a team of enforcers whose job is to report back to the leader about what everyone else is up to. Those people get to make sure everyone else obeys all the rules and doesn't get out of line."

"Who are Metwater's enforcers?" she asked.

"I met one guy who fits the bill," Walt said. "A big, bearded man who goes by the name of Kiram. Apparently he's been with Metwater a long time, and the others seem wary of him. There are probably one or two others."

"What happens if someone breaks a rule?" she asked.

"I don't know. But I intend to find out." They had reached the edge of the camp, at a point farthest from Metwater's RV, and farthest from the trail that led into the clearing. Walt shone his flashlight on a large, leaning juniper. "How about here, under this tree?" he asked. "We'd be out of the way and have some shade in the daytime."

"Sure." She unzipped the tent bag and pulled out the stiff bundle of green-and-black polyester. "Why did that officer, Carpenter, call you out this afternoon?" she asked. "He could have ruined everything."

"Lance just got back from his honeymoon. And Michael was on assignment in another part of the state." He began fitting the shock-corded tent poles together. "My guess is the missing persons call came in and they decided to check out the camp without checking in with headquarters, and no one had briefed them. It worked out okay, though. I think Metwater believed my story about the ticket."

"What do you think this training is going to consist of?"

"I don't know, but maybe we'll get lucky and won't have to endure it for long." He laid aside the completed poles and looked at her. "What happened in the RV this afternoon after I was escorted out?" he asked.

She made a face. "He asked how we heard about

him, why we wanted to join up—about what you'd expect."

"Did he make a pass at you?"

She laughed.

"What's so funny?" he asked.

"It's just not a question I expected."

"Well, did he? He was certainly leering at you enough."

"No, he didn't make a pass at me. Not exactly."

"Did he or didn't he?"

She shrugged. "He put his arm around me. He said he thought marriage was an outmoded concept."

"He would just as soon get rid of me and have you stay to be one of his faithful female followers."

"Are you jealous?" She wasn't laughing anymore—instead her blue eyes searched his, making him feel a little too vulnerable.

"I'm not jealous," he said. "But I don't trust Metwater. He clearly has a lot of beautiful women hovering around him, and I think he sees you as another one."

"No chance of that," she said. "I've never been attracted to men who think they're God's gift to women."

What kind of man are *you attracted to?* he wondered, but pushed the thought aside. He didn't have the best track record with women and he ought to be focusing on the job at hand. "I don't trust all his talk of living peacefully and promoting harmony," he said. "That's not the impression I got when I talked to some of the men."

"What did you find out?"

"They didn't say anything specific, but they hinted that people who didn't follow Metwater's rules—or people who asked too many questions—were punished."

"He said something to me about punishment, too," she said. "That they had their own rules and answered to a higher power—which I interpreted as another way of saying he thinks he's above the law. Did you get any idea of what kind of punishment they use? He wouldn't tell me."

"The men I was talking to wouldn't say, either. And they changed the subject when I tried to find out more. But when I mentioned Emily, I got the impression at least a couple of them knew who I was talking about, though they pretended not to."

"You asked about Emily?" She clutched his wrist. "What did you say? What did they say?"

"One of the men said he thought she had been here in the spring. Does that sound about right?"

"Yes. That would have been about the time she left home to follow Metwater. The first letter she sent me arrived in May." She bent and began threading the poles into the channel across the top of the tent. "I asked Metwater about her, too."

He froze. "I thought we agreed you weren't going to say anything about her."

"I couldn't pass up the chance to learn about her. I didn't say she was my sister—I told him she was a friend."

"What did he say?"

"He said he'd never heard of her. But I think he was lying."

"I'm going to try to find out more, but we have to be careful asking questions." He slid the pole into the other channel of the tent, and together they tilted the structure upright. "You try to make friends with the women and find out what you can about your niece—though you realize she may not be here."

"I know. But I feel like she is."

He began hammering in stakes to secure the tent. "You can go ahead and go inside and get ready for bed," he said. "I'll join you in a minute."

"All right." She crawled into the tent and zipped it up after her.

Walt pounded the stakes in with a mallet, hitting them harder than necessary, working off some of his frustration. He needed to get a grip on his feelings before he crawled into that tent to spend the night with Hannah. He had thought pretending to be her husband would be just another undercover gig, one that he would handle professionally. But being this close to her, seeing Metwater leer at her, had triggered something primitive in him—a possessiveness and desire to protect her that caught him off guard.

Now they had a long night ahead of them in a small tent. He couldn't let himself be the man who was attracted to a smart, beautiful woman. He had to be a cop with a job to do—and that job didn't include letting emotion get the better of his good sense.

HANNAH HUDDLED IN a sleeping bag on one side of the tent and waited for Walt to come in. She had changed under the covers, wishing she had opted for sleepwear that wasn't quite so revealing. At the time she had packed, she hadn't been thinking about the fact that she'd be spending the nights alone with Walt. She had pictured them sleeping in a cabin or a travel trailer, not a small tent with only inches separating them.

The tent zipper slid open and Walt crawled in, flashlight illuminating the interior. "Comfortable?" he asked.

"It's not too bad," she lied. She had never slept on the ground like this before—had never realized it could be so hard.

He crawled to the other sleeping bag and began removing his boots. Boots off, he pulled his shirt off over his head. She closed her eyes, but not before she caught a glimpse of his lean, muscular body and felt the instant jolt of arousal.

The light went out and darkness closed around them, so that Walt was only a denser shadow across from her, though in the small space she could hear his breathing, and take in the spice-and-sweat scent of him. She felt the heat of his presence beside her, more intimate somehow than if they had been touching. The idea made her heart race, and she kneaded her hands on her thighs, listening to the sounds of him finishing undressing— the lowering of a zipper and the soft hush of cloth being shoved down, then the crisper rustle of the sleeping bag as he crawled inside. "At least we don't have to worry about it getting really cold at night," he said.

"I've never been camping before," she said.

"Never?"

She shook her head, then realized he couldn't see her. "I guess I've always been a city girl."

"It can be fun," he said. "I've spent the night in a tent in some beautiful spots all over the country."

"I guess it's different when you're by yourself," she said. "Not with a group like this, with other people all around you."

"Camping's nice with one other person," he said. "The right person."

"Did you and your girlfriend go camping?" she asked.

"Once. She didn't like it. Maybe that should have been my first clue things weren't going to work out."

"Relationships are hard," she said. "We don't always know who to trust."

"Sometimes the hardest part is trusting yourself."

"What do you mean?" She rolled onto her side to face him. She could almost make out his features in the dim light.

"I didn't pay attention when my gut told me something was off between me and my girlfriend," he said. "I didn't trust my own instincts, but I should have."

"I guess we all doubt ourselves from time to time," she said. She certainly wasn't one to give advice on handling relationships. She'd done a lousy job of that in her own life. She hadn't even been able to keep her own sister close, much less a lover.

"You're doing great so far," he said. "Just keep it up and we'll get out of here as soon as we can." He rolled over to face the wall. "Good night."

"Good night," she said, but didn't close her eyes. Even though she longed to find her niece and leave Metwater's camp as soon as possible, she was going to miss Walt. She was going to miss lying beside him like this, pretending that in another life, they might have been a real couple, camping together because they wanted to, not because circumstance had forced them together into a relationship that felt so real, but wasn't.

"SERENITY!"

Hannah and Walt were shaking out their sleeping

bags the next morning when they turned to see a pale woman moving toward them. Her hair was so blond it was almost white, and despite the intense sun here in the wilderness, her skin seemed almost devoid of color. Even her eyes were pale, a silvery gray that added to her ethereal appearance. "My name is Phoenix," she said. "I came to fetch you to come help us prepare breakfast."

"Call me Hannah. I prefer it." She rose and brushed off her skirt. "I'm happy to come and help."

Phoenix turned to Walt. "You can gather firewood. Now that we've been here awhile, the best wood is farther away and harder to haul."

"Sure." He rose also. "I'm happy to help."

"It's your job to help if you want to be one of us." Phoenix grabbed Hannah's hand and tugged her, with enough force that Hannah stumbled, then had to hurry to keep up as Phoenix led her back toward the center of camp.

"She's right. Your job is to work for the good of the Family."

He whirled to find Kiram standing behind the tent, next to the tree trunk. He held a long-bladed knife—the kind hunters used for skinning animals. How long had he been lurking back there, listening in on Walt and Hannah's conversation? Walt forced himself to remain passive. "I thought no weapons were allowed in camp," he said.

"This knife is for ceremonial purposes," Kiram said. "And I use it for hunting." He moved away from the tree and walked around the side of the tent, studying it. "Why did you decide to camp back here, far away from everything and everyone?" He stopped beside Walt—close enough to lash out with that knife.

Walt bent and picked up the mallet he had been using to drive in stakes. He felt better with a weapon of his own, feeble as it might be against the knife. He didn't want to risk drawing the gun he wore in an ankle holster unless he absolutely had to. "We're newlyweds," he said. "We like our privacy."

"There's no such thing as privacy in a camp like this," Kiram said. "There's always someone watching you, listening to you. Before very long, everyone will know all your secrets."

Walt knew a threat when he heard one. He met Kiram's cold stare with a hard look of his own. "What's your secret?" he asked. "Why do you feel the need to sneak around in the woods with that big knife?"

"I already told you it isn't a good idea to ask too many questions." Kiram thrust the knife into the scabbard at his side.

"You told me, but you didn't tell me why. Questions can be a good way to learn things I need to know."

"People who ask questions have to be punished," Kiram said. He looked Walt up and down, as if taking his measure.

"I guess that's for the Prophet to decide, not you."

"The Prophet decides," Kiram said. "Then I do his will." He shoved past Walt, then paused a few steps away and looked back. "You didn't ask me what I was hunting."

"Why should I care what you do?" Walt said.

Kiram grinned, showing crooked bottom teeth. "I hunt rats. It's my job to keep them under control." He turned back around and strode away, leaving Walt to stare after him, gripping the mallet at his side, cold sweat beading on the back of his neck.

Chapter Seven

Hannah let Phoenix drag her to the center of the camp, where three other women were already working at two long picnic tables set up beneath a shelter fashioned of logs and branches. One table served as a prep area for the morning's meal, while the other table held two propane-fueled cooking stoves, on which bubbled two large stockpots full of oatmeal. "This is Serenity," Phoenix said by way of introduction. She handed Hannah a paring knife. "You can peel the potatoes." She indicated a ten-pound bag of potatoes at the end of the table.

"Call me Hannah," Hannah said.

"The Prophet named her Serenity," Phoenix said, and moved to stir one of the cooking pots.

"He must like you, if he gave you a name already." Starfall said. Tears streamed down her face from the onions she was chopping. She nodded to the pregnant woman across from her—Andi Matheson. "This is Asteria. And the redhead over there is Sarah."

"It's good to meet you," Hannah said. "And I am flattered that the Prophet would give me a name, but I don't feel like a Serenity. I'm just—Hannah."

"I don't care what you call yourself, as long as you

peel those potatoes." Phoenix added salt to the pot and stirred. "We need them to fry up with the onions."

Hannah picked up the knife and a potato. "Does everyone eat all their meals together?" she asked.

"Usually," Starfall said. "It's more efficient that way, and it fosters a sense of family." She swept chopped onion into a bowl and picked up another onion.

"We take turns cooking and watching the children," Asteria said. "The work is easier with more people to do it."

"I love children," Hannah said. "How many are there in camp?"

"Gloria has a five-year-old son," Asteria said. "Starfall has a son, who's seven months old. Solitude has a three-year-old, too. A boy. Zoe has six-year-old twins. And Phoenix has a fourteen-year-old daughter and a baby girl."

"My husband and I knew this was a good place to be when we saw so many children," Hannah said. The word "husband" sounded odd to her ears, but it was easy enough to say, even though she had never thought of herself as very good at lying.

"That's a good-looking man you have," Sarah said.

"Um, thanks." Hannah wasn't sure how to respond to this comment. Walt was handsome, but it wasn't as if she could claim responsibility for that. "He's a good man." She thought that much was true, at least.

"Maybe he'll be one of the rare ones who stick," Starfall said.

"What do you mean?" Hannah dropped a peeled potato into the empty pot Asteria had set in front of her and picked up another.

"A lot of guys don't adapt well to life in the Family," Asteria explained. "We have a few who have been here awhile, but a lot of them end up leaving after a few months or weeks because it's not what they expected."

"It's not a lifestyle for everyone," Phoenix said. "But the Prophet changes lives. I'm proof of that." She moved one of the pots off a burner and set another in its place.

"Mom, I need a bottle for Vicki." A lanky teenage girl, her long brown hair in pigtails, raced up to Phoenix. Dressed in shorts and a T-shirt, she looked like any other young teen, except for the baby on her hip. The infant, dressed in a pink sleeper, gurgled happily as the girl hoisted her up higher.

"Give me a minute." Phoenix added salt to the pot in front of her and tasted.

"She's been really fussy," the girl said. "I think she's hungry."

"All right." Phoenix set aside the spoon she'd been using to stir and walked to the row of coolers along the shadiest side of the shelter.

Hannah moved around the table to where the girl stood. "I'm Hannah," she said. "I'm new here."

"I'm Sophie, and this is Vicki." Sophie hitched the baby up again. "Well, her name's really Victory, but no one calls her that, except the Prophet."

"How old is she?" Hannah had to restrain herself from reaching for the infant, who kicked her little legs and waved her chubby arms, letting out a wail of protest.

"Almost four months. Would you like to hold her?"

Before Hannah could even form an answer the girl was putting the baby in her arms. Hannah cradled the child against her, patting her back and delighting in her chubby sweetness. The child quieted and stared up at Hannah with wide blue eyes.

Emily's eyes. The recognition hit Hannah like a slap. She touched one finger to the tiny dent in the baby's chin. Hannah had a dent like that in her own chin.

"She must like you. She's not usually that good with strangers." Phoenix had returned and stood at Hannah's elbow, a baby bottle in one hand.

When she leaned in to take the baby, Hannah's first instinct was to hold on tight. She could run away, find Walt and they could leave on his motorcycle. They could reach Ranger headquarters before anyone would have time to pursue them.

Logic—and probably all the lectures she had endured from Walt and his boss about needing proof that any child she found in the camp really was Emily's baby—made her reluctantly release the child to Phoenix. "You don't breast-feed?" she asked as the child latched on to the bottle.

Phoenix frowned at her. "I couldn't. I got sick right after she was born and lost my milk."

"I'm sorry," Hannah said. "That was a terribly rude question. I'm just so curious about anything to do with babies these days."

Phoenix's expression softened. "I understand." She smiled down at the baby. "I never thought I'd have another little one and now I have her. She's been a special blessing in my life."

Hannah clenched her jaw, fighting back the questions she wanted to ask. Who was this baby's father? When had she been born? Where had she been born? Did Phoenix know a woman named Emily? Instead, she held her tongue and returned to peeling potatoes, her mind working furiously. She had to find a way to prove that little Vicki wasn't Phoenix's child, but Emily's. Maybe Phoenix had taken over care of the baby because no one else was available at the time of Emily's death. Hannah was grateful to her if that was the case. But if that was so, why pass the baby off as her own? And surely she hadn't taken in the baby without Daniel Metwater's knowledge. So why had the Prophet lied about having Joy with him?

"Did you hear what those cops said about that missing girl?" Sarah heaved a large watermelon onto the table and plunged a knife into it.

"She never should have left camp," Asteria said. "She would have been safe here."

Hannah almost dropped her potato. "You mean the girl the police were looking for was here?"

"For less than a day." Starfall scraped the last of the chopped onions into a pot. "The Prophet told her she couldn't stay, since she was underage, and she left."

"Why didn't anyone tell the Rangers that?" Hannah asked.

"One thing you need to learn if you stay here is that we don't speak to the cops," Starfall said. "It's one of the Prophet's rules."

"But if it would help them find her, why not say something?" Hannah asked. "Her poor parents must be worried sick."

"It won't help her, and it will only focus unnecessary attention on us," Starfall said. "The point is, she's not here now, and no one in the Family had anything to do with her disappearance, so the cops should look elsewhere instead of hassling us."

"Don't you go saying anything to anyone," Phoenix said. "It will only cause trouble. You don't want to start out like that."

Why would any reasonable person want to be a part of a group that hid evidence from the police? Hannah thought, but she only nodded and went back to peeling potatoes. She would have so much to tell Walt tonight—not only this bit of news about the missing young woman, but that she was sure she had found her sister's baby. All she needed was a little proof.

WALT SET OUT with Jobie and a guy who introduced himself as Slate to gather firewood. They had one hand ax and a rusting bow saw between them, and apparently Jobie and Slate had never been Boy Scouts, because they seemed to have no clue what actually made good firewood.

"I don't think that rotten stuff is going to burn very well," Walt said as Slate tugged at a fallen tree trunk that was so rotten it was growing a healthy crop of mushrooms.

The log crumbled as soon as he tried to lift it. "Guess not," he said, and straightened.

"Do you do this every day?" Walt asked.

"Pretty much," Jobie said. "We keep telling the Prophet if we had a chain saw we could cut a bunch at once and not have to work so hard, but he says the noise would draw the wrong kind of attention."

"Yeah, the cops have already got it in for us," Slate said. "They're always around here hassling us."

"Why do you think that is?" Walt asked.

"Because they're suspicious of anyone who colors outside the lines," Slate said.

"We don't bother anybody and we ask the same of them." Jobie tugged on the end of a branch that lay beneath a tree and held up a four-foot length of juniper. He grinned and added it to his pile.

"What do we need all this wood for, anyway?" Walt asked. "Do the women cook over a fire?"

"They mostly use the camp stoves for cooking," Jobie said. "But every night after supper we have a campfire. Sometimes there's singing or dancing, like last night. Sometimes the Prophet has a message for us, and sometimes there's a ceremony."

"What kind of ceremony?" Walt asked.

"Oh, you know, like when new members join or if the Prophet has had a vision that tells him we need to perform some kind of ritual."

"You mean like saying prayers or something?"

"Not that, so much," Slate said. "Cooler stuff. Once we did fire walking, and another time everyone had to bring something to burn that represented stuff they were letting go of."

"The Prophet is really big on letting go of the past," Jobie said. "Like, if you've made mistakes or whatever, none of that has to hold you back now."

"That's what makes being part of the Family so great," Slate said. "Nobody judges you based on what you did before. You start over clean. That's why I chose the name I did. I'm a clean Slate."

Walt had read Metwater's writings about new beginnings and fresh starts. But he wondered if those teachings might not have a special appeal for people who wanted to get away with bad behavior with no consequences. Simply join up with the Prophet and all your sins are forgiven. You could get away with anything—maybe even murder.

Walt figured this wasn't the time to share his skepticism about the Prophet's message. "I guess that takes lots of firewood," he said.

"Yeah." Jobie swung the ax ineffectually at the spindly branch of a pinyon. "The Rangers think we relocated our camp because our permit expired, but really, it was just that we ran out of firewood."

Walt joined in their laughter and led the way to the next clump of scrubby trees. He estimated they were about a mile from camp, in a part of the Curecanti wilderness that he had never visited. Probably very few people came to this roadless site. "Do you ever run into wild animals out here?" he asked. "Bears or mountain lions or anything like that?"

"Sometimes we see coyotes," Jobie said. "And lots of rabbits."

"We've found other weird stuff, though," Slate said. "An old junk car, shot full of holes. A whole skeleton of some big animal, like a horse or something."

"Once we found a sofa, just sitting out in the middle of nowhere," Jobie said. "We hauled it back to camp and Kiram has it in this shack he built."

Walt pushed through a tangle of tree branches and vines and emerged in a small clearing, no larger than the average living room. A wall of green surrounded it, with a circle of blue sky high overhead. No shot-up car or skeleton occupied the space, but a different kind of oddity that sent a cold chill up Walt's spine. "Is that a grave?" he asked, pointing to the mound of disturbed earth, a makeshift cross at its head.

Chapter Eight

"The Prophet is not going to like this." Jobie shook his head as the three men stared at the grave in the middle of the clearing.

Walt studied the area around the burial site. There were no clear footprints, and the soil had settled some, though he couldn't tell if the grave had been dug in the past few days or the past few weeks. No plants grew on the surface of the mound, and the wood on the cross was new enough the cut edges were still fresh. "We need to notify the Rangers," Walt said. "They'll want to investigate."

"Cell phones don't work out here," Jobie said. "So none of us have them."

"We'll have to talk to the Prophet," Slate said. "It's up to him."

Walt started to point out that the grave was on public land and it wasn't up to Daniel Metwater to decide whether or not it should be reported, but he didn't waste his breath. "Come on," he said. "Let's get back to camp."

They gathered up the firewood they had collected and Walt led the way back toward camp. Kiram met them at the edge of the clearing. "What took you so long?" he asked.

"We have to talk to the Prophet," Slate said.

"He doesn't like to be disturbed before dinner," Kiram said.

"He's going to want to know about what we found while we were looking for wood," Jobie said.

"What did you find?" Kiram asked.

"We'll tell the Prophet," Walt said. He pushed past the bearded man, dropped his load of wood beside the fire ring then strode toward Metwater's RV. Jobie and Slate hurried to catch up with him, Kiram following, his face like a thundercloud.

Metwater opened the door before Walt could even knock. "Is something wrong?" he asked, letting his gaze drift over the four men who gathered on the steps of the RV.

Jobie, Slate and Kiram all looked at Walt. "We found a grave while we were looking for firewood," he said. "It looks pretty fresh."

"Whose grave?" Metwater asked.

"The marker didn't say," Jobie said—as if this was a perfectly reasonable question.

"We need to notify the Rangers," Walt said. "They can determine who's in the grave."

"Maybe it's that girl the cops were looking for," Jobie said.

"If the grave is hers, I'm sure the police will find it before long," Metwater said. "We should stay out of this."

"It's too late for that," Walt said. "We found it and now we have to report it."

Metwater put his hand on Walt's shoulder and

looked into his eyes, his expression that of a father dealing with an unruly—and perhaps stupid—child. "You aren't a part of that outside world anymore," he said. "Here in the Family we don't concern ourselves with the world's evil. That is for others, not us."

"You can't divorce yourself from responsibilities that way," Walt said.

"That's exactly what we're doing, living here in the wilderness," Metwater said.

"Wilderness supported by taxpayer money. You're happy enough to take advantage of that."

Metwater shook his head. "You have a long way to go toward gaining the understanding necessary to be a true member of the Family," he said. "Your wife is much more in tune with our purpose than you are."

"And you know that from talking with her for what, twenty minutes?"

"Women are much more intuitive about these things than most men. It's one of the reasons they are so drawn to my teachings."

And it has nothing to do with naked muscles and flowing hair, Walt thought cynically. "You can't let that grave go unreported," he said.

"That's exactly what we will do," Metwater said. "Although I will meditate on the problem and if I receive different guidance I will act on it." He clapped a hand on Walt's shoulder. "Come. We are having a special meal to welcome you and Serenity to the fold."

"Her name is Hannah," Walt said, reluctantly falling into step beside Metwater, since the alternative seemed to be wrestling with the man, which probably wouldn't go over well with Kiram and the others.

"But you and she are starting a new life here. Serenity suits her. She strikes me as someone who is looking for peace in her life."

Hannah was looking for her missing niece—but maybe Metwater wasn't so far off track. Maybe having the baby in her life would bring Hannah more peace of mind, and ease some of her grief for her sister. Walt wanted to help her find the baby, and the closure adopting her niece might bring.

In order to do that, he had to walk a fine line between doing anything that might blow his cover or anger Metwater to the point where he threw them out of camp, and continuing to uphold his duty as a law officer.

They reached the camp's outdoor kitchen, where most of the residents were already lined up awaiting the meal. Jobie and Slate took their places in line, while Kiram hovered near Metwater. Was he some sort of bodyguard, or simply awaiting more orders from the Prophet?

Kiram looked over and caught Walt watching him. Certainly there was little peace and love in his eyes. Walt spotted Hannah and started toward her, but Kiram grabbed his arm. "Don't get any ideas about sneaking out of camp to go to the police," he said, keeping his voice low. "Try it and you will be punished."

"I'm trembling in my boots," Walt said.

"You should be." He gave Walt's arm a shake, then released his hold. "And remember—you won't be the only one hurt." He turned to Hannah, and the icy hatred in his eyes chilled Walt to the bone.

"WHAT'S WRONG WITH YOU?" Hannah asked when she finally cornered Walt at their tent after supper that evening. They hadn't been able to exchange more than a few words during the day, constantly surrounded as they were by Family members who were either eager to welcome them, curious to know more about them or both. After breakfast, they had both been assigned to work teams to clean up, and after that had been a speech—or more like a sermon—from Metwater. Though Hannah could admit he was a charismatic speaker, she was too focused on Walt to pay much attention to Metwater's message. He sat across from her with a group of men, scowling at the Prophet as if the man had just kicked his dog.

The afternoon was taken up by more work. Hannah stayed with the women and did her best to avoid Metwater. She spent most of her time with Phoenix, taking every opportunity to hold the baby, growing more and more sure that this was her sister's child. She was relieved to finally have the chance to be alone with Walt again after supper, to tell him all she had learned.

"I have to find a way to sneak out of here for a few hours tonight without anyone noticing," he said.

The thought of him leaving her alone here sent a spike of panic through her. "Why do you have to leave?" she asked.

He glanced around. "Let's not talk out here." He unzipped the tent flap. "Inside. And keep your voice down."

She crawled into the tent ahead of him and sat cross-legged on one of the sleeping bags he had unrolled. He moved in after her, zipping up the tent behind him. "Why do you need to leave?" she asked, her voice just above a whisper.

"When I was out gathering firewood this morning with two other men, we found a grave."

"A grave? A *person's* grave?" Her voice rose on the last word and he gripped her hand.

"Keep your voice down," he said.

She nodded, then, realizing he probably couldn't see her, said, "Okay, but what are you talking about? You found someone buried out here in the middle of nowhere?"

"I don't know what's in the grave, but I need to get word to the Rangers so they can investigate."

"You don't think it was from some pioneer ranching family or something?" she asked. "I mean, wasn't some of the parkland private land at one time?"

"This wasn't like that," he said. "I'm pretty sure it was more recent. Much more recent."

A chilling thought struck her and she gripped his hand more tightly. "That girl the Rangers are looking for?"

"I don't know," Walt said. "It's a possibility."

"The women I was working with this morning said she was here—in camp," she said. "But that she left after less than a day. Metwater supposedly sent her away because she was too young."

"I'll be sure and let the Rangers know when I talk to them. If Metwater and his followers are lying about not knowing her, I have to wonder what else they're covering up."

"The men you were with—do they know about this grave?"

"Yes. They saw it, too. Two men, Jobie and Slate. We told Metwater when we got back to camp and he refused to go to the police, or to let us go."

"He can't keep you from telling them," she said. "We came here voluntarily. He can't make us stay."

"He thinks he can."

Something in his words ratcheted her fear up another notch. "Did he threaten you?"

"He didn't, but a man named Kiram did. He's the guy I told you about—Metwater's enforcer. He said if I tried to leave, I would be punished." He took her other hand. "He said you would be, too. In fact, instead of me leaving and coming back, I'm beginning to think we should leave together and not come back. Maybe this undercover op was a bad idea."

"No, we can't leave." She pulled her hands from his. "Not when we're so close to finding Joy and learning what happened to Emily. In fact, I think I've already found Joy."

"What? Where?" He shifted toward her.

She took a deep breath, trying to organize her thoughts, but all that brought her was his scent, distracting and sensual. Heat curled through her, and the space inside the tent suddenly seemed too intimate. If she leaned over just a little, they would be touching, and her skin tingled in anticipation…

"Do you think one of the children in camp is your niece?" Walt prompted.

"Yes. The woman who came to get me to help with breakfast this morning—Phoenix—is a little older than some of the rest of the women here, maybe in her early forties. She has a fourteen-year-old daughter, Sophie. But she also has a baby. A little girl, about four months old."

"Why do you think this baby is Joy?"

"Phoenix isn't breast-feeding her. She's using formula. She told me she wasn't able to breast-feed, but I think she's lying."

"Lots of women use formula. It doesn't mean the baby isn't hers."

"No, but I held this baby. I looked into her eyes. They were Emily's eyes. The same shape—the same color." She wished she could see his face more clearly, to judge if he believed her, but the light was too dim to make out his features.

"What color are Phoenix's eyes?" he asked.

The question caught her off guard. She tried to bring Phoenix to mind, to remember her eyes, but she couldn't. "I don't know," she admitted.

He took her hand again, gentle this time. His voice was gentle, too, when he spoke. "I know you want to find your niece, and that you have good reason to believe she's with Metwater. But you can't let your natural biases lead you into a mistake. Think about how much pain it would cause Phoenix if this baby really is hers, and not Joy?"

She wanted to insist that she knew this baby was Emily's daughter, but the part of her that relied on logic instead of emotion told her that everything he said made perfect sense. "Then we have to stay here and look for proof," she said. "If I make friends with Phoenix, and with Sophie, maybe I can persuade them to tell me the truth about the baby."

"I still have to let the Rangers know about the grave we found."

"Of course." She slid her hand from his and clenched it in her lap. "I'll be fine. After all, it's nighttime. Everyone will be sleeping."

"Stay in the tent. I should be back before morning." He moved toward the door.

"Let me come with you to the bike," she said. "I can serve as a lookout until you get safely away." And she wanted to prolong the time before he left her alone.

"All right. We'd better go now. The sooner I can get away, the sooner I'll be back."

They crept through the darkened camp, keeping to the edges, skirting any lights that still shone outside tents or trailers. Walt held Hannah's hand, and she took comfort from his strong grip pulling her along, his sure steps guiding hers as they moved through the darkness.

They found the bike where they had left it, on the edge of the parking area. Walt had cut tree branches and draped them over the motorcycle to hide it from curious eyes. He quickly pulled these away and pushed the bike toward the road. "I won't start it until I'm farther from camp," he said. "If anyone comes to the tent looking for me, tell them I'm asleep."

"I will."

"And take this." He pressed something hard into her hand.

She looked down at a knife—similar to the one she had used to peel potatoes this morning. "I palmed it at dinner," he said. "It's not much, but I didn't feel right leaving you defenseless. You can keep it in your pocket."

"All right." She slipped the knife into the pocket of her skirt, where it rested, heavy and awkward, a reminder of the danger they might be in here, but an even stronger reminder that Walt was looking out for her, even when he couldn't be with her. The knowledge shook her—she had spent so many years alone.

She was used to looking after herself, so what did it mean that knowing he was on her side felt so good? She looked toward the road, a faint pale strip in the light of a quarter moon. It would take Walt more than an hour to reach a good phone signal he could use to report his find—an hour traveling over rough, narrow roads in pitch-blackness. An unseen pothole, an animal running out in front of him—or one of Metwater's men in pursuit—and he might never reach his destination at all.

"Be careful." She took hold of his arm and leaned toward him, intending only to kiss his cheek. But he turned toward her and their lips met, and she realized this was what she had wanted all along—what she had wanted in that dark, intimate interlude in the tent. He brought one hand up to caress her cheek and she angled her mouth under his. He kissed the same way he did everything—with a quiet strength that moved her more than Metwater's overt seduction ever could. The brush of his unshaven cheeks abrading her skin sent a shiver of arousal through her, and she leaned in closer, wanting to be nearer to him, wanting this moment to never end.

But at last he pulled away, though his hand remained on her shoulder, steadying her. "I'll be back as soon as I can," he said. "Stay safe."

"You, too." Reluctantly, she stepped back, one hand to her mouth as if to preserve the memory of his kiss. She watched him as he walked away, pushing the motorcycle, until he was out of sight, disappearing into the darkness. Then she crossed the bridge back into camp.

She retraced the route they had followed back to the tent, seeing and hearing no one. The few lanterns that had previously been lit were out now, plunging the compound into silent blackness. Hannah felt her way from tree to tree, wishing she had thought to bring a flashlight with her. She let out a sigh of relief when she spotted the tent, by itself on the edge of the camp.

She had almost reached the safety of that shelter when someone clamped a hand over her mouth and dragged her back against him. She kicked out and tried to struggle free, but the unseen man held her fast. "Where is your husband now?" a voice growled in her ear. "And why isn't he here to protect you?"

Chapter Nine

Walt estimated he had walked the heavy motorcycle the better part of a mile before he dared climb on and start the engine. It roared to life, echoing in the midnight stillness. If anyone in camp heard him and figured out what was going on, he would be long gone before they could come after him.

He raced the bike as fast as he dared over the rough washboard road, barely maintaining control of the big machine as it bounced over the rugged dirt track. His headlight seemed to scarcely penetrate the inky blackness, illuminating only a few yards in front of him. More than once eyes glowed from the brush alongside the road—coyotes or foxes or other wild creatures observing his passing.

He tried not to think of what might happen to Hannah while he was away. Instead, he focused on the memory of that goodbye kiss. Working with her on this undercover op, he had grown close to her in a very short period of time. Even though they weren't married, at times he felt that close connection to her—or at least, what he hoped the connection between a husband and wife should feel like.

The kind of connection he had wanted with his former girlfriend, but had clearly never had. Looking back, he remembered how stunned he had been when he learned she was seeing his brother. But he saw, too, how part of him wasn't surprised she had betrayed him. Wanting someone to love you deeply wasn't the same as having that love be a reality. It was a lesson he had had to learn the hard way.

So why was he even thinking about love and Hannah in the same breath? As beautiful as she was, and as close as he felt to her at times, she was here to find her niece. She wanted to return to her home in Texas and start a new life with the baby—nowhere in that plan did he see room for a backcountry cop. He was doing it again—wishing for a relationship that couldn't exist.

It was almost two in the morning when he finally reached the paved highway that led toward Black Canyon of the Gunnison National Park and Ranger Brigade headquarters. He raced the bike over the blacktop to the headquarters building and let himself in with his key, then dialed the commander's number on the office line, more reliable than cell service out here.

Ranger Brigade commander Graham Ellison didn't sound groggy when he answered the phone. "Ellison. What's up?"

"It's Walt Riley, sir. There's been a development near Metwater's compound that you need to be aware of." He explained about the grave and its approximate location, as well as Metwater's stricture against reporting it. "I took a chance, sneaking out of camp," Walt said. "I need to get back as soon as possible."

"Wait there at headquarters. I'll have someone there

in half an hour or less. We need you to show us the area on a map and fill in some details."

"Yes, sir." He hung up the phone and settled in to wait.

Kɪʀᴀᴍ ᴡʀᴇɴᴄʜᴇᴅ Hᴀɴɴᴀʜ's arm behind her back, hurting her. "I'm going to uncover your mouth," he said. "But if you cry out, I'll break your arm."

She nodded to show she understood and he removed his hand. "Let me go," she said.

"Where is your husband?" he asked.

"He's asleep in the tent."

"I was just there. He isn't there."

"Maybe he got up to go to the bathroom." She began to struggle again, frantic over what he might do to her if she didn't get away. He started pulling her toward the parking lot—toward the deserted road and the empty wilderness, away from the rest of the camp, where there were people who might help her. "What are you doing?" she asked. "Where are you taking me?"

"I warned your husband what would happen if he disobeyed the Prophet's orders."

"I don't know what you're talking about. Let me go. Help!"

The savage jerk he gave her didn't break her arm, but it hurt enough that she gasped in pain. "You're making a mistake," she said. "Let's go to the Prophet now. I'll prove to you that you're making a mistake." She had no idea what she would say to Metwater, but demanding to see him would at least get her back to the camp, where surely someone would help her.

Kiram stopped. "You want to see the Prophet?"

"Yes. He's the leader of this camp. If he thinks I need to be punished, I want to hear it from him."

"Fine. We'll go to him." He turned and headed back toward camp, still gripping her arm. She had to run to keep from being dragged. The clearing in the midst of the tents and trailers was empty and silent, the only light from the dying coals of the bonfire they had gathered around earlier. Metwater's motor home was dark and silent also.

Hannah slowed her steps as they neared the RV. "The Prophet won't like being awakened," she said.

"You should have thought of that before your husband disobeyed him." One hand gripping her arm, he raised the other hand to knock on the door of the motor home.

Hannah didn't wait for someone to answer Kiram's knock. She had no intention of going into that RV with him—not in the middle of the night, with no witnesses around to notice if the two men decided to make her disappear altogether. She slipped her hand into the pocket of her skirt and gripped the knife Walt had given her. As her fingers closed around the blade, she summoned all her courage. She was doing this for Joy, she told herself. For Emily.

She jabbed the knife hard into Kiram's shoulder. He yelped and released her, and she ran to the far side of the dying bonfire. Snatching a smoldering branch from the fire, she brandished it in one hand, the knife in the other. Then she began to scream. "Help! Someone help me, please! Kiram attacked me! Help!"

As she had hoped, heads poked out of the tents and trailers surrounding the area. Kiram clutched his shoulder, blood trickling between his fingers. "She stabbed me!" he roared, and started toward her, his face a mask of rage.

"Only because he attacked me first. Look at the bruises on my arm if you don't believe me."

No one moved to help her, but none of them went back inside, either. Kiram glared at her. The light outside the motor home went on and the door opened to reveal Daniel Metwater, clad only in pajama pants, scowling at them. "What is going on?" he asked.

"The new man, Walt, left tonight," Kiram said. "I'm sure he went to the police."

"Of course he went to the police," Hannah said. "There's a fresh grave out there, not far from camp, and the police are looking for a missing woman. Her family is probably beside themselves, trying to find her."

"We don't have anything to do with that," Metwater said.

"Trying to hide it makes you look like you do." Hannah slipped the knife into her pocket but kept hold of the smoldering branch. "And the fact that Walt went to tell someone about the grave doesn't give Kiram any right to attack me."

Metwater turned to Kiram. "Did you attack her?"

"I warned her husband if he disobeyed your orders and left the camp, they would have to be disciplined." He lifted his hand from his shoulder. "And she stabbed me."

"When a man puts his hands on a woman against her will, she has a right to defend herself," Hannah said.

Murmurs of agreement rose from the crowd of onlookers. Metwater held up a hand. "Part of being a member of the Family is agreeing to abide by my rules," he said.

"One of your rules is that women are to be treated with respect."

Hannah turned to see who had spoken. Phoenix stepped into the circle of light from a lantern that hung outside her tent. She cradled the baby in her arms. "If Kiram attacked Serenity in the darkness, when her husband wasn't there to defend her, that isn't treating her with respect."

"What about respect for me and my role of carrying out the Prophet's will?" Kiram growled the words. At that moment, he reminded Hannah of a wounded bear.

Everyone was focused on Metwater, as if he really was some king or Old Testament prophet who had authority to rule their lives. Hannah realized she was holding her breath in anticipation, as if she believed he had power over her, as well. Had Emily stood before him like this, waiting while he decided her fate?

Of course, all she had to do was declare she had had enough of this nonsense and walk away. But doing so would end her best chance of finding out what had happened to Emily and her baby. She shifted her gaze to where Phoenix stood, cradling the child. That baby might be Joy. Hannah couldn't walk away until she knew for sure.

"Tomorrow, after Serenity's husband has returned, we will hold a council," Metwater declared. "At that time, we will decide the appropriate response to their willful and disobedient behavior." He fixed his gaze on Hannah. A shiver crept up her spine. Did no one else see the malevolence in those dark eyes? "Until tomorrow, I put you in Phoenix's care. She will watch over you."

"I don't need a guard," Hannah said.

Metwater's smile held no warmth. "But clearly, you do."

Phoenix crossed the clearing to Hannah's side. "Come on," she said. "I'll fix a comfortable place for you in my trailer." She leaned closer, her voice so soft Hannah scarcely heard her words, and she was sure no one else could. "You'll be safer with me than alone in your tent—just in case Kiram gets any ideas."

Hannah glanced at Kiram, who was still glowering at her. Her aching arm reminded her of how easily he could overpower her. She nodded. "Thanks," she said. She wouldn't think of this time as imprisonment. She would use the opportunity to get to know Phoenix and her baby better. Maybe this would be the key to learning the truth she needed to know.

MEMBERS OF THE Ranger team started showing up at headquarters within half an hour of Walt's call—Lance Carpenter arrived first, followed by Michael Dance, Ethan Reynolds and the commander. Walt had made coffee and they helped themselves to mugs before settling down to consider the case. "Sorry for almost blowing your cover out there yesterday," Lance said as he settled at the conference table across from Walt. "We should have checked in with the commander before we headed out there."

"It worked out okay," Walt said. "Now Metwater and the rest think I'm as disgruntled with the cops as they are."

"Tell us more about this grave you found," Commander Ellison said, settling into the chair at the head of the table.

"It looks fairly recent, though I'm no expert," Walt

said. "It was in a small clearing, not visible until you were right up on it, about a mile from camp, at least that far from any road."

"And you're sure it was a grave?" Michael asked.

"It was an oblong mound of earth, maybe two feet wide and four feet long, with a homemade wooden cross at one end. No writing on the cross. No footprints on the surrounding ground. The dirt had dried out and settled a little, but no vegetation was growing on it, and the sawed ends of the cross were fresh, not weathered." He sat back in his chair. "And Metwater was very annoyed when I told him I intended to report it."

"What was his argument against doing so?" Ethan asked.

"It would bring law enforcement into camp again."

"What is he afraid we're going to find?" Lance asked. "He sounds like a man with something to hide."

"Do you think he knows anything about the missing woman—Lucia Raton?" Graham asked.

"Hannah spoke to some Family members who said she came around wanting to join the group," Walt said. "Metwater supposedly sent her away because she was too young."

"And they didn't bother to mention this to us," Michael said. "I think this warrants questioning him again. Maybe we should bring him in."

"Let's see what we find in the grave first." Graham sat back in his chair. "We'll get a team out there at first light, though we'll have to wait for a forensic anthropologist to excavate it properly. That could take a while, depending on where he or she has to come from. If it's Denver or Salt Lake, it could mean an extra day's wait."

"You should at least get someone out there to guard

the site," Walt said. "Now that Metwater knows I know about this, if he is involved somehow, he may try to destroy evidence."

"We'll do that," Graham said. "What else have you learned?"

"Metwater preaches a message of peace and love, but he's set a lot of rules for his followers. He's got at least one guy, calls himself Kiram, whose job is to enforce the rules. He threatened me—and Hannah—if I came to you."

"Threatened you with what?" Lance asked.

"Nothing specific. I told Hannah I'd feel better if she came with me tonight," Walt said. "I gave her the opportunity to call off the operation altogether, but she wanted to stay and see it through."

"Any news about her sister or the baby?" Ethan asked.

"Everyone denies knowing anything about the sister, but I think they're lying," Walt said. "There's a woman in camp who has a little girl the right age to be Hannah's niece, but we don't have any proof she isn't the woman's child. Hannah thinks if she makes friends with the woman, who goes by Phoenix, she can find out more."

"We'll give it another day or two, but if either of you feel at any time that you're in danger, get out of there," Graham said. "If this bunch really is responsible for Lucia Raton's death, we don't want to give them a chance to add to the body count."

"When I described Hannah's sister to some men in the camp, one of them told me she sounded like a woman who was there in the spring," Walt said. "Hannah said Metwater reacted to the name, though he denied knowing Emily."

"Before I forget, we managed to get hold of Marsha Caldwell." Marco leaned back to snag a notebook off a desk. "The nurse who witnessed Emily Dietrich's will."

"What did she say?" Walt asked, tensed on the edge of his chair.

"She remembered Emily—described her as a sweet young woman with a beautiful baby. Caldwell said Emily didn't strike her as particularly fearful. She came to the hospital with another woman—the Anna Ingels who also witnessed the will. She thought Ingels was a friend or maybe an older relative."

"Did you get a description of Ingels?" Walt asked.

Marco consulted his notes. "Nothing really useful. Medium height, late thirties, blond hair and light eyes."

That description could fit a few of the women in camp, but it wasn't specific enough to zero in on anyone. "How could she say Emily wasn't fearful when she wanted Caldwell to witness a will?"

"She said it wasn't the first will she had witnessed," Marco said. "Apparently, labor and delivery is traumatic for some women. She said it makes them aware of their own mortality. Add in the responsibility for a new life, and a will outlining who should care for the baby in the event of the mother's death is a sensible response."

"So she didn't think Emily was afraid someone was going to kill her?" Walt asked.

"She didn't think so, no."

Was Hannah wrong, then? Had her sister died of an unfortunate bout of ill health, and Metwater had nothing to do with it? So why was he trying to hide the child—assuming Phoenix's baby really was Hannah's niece, as she asserted? He shoved back his chair. "I had better get back to camp," he said. "Even though I don't think Kiram would be foolish enough to try anything, I don't like leaving Hannah there too long."

"You may be in the best position to learn what happened with Lucia Raton," Michael said. "Whatever evidence you can find could be crucial to making a case."

Walt nodded. As long as Metwater and his people saw Walt and Hannah as prospective members who were interested in the Prophet's teachings, they were more likely to let down their guard and reveal information that could help solve one or more crimes. Provided Walt could hold on to his cover long enough and get back in Metwater's good graces after disobeying orders and coming here tonight. He was going to have to do some fast talking to do so, but maybe Metwater's desire to keep Hannah around would work in their favor. "I'll try to learn as much as I can," he said.

Graham walked with him to the door and shook his hand. "We'll be back in camp after we've searched the grave. We'll let you know what we find then."

"By that time, I hope Hannah and I are ready to leave. Everything in camp looks innocent enough, but something about the whole setup rubs me the wrong way. Metwater is up to something—we just haven't figured out what yet."

Chapter Ten

Hannah spent a restless night on a sofa on one side of the travel trailer Phoenix shared with her daughter Sophie and the baby. Worries over where Walt might be and what he might be doing competed with nightmares of Kiram or Daniel Metwater leering over her to prevent sleep. Had Walt made it safely to the road? What would the Rangers do with the information he gave them? Was the grave that of the missing young woman? Who had killed her and put her there? Had Kiram merely been trying to frighten her when he had grabbed her earlier, or had he really intended to hurt her? Had Emily suffered a similar fright, which had eventually led to her death?

She tried to distract herself by focusing on the baby. Little Vicki slept in a porta-crib next to Phoenix's bed, and Hannah could just see her from the sofa. The child slept peacefully, fist in her mouth, clad in a pink fleece sleeper. Hannah fought the urge to take the baby from the crib and cuddle her. But that would only awaken Phoenix and the baby and arouse suspicion. And it wouldn't really tell Hannah anything, only satisfy her longing to hold the child in her arms.

Phoenix awakened at dawn to tend to the baby.

Hannah sat up on the sofa, a blanket wrapped around her, and watched as the older woman prepared a bottle of formula. "Would you like to feed her while I get dressed?" Phoenix asked.

"Yes." Hannah held out her arms and took the child, who stared up at her with sleepy eyes. Vicki took the bottle readily and Hannah settled back to marvel at the baby's sweet perfection. Sophie got out of her bunk and came to sit beside her.

"She eats like a little piglet," the girl said, letting the baby latch on to her index finger.

"She's always had a healthy appetite." Phoenix emerged from her bedroom and joined them. "I'm grateful for that."

"Would you think I was terribly nosy if I asked about her father?" Hannah kept her eyes focused on the baby, though she braced herself for Phoenix's answer.

"The Prophet is her father," Phoenix said, unflustered by the question.

"Oh. I didn't know."

Phoenix removed the now-empty bottle from Vicki's mouth. "I'll take her now," she said, and raised the baby to her shoulder and began patting her back. "He's the father to all the children here," Phoenix said. "If not physically, then certainly spiritually."

Sophie made a face. "He's not my father," she said.

"Now, Sophie," her mother said.

Sophie turned to Hannah. "My father is a musician in San Francisco. But we don't see him much." She shrugged. "It's okay. He's kind of messed up."

"Sophie, why don't you run ahead to help Starfall and the others with breakfast," Phoenix said. "Serenity and I will be along soon."

"She doesn't like it when I talk about my dad," Sophie said, standing. "She and the Prophet are big into forgetting the past, but I don't see how anyone can really do that, do you?"

"Sophie!"

"I'm going." Grinning, the girl skipped from the trailer.

Phoenix settled onto the sofa beside Hannah. "I'm sorry about that," she said. "I guess Sophie is a little young to understand all the spiritual concepts the Prophet is trying to teach us."

"You mean, about forgetting the past."

"Maybe not forgetting." She laid the baby across her lap and began removing her diaper. "But putting it behind us. She and I made a fresh start when we came here. It's time to look forward, not backward." Her eyes met Hannah's. "We all have things in our past we would like to not dwell on."

"Yes. But the past shapes us," Hannah said. "We are who we are because of it."

"I would rather not remember the pain," Phoenix said. "I want to focus on the future." She fastened the baby's diaper and smiled down at the child. "Let's go to breakfast," she said.

"The Prophet said last night you were in charge of me," Hannah said as they made their way through camp toward the outdoor kitchen. "Does that mean you're my guard? Will you get in trouble if I leave?"

"Think of me as your companion." She hooked her arm in Hannah's. "I'm watching out for you and helping you. There's no need for you to be alone."

"My husband will be back soon," she said, resisting the urge to pull away from the other woman.

"He'll be assigned a companion, as well. The two of you will be kept apart until the council."

Hannah stopped. "Why?"

"It's for your own good," Phoenix said. "So that you can think more clearly, and so that you will be fairly judged separately and not as a single unit. His crimes don't have to reflect on you."

"Walt hasn't committed any crime," Hannah said. "He did the right thing, notifying the police about that grave."

Phoenix's gaze shifted away, and her mouth grew pinched. "Disobeying the Prophet is wrong," she said. "He has good reasons for all of his decisions. If you want to be a part of the Family, you need to realize that." She took Hannah's hand. "Come on. We'll be late for breakfast. You'll feel better after you eat."

Hannah tugged her hand free, but walked beside Phoenix to the cook tent. She left her with the other women and got in line for oatmeal and dried berries, then found a seat on a bench next to Sophie. "Did you and Mom have a fight about something?" Sophie asked.

"Your mother thinks my husband should be punished because he disobeyed the Prophet, even though he was doing the right thing," Hannah said.

"It's a big deal to disobey the Prophet," Sophie said. "It almost never happens."

"Who was the last person to break one of his rules?" Hannah asked.

Sophie dug into her bowl of oatmeal. "We're not supposed to talk about it."

"I didn't know the person, so what could it hurt?" Hannah said. "Maybe by telling me who they were and what they did, you could help me not to make the same mistake."

Sophie considered this. "It was a girl called Freedom. Well, that's what the Prophet called her. I don't think it was her real name."

"What did she do that was so wrong?" Hannah asked.

"She wanted to run away."

Hannah set aside her own spoon, a cold hollow in the pit of her stomach. "I thought anyone was free to leave here whenever he or she chose."

"Most people are. But Freedom had a baby, and all children belong to the Prophet. So she could have left, but she would have had to leave her baby behind."

"No mother would do that," Hannah said.

Sophie shrugged. "I guess she wanted to leave badly enough that she did."

Hannah stared at the girl for a moment, letting this information sink in. "You mean, she left the Family, and didn't take her baby with her?"

Sophie ducked her head. "I shouldn't have said anything. Please don't tell Mom. I'll get in trouble."

"I won't tell her, I promise." Hannah covered the child's hand with her own and lowered her voice to a whisper. "That's why you have Vicki, isn't it?" she asked. "She was Freedom's baby."

Sophie nodded. "Please don't tell."

Hannah squeezed her hand. "I won't. I promise." Freedom must have been Emily. Vicki—Victory—was Joy. And she belonged to Hannah now. Not Phoenix or the Prophet or anyone else.

WALT HALF EXPECTED to be met in the parking area outside the camp by Kiram and a crowd of angry Family members, but the lot was vacant, only the chattering of a scolding squirrel greeting him. He parked the bike, covered it with the branches he had cut earlier and crossed the bridge into camp. Jobie met him at the other side, a staff in one hand, a breakfast burrito in the other. "Hey," he said by way of greeting. "You missed all the excitement with your wife and Kiram last night."

Walt froze, one hand automatically reaching for the service weapon that wasn't at his side. "What happened with Hannah and Kiram?" he asked, his mind racing. If that thug had hurt Hannah...

"She says he was manhandling her and she called him on it and made a big fuss in front of the Prophet and everyone." He took a bite of his breakfast and chewed.

"Was he hurting her?" Walt asked. "And why?"

"He said she needed to be punished because the two of you were disobeying the Prophet's orders." He shrugged. "One of his jobs is to keep people in line, but he has a rep for taking things too far. A couple of other women have complained, but I guess the Prophet has let him get away with it until now. No way he could ignore the stink your wife was making last night, though."

Good for Hannah, Walt thought. "What did the Prophet do?"

"He sent Serenity off to stay with Phoenix and told Kiram to leave her alone. There's going to be a special council tonight to decide what your punishment should be for breaking the rules and leaving camp to go to the police."

Let them try to lay a hand on him or Hannah and see

how far they got. Walt started to push past Jobie. "Her name isn't Serenity, it's Hannah, and I need to see her."

Jobie tried to block him and Walt raised his fist, as if to take a swing. Jobie took a step back. "Hey, chill, dude! I was just going to tell you it's a good idea to play it cool. Kiram is still really ticked about being called out in front of the whole camp, so it would be smart to steer clear of him until tonight."

What he wanted was to confront Kiram right now and maybe pound his face for laying a hand on Hannah, but doing so would be letting emotion take the lead instead of using common sense. "What happens at these council meetings?" he asked.

"The Prophet usually gives a talk, then each side gets to present their case, then the Prophet makes a ruling." He shrugged. "He'll probably just have everyone involved do some kind of community service like pick up trash or build a new shelter. It's no big deal."

"Where is Hannah now?"

"She's eating breakfast with Phoenix and Sophie. She's fine."

"I still want to see her." He started forward once more and this time Jobie stepped aside to let him pass.

Conversation stopped abruptly when Walt walked into the open-sided shed that served as the Family's dining hall. Kiram looked up from his seat at the end of one of the long wooden picnic tables and glared at Walt, but remained silent. Everyone else stared, some openmouthed with avid curiosity, others avoiding his gaze, clearly fearful. Walt spotted Hannah, sitting next to a young girl, and started toward her. She rose to meet him and, without speaking, he took her arm and led her away from the shelter.

The murmur of conversation rose again behind them. Hannah gripped his arm. "How did it go?" she asked. "Are the Rangers on their way?"

"They're sending a team out to investigate the grave, then they'll want to question Metwater and others in the camp."

"That won't go over well," she said, glancing back toward the tables. Kiram had moved from his seat and stood at the edge of the shelter, watching them.

"They need to explain why they lied about Lucia Raton having been in camp," Walt said. "And why Metwater was so insistent I not report the grave to law enforcement."

"Some of the people here feel the police are invading their privacy with all their questions."

"It's our job to invade people's privacy, if that's what it takes to solve a crime."

"I know." She patted his arm. "But I see their point, too. Not wanting the police here doesn't make them guilty of anything."

"Maybe not. But lying is almost always suspicious." He smoothed his hand down her arm and she winced. "What's wrong?" he asked, immediately tensed. "Are you hurt?"

"Just a little bruised where Kiram grabbed me." She rubbed the arm. "He caught me walking back toward our tent after you left last night."

"Jobie told me you called him out in front of a crowd and that Metwater ordered him to leave you alone."

"Yes. Kiram says he was acting on Metwater's authority, but I'm not so sure. I think he's just a bully." She glanced over her shoulder at the glowering young man. "I'm probably his least favorite person right now."

"He's my least favorite person, so that makes us even." He glared at Kiram. The man was going to be trouble, but Walt would wait to deal with him. He turned back to Hannah. "You're sure you're all right?"

"Yes." She took his arm and led him farther away from the crowd. "Better than all right," she said. "Phoenix's daughter, Sophie, admitted this morning that the baby isn't her mother's. She belonged to a Family member who called herself Freedom. I'm sure she means Emily."

"How did Phoenix end up with the baby?"

"Sophie said the mother, Freedom, wanted to run away. The Prophet said she could leave, but she would have to leave her baby behind, because all children belong to him or some such nonsense." She frowned. "Phoenix told me Metwater was the baby's father, but I know that isn't right. But apparently, he claims to be the father of all the children in the camp, whether he actually is or not."

"So what happened when he told her she could leave but he would keep her baby?" Walt asked.

"Sophie said Freedom left anyway, and Phoenix was given the baby to care for. But I know Emily wouldn't have left the baby behind. Not voluntarily."

"It sounds as if Sophie doesn't know Emily—if Freedom really is Emily—is dead," Walt said. "Maybe she wasn't told because she's still a child."

"Or maybe no one was told because Metwater didn't want anyone to know about his involvement in her death. Emily died in Denver, when the Family was already living here on park land. It would have been easy enough to bring the baby back from Denver after Emily died and tell everyone the mother had abandoned her."

"Maybe Emily left, intending to come back, and died before she could," he said.

"Emily would never have abandoned her baby. Never." Hannah's voice shook and she sounded on the verge of tears.

Walt took her by the shoulders. "It's okay," he said. "Keep talking with Phoenix and Sophie and see what else you can learn. There's still a chance the baby belongs to some other woman and not your sister."

"Vicki is Emily's baby, I know it." She clutched his arm. "Why can't we just take the baby and leave now? The DNA tests will prove I'm right."

"We need to stay as long as we can and learn as much as we can," he said. "We may never have a better opportunity to find out not just what happened to your sister, but to Lucia Raton."

She looked stubborn and Walt braced himself for her arguments. He was prepared to tell her that she could leave with the investigative team when they showed up to question Family members about Lucia, but that he needed to stay behind to gather more information. While Hannah had a court order granting her temporary custody of her sister's child, they needed a positive identification of the baby before Hannah could take her. And as long as Daniel Metwater claimed to be the child's father, and his name was on the birth certificate, he could fight Hannah in court to regain custody of the baby.

Hannah changed the subject. "There's supposed to be some kind of meeting this evening to decide our fate," she said. "I'm guessing after the cops descend on camp, everyone will vote to throw us out."

"They might," he said. "We'll have to work hard to persuade them that we're sincere."

"Do you really think the grave you found belongs to that poor girl?"

"I don't know. We'll have to wait and see."

"I've never been very good at waiting," she said. "I've always been the type to make a decision quickly and follow through." She stared at the ground between their feet. "That hasn't always worked out well for me."

"I'm more deliberate, but that doesn't mean the decisions I've made have always been the right ones," he said.

"Serenity!"

They looked up to see Phoenix hurrying toward them, a worried expression on her face. "Is something wrong?" Hannah asked. "Is Vicki okay?"

"We're fine." She stopped in front of them, a little out of breath. Up close, Walt noted the fine lines at the corners of her eyes and the deep furrow between her eyes. Hannah was right—Phoenix did look closer to forty than thirty—older than the majority of Metwater's followers. How had she ended up with the group? "You need to come with me now," Phoenix said to Hannah. "I'm supposed to watch over you until the meeting tonight."

"Surely the Prophet won't be upset about me talking with my husband," Hannah said.

"Sometimes when two people talk together a lot, away from the group, it can look like they're plotting," Phoenix said. "It sets a bad example."

"Is that one of the lessons the Prophet teaches?" Walt asked.

Phoenix glanced at him. "The Prophet teaches many

lessons," she said. "Some of them have saved my life." She took Hannah's hand and laced her fingers with the younger woman's. "Let's go. You said before you enjoy working with children. You can help me with that job this morning."

She started to lead Hannah away. "What about me?" Walt called. "What am I supposed to do until the council this evening?"

Phoenix looked over her shoulder at him. "Someone else has been assigned to watch over you," she said, then ducked her head and hurried away.

Walt heard heavy footsteps behind him. He tensed, prepared to defend himself if necessary. The new arrival said nothing.

"Kiram, I've got a score to settle with you," Walt said, turning around.

"If I ever catch you away from camp, believe me, we'll settle that score," Kiram said. "For now, you're to come with me."

"What if I refuse?" Walt asked.

"I'd be fine with you leaving camp right this minute," Kiram said. "But the Prophet wants to see you. He has a proposal for you—one you ought to listen to."

"The Prophet wants something from me?" Walt asked. That was a new twist. "What is it?"

"Come with me and find out. I'm hoping he wants me to take you out and beat you to a pulp, but then, I seldom get so lucky."

Chapter Eleven

"Where is Kiram taking Walt?" Hannah tried to pull away from Phoenix when she saw Kiram lead Walt away.

"Your husband will be all right." Phoenix was stronger than she looked and almost yanked Hannah off her feet. "You'll see him tonight, after the council. In the meantime, you can help me with the children. That's our job for the day."

"This isn't right," Hannah said, reluctantly falling into step beside Phoenix. "We shouldn't be separated like this."

"It's for your own good," Phoenix said. "After all, you have to think for yourself, even though you're married. And remember—whatever punishment the Prophet decides for you, it will make you a better person in the end."

"Have you ever been punished by the Prophet?" Hannah asked.

"When I first came here, yes. But I needed to learn an important lesson, and I was grateful for it later."

"What did you do that you needed to be punished for?" Hannah asked. The older woman looked so serene and devoted to Metwater. Hannah couldn't imagine she had ever done anything to displease him.

"That is all in the past and we don't talk about the past," she said. "Come, let's get the children. You'll feel better when you're with them."

Sophie was waiting with the other children, and a duffel bag filled with balls and stuffed animals and other toys. While Sophie and her mother organized the children into play groups, Hannah took charge of Vicki. She was an easygoing baby, seldom fussy, happy to be held and admired.

"You're so good with her," Phoenix said, coming to sit at the picnic table beside Hannah. "Do you have children?"

Hannah couldn't hold back the gasp that escaped her. "Wh-why would you ask that?" she stammered. "If I had children, they'd be here with me."

"Not necessarily. They might be with their father, or a grandparent. Not every child lives with her mother. Sometimes that isn't even the best thing."

Hannah clutched the baby more tightly. "No, I don't have any children." It wasn't a lie. Not really.

"Sophie lived with my parents for a while," she said, her expression calm as she watched her daughter. "I wasn't able to take care of her, so I signed over custody to them. One of the best things about coming here is that she's able to be with me again."

Were Phoenix's parents really happy that she was living in a trailer in the middle of nowhere, following a self-proclaimed prophet? Hannah wondered. Then again, maybe Phoenix's folks were in poor health, or simply tired of taking care of the child. It wasn't Hannah's place to judge. "She seems very happy here," she said.

"She doesn't like the Prophet, but I hope in time she'll understand his wisdom."

"Do you really think he's wise?" Hannah asked.

She smiled serenely. Or was her serenity merely a kind of naïveté? "The Prophet saved my life. I owe him everything. Apollo, what is that in your mouth? We don't eat bugs." She jumped up and hurried to persuade the little boy to spit out his find. Hannah cradled the baby and studied the other woman. Surely she didn't mean that Daniel Metwater had literally saved her—rescuing her from drowning or pulling her from a burning car? Following the Prophet had clearly sent Phoenix's life in another direction—away from a bad situation or wrong choices?

Phoenix returned. "How long have you and your husband been married?" she asked.

"Not long. A few months." Hannah hoped her response sounded natural. She wasn't used to lying, though she agreed that in this case, it was necessary.

"I thought about marriage a couple of times, but it never happened," Phoenix said. "Just as well, since I never stayed with any man very long." She laughed. "Good thing, or I wouldn't have met the Prophet."

"Are you and he, well, lovers?" Hadn't Phoenix hinted as much, when she said Metwater was the baby's father? Or had she said that because she believed Emily and Metwater had been a couple?

Phoenix's smile struck Hannah as a little smug. "I've enjoyed the Prophet's attentions from time to time," she said. "He tries to spend special time with each of his female followers—it's really a privilege." She patted Hannah's arm. "I'm sure your turn will come."

Hannah shuddered. She had no intention of enjoying any such "attention" from Metwater. "I doubt my husband would appreciate that."

"Oh, he'll come around in time. After all, marriage is such an outmoded concept."

Hannah recognized Metwater's words. "I think two people pledging to love each other and care for each other for the rest of their lives is timeless," she said. "An ideal that never goes out of style."

Phoenix wrinkled her nose. "But how many people actually live up to that ideal?"

"A lot whom I know," Hannah said.

"And no one I know."

Before Hannah could come up with a suitable answer, the baby began fussing. Hannah shifted and tried to comfort the infant, but her fussing soon grew to wails. "Let me take her." Phoenix reached for the baby. "Maybe she needs changing."

As she took the child, one sleeve of her loose peasant blouse pushed up, revealing several lines of thin, dark scars on her forearms. "What happened to your arm?" Hannah asked.

Phoenix flushed and quickly yanked the sleeve down and cradled the child. "It's nothing. I'll go get a fresh diaper," she said, already heading toward the trailer. "You watch the children."

A chill swept through Hannah, as if someone had opened a door that should have been left closed. She wished she was home, with Joy safe and the future not so uncertain. There were too many secrets in this particular family.

"I WANT TO know what you told the police."

Daniel Metwater didn't waste any time getting to the point when he hauled Walt in front of him. At least the Prophet was fully dressed today, in faded jeans and a white button-down with the sleeves rolled up. He sat in an upholstered chair in the living room of the RV like a man on a throne. Walt still thought he looked out of place here in the backcountry—like the kind of man who, instead of taking a five-mile hike to see the sights, would order a flunky to take the hike for him and report back.

"Why do you want to know?" Walt asked.

"Lose the attitude," Kiram said, and punched Walt in the shoulder.

Walt turned on him. "Hit me again and you'll be sorry," he said. "You can't shove me around the way you did my wife."

"Leave us, Kiram," Metwater said.

Kiram's face reddened and he worked his mouth as if trying to come up with a response. But when Metwater fixed him with a stare, the bearded man bowed his head and stormed out. Walt waited until the door closed behind him before he spoke. "Hannah has bruises on her arms where Kiram roughed her up last night," he said. "I'm not going to stand for that." He had every intention of filing assault charges against Kiram, though he hadn't discussed it with Hannah yet.

"Kiram can be a little intense in his zeal to protect the Family—and to protect me," Metwater said.

"He's a bully. If you don't rein him in, I will."

"I can take care of Kiram."

"Keep him away from me—and away from Hannah."

Metwater hesitated. Walt was sure he was going to say something about Walt needing a minder until tonight's council meeting, but after a tense few seconds, he relented. "I'll tell him to stay away."

"See that he does."

"I didn't bring you here to talk about Kiram. I want to know what you told the police."

"I told them the truth," Walt said. "That I was out looking for firewood and found what appeared to be a fairly fresh grave. They agreed it was worth checking out, especially with a young woman missing."

"No one in this camp had anything to do with that unfortunate young woman's disappearance," Metwater said.

"I've learned she was here in the camp, yet you lied when the Rangers asked if you had seen her before."

"Who told you that?" Metwater demanded.

Walt leaned against the wall that separated the RV's living area from the rest of the space, arms crossed in a deliberately casual, some might have said disrespectful, pose. "Why does it matter if it's true?" he countered.

"Because of you, officers will be disrupting our lives with their questions," Metwater said.

"No. They'll be doing that because you lied to them and tried to conceal what could be evidence of a crime. Guilty people behave that way."

"Or people who value their privacy," Metwater said.

"Sometimes it's the same thing." Walt had to force himself not to smirk. He was enjoying this too much.

"When the Rangers arrive, I want you to talk to them," Metwater said.

Walt hadn't seen this coming. "Why me?"

"Since you're the one who went to them, they'll be

more likely to trust you. Tell them we had nothing to do with the grave you found or the woman who disappeared."

Walt straightened. "You tell them. I'm not your official spokesperson."

"I have more important things to do than waste time talking with the police," Metwater said.

"Such as?" Walt looked around the trailer. "Writing blog posts and preaching sermons can't take that much of your time."

Metwater stood and moved closer to Walt. They were about the same height, and had no trouble looking each other in the eye. "Why did you come here?" Metwater asked. "I don't believe it was because you want to be one of us. You have no respect for our way of life."

Sticking to his cover required Walt to lie and pretend to be a fan of Metwater and his philosophy, but after the better part of two days in camp, he didn't have the stomach for it. As long as he didn't reveal he was a law enforcement officer, sticking closer to the truth should be safe. And it might even nudge Metwater into revealing something useful. "I came here looking for a friend," he said. "She disappeared a while back and her family is worried about her."

Metwater lifted one eyebrow. "Lucia Raton is a friend of yours?"

"Not her. I'm looking for Emily Dietrich."

"Your wife's friend from school." Metwater nodded. "You think she was one of my followers?"

"She was pregnant. Her fiancé was killed and she became one of your followers. She was living with your followers the last time her sister heard from her."

"Her sister, your wife."

Walt didn't let himself react. "Why do you say that?" he asked.

"The resemblance is there."

"So you do know Emily?"

"I knew her. But she was only with us a short time."

"What about her baby?"

Metwater turned away. "I can't help you there."

"Can't—or won't?"

"You may leave now," Metwater said. "I'll see you at the council tonight."

"Tell me what happened to Emily Dietrich," Walt said.

Metwater sat and looked up at Walt, his expression calm. "I can't tell you what I don't know," he said.

Walt wanted to grab the man and shake him. But all that would probably achieve was a beating by Kiram and friends, and possible assault charges himself. "I'm going to keep asking questions," he said. "I'm going to find answers."

"I can't stop you," Metwater said. "But you might not like the answers you find. Sometimes it's wisest to let the dead rest in peace."

"What makes you say she's dead?" Walt demanded. "You do know something, don't you?"

Metwater's gaze shifted away and he waved his hand dismissively. "I was using a common figure of speech. If I said 'let sleeping dogs lie' you wouldn't think I was calling your friend a dog, would you?"

"I'm not buying it," Walt said. "You know something, and I'm going to find out what it is."

"Don't waste any more of my time." Metwater left the room. Walt stared after him. The Prophet was going to be on guard now that he knew he was being watched, but that wouldn't keep Walt from finding out the truth.

When Walt emerged from the trailer, Hannah was waiting for him—along with Kiram. Walt ignored the bodyguard and addressed Hannah. "I thought you were with Phoenix." Before she could answer, Kiram stepped between them. "You aren't supposed to be together until the council meeting tonight," he said.

Walt studied the other man for a long moment. Kiram was clearly devoted to Metwater and his rules, but if the two of them hung around much longer he had no doubt one of them was going to lose his temper. "The Prophet has decided I'll be okay on my own." He nodded toward the door of the motor home. "If you don't believe me, go ask him."

Kiram looked from Walt to the motor home and back again. "You're trying to trick me."

"No trick," Walt said. "Go on and ask him. It's not as if you can't find me easily enough if it turns out I'm lying."

Kiram glared at Walt, then stormed up the steps and knocked. After a moment, he was admitted. Walt took Hannah's arm. "Let's get out of here," he said.

Hannah pulled him around behind the RV, out of sight of the rest of the camp. "When Phoenix went inside her trailer to get a diaper for Vicki, I walked away," she said. "I was getting worried about you. What did Metwater want?"

"He wanted to know what I told the police. And he wanted to know why we're here," he said. "He wasn't convinced we're true believers."

"What did you tell him?"

"The truth—or part of it. I told him we came here looking for Emily."

All the color left her cheeks and she released her hold on him. "What did he say?"

"He said she was here for a short time, but he didn't know what happened to her—or to her baby."

"Do you believe him?"

"Do you?"

"No." She glanced around, then pulled him farther into the woods, away from the campsite. "I think the people here are lying to us about a lot of things," she said. "And some of the things that might be the truth make me very uneasy. I think we should take the baby and get out of here as soon as possible."

She was still pale, and her hands shook as she smoothed back her hair. "What's got you so upset?" he asked.

"Phoenix told me Metwater has slept with most of the women here. She said she'd slept with him—that it was an honor. She said my turn would come—it doesn't matter that I'm married. Or, you know, that he thinks I'm married."

He smoothed his hand down her arm, trying to comfort her. "I'm not going to let him hurt you," he said.

"I won't be alone with him again," she said.

"Agreed. What else did Phoenix tell you? Did you learn anything more about Emily or Joy?"

She shook her head. "She only talked about the Prophet, and how he changed her life. And she said she had to give custody of Sophie to her parents for a while, but joining up with the Family made it possible for her to have Sophie with her again. But that didn't make a lot of sense to me. Would grandparents really turn over their granddaughter to live with a wandering bunch of modern-day hippies?"

"Maybe they would if they thought it was best for Sophie and for Phoenix."

"There's something else that's bothering me. Not anything Phoenix said, but something I saw."

"What is it?"

"You know how she always wears long sleeves?"

"I hadn't noticed."

"I had. All the other women wear tank tops or short sleeves—it can get pretty warm here during the day, especially in the kitchen. But Phoenix always stays covered up to her wrists. But this morning, when she reached for the baby, her sleeve pushed up and I saw that she has scars." She traced a line on the back of her arm, from elbow to wrist. "Thin lines. I wondered—could it be from drugs?"

"Maybe," Walt said. "Have you noticed any signs that she's using now?"

"No. I don't think she is. She says Daniel Metwater saved her life—do you think she means he helped her get off drugs?"

"I don't know."

She looked back toward the camp. "I don't like it here, and I can't shake the feeling there's a lot going on we don't know about. But maybe it's also possible that Metwater is doing some good, at least for some people."

"I guess no one is all good or all bad, but I still don't trust him."

"When can we leave and take Joy with us?"

"Soon," he said. "When the Rangers get here, I'm going to request a court order for us to take the baby into temporary custody, until a DNA test confirms her identity."

"Will they be able to get it?"

"I think so. In the meantime, I'd rather stay here to make sure they don't try to leave with her."

"I won't let them take her away," Hannah said. "When will you hear from the Rangers again?"

"They can't open up the grave until a forensic anthropologist can be on site. That might take a day or two. They'll want to see what's in there before they question anyone in the camp."

"In the meantime, we've got this council tonight," she said. "What do you think they'll do?"

"I think they'll make a lot of noise and try to scare us," he said. "Just remember they don't have any authority over us."

"That doesn't mean they won't try to hurt us—that they didn't hurt Emily, or Lucia."

"Serenity!" Phoenix raced up to them, her face flushed and out of breath. "There you are," she said, gasping. "I thought you had run away."

"I had to see Walt," Hannah said.

Phoenix glanced at him, then took both Hannah's hands in hers. "You shouldn't keep breaking the rules," the older woman said. "It will only go against you at council tonight."

Hannah pulled her hands free. "I won't blindly obey arbitrary rules that don't make sense," she said.

"Without rules, there's only chaos," Phoenix said.

"But rules have to have a larger purpose than merely controlling people," Walt said.

Phoenix shook her head and grabbed Hannah's

hands again. "Please come back with me," she said. "Or I could get into trouble."

This time, Hannah didn't pull away. "All right," she said. "But Walt has to come with me."

"Where's Kiram?" Phoenix asked. She looked around as if she expected the bearded young man to pop out from behind a tree.

"The Prophet and I talked and he agreed I didn't need a babysitter." Walt put his arm around Hannah again. "Hannah and I can stay with you this afternoon," he said. "And we'll try to keep out of trouble."

"Tell me another one," Phoenix said. "Men like you have trouble written all over them."

She turned and started walking away. Walt and Hannah followed. Hannah leaned in close. "She's right," she whispered. "You do look like a man who wouldn't shy away from trouble."

"Is that such a bad thing?" he asked.

"Oh, not at all." She squeezed his arm. "I'm beginning to think it's a very good thing."

THEY RETURNED TO Phoenix's trailer, where Sophie sat at the small table, surrounded by books, and Vicki played on a quilt on the floor. Hannah moved past Phoenix to scoop the baby up from the floor. "This is Vicki," she said, turning to Walt.

"Hey there, cutie." A huge grin split his face and before she could protest, he was lifting the baby from her arms and cradling her against him. Vicki stared up at him in wonder, then reached up one chubby hand to pat his cheek. "What do you think, little one?" he asked. "Do I look like trouble to you?"

Hannah's stomach quivered and her knees felt unsteady. The sight of this tough, rugged man being so tender with the baby stirred her emotions. Walt was trouble all right—a big disruption to the smooth path she had laid out for herself. She needed to focus on getting Joy safely home and building a stable life for the two of them. She didn't see how she could do that without Walt's help. But it had been so easy to move from wanting his help to wanting more.

"What are you studying?" Walt asked. Still cradling Vicki, he had moved over to the table and was looking down on the books scattered around Sophie.

"It's my homeschool correspondence course," she said. "It's supposed to be Introduction to Algebra, but I'm all confused."

"Maybe I can help." He leaned over her. "What are you having problems with?"

"You definitely need to have children soon." Phoenix moved to Hannah's side. "He's great with them."

"Yeah, he is." Judging from Sophie's smiles, his explanation of algebra was helping her, and Vicki seemed more than content to gaze up at him and gnaw on his thumb.

"Tell me about Vicki's mother," Hannah said, hoping she wasn't making a mistake asking the question.

Phoenix stiffened. "I'm Victory's mother."

Hannah squeezed the other woman's hand. "You've done a wonderful job of caring for her, but I heard her birth mother was a young woman who called herself Freedom."

"Who told you that?" Phoenix looked toward the table, where Walt now sat beside Sophie.

"In a camp this small, there are no secrets," Hannah

said. "Someone told me that when we first came here. What can you tell me about Freedom?"

"She was a troubled young woman who was looking for peace," Phoenix said. "She hoped to find it here, but she had a hard time obeying the rules." She sighed. "She was a lot like you in that respect—always wanting reasons, not willing to simply be and accept."

"You really think she was like me?" Hannah had focused so long on the differences between her and her sister that she hadn't considered all the ways they might be alike.

"She wasn't as lucky as you in love." Phoenix's gaze shifted to Walt. "She said the man she had been engaged to marry was killed. She needed the love of a family to surround her and her baby, and she hoped to find that here."

"What about her own family?" Hannah's voice was strained from the tears she was fighting to hold back.

"She never talked about them. Sometimes it's easier to turn to strangers than to family—families know all your mistakes, and that can make them harder to put behind you."

And you know all your family's mistakes, which can be harder to forgive, Hannah thought. She recalled the last argument she had had with Emily, before her sister left to join Metwater's group.

She pushed the painful memory away. "What happened to Freedom?" she asked.

"She left us. It was for the best, since she wasn't happy here."

"But how could she leave her baby behind?" Hannah asked.

"I don't know," Phoenix said. "It struck me as out

of character, but when people are desperately unhappy, they don't always act like themselves."

"Mind if I join you?" Walt returned to the living area.

"We were just talking about Freedom," Hannah said.

Phoenix frowned. "You told him?" she asked Hannah.

"He's my husband. Of course I told him." How easily the lie flowed off her lips. The longer she was with Walt, the easier it was to imagine him as her partner— which was crazy, considering how little time she had known him. Being thrown together like this, with the underlying current of danger, was obviously getting to her.

"What happened the day Freedom left?" Walt asked.

"She went with the Prophet to Denver," Phoenix said. "He was speaking there and he asked her to go along. He wanted to spend more time with her, to try to persuade her to stay with the Family."

"I thought he had told her she should leave," Hannah said. "That he was punishing her for wanting to run away."

Phoenix nibbled her thumbnail. "Well, yes, he had told her that, but he wanted to give her one more chance. He thought the trip to Denver, just the two of them, would help him persuade her to stay."

"She didn't take the baby with her?" Hannah asked.

"No. She left Victory with me." She took the child from Walt, who didn't protest. "I've taken care of her practically since she was born."

"Did the Prophet say what happened while they were in Denver?" Walt asked.

Phoenix smoothed the baby's curls. "He said Freedom decided to stay in the city and he came back with-out her."

"That didn't strike you as odd?" Walt asked. "That she didn't come back for her baby?"

"I thought she would, at first," Phoenix said. "But then…" She shrugged. "The Prophet said her mind was made up and he wasn't able to stop her from leaving. He doesn't keep people here against their will."

"So he would have been fine if she had taken Vicki with her when she left?" Hannah asked.

Phoenix stood. "I think the baby needs changing," she said, and disappeared into the back room before they could protest.

"Mom says the Prophet would have changed his mind about making Freedom leave her baby behind if she had come back for Victory." Sophie looked up from her books. "She refuses to believe he would ever do anything cruel."

"What do you think?" Walt turned to look at the girl.

She shrugged and doodled in the corner of her note-book. "I think people do cruel things all the time. Why should he be different?"

A knock on the door interrupted them. Hannah looked toward the back of the trailer, but Phoenix didn't emerge. The knocking persisted.

"I'll get it," Sophie said, but Walt got to the door before her.

He opened it and Agent Marco Cruz moved past him into the room. "I'm looking for a woman named Phoenix," he said. "We have questions for her related to the disappearance of Lucia Raton."

Chapter Twelve

Walt bit the inside of his cheek to keep from blurting out the questions Marco's announcement brought to mind. Of all the suspects Walt might have singled out as having something to do with Lucia's disappearance, Phoenix wouldn't have even made the list.

At Marco's words Phoenix emerged from the back bedroom, her face even paler than usual. She took one look at the officers, then thrust the baby into Hannah's arms and bolted for the door, but Michael Dance stepped in behind Marco and caught her. "Calm down, ma'am," he said, leading her back to the sofa. "We just need to ask you some questions."

"What is this about?" Sophie had moved from her place at the table and stood behind the two officers, eyes wide with fear.

"Hannah, maybe you should take Sophie and the baby and wait for Phoenix outside," Walt said.

"No." Hannah cradled the infant to her shoulder and beckoned Sophie to her side. "I won't leave Phoenix alone with three strange men." She glared at Walt, as if she blamed him for this turn of events. "Can't you see she's terrified?"

"Why don't we all sit down?" Marco moved farther

into the room, while Michael stayed by the door. Phoenix wrapped her arms across her stomach, as if trying to make herself as small as possible. "Ma'am, do you want your friends to leave?" Marco asked.

Phoenix raised her head to look at Hannah. "I want Hannah to stay," she said.

"If Hannah stays, so do I." Walt crossed his arms over his chest.

"I'll take the baby," Sophie said. She reached for the infant and Hannah surrendered her. Then Sophie turned and fled from the trailer, shoving past Michael and slamming the door behind her.

Marco brought a chair from the table and set it in front of the sofa where Phoenix and Hannah now sat next to each other.

"What is this about?" Hannah asked. "Are you charging her with some crime?"

Walt frowned at her and shook his head. She needed to be quiet and let the Rangers do their job. But she looked away from him.

"Ma'am, before we start, I need to know your real name," Marco said.

"My name is Phoenix."

"That isn't the name you were born with," Marco said.

She glared at him. "Phoenix is my name."

Marco consulted his phone. "But weren't you born Anna Ingels?"

Hannah gasped. Walt recognized the name, too—Anna Ingels was the other witness on Emily Dietrich's will.

"Anna is dead," Phoenix said. "I left her behind when I came here."

Marco took something from his shirt pocket and

handed it to her. "Isn't this your driver's license?" he asked. "The picture is yours and the name is Anna Ingels."

Walt leaned over to peer at the picture, which did indeed look like Phoenix. It was a Colorado license, showing an address in Denver, with an expiration date two years from now.

Phoenix clutched the license. "Where did you get this?" she asked.

"Our forensics team found it, along with some other items belonging to you, in a grave in the woods not far from here," Marco said.

Walt sent his fellow agent a sharp look. *What else did you find in that grave?* he wanted to ask, but knew he would have to wait for the answer.

Phoenix bowed her head. Hannah put her arm around the older woman and rubbed her shoulder.

"Why don't you tell us how your license ended up in that grave?" Marco said, his tone gentle.

"I buried the license, along with some clothes and books and other things," Phoenix said. "Anna's things. Part of my old life. I have a new life now. I'm a new person. I didn't need those reminders of what I used to be."

"What did you used to be?" Marco asked.

She raised her head to meet his gaze, her face a picture of misery. "I'm not that person anymore. The Prophet saved me. He changed me. I don't have to think about that life anymore," she said.

"We ran your license," Marco said. "You have a criminal record for possession of heroin and prostitution."

That explained the tracks on her arm, Walt thought.

And maybe why she had lost custody of Sophie temporarily.

"That was Anna. It wasn't me. I'm not like that anymore."

"There's no crime in starting over," Hannah said. "And no crime in burying some old clothes and papers."

Marco ignored her and leaned toward Phoenix. "When did you bury those things?" he asked.

"A couple of weeks ago," she said. "The Prophet had a vision that we should divest ourselves of anything from the past that was holding us back. Some people burned items, or boxed them up and mailed them to their families. I held a funeral to say goodbye to my old self, and buried everything that belonged to Anna." She smiled and the light returned to her eyes. "It was wonderful—like being reborn. I truly was a Phoenix, rising from the ashes of my former self."

"Tell us about Lucia Raton," Marco said. "When did she come to the camp?"

Phoenix sighed. "The Prophet said we shouldn't talk about Lucia. Especially not to the police."

"Lucia is missing," Marco said. "She could be dead. I need you to tell me about her. When was she in camp?"

The lines on Phoenix's forehead deepened. "I don't know. We don't keep track of time here." She looked around the trailer. "I don't even have a calendar."

"Guess. How long ago was she here?"

She considered the question a moment longer. The sound of someone laughing somewhere outside drifted through the open window, along with hammering— ordinary sounds of life in the camp in sharp contrast to the surreal atmosphere inside the trailer. "I buried Anna's things when the moon was full," she said. "Lucia was here a few days after that—maybe a week."

Marco typed the information into his phone. "How long was she here?" he asked.

"Only a day. Less than that, really. She didn't spend the night."

"You're sure about that?" Marco asked.

"I'm sure. The Prophet told her she had to leave because she was underage. She was only seventeen." Her expression grew troubled. "I hope she's okay. She seemed like a sweet girl—a little defiant and confused, but that's part of what being a teenager is about, isn't it?"

"Did you spend a lot of time with her while she was here?" Marco asked.

"No. She came around and introduced herself to me and some other women who were preparing dinner, but we didn't really talk."

Marco took something from his shirt pocket and held it out to her. It was a plastic evidence bag that contained a necklace—a locket on a blackened silver chain. "Do you recognize this?" he asked.

Phoenix shook her head. "It doesn't look familiar."

Marco pressed a catch on the side of the locket and it opened to reveal a photograph of a man and woman. "Who is that?" Phoenix asked.

"Read the inscription," Marco said.

She leaned closer and read. "'To Lucia. We love you. Mami and Papi.'"

"So the locket belongs to Lucia Raton?" Hannah asked.

"Her parents described it when they listed the things

she was wearing the last time they saw her." Marco returned the evidence bag to his pocket. "Are you sure you don't remember it?"

Phoenix shook her head. "No. I only saw her for a few minutes."

"Was she with anyone else when she came here?" Michael Dance spoke for the first time from his position by the door. "Was there anyone she hung out with while she was here?"

"Not really." Walt sensed her hesitation; Marco must have, too.

"What is it?" Marco asked. "Was there someone she spent time with here?"

"Easy offered to give her a ride back into town," she said.

"Who is Easy?" Hannah asked before either of the officers could speak. "I haven't met anyone here by that name."

"He's not a member of the Family," Phoenix said. "He just visits sometimes. He delivers groceries or gives people rides if they need to go somewhere and don't have their own car. Sometimes he runs errands for the Prophet."

"What kind of errands?" Walt hadn't meant to speak, but he couldn't keep the question back.

Phoenix shrugged. "I don't know. He buys stuff he needs or takes him to the airport when he flies somewhere to give a talk."

"When was the last time you saw Easy?" Marco asked.

"A few days ago. I don't remember." She shifted. "What does any of this have to do with me? I'm sorry the girl is missing, but I can't help you."

She looked up as the door to the trailer opened. Michael whirled to face the newcomer, one hand on the duty weapon at his side. Daniel Metwater stepped into the trailer. His hair was wet and he smelled of soap. He wore the same loose linen trousers he usually favored, and a flowing tunic of the same white linen. Walt thought of it as his official Prophet uniform. "What is going on here?" Metwater demanded, taking in the scene.

Marco stood and faced the newcomer. The door was still open and Sophie, carrying the baby, slipped past the officers and joined her mother on the sofa. The girl must have summoned the Prophet to help her mother. Kiram followed her, taking his place behind Metwater, his expression sullen, as usual. The small trailer was too crowded, and the air fairly crackled with tension. Walt thought of the gun in his ankle holster and hoped he wouldn't have to use it. He took a step closer to Hannah, prepared to shove her to the floor if bullets started flying.

"We're investigating the disappearance of a young woman who visited your camp shortly before she disappeared," Marco said.

"We had nothing to do with that," Metwater said.

"Why did you lie to us about having seen Lucia Raton?" Michael asked. "What are you trying to hide?"

"She was here for only a few hours," Metwater said. "And she was fine when she left here."

"Then why lie?" Marco asked.

"I'm entitled to my privacy. And you're trespassing in my home. You need to leave."

"This is public land," Marco said. "You are camping here because you have a permit, but that doesn't give you the right to exclude anyone—especially not officers of the law who are conducting an investigation."

"Why didn't you want us to know about the grave in that clearing?" Michael asked.

"I don't have to answer your questions." Metwater looked sullen, and less handsome and in-control than usual. "You need to leave."

Marco ignored the order, deliberately turning his back to Metwater to face Phoenix once more. "We found Lucia's locket in the grave with your belongings," he told her. "Can you explain how it got there?"

IF SHE WAS feigning shock, she was doing an amazing job, Hannah thought as Phoenix stared up at Marco. "That's impossible," she said. "I buried those things before Lucia ever visited the camp."

"Is there anyone who can confirm that?" Marco asked. "Anyone who helped you with the burial?"

She shook her head. "No. I did it alone. It was important that I do it alone."

"Did you tell anyone what you planned to do?" Marco asked. "Could someone have followed and seen you?"

"I only told the Prophet," Phoenix answered. "And why would someone have followed me?"

Hannah hated seeing the other woman so distressed. "Did you find anything else in the grave that belonged to Lucia?" she asked.

"The forensics team is still sorting through their findings," Marco said.

"You're wasting your time here," Metwater said. "You need to leave."

"We'll go, after we've questioned Mr. and Mrs. Morgan." He motioned to Walt and Hannah. "If you two will come with me, please."

Kiram moved to block the door. "Why do you want to talk to them?" he asked.

"We think it's a little suspicious that they showed up here about the time Lucia disappeared," Marco said.

Even though she knew the words were a lie, Hannah felt a tremor of fear. How much worse must Phoenix feel, being accused by these men who had so much power to destroy her life? She squeezed the older woman's hand, then stood and prepared to follow Walt and the others out of the trailer.

A hand on her shoulder stopped her. Metwater moved close to her—too close. His gaze locked to hers and he smoothed his hand down her arm in a possessive way that sent a shiver up her spine. "Don't be too long," he said. "You have to prepare for tonight's council."

Walt took her hand and tugged her toward the door. They followed Marco and Michael a short distance away, down a path that led into the woods along the creek. The noise of the water rushing over the rocks was a soothing contrast to the tension knotting tighter inside her with each passing minute.

"You're on the wrong track here," she said when the two lawmen stopped and faced her and Walt. "Phoenix couldn't have had anything to do with Lucia's disappearance. She's not the type to harm someone else."

"I got the impression she would do just about anything for Metwater," Marco said. "You heard her—he saved her life."

She looked at the ground, unable to think of a response. Phoenix did have a blind spot when it came to the Prophet.

"How did that locket get in the grave if she didn't put it there?" Walt asked.

"Don't know." Michael leaned against a tree, his posture relaxed. "What do you make of her story about burying her past?"

"I believe it," Walt said. "It's the kind of thing Metwater would preach. They're very big into rituals and ceremonies around here."

"What is this council he mentioned?" Marco asked.

"Some kind of meeting to decide on the appropriate punishment for me disobeying Metwater's orders and going to you guys to report the grave," Walt said.

"Punishment?" Michael asked. "What kind of punishment?"

"I don't know." Walt turned to Hannah. "Have you heard anything?"

"Phoenix said it will probably be extra work or something like that—something to impress upon us the importance of putting the Family ahead of ourselves. We have to prove we're serious about our intentions to become one of them."

"How serious are you?" Marco asked. "Why not just leave now? You've probably learned all you're going to learn at this point."

"We know Phoenix's baby is really my niece," Hannah said. "She told us this afternoon—right before you arrived—that the baby belonged to a woman who called herself Freedom. And Phoenix's real name on my sister's will proves she was at the hospital when the baby was born."

"There's still the problem of Metwater's name as the father on the birth certificate," Walt said. "He can fight any attempt to gain custody."

"Not if we have a DNA test proving paternity," Hannah said. "And not if we prove he was involved in Emily's death." She turned to Marco. "Phoenix said Metwater took Emily to Denver with him and came back without her. He told everyone here that she had left—she had abandoned her baby. Why would he lie about her having died in the hospital, unless he had something to do with her death?"

"He lies about a lot of things," Michael said. "But in most cases, lying itself isn't a crime."

"Why didn't you ask Phoenix about the will?" Hannah asked.

The two officers looked at each other. "We were so focused on the search for Lucia we weren't thinking about your sister's will," Marco said.

"Were you able to get the warrant for the DNA test on the baby?" she asked.

Another look passed between them. "Not yet," Marco admitted.

"I can't leave camp without the baby," she said.

"Taking her without the court order could backfire if Metwater decides to press charges," Walt said. "Child Welfare and Protection has already indicated they're on his side. They could ask the court to award temporary custody to Metwater, pending the outcome of the DNA test, and while we're waiting on results, he could leave the area with the baby."

"I won't risk it," Hannah said. "I have to stay here until I can legally take her away."

Michael straightened. "We'll push harder for the court order. In the meantime, see if you can find out anything that would link Metwater to Lucia's disappearance."

"We also need to find this Easy fellow and interview him," Marco said. He clapped a hand on Walt's shoulder. "Let us know if you discover anything useful. And try to stay out of trouble."

"Right," Walt said. He took Hannah's arm and they walked silently back to camp. She fought the urge to lean into him, to let his presence shield her from the anxiety coiling inside her. Maybe it was seeing Phoenix so frightened, or maybe this was simply the emotional side effect of digging so deeply into Emily's last days, but she felt overwhelmed and a little out of control. As if sensing her struggle, Walt put his arm around her. "It's going to be all right," he said. "It will all be over soon."

Chapter Thirteen

"Phoenix is waiting for you," Kiram told Hannah as she and Walt approached Phoenix's trailer. "She will help you prepare for tonight." He motioned to Walt. "You come with me."

Walt started to protest, but Hannah interrupted. "It will be all right," she said, repeating the words of comfort he had given her. She kissed his cheek. "I'll see you soon."

Much as she would have liked to stay with Walt, she would learn more from Phoenix without him there. She made her way back to Phoenix's trailer and found her laying an assortment of supplies on the table—soap, paints, hair ribbons and a simple white garment Hannah suspected was sewn from a bedsheet. "What is all this?" she asked, surveying the array.

"This is for tonight." Phoenix smiled at her. "You want to look your best for the council." She picked up the soap. "First, bathe with this. Then we'll do your hair and makeup."

The soap was obviously homemade and smelled astringent—not the moisturizing bar Hannah preferred. But she didn't argue, and walked with Phoenix to the outdoor shower someone had built, utilizing a plastic drum to store water that was heated by the sun. After a quick soap and rinse, they walked back to the trailer, where Phoenix seated Hannah at the table and began combing out her hair, humming to herself.

"I told the officers I thought you were innocent," Hannah said after a moment. "I'm sure you didn't have anything to do with that girl's disappearance."

"I have faith they'll learn that soon enough." She picked up a ribbon and began braiding it into a section of Hannah's hair.

"When I heard your real name—your old name—I realized it was familiar to me," she said.

Phoenix's fingers stopped moving. "Did we know each other before?" she asked, her tone puzzled.

"You were one of the witnesses on Emily—Free-dom's—will." She waited for Phoenix to ask how she knew about the will, but the other woman merely went back to braiding Hannah's hair.

"She asked me to sign some papers for her, so I did," Phoenix said. "A nurse from the hospital was there and she signed, too."

"Why did she decide to write a will?" Hannah asked. "What was she afraid of?"

"Oh, she wasn't afraid. Not exactly."

"But she was upset about something?" Hannah prodded. "Why else would she be so anxious to have a will that she wrote it right there in the hospital?"

"She had had a fight with the Prophet. That upset her."

Hannah turned to look at her. "A fight? What about? Did he threaten her?"

"The Prophet doesn't threaten—he disciplines. And

only because we need it. Just as a loving father disciplines his children."

Hannah could guess where those words had come from. "How did he discipline Emily?" she asked, stomach cramping in anticipation of the answer.

"I don't know. And I don't know what they argued about, either. That was between Freedom and the Prophet."

"I don't think an adult has the right to 'discipline' another adult," Hannah said.

"You just don't understand because you haven't experienced it." She picked up another ribbon and began braiding another section of Hannah's hair. "For instance, when I first came here, I was still trying to get off heroin. The Prophet locked me up in his motor home and looked after me while I went through withdrawal. He wouldn't let me leave, even though I tried to run away. Some people might have seen it as cruel that he kept me prisoner that way, but he saved my life."

"Emily wasn't a drug addict," Hannah said. She took a deep breath, reining in her anger. "She was a grieving young woman with a new baby. She didn't need to be punished for anything."

"I'm sure the Prophet had his reasons," Phoenix said. "I've never known him to be wrong."

Hannah turned to face her once more. "Do you think he's going to punish me for Walt going to the police?" she asked.

Phoenix brushed a lock of hair from Hannah's forehead. "He likes you. I can tell by the way he looks at you. You're going to be one of his favorites. Whatever he does, it will only be because he cares for you."

Hannah felt sick to her stomach at the words. She

didn't want Daniel Metwater's brand of caring. She had to find a way to safely leave here, and to take Joy with her. *What about Walt?* a voice in the back of her mind whispered. *Will you take him with you, too—or leave him behind?*

"I'M NOT GOING to walk out there in front of a whole camp full of people naked." Walt folded his arms and glared at the scrap of cloth Kiram was holding out for him to put on.

"Everyone else will be dressed this way," Kiram said. "It's to show we have nothing to hide from each other."

Walt took the loincloth. He definitely wouldn't be able to hide a weapon in this getup. He would bet Kiram and Metwater's other "bodyguards" would be wearing their knives along with this primitive excuse for a Speedo. But he didn't see any way to get out of wearing the thing if he wanted to avoid raising further suspicion. "I'll wear it," he said. "But I'm putting my regular clothes back on as soon as this is over."

Kiram shrugged. "What did those cops want with you and your wife?" he asked.

Walt had been waiting for this to come up. "They asked if we knew the missing girl—if we had ever met her or seen her or knew anything about her."

"What did you tell them?"

He pretended to examine the loincloth. "We told them the truth—we didn't know anything."

"Seems like they could have asked you all that when you told them about the grave site."

"Yeah, well, they didn't." He stuffed the loincloth

into his pocket. "I guess I'll go back to my tent and change."

"You can change at my place." He pointed to the shack behind them.

"What do I do with my clothes?"

"Leave them here. They'll be fine with me."

And Kiram would be going through his things as soon as Walt was out of sight. "Okay." He headed for the shack. He'd have to find a hiding place for his gun while he was at the council—someplace Kiram wasn't likely to look.

He stripped off quickly, folded his clothes and left them on the end of Kiram's cot. He thought about hiding the weapon under the bed, but ended up stashing it behind a rafter overhead. In the dim light, it would be almost impossible to see. Then he took a few minutes to poke around in the room. Kiram had a small collection of manga novels and another of porn magazines, stashed in a wooden crate that served as his bedside table. He had a wardrobe of mostly shorts and cargo pants and T-shirts; a toolbox with an assortment of screwdrivers, wrenches and a hammer; and a dartboard with only three darts. A sagging, faded sofa sat against one wall.

Walt eyed the footlocker that sat at the end of the cot. He wished he had the time to check the contents of it, but he didn't dare risk it right now.

The door opened and Kiram stepped in. "What's taking so long?" he asked. "You'd better not be messing with my stuff."

"It took me a while to figure out how to get this thing on." Walt snapped the waistband of the loincloth, which was a little too breezy for comfort.

"Come on, let's go." He stepped aside and motioned for Walt to move ahead of him.

A soft drizzle had begun to fall—enough moisture to make everything damp and uncomfortable, but not enough to get them really wet. The murmur of voices drifted through the trees, swelling as they neared the center of the camp. A bonfire blazed, flames bright against the surrounding blackness, popping wood sending out showers of sparks like fireflies. It looked to Walt as if everyone in camp had gathered, most dressed in the same kind of faux-native garb he and Kiram wore. The crowd parted as he followed Kiram to a spot by the fire, and he looked across the circle and saw Hannah with Phoenix and Sophie.

For the briefest moment, he couldn't breathe, as if he had forgotten how. Her hair was down, spilling around her shoulders in a mass of tiny braids threaded with purple and pink and blue ribbons. She wore a simple sheath which, though it covered her from her collarbone to just above the knees, did nothing to hide her feminine curves. If anything, it made him more aware than ever of his attraction to her. He wanted her, yes, but he also wanted to protect her and champion her and work alongside her.

Kiram prodded him in the side. "Close your mouth and stop gaping," he said. "You'd think you'd never seen your wife before."

A clap of thunder shook the air and a murmur swept through the crowd like a wave, and the mass of people parted to reveal Daniel Metwater striding toward the fire. Walt wondered how long he had waited in the background for that thunderclap to announce his entrance—he doubted it was merely coincidence. Like most of the other men he, too, wore a loincloth, revealing muscular legs and the body of someone who spent a lot of time working out. His chest and face were painted in primitive symbols rendered in red, white and black—his eyes circled in white, a black streak down his nose, and more lines on his cheek and chin. It reminded Walt of a poor copy of an African tribal mask he had once seen in a museum. The effect was eerie, firelight flickering on his familiar, yet not familiar visage.

Metwater raised both hands over his head and the crowd quieted. "Thank you all for gathering with me tonight," he said, his voice booming in the sudden silence. "Thank you for recognizing the importance of coming together as a family, and of working as one to build something beautiful—something the outside world doesn't understand."

Walt recognized the technique—build cohesiveness in a group by pitting the members against an outside enemy—a mysterious "them."

"We are here tonight to consider the fate of two who have petitioned to join us," Metwater continued. "Serenity—" He gestured to Hannah. "And Walter."

Walt was sure the use of names neither he nor Hannah preferred was deliberate, another way of saying *I'm the one in charge here.* "They have expressed a desire to become part of our family, but their actions show they yet lack the discipline and commitment required to build a strong unit," Metwater said.

Walt caught Hannah's eye across the circle. She gave him a half smile, then made a face at Metwater. *Attagirl.*

"I have spent much time in meditation on their fate, and I have received a vision."

Walt watched the faces of those around him as they listened to Metwater. They stared fixedly at him, some almost trancelike as his words rose and fell, his voice having the rhythm and cadence of a hypnotist. He was good, Walt had to admit. But if you had to trick people into listening to you, how good of a leader could you really be?

Metwater spent some time describing his vision—something to do with a figure all in white—an angel—coming to him with a tablet, on which was written the solution to their problem. Were people really buying this? Apparently so, as they began to murmur and nod their heads in agreement.

Suddenly, Metwater reached out and grabbed Hannah's hand and yanked her to his side. Walt hadn't even realized he had lunged forward until Kiram pulled him back. The blade of Kiram's knife pressed to his throat. "I wouldn't make another move if I were you," the bearded man said.

Walt probably could have fought off the other man. He'd been trained in self-defense and was confident of his abilities. But he couldn't fight off a whole camp full of men, and the way this bunch was hanging on Metwater's every word, if the Prophet had commanded them to kill Walt, they wouldn't have hesitated to fall on him like a pack of rabid dogs.

Hannah tried to pull away from Metwater, but he held her fast. She settled for glaring at him. Clearly, she hadn't fallen under his spell like so many others. "My vision told me to welcome Serenity to our fold with open arms," Metwater said. "She has a true gentle spirit and will be an asset to us. With proper guidance, I believe she will come to be a revered and respected member of the group."

Hannah's expression didn't soften. Walt imagined she was grinding her teeth to keep from reminding Metwater that her name wasn't Serenity and she wasn't interested in his guidance.

"As of tonight, Serenity will live with me and I will take personal responsibility for her education and training."

A murmur rose from the crowd. Phoenix clapped her hands together, apparently thrilled. Hannah paled and tried, in vain, to pull away from Metwater. *That does it*, Walt thought. They were leaving tonight. He wasn't going to give Metwater a chance to "educate" Hannah, whatever form that might take.

At last Metwater handed Hannah off to Phoenix again. "Now to the question of Walter," he said. The crowd shifted to stare at Walt, who glared back.

"I fear, and my vision confirmed, that he does not have the proper spirit of cooperation that would allow him to be a valued member of our group," Metwater said. "He has shown a blatant disregard for our rules and an unhealthy defiance."

Or maybe just a healthy skepticism that you would have anyone's benefit but your own in mind, Walt thought.

"For the good of the Family, Walter must be banished," Metwater declared.

"No!" The cry came from Hannah, who was being held back by Phoenix and another woman.

"Fine by me," Walt said. "I'll leave tonight." And he

would be back before morning with a team of Rangers to free Hannah and arrest Metwater for kidnapping.

Metwater ignored him. "In order that he may learn a valuable lesson, and have time to reconsider his rebellious attitude, he will undergo a trial."

"I've had enough of this nonsense," Walt muttered.

Kiram took a firmer hold on him. "Don't try anything," the bearded man whispered.

Metwater turned and strode toward him. There was nothing natural in his movements—he was a performer on stage, playing to his audience. He stopped in front of Walt. "You will be taken out into the wilderness. From there, you can make your own way back to the world. You are never to come here again."

"I have my bike," Walt said.

"No. I have your bike." Metwater smiled. "Or rather, you are leaving it behind for your lovely wife."

"You can't do this," Walt said.

"If you could speak with others who have tried to defy me, you would learn that I can." He turned his back on Walt and crossed the circle to Hannah.

"I won't stay with you," she said. "I'm leaving with my husband."

"I am your husband now," Metwater said. "And your father and your brother and all you need." The words were beyond cheesy, but the frightening thing was, Metwater had managed to brainwash these people into believing them. He took Hannah's hand and held fast when she tried to turn away.

Walt shoved aside Kiram's hand, not caring that the knife grazed his arm, drawing blood. "Let her go!" he shouted.

His eyes met Hannah's, and behind her panic he saw

strength, and then alarm. "Walt, look out!" she cried, and then he felt a sharp pain at the back of his head, and everything went black.

Chapter Fourteen

Hannah couldn't believe this was happening. Up until now everything about the evening—from the ridiculous dress-up clothes to Metwater's bombastic speech—had seemed like a silly game. It hardly seemed credible that anyone could get away with things like kidnapping and banishment in front of a crowd of people in this day and age.

But they were in an almost roadless wilderness area, far from other people and laws and even cell phones. That isolation—and his followers' willingness to be hypnotized by his words—gave Metwater more power than he might otherwise have had.

But she wasn't going to allow him to have power over her. "Stop!" she shouted, as two men carried Walt's inert body away from the fire, into the darkness. She kicked and clawed at the men who had moved in to help the women contain her, but they only tightened their hold.

"Serenity! Hannah! You need to calm down." Phoenix grasped her hand and patted it, her face twisted in concern. "You don't need to get so upset."

"They hurt Walt," she said, fighting a mixture of rage and dismay.

"I'm sure they didn't." Phoenix squeezed her hand. "He'll be fine. Meanwhile, you've been given a great honor."

Hannah stared at her friend, confused.

"You're going to live with the Prophet." Phoenix stroked her hair. "He rarely takes such an interest in anyone. It's really a privilege."

Hannah winced. "He can take his privilege and stick it where the sun doesn't shine!"

"Freedom was the same way when he chose her," Phoenix said. "Don't make the same mistake she did and fight with him. In the end it will only do you more harm than good."

"He did this to my sister?" Hannah stared at her. "He forced himself on her?"

Phoenix looked flustered. "I don't know about your sister. I was talking about Freedom."

"Freedom was my sister," Hannah said. "Her name was Emily Dietrich, and her daughter's name is Joy. I have Joy's birth certificate, and the will you witnessed. I know."

Phoenix shook her head, as if trying to clear it. "Have you seen her? Spoken to her? Did you ask her why she left her baby?"

"She didn't leave her." Hannah was crying now, tears streaming down her face, even as the two men who held her dragged her toward Metwater's RV. "Emily couldn't come back to her baby because she's dead," she said.

"I don't understand," Phoenix said.

"My sister—Emily—Freedom—is dead," Hannah said. "She died in Denver, when she went there with the Prophet. I believe he killed her."

Phoenix stopped at the bottom of the steps leading to the motor home's door. "That isn't possible," she said. "He told us she had left."

"She would never have left her baby," Hannah said. "You know that."

"I don't—" Phoenix began.

"Come on." One of the women had opened the door to Metwater's RV and held it while the men dragged Hannah backward up the steps. They must have heard what she told Phoenix, but they showed no reaction. "You don't want to keep the Prophet waiting," the woman said.

They dragged Hannah into the RV, which appeared to be empty. If Daniel Metwater was there, he wasn't showing his face. They shoved her into a room and the lock clicked behind her. She stood for a moment, catching her breath and taking stock of her surroundings. The room contained a futon and a single chair. One window. She dragged the chair over to the window, climbed up on it and tried to force up the sash. It wouldn't budge.

"You won't get out that way."

Metwater stood in the doorway. He had removed the paint and the loincloth, and changed back into his loose linen trousers. "The window is nailed shut from the outside," he said. "And there's mesh over the pane so you can't break the glass." He moved closer to her and held out his hand. "Come down from there and let's talk."

He led her to the futon and pushed her down, then sat beside her. "You're even prettier than your sister," he said.

"What did you do to Emily?" she asked.

"I tried to help her, but she wouldn't accept my help." His smile sent a cold shiver through her stomach.

"She didn't need your help," she said.

"You say that because you want to believe that you were all she needed. But if that had been true, she wouldn't have left you and come to us."

His words were like a knife to her heart. No matter how long she lived, she would never stop believing she had somehow failed her sister. "What did you do to her?" she asked. "Why did she die?"

"An unfortunate accident," he said. He reached for her and she pulled away.

"I want to know what happened in Denver," she said. "Why did my sister die alone?"

He sat back, his expression hard. "I took her to the hospital. There was nothing else I could do for her."

She shivered, struck by his coldness. "You could have stayed with her. She was probably terrified."

He said nothing.

"Why did you lie and tell everyone she had run away?" she asked.

"There was no sense upsetting the rest of the Family. I don't believe in dwelling on negatives. What's important is the future." He reached for her again, but she pushed him away.

He scowled. "You're upset," he said. "But I can be patient—for a while." He stood. "We'll talk again in the morning."

"What did you do with Walt?"

"I didn't do anything," he said.

"That's how you operate, isn't it?" Anger made her bold. "You have other people do your dirty work for you."

"Go to sleep," he said. "We'll talk in the morning."

He shut off the light and closed the door. Her instinct was to run after him, to pound on the door and shout for him to let her out. But no one would pay any attention to her, least of all Metwater. She sank onto the futon and glared at the shut window. She had to figure out a way to get out of here. She had to find Walt, and together they had to get Joy and take her to safety.

She thought of Emily, trapped in this same room, missing her baby and desperate to escape. She hadn't been lucky enough to get away. Maybe she hadn't been strong enough. But Hannah would be strong enough for both of them. She would take care of her sister's child. Failure wasn't an option.

WALT CAME TO lying flat on his back in the darkness. He was wet and cold, and something hard was digging into his spine. Groaning, he shoved himself into a sitting position and wiped dripping water out of his eyes. It was raining—a steady drizzle that ran in rivulets across the rocky ground around him. He could make out little in the darkness, except that he was somewhere away from camp, presumably in the wilderness.

He was still wearing the stupid loincloth and was barefoot. He wouldn't get far in this country full of rocks and thorns in such a state of undress. Of course, before very long he'd probably die of hypothermia, what with the rain soaking him and nighttime temperatures in the fifties. Or he'd starve or die of thirst, since the rainwater would dry up in a matter of hours once the sun rose. Metwater was counting on that. It was a good way to kill someone without actually having to pull the trigger. If the body was found later, Metwater could always claim Walt had wandered into the wilderness on his own.

But he didn't have to get far—he only had to get back to camp. He wasn't going to die out here. He would rescue Hannah, recover his clothes and his bike, and head back to Ranger headquarters. Then Metwater would discover how hard paybacks could be.

He struggled to his feet, swaying a little, dizzy from the pounding in his head. He ran his fingers over the knot at the back of his skull, his hair sticky from what he imagined was drying blood. He took a few steps, wincing as rocks dug into his feet. He stumbled over something—a log or a boulder—and fell, hitting the ground hard and cursing loudly. The only answer was the steadily falling rain.

This wasn't going to work. It was too dark to see where he was going. He'd have to wait until it was light. Then he could take his bearings and determine the most likely route back to the camp. Otherwise, he might break his leg or stumble over a cliff. He wouldn't be any help to Hannah, lying at the bottom of a ravine.

Moving carefully, hands outstretched like a blind man, feet shuffling along, he made his way to a tree and huddled at the base of the trunk. Knees drawn up and arms wrapped around his legs, he tried to warm himself. Distraction—that was what he needed. He just had to stick it out here a few more hours. He started by thinking of all the ways he would make Metwater and Kiram pay for their treatment of him and Hannah. He had compiled a long list of possible charges against them, from kidnapping and assault to fraud and violating the county burn bans.

The idea was satisfying, but it couldn't keep his

thoughts from straying to his chief worry—not fear for his own life or concern that he might not find the camp again, but worry for Hannah. He felt physically ill, knowing she might be in danger and he was out here, powerless.

She's tough, he reminded himself. *She isn't afraid to stand up to Metwater. She's smart, too.* She was the most amazing woman he knew, and out here in the darkness, with nothing between him and his feelings, he realized he had fallen in love with her. It wasn't something he had intended to happen, but there it was. He'd lost his heart to a woman who lived in another state, who was focused on making a new life with her orphaned niece and who clearly had no room in her life for an ordinary cop.

HANNAH MOVED THE chair from the window and wedged it under the bedroom doorknob. She'd have to remove it eventually, but at least Metwater wouldn't be able to come into the room while she slept.

If sleep were even possible. She lay down on the futon, her mind racing with thoughts of her sister, of Joy, of Metwater—and of Walt.

Where was he right now? Had Kiram taken him out into the desert and killed him? Or left him to die? Her throat constricted and she swallowed tears. How had the lawman come to mean so much to her in such a short time? He wasn't like any of the other men she had known—he didn't try to change her or expect anything of her or judge her choices. He didn't need her for anything, yet when she was with him she felt stronger and smarter and more confident. Time spent with him seemed better than time spent alone—and that had never been the case with anyone else.

Her breath caught, and she sat up in bed. Was she falling in love with Walt? Was that even possible when she had known him such a short time? She didn't want a man in her life—didn't need one. She had work and Joy and so much going on. How could that leave any room for a relationship?

She tossed and turned until the window changed from a square of black to a square of silvery gray. She returned to the window and stood on tiptoe to see out. No one moved out there at this hour. Not that she would expect to see anyone at any time of day, really. The back of the RV looked out onto a choked mass of trees and underbrush that bordered the creek.

She shoved at the window sash again, and scowled at the wire mesh that covered the glass. If only she was strong enough to throw up the sash despite the nails. Would it help if she had listened to her friends and taken up weight training?

A scraping noise outside the RV made her freeze. Heart racing, she rose on tiptoe again and took a look outside. A scream stuck in her throat as a figure loomed up on the other side of the window. She jumped back, then sagged with relief when she recognized Phoenix. The other woman held up a hammer, then used it to pry the nails from the sill. Moments later, the sill shot up and Phoenix leaned her head in.

"I couldn't sleep," she said. "I've been thinking about what you said—about your sister. Do you think the Prophet really killed her?"

Hannah wanted to suggest Phoenix help her get out of the RV without Metwater knowing, and then they could have this discussion, but she couldn't be sure whose side the other woman was on. She was such an ardent fan of the Prophet that the odds seemed about even that she would alert him of any attempt Hannah made to escape. Better to try to win her over to Hannah's point of view. She moved closer to the window and kept her voice low. "I don't know. She died in the hospital emergency room, of an asthma attack."

Phoenix looked thoughtful. "I remember she had an inhaler she used. She said she was going to get her prescription filled while she and the Prophet were in Denver."

"Maybe he didn't let her fill it."

"Why wouldn't he? I mean, it wasn't as if she used it very much at all."

"No, but stress can make asthma worse. If she and the Prophet were fighting, she would be stressed."

Phoenix frowned. "But that doesn't mean he killed her."

"No. But he left her at the hospital alone." Hannah struggled to hold back her anger. "And he lied to you and everyone else here about what happened to her."

"That's what troubles me most," Phoenix said. "Why would he do that?"

"I don't know. Help me down, will you?"

"I'm not sure I should help you leave."

"I don't want to be here. The Prophet is holding me against my will. Do you think that's right?"

Phoenix hesitated so long, Hannah began to despair. Maybe she should rush the window and try to move past the other woman. "He's not going to like you leaving," Phoenix said. "He'll probably send Kiram and others after you. They might even try to hurt you."

"I know. They might already have hurt Walt. But I have to risk it. I can't stay here."

"All right, I'll help you," Phoenix said. "But wait just a minute. I'll be right back—I promise."

Before Hannah could protest, Phoenix shut the window and climbed down the ladder. By the time Hannah had the window open again, Phoenix had laid the ladder on the ground and left. Hannah moaned softly. The sun was already higher in the sky. She had no idea if Metwater was an early riser, but what if he was and decided to pay her a visit?

THE RAIN SLACKED off and Walt fell into a doze. When he woke again, stiff and cold, the sky was pale with the first hint of dawn. Standing, he pushed out of the underbrush and studied his surroundings. Nothing about this area looked familiar. Maybe if he had been on the job longer he would be more familiar with the wilderness backcountry, but his work thus far had kept him mostly in the national park and along roads. Before him spread a landscape of brown dirt, red and gray rock, and clumps of gnarled trees and sagebrush.

He tried to retrace his steps from the night before, and found the place where Kiram had left him, drag marks in the mud clearly showing where the bearded man had dumped him. Following the drag marks, he came to the impression of tires, showing where Kiram had parked his vehicle. The treads led away from the parking spot in a clear path across the prairie.

Heart pounding, Walt moved faster, trotting now, ignoring the pain in his feet as he followed the faint impressions in the mud. With a little luck, he'd be able to follow these tracks all the way back to the road, and from there to the camp.

An hour later, just as the first hints of pale blue were showing in the sky, Walt crept into the woods on the outskirts of camp. Moving stealthily, seeking cover behind trees and the random piles of junk that had accumulated among the trailers, tents and shacks, he peered out at the center gathering area. No one was moving about yet. A tendril of smoke rose from the remains of last night's bonfire, and the air smelled of wet ashes and earth.

Satisfied that no one was about, he made his way to his tent and quickly dressed. His only shoes were in Kiram's shack, along with his gun. Not wanting to be unarmed, he crept to the camp kitchen and found a knife. Suddenly ravenous, he ate some bread and cheese he found, then stuffed his pockets with several energy bars. Then he headed for Metwater's RV.

Barging into the motor home would be a bad idea. Reports he had read at Ranger headquarters indicated Metwater owned at least one firearm, and Walt couldn't be sure the Prophet was in the RV alone.

Alone except for Hannah. Walt needed to find out where she was, then make a plan for freeing her. He crept around the motor home, listening for any sign of movement inside. Most of the windows were too high up for him to see into, and he couldn't tell much about the layout of the vehicle. He thought the bedroom or bedrooms were to the left of the door, but he couldn't be sure.

He stood at the back of the RV, considering his next move, when a voice from behind him made him freeze. "Walt! You're not supposed to be here."

Slowly, he turned and stared at Phoenix. She stood at the far end of the RV, paler than ever in the early-morning light. And was that a bow and arrow she had trained on him?

HANNAH LEANED HER head against the windowsill and listened for any signs of movement in the other parts of the RV. If she heard anyone coming, she would jump out the window. Maybe she'd get lucky and wouldn't break any bones.

She wasn't sure how many minutes had passed when she heard voices outside. She looked toward the end of the RV where they seemed to be coming from and gasped as she recognized Walt and Phoenix. He was standing with his hands over his head, and Phoenix was pointing something at him. Hannah craned her neck for a closer look and gasped. Was that a bow and arrow?

THE BOW AND arrow Phoenix held looked crude, but effective. Walt had no doubt the arrow could do serious damage, especially at such close range. "I'm here to help Hannah," he said.

"Phoenix, what are you doing?"

Walt didn't dare turn around, but he recognized Hannah's voice behind him. Phoenix shifted her gaze to over his shoulder. "He's not supposed to be here," she said.

"No, I'm supposed to be dead," Walt said. "Kiram took me out into the desert and left me to die of exposure or thirst or whatever it took."

"How did you get back?" Phoenix asked.

"He was too stupid to realize his truck would leave

tracks in the fresh mud. As soon as it was light enough, I followed his trail back to camp."

"Could we discuss this later?" Hannah asked.

Phoenix lowered the bow, and together she and Walt hurried to the window where Hannah waited. He spotted the ladder and propped it against the RV, then together he and Phoenix helped Hannah climb out.

She wrapped her arms around his neck. "I was so worried about you," she said.

He held her close, unable to let go. "Are you okay?" he asked, studying her face.

She nodded. "I am. Especially now." She turned to Phoenix. "What are you doing with that bow and arrow?"

"Some guys made them a while back to hunt rabbits. They didn't have any luck but since you said you were leaving camp, I thought you might want one. You know, for self-defense."

"Is that why you left—to get something to help me protect myself?"

Bright color flooded Phoenix's normally pale cheeks. "I wedged the front door of the motor home shut. If the Prophet saw you escaping, I wanted to slow down his pursuit."

Hannah moved from Walt's arms into Phoenix's. "Thank you," she said, and kissed the older woman's cheek.

"We need to leave before everyone wakes up," Walt reminded her.

"First we have to get Joy—Vicki." She squeezed Phoenix's arm. "She has to go with us."

"No!"

Walt flinched at Phoenix's loud cry, and looked around to see if anyone had heard.

"Yes," Hannah said. "Emily—Freedom—wanted me to have the baby. She said so in her will."

"If the Prophet finds out I gave her to you, he'll punish me." Phoenix looked on the verge of tears.

"Then tell him I stole her."

Phoenix shook her head, tears streaming down her face. Walt clenched his jaw, hating how helpless he felt. He wanted to tell Hannah to leave the baby—that they would come back for her later. But he might as well have told her to leave her right arm behind. She wouldn't go without the child, and he wouldn't go without her, so they were stuck at an impasse.

"Mom, we have to give Vicki to her."

Sophie stepped from the edge of the woods, the baby cradled on her shoulder. The girl was barefoot, dressed only in a thin cotton nightgown.

"Sophie!" Phoenix cried. "What are you doing here?"

"I saw you take the bow and arrow from under the bed and I wanted to know what you were doing." She moved closer. "You always said you would give Vicki back to Freedom if she came for her," she said. "If Hannah is her sister, she's the next best thing."

Phoenix touched her daughter's cheek, then laid her other hand on the baby's back.

"You always said children belonged with family," Sophie said.

"I did, didn't I?" She turned back to Hannah. "You're not lying to me, are you?"

"Everything I've told you is the truth," Hannah said.

Except that she and Walt weren't really husband and wife, he thought, but what bearing did that have on any of this?

Phoenix handed the bow and arrow to Walt, then

took the sleeping infant from Sophie and put her in Hannah's arms.

Sophie slipped the diaper bag onto Hannah's shoulder. "Some of her things are in here, including some bottles of formula and some diapers."

"Thanks," Hannah said, and patted the girl's hand.

"Take good care of her," Phoenix whispered.

"I will," Hannah said. "And thank you—for being my sister's friend, for taking care of her baby and for helping me. You're a good woman, Phoenix."

She said nothing, but took Sophie's hand and turned away. "I'll light a candle for you," she said.

"Wait!" Hannah called.

Phoenix looked back over her shoulder.

"You should come with us," Hannah said.

"No." Phoenix took a step back. "This is my home. This is where I belong."

"But what if someone tries to hurt you?" Hannah asked. "Because you helped us?"

Phoenix smiled. "I'm sure that won't happen. We're safer here than we would be anywhere else."

Walt could see Hannah didn't believe that, but he doubted she would ever convince the older woman she was in danger. Phoenix still believed in the Prophet, despite everything that had happened. "We'll stay in touch," Hannah said. "We'll make sure you're all right." She would ask the Rangers to keep an eye on mother and daughter—to make sure no harm came to them.

WALT SHOULDERED THE crude bow and arrow, then took Hannah's hand. "Come on," he said. "We'd better go."

"I can't wait to get out of here," she said, hurrying along beside him.

"We have to stop by Kiram's place first," he said.

She balked. "Why do we have to go there?"

"I have to get my shoes—and my gun."

She glanced down at his bare feet. "Are you sure it's worth the risk?"

"We won't let him see us. You can hide somewhere nearby while I go inside."

She tucked the blankets more securely around the baby. "Let's get it over with, then."

They found a spot in the woods away from the camp but close enough to give them a view of Kiram's shack. People were beginning to emerge from some of the other trailers and tents, but there was no sign of life around the makeshift dwelling. Walt was beginning to wonder if they had missed the bearded man. "Maybe I should see if the place is empty," he said.

"No." Hannah's fingers dug into his arm. When he turned to look at her, she fixed him with a fierce gaze. "I almost lost you to that bully once," she said. "I don't want to risk it again."

Her words made him feel a little unsteady, as if reeling from a punch. He wanted to demand she explain what she meant, but now didn't seem the right time. Instead, he covered her hand with his own and nodded. "All right. We'll wait a little longer."

Just as he turned back to the shack, the door opened and Kiram emerged. As usual, he wore the knife at his waist. He looked around him, then headed away, toward the center of the camp, where other Family members were gathering for breakfast.

As soon as he was out of sight, Walt rushed forward. He took cover around the side of the shack for a moment, catching his breath. No one shouted or gave any other sign they had seen him. Quickly, he moved to the door and slipped inside.

He went first to the rafter where he had hidden the gun, and breathed a sigh of relief when he found it still there. He checked that the weapon was still loaded, then tucked it into the waistband of his jeans. His shoes were also where he had left them. He put them on, then looked around to see if he had missed anything. Moments later, he rejoined Hannah. "Let's get the bike and get out of here," he said.

"Do you think it's safe to take the baby on the motorcycle?" she asked as they made their way along the creek toward the parking area.

"It's not the safest choice," he said. "But I don't think we have any other option."

"No. I don't suppose we do."

On the way to the parking area, he dumped the bow and arrows into the brush. "I appreciate Phoenix looking out for you," he said. "But I'm more comfortable with my service weapon than those."

"I guess a gun would be more reliable," Hannah said. "Though I hope it doesn't come to that."

They emerged on the edge of the gravel parking area. As usual, the area was empty. They kept to cover until they came to the place where Walt had left the bike, camouflaged with branches. He peered into the thick underbrush and saw a few loose branches on the ground, but no bike.

"I don't see it," Hannah said.

He swore under his breath and kicked at the dirt, where the imprint of the motorcycle's tires clearly showed. "It was here," he said. "Someone took it."

"Metwater wanted it," she said. "He must have hidden it away somewhere."

"That would be my guess." Add theft to his list of charges against the so-called prophet.

"What are we going to do?" she asked.

"We start walking."

"That's right. You can turn around and walk back into camp." The underbrush behind them moved and Kiram emerged. Though Kiram still wore his knife, he aimed a pistol at Walt. "Start walking," he said. "Or I'll take a great deal of pleasure in shooting you."

Chapter Fifteen

Walt stepped in front of Hannah and the baby. He had to give them a chance to get away. Metwater wanted Hannah, but Kiram hated Walt, and Walt could use that fact to his advantage. "What's with the gun?" he asked. "I thought you were a peace-loving guy focused on spiritual matters."

"Shut up and start walking." Kiram motioned with the gun toward camp. The way he was waving the weapon around made Walt think he hadn't handled guns a lot—or at least he hadn't been trained to handle them safely. Which made him more dangerous, but less likely to be a really good shot.

Walt reached back and took Hannah's hand. "We'll come quietly," he lied. "Just allow us one more kiss before you tear us apart again." Before Kiram could respond, he pulled Hannah close and kissed her soundly on the mouth. She stiffened, then melted into his arms. He would have liked to prolong the moment, to savor the feel of her lips on his. But they didn't have a moment to lose. With his back partially shielding her from view, he moved his mouth to her ear.

"When I give the word, run," he said. "I'll be with you as soon as I can."

"Yes," she whispered.

He released her and turned to face Kiram once more. "Get going!" the bearded man shouted.

"I'm going." He took two steps toward the other man, then launched himself at Kiram's legs, sending him flying. "Run!" he shouted, and prayed that Hannah wouldn't hesitate to flee.

Kiram grunted as he landed hard on his back, but he kept hold of the gun. By the time he sat up, Walt had drawn his own weapon. Kiram fired, but the shot went wild. He rolled to the side as Walt fired, so that the bullet struck him in the shoulder, instead of the chest. Kiram's eyes widened in shock. He dropped his weapon and clutched at his shoulder, where blood blossomed, seeping through his fingers.

Walt kicked Kiram's gun away as loud voices approached. The others in the camp must have heard the shots. "Help!" Kiram shouted. "He's getting away!"

Walt didn't wait to hear more. He took off in the direction Hannah had fled. He had run several hundred yards, away from the road and the camp, when he heard her call his name. "Walt! Over here!"

He found her huddled in a thick growth of scrub oak, the baby clutched to her chest. "Are you all right?" she asked, her expression pale and stressed.

"I'm okay." He crouched in front of her. He needed to touch her, to reassure himself that she really was okay. He smoothed her hair back from her face. "What about you?"

"I'm okay." She put one hand to his cheek. "I heard gunshots and I was so worried."

"Kiram fired on me, and I shot him."

"Is he dead?"

"No. I hit him in the shoulder, but he should recover."

"As long as you're safe." She pulled his mouth down to hers and kissed him hard, as if trying to drive away all fear and doubt. He gripped her shoulders and returned the kiss, not holding back any of the emotion he felt. He didn't care that this thing between them was impractical and poorly timed and likely doomed—he was going to enjoy it now, for whatever time together they had.

Voices rose in the direction of camp and he pulled away. "We'd better go," he said. "The more distance we can put between us and Metwater's followers, the better."

He stood and helped her to her feet. The baby began to cry. "I need to change her diaper," Hannah said.

"Hurry." He looked over his shoulder, the way they had come. Though he couldn't see anyone headed toward them, Metwater's enforcers were bound to pursue them as soon as they got the story from Kiram. When he turned back to Hannah, she had laid the baby out on the blanket and removed the old diaper, which she placed in a plastic bag and stuffed in the diaper bag. "I guess we can't count on help from anyone in camp," she said.

"Some of them, like Phoenix, might want to help, but I think Metwater has most of them firmly under his thumb. I don't think we can risk it."

She nodded and fastened the new diaper around the baby, who kicked her feet and babbled. Walt smiled and held out his finger for her to grip. "You're going to be a great mom," he said.

She stared at him. "Do you really think so?"

Clearly, his answer mattered to her. He patted her shoulder. "You already love her, and that's what's most important."

Nodding, she rewrapped the blanket and zipped shut the diaper bag. "What do we do next?"

"We head for Ranger headquarters." He stood and helped her to her feet. "We'll have to travel cross-country. Metwater's people are likely to be looking for us along the roads."

They set out, trying to stay in cover as much as possible, alert to any sounds of pursuit, which didn't come. The sun climbed overhead, the day already hot. Walt wished he had thought to bring water. The creek that ran alongside Metwater's camp was the only water source he knew of around here and they couldn't risk detouring back that way. But it should only take them a few hours to reach the main road. From there they might be able to catch a ride to Ranger headquarters or into Montrose. They could call for help from there.

They paralleled the road leading away from the camp, but the going was slow, the ground rocky and uneven. Every hundred yards or so they had to detour around a pile of boulders or a dry wash or an expanse of cactus. All signs of the previous night's rain had vanished, the ground dry as powder beneath their feet, the air heavy with the scent of sagebrush and cedar.

Though they kept out of sight of the road, the rumble of passing traffic reached them, and dust clouds from the passing cars rose up in the air. "Do you think it's Family members looking for us?" she asked.

"I can't think who else it would be." Walt followed yet another dust plume with his eyes. "These roads normally get hardly any traffic."

"Maybe one of the Rangers will stop by the camp and someone will tell them we're gone," she said.

"We should have headed toward the grave site," he said. "The forensics team might still be working there. I don't know why I didn't think of that before."

"It was too close to camp," she said. "It's probably one of the first places Metwater will look. And you don't even know if anyone is still there."

"No." He wasn't even sure he could find the grave site now—not without returning to the camp as his starting point, and that was far too risky.

They had walked only an hour or so when he noticed Hannah limping. "What's wrong?" he asked, stopping. "Are you hurt?"

She grimaced. "Blister."

"Let me take the baby." He held his arms out and after a moment's hesitation, she handed the child over.

He settled the infant into the crook of his arm, a warm weight. She smiled up at him and he smiled back, enchanted.

"She's just like her mother," Hannah said. "Emily could always charm any man."

"You're pretty charming yourself," Walt said.

"Ha! I'm a lot of things, but charming is not one of them."

"All right, what about—alluring."

Pink warmed her cheeks, but she said nothing, merely set out walking again.

He caught up with her. "Why does that catch you so off guard?" he asked. "Me saying you're alluring?"

"Because I'm not," she said.

"You can't pretend you don't know I'm attracted to you. And you're attracted to me."

"I don't want to be."

He recognized truth when he heard it. "I get that, but I don't understand why."

She glanced at him, then went back to focusing on the ground. "You don't have to understand."

"But I want to."

She said nothing, only quickened her pace. He lengthened his stride to keep up with her. "When I first met you, I thought I had you figured out," he said. "I saw a smart career woman, someone used to being in charge. You became the guardian of your dead sister's baby and you threw yourself into preparing for motherhood the way you would any other project."

She said nothing, so he kept talking, refusing to let her silence shut him out. "You had probably researched all the best products and techniques, maybe arranged for child care, found a pediatrician, furnished a nursery. You had a plan for what things would be like when you got back to Texas."

"Is there something wrong with that?" she asked.

"Nothing. Except then we started working together and these feelings grew between us and I'm not a part of your plan."

"I can't be in a relationship right now."

"Why not? You don't think you can love that baby and me at the same time? People do it every day."

"I'm not every person," she said.

"No, and that's why I love you." He grabbed her hand, stopping her and turning her to him. He waited for her to rebel, to tell him he couldn't possibly love her, she didn't love him, they lived in different states, the whole situation was impossible...

Instead, she stared at him, eyes wide and shimmering with tears. "You can't love me," she said.

"Why not?"

"Because you don't know me. You don't know the awful things I've done."

"Awful things? What awful things?" A chill crept into his chest as he studied her grave expression and read the mixture of pain and fear in her eyes. Had he misjudged her so badly?

Tears were streaming down her face now. She turned away, hugging her arms across her body. Walt shifted the baby to his other arm and moved up behind her, caressing her shoulders. "I can't believe you've ever done anything so awful it would change the way I feel about you," he said.

"Emily knew. It was one of the reasons why she ran away."

"But she gave you her baby. That must mean she forgave you."

She nodded. "Yes. Yes, I think she forgave me."

"Tell me," he said. "You need to tell me or we'll both always wonder what would have happened if you had."

She sniffed, but a fresh wave of sobs shook her. He handed her his handkerchief and waited while she dabbed at her eyes and blew her nose. "I had a baby once," she said.

He blinked. He had never expected this. She had a baby? When? With whom? But none of those questions spoke to the pain in her eyes. "What happened?" he asked.

"I was nineteen. I had just started college and I had a…a fling. Nothing serious. When I got pregnant the guy freaked out. We both agreed we couldn't raise a child, so I decided to give the baby up for adoption."

"I'm sure that wasn't an easy decision. But it doesn't make you a bad person. You gave someone else who badly wanted to be a parent the chance to do so."

"It was the hardest decision I ever made." She drew in a ragged breath. "I chose an open adoption, because I wanted to know what happened to my child. Everything went well. The couple was very nice. Then, when she was three months old, little Madison died."

Another sob shook her. He gathered her close and held her tight. "I'm so sorry," he whispered, stroking her hair.

"They said it was crib death—just something that happens sometimes. But I can't help thinking, if I had been there, I could have kept her safe. If I had taken care of my own child, that wouldn't have happened."

"You can't know that," he said. "Terrible things happen sometimes, for no reason."

"I know. That's what the counselors I saw said, too. But it's haunted me. It made me believe I didn't deserve to be happy. I threw myself into my work because that was something I could control—something that didn't depend on emotion and chance. And then Emily gave me this second chance to be a mother." She smiled down at Joy, who lay sleeping in his arms.

"You're going to be a great mom to her," Walt said. "I believe that."

"But I can't take any chances," she said. "I can't let myself be distracted. Not even by you."

He could argue that he wouldn't be a distraction— that he could help her with the baby and everything would be all right. But he wasn't the one whose baby had died. He wasn't the one who was suffering.

And he couldn't think of any argument that would change her mind. Only time and experience could do that. She stepped away from him and he let her go. "Just know you're not alone," he said. "I will be there for you if you need me."

Her expression grew less bleak. "Thank you," she said. "That means a lot."

"Thank you for trusting me with your story," he said. "Hearing it doesn't change how I feel about you. If anything, it makes me admire you all the more."

"How can you say that?"

"You suffered something terrible. But you didn't let it defeat you. You came out the other side. I've seen the kind of courage you have and now I know some of what's behind it."

She studied his face, as if searching for something there. "I never met anyone like you," she said.

"I hope that's a good thing."

The baby woke and began to cry. Hannah took the child from him. "She's probably hungry," she said. "We should stop and feed her."

He looked around, then led the way to the meager shade of a stunted pinyon. Hannah settled herself against the trunk and pulled out a bottle of formula for the baby. Walt sat beside her and tried not to think about how thirsty he was.

A loud vehicle passed on the road a quarter mile distant, the rumble of an exhaust system with a hole in it echoing across the empty landscape. "Why are they pursuing us like this?" Hannah asked.

"Because Metwater knows we'll go to the police,"

Walt said. "We'll tell them about him kidnapping you and assaulting me, stealing my motorcycle, lying about your sister—all the things he's done. That will lead to more digging into his activities. My guess is that an investigation will turn up more crimes—things he doesn't want us finding out."

"He's built a little kingdom out here and he thinks he can control everyone in it," Hannah said. "He thought he was safe."

"He wasn't able to control us," Walt said. "And that's made him angry—and dangerous."

"How much longer before we reach somewhere safe?" she asked. She stowed the bottle and zipped up the diaper bag, then rested the baby on her shoulder and patted her back. She looked so comfortable and natural with the infant—he started to point this out, but then thought better of bringing up what was obviously a painful topic.

"We've only got another hour or two to walk and we should be able to flag down a car," he said. "Once we're in the park, there will be more tourist traffic. Someone will help us."

"I hope so." She held up her hand and he pulled her to her feet and they set out walking again.

They hadn't gone far when they came to a deep gash in the landscape—a narrow, rocky ravine. Walt peered into the shadowy, brush-choked canyon. "It's too steep to climb down into and out again," he said. "Especially with the baby."

Hannah shielded her eyes and peered down the length of the ravine. "It looks as if it goes on for miles."

"We'll have to walk up to the road. There's a culvert and a bridge there."

Hannah drew back. "Is that safe?"

"We can hear and see cars approaching from a long way off," he said. "We'll hide until we're sure the coast is clear, then make a dash for it."

They turned and followed the ravine up toward the road. As they drew closer, the rumble of an approaching vehicle sent them diving for cover behind an outcropping of pocked rock. Heat radiated from the scarred red granite, but the ground on its shady side still gave off a damp coolness.

Walt peered over the top of the boulder and watched a faded brown Jeep move slowly past. A bearded man sat behind the wheel; Walt was sure it was Kiram, but was that even possible, considering how recently he had been wounded?

When the vehicle had passed, they moved forward again. The bridge over the ravine was a plank affair one lane wide, laid over a rusting metal culvert. No railings separated traffic from the chasm below, and only a single orange reflector on a post marked the beginning of the bridge.

"It didn't seem this narrow when we were on the motorcycle," Hannah said.

"All we have to do is walk across it and we can move away from the road again." Walt held out his hand and she took it.

Their feet made a hollow sound on the wood planks, but the bridge was solid underfoot, and only about twenty feet across. Halfway across, the baby began to fuss and squirm. Hannah stopped and shifted her. "Her diaper's soaking," she said, feeling around one chubby leg. "No wonder, considering the way she sucked down that bottle."

"You can change her in another couple of minutes," Walt said. Standing out here in the middle of the bridge felt too vulnerable. The hair rose on the back of his neck, and he couldn't shake the feeling they were being watched. A hot wind ruffled his hair and he squinted across the prairie, his unease growing.

"What was that noise?" Hannah looked up from tending the baby.

Walt didn't have to ask "what noise?" He heard it, too—the low rumble of an engine turning over. He pivoted toward the sound, and saw what he hadn't noticed before—an old wooden corral, the boards forming the sides almost obscured by several decades' growth of sagebrush and prickly pear cactus. The corral made the perfect hiding place for someone in a vehicle to park and watch the bridge and wait.

The driver wasn't waiting anymore. His vehicle—a faded brown Jeep—shot out from the screen of boards and brush, headed straight for the bridge, and Walt and Hannah standing in the middle of it.

Chapter Sixteen

Hannah froze, transfixed by the sight of the Jeep barreling toward them. She was like someone in a dream, wanting to move but unable to do so.

"Climb down!" Walt tugged on her arm. "Over the side. Into the culvert." He pulled the infant from her and dragged her toward the edge of the bridge. He dropped to his stomach and pulled her down alongside him. "Go!" he urged.

She swung her legs over the side, clinging to the edge of the bridge, the boards shaking as the Jeep hit the bridge, the roar of the engine filling her ears. The baby clutched to his chest, Walt swung down beside her and dropped to the ground. She released her hold on the bridge as the Jeep thundered over them.

She hit the ground hard, the breath jolted out of her, but managed to roll into the culvert. Walt helped her to her feet and shoved the baby into her arms. "Get behind me," he said, drawing his gun and moving into the shadows.

Tires skidded on gravel as the Jeep braked to a halt. Car doors slammed and footsteps crunched. Hannah shrank into the deepest shadows, heart thudding so hard in her chest she had trouble drawing breath. Walt guided her into the middle of the tunnel formed by the culvert, into a corner formed by wooden bracing. He settled her into this hiding place, then turned, his back to her, shielding her with his body. She stared over his shoulder toward the opening at the end of the culvert, a circle of bright light like a spotlight, blinding in its intensity.

Each footstep overhead seemed to echo through the tunnel. Obviously, their pursuers were making no attempt at stealth. The movement above stopped. "We know you're in there, Walter!" Kiram shouted. "Come on out and we'll go easy on you."

Walt remained silent, still as a cornered stag—or a waiting lion.

Two heavy thuds signaled that their two pursuers had dropped into the ravine—one on either side of the culvert. Hannah stiffened. They were trapped now, caught between the two.

Walt reached back and squeezed her hand. The gesture shouldn't have calmed her, but somehow it did. Without uttering a word, he was letting her know he had a plan. She had to trust him.

She took a deep breath and squeezed back. *I trust you.*

A shadow darkened the opening to the tunnel—the silhouette of a tall, muscular man. "You can't escape now," Kiram said. "We've got you cornered."

He raised his right arm, and Hannah recognized the silhouette of a gun before it melted into the shadow of his body. But he was aiming it at the opposite side of the tunnel from where they were standing. He hadn't yet seen them. They were hidden in the deepest, darkest recesses of the tunnel, and his eyes, attuned to the brightness outside, hadn't been able to make them out. The man at the other end of the tunnel wouldn't be able to see them either, especially since the wooden support completely blocked them from his view.

Kiram took a step into the tunnel. Walt would have a clear shot at him now. Didn't Kiram realize this? Or was he so sure of his own superior position that he wasn't thinking? But would Walt fire? As soon as he did so, he would give away their position to the other man.

"It's too late to save yourself," Kiram said. "I promised to kill you and I will. But you can save the woman. The Prophet wants her and the baby safe and alive. Give yourself up now and I promise to take them to him. Try to take me and…well, I can't help it if they get caught in the cross fire, can I?" He took another step toward them.

The shot was a loud, echoing explosion in the metal culvert. Hannah choked back a scream and sank to her knees, her body arched over the baby, who began to wail. A second shot followed the first, then two more in rapid succession. Head down, eyes squeezed tightly shut, Hannah couldn't tell where they came from.

Her ears rang, and the smell of gunpowder stung her nose, but even half-deaf, the scuffle of retreating footsteps was clear. Opening her eyes, she turned to see Walt racing toward the far end of the tunnel. Before he had reached the end, an engine roared to life overhead, and tires skidded as the Jeep raced away.

Walt returned to her, the gun still in his hand. "Are you all right?" he asked.

"Yes." She started to rise, and he bent to help her. "What happened?" she asked.

"I'm going to check on Kiram," he said, and left before she could say more. Too shaken to move, she leaned back against the support and held her breath as he moved slowly toward the slumped figure at the tunnel opening.

She knew Kiram was dead by the heavy, sack-of-cement way his body rolled over when Walt nudged it. Walt knelt and put a hand to the bearded man's neck, then eased the gun from his grip and tucked it into his belt. He took something else from the body, then returned to her side.

"Here." He pressed something heavy into her hand. "He was wearing this on his belt."

She realized she was holding a water bottle, and hurried to twist off the cap and drink. The cool, sweet water flowed over her tongue and tears stung her eyes at the sheer pleasure of it. She forced herself to hold back from drinking it all and passed it to him.

"The other man got away," she said, when Walt had finished drinking and re-capped the bottle.

"Yes. He'll tell the others we're in this area. We need to move quickly."

"Why did he come after us?" she asked. "I thought you shot him back at the camp."

"I wounded him, but it obviously wasn't enough to stop him. His shoulder was bandaged, but my guess is he hated me enough that he was determined to find me. That kind of emotion can lead people to do incredible things."

"But he didn't stop us," she said. "He won't stop us."

"No, he won't." He started to lead the way out of the culvert, but she took hold of his arm, turning him toward her.

"What—?" She cut off the question, her lips on his, her body pressed against him. All the fear and anxiety and the giddy relief of simply being alive and with him at this moment coalesced in that kiss. All the passion she felt for him but was afraid to put into words found expression in the melding of her body to his.

He wrapped his arms around her, crushing her to him. There was no hiding her body's response to him, or his to her. Heat and hunger and need washed over her like a wave, and she moaned softly as he caressed the side of her breast and lowered his mouth to nibble the soft underside of her jaw. Every kiss, every caress, reached past the barriers she had erected long ago and touched some vulnerable part of her deep inside, coaxing her to let go a little bit more, to surrender. To trust.

He rested his forehead against hers, his breathing ragged, his voice rough. "This isn't the best time for this," he said.

"I know." She rested her palms against his chest. "We have to go. I just…I wanted you to know how I felt."

"I got the message, loud and clear." He wrapped both hands around her wrists and kissed the tips of her fingers, a gesture that set her heart to fluttering wildly.

Then he released her, and she wanted to cry out, but instead bit her lip and bent to pick up the baby, who smiled up at her with such an expression of happiness that tears stung her eyes. Talk about an emotional roller-coaster ride! The last thirty minutes had taken her through almost every feeling imaginable.

They moved out of the tunnel, the light momentarily blinding them after so much time in the shadows. Joy wailed, and Hannah rearranged the blanket to shade her face. "We'll stick to the ravine," Walt said. "It'll be rough going, but we'll be out of sight of the road."

Navigating the ravine was akin to negotiating an obstacle course. Uprooted trees, boulders the size of furniture, loose gravel and tangles of thorny vines necessitated frequent detours and stumbles. After a short distance Walt took the baby so that Hannah had both hands free to steady herself as she climbed up boulders and teetered along downed tree trunks. She stumbled often, scraping her hands and muddying her skirt. But she plowed doggedly on. As difficult as this was, at least they weren't out in the open, where anyone looking for them might easily spot them.

They had been walking less than an hour—and covered maybe half a mile—when the roar of approaching vehicles made them freeze in midstride. "It sounds like at least two of them," Walt said.

"Are they on the road?" Hannah asked, straining her ears.

As if to answer her question, the engine sounds faded, followed by crunching gravel, then the engines revved with a different pitch than before. "They turned off the road," Walt said. "They're headed this way."

He turned and continued moving up the ravine. "What are we going to do?" she asked, hurrying after him.

"As long as they stay in the vehicles, they can't see us down here," Walt said. He reached out a hand to pull her up over a large section of dead tree that was wedged across the ravine. "As long as they don't stop and get out, they're just wasting gas racing around up there."

"How did they find us so quickly?" she asked.

"They might have radios."

The engine noises faded again, and car doors slammed. Hannah looked up, and wished she knew what was going on up there.

"We'd better find a place to hide," Walt said.

They moved farther down the ravine, losing their footing often on the rough ground, but pressing on. The ravine forked and Walt led her down the narrower branch, which was scarcely wide enough for them to walk side by side. This channel was more deeply eroded, but less clogged with debris, though tree roots reached out from the bank like bony fingers, snagging at their clothing and hair.

"In here." Walt indicated a place where the bank was undercut behind a snarl of tree roots, forming a recess. Hannah balked, staring at what was really a mud-lined hole in the ground. It looked like the perfect home for spiders, snakes and who knew what else.

"Come on," Walt urged. "We have to hide before they decide to search here."

He was right, and there was no sense being squeamish. She followed him into the niche. He handed her the baby, then pulled the tree roots and a couple of loose branches to cover their entrance.

Sunlight filtered through the network of limbs and branches that formed one wall of their shelter, dappling their faces and making the niche a little less threatening. Hannah settled back into an almost-cozy spot and took out a fresh diaper and a packet of wipes. At least she could make Joy more comfortable. She stashed the dirty diaper in a plastic bag and stuffed it into the diaper bag, which she used as a kind of pillow at her back.

"Here." Walt handed her a protein bar. "Dinner."

"Thanks. You think of everything."

"Yeah. I really know how to show a woman a good time." He unwrapped a bar for himself. "Take this out-of-the-way bistro. You can't imagine how exclusive this place is."

"And it's so romantic." She laughed, and he grinned and rested his hand on her knee. "Anyplace with you seems romantic to me."

She debated kissing him again, but the narrow confines of their hideaway—not to mention the baby on her lap—made that difficult. So she settled for lacing her fingers in his and soaking in the feeling of contentment that filled her. She was dirty, hungry, thirsty and exhausted, terrified of the killers who hunted them, and confused about what lay ahead for her and Joy. But all of those worries and fears faded into the background here beside Walt.

They shared the last of the water, munching in companionable silence while straining their ears for any sound from the searchers overhead. "It doesn't sound as if they've come this way," Walt said after a while. "They probably didn't expect us to get this far. They might even suspect we went another direction."

He shifted to turn toward her. "What happened last night?" he asked. "When Metwater took you to his RV?" Tension radiated from him, as if he was bracing for bad news.

"Nothing, really," she said. "He seemed to think I ought to be flattered that I'd been singled out for attention from the great and mighty Prophet." She made a face. "The guy has an ego bigger than his biceps."

"So he didn't try to force himself on you?"

"He intended to keep me prisoner until I came around to his way of thinking." She sighed. "I think that's what he did with Emily. At least, Phoenix told me he had moved her in with him a week or so before she died. Taking her with him to Denver was a special privilege—maybe an attempt to persuade her to give in to his demands. I think the stress of the whole ordeal, and being without her baby, brought on her asthma attack. Plus, Phoenix told me she had run out of her inhaler prescription."

"It would be tough to prove murder, though if what you say is true, he could have definitely contributed to her death."

"I know. But then, why lie and say she had run away instead of telling people she had died?"

"Because he didn't want to upset the rest of his followers?" He put his arm around her. "We may never know. Though when I bring in Metwater, I intend to ask him."

She settled against him, her head on his shoulder. "Knowing you care means a lot."

He kissed the top of her head. "I do care."

Yes. And she cared for him. But if caring were enough, her baby never would have died. She had made a mistake then, trying to do the right thing. She couldn't afford to make another mistake.

Despite the discomfort of her surroundings and the lingering fear for their safety, the sleepless night in Metwater's RV, coupled with the physical hardship of fleeing across the wilderness, overcame Hannah's attempts to stay awake, and she sank into a deep slumber.

She woke to Joy's cries the next morning, sunlight streaking down from above. Next to her, Walt stirred.

"I'm going to go up and check things out," he said. "See if it's safe for us to move on."

He moved out of their shelter, and she took advantage of his absence to spread out the contents of the diaper bag and organize them. She had one more bottle of formula, which she would feed Joy this morning—and only two more diapers. No more water or food for her and Walt. But surely this morning they would reach safety. They couldn't be that far from the highway after they had walked so much yesterday.

A shower of dirt signaled Walt's return. "Everything's quiet up here," he said. "I think it's safe to go."

"Let me change Joy," she said. "She can have her last bottle while we're walking."

"I don't suppose you've stashed any coffee in there," he said, eyeing the diaper bag.

"I wish. I guess all the coffee shops up there are closed?"

"Every one of them." He waited while she finished diapering the baby, then reached down to help them out of their hiding place.

She groaned as she put weight on her cramped limbs. "I think every bone in my body hurts," she said.

"We'll have to complain to management about the mattresses in this place," Walt said.

They climbed out of the ravine and she paused at the top to stretch and breathe in the fresh, clean air, which smelled of sage and wildflowers. After spending so much time out here, she would never look at the wilderness as barren again. "Which way do we go?" she asked.

Walt turned in a slow circle, taking in the surrounding landscape. The land was gently rolling, and devoid of any sign of human habitation. Only scrubby prairie and the occasional rock uplift defined the empty expanse. Hannah had hoped to see a road, but no such luck. "Does anything look familiar to you?" he asked.

"Everything out here looks the same to me," she said.

"Me, too."

His grim expression alarmed her. "Are you saying we're lost?"

"I'm saying I'm not sure which way we should go to find the road."

She turned to look behind them, at the ravine they had just climbed out of. "Can't we just follow this back to the BLM road, then parallel that to the highway?" she asked. As much as she hated the thought of backtracking, it would be better than wandering aimlessly in the middle of nowhere.

"We could. If we knew which ravine to follow." He indicated the network of half a dozen similar ditches that spread out in every direction.

"I don't remember those," she said. "When we were down in there, there was only one way to go, at least, after we took the fork off the main channel."

"There were other forks," he said. "Now I'm not sure which one we should take."

She looked down into the chasm again. The thought of repeating the torturous crawl of the day before made her want to sink to her knees and weep. But she was stronger than that. "Do you know which direction the road was from Metwater's camp?" she asked.

"East," he said.

"The sun rises in the east, so we can walk that direction," she said.

"Except we don't know where we are in relationship to Metwater's camp," he said.

"So you're saying we're lost."

He squinted up at the sky. "Yeah. I guess I'm saying we're lost."

The words seemed to bounce up against her brain, refusing to sink in. After all they had been through, this couldn't really be happening. "You work out here," she said. "Don't you have some idea of where we are?"

"I've only been on the job two months," he said. "And it's a lot of territory. It would take years—decades—for any one person to know it all."

"So what are we going to do?" She hated that they were in this situation—and she hated that she was looking to him for answers. She wasn't the kind of person who depended on other people. She was used to solving her own problems. But this wasn't a chemical formulation that needed tweaking or a budget item she needed to finesse. She had nothing to draw on to get them out of this jam.

"Right now, I think we've got an even bigger problem to worry about," Walt said.

"What are you talking about?" What could be bigger than being lost in the middle of nowhere?

"If I'm not mistaken, we've got a prairie fire headed this way."

She turned to follow his gaze and gaped at the line of leaping orange flames that filled the horizon.

Chapter Seventeen

Walt stared at the line of flames inching toward them, the lessons from a wildland firefighting course he had taken as part of his training repeating in his head. The wind was pushing the fire in this direction, and there was nothing to stop it, and plenty of dry tinder to feed it. Firefighters carried flameproof shelters which—sometimes—could save their lives if they were overtaken by an out-of-control burn, but he and Hannah didn't have anything like that.

He took hold of her arm. "We have to get back into the ravine," he said. "If we're lucky, it will divert the flames, or they'll pass over it."

She didn't hesitate or argue, merely wrapped the baby more securely and started half climbing, half sliding into the ditch they had only recently climbed out of. "Try to find the cave where we spent the night!" he shouted after her. Already the roar of the fire was growing louder, like a jet engine revving for flight. The wind blowing toward them carried the scent of burning wood—like the world's largest campfire.

He caught up with her at the bottom of the ra-vine and together they scrambled over boulders and branches, watching for the opening to the undercut that had sheltered them last night.

"There!" Hannah pointed to the place where they had pushed aside a knot of tree roots as they had exited their shelter.

"Hurry!" He took the baby from her and started up the slope. The fire was almost upon them, a hot, shrieking turbulence created by the flames sending debris flying, branches and even whole trees exploding into flames like hand grenades going off as the sap superheated inside the bark.

He shoved the baby, who was crying now, into the mud-lined shelter, then reached back to haul Hannah up by both arms. He pushed her into the opening, then crawled in after her, shielding both her and the child with his body, his back to the world above that was already being consumed by flames.

Hannah crouched over the infant, whose wails rose over even the sound of the inferno, a siren song that seemed to intensify his own fear and anxiety. He wrapped his arms around Hannah and buried his face against her neck, breathing in deeply of her sweet scent, trying to block the acrid stench of smoke. She gripped his arm, fingers digging into his flesh. The roar of the flames was even louder now—he winced as the heat intensified, searing his back. It was growing harder to breathe, and the baby's wails silenced. He slid one hand beneath Hannah's to touch the child, reassured that she was still breathing.

Hannah coughed, and he held her, then gave in to spasms of his own. But as the pain in his chest eased, he opened his eyes and realized the roaring of the blaze had faded, and light was once more seeping into their shelter. The heat had lessened, as well. Hannah turned her head and her eyes met his. "Is it over?" she asked.

He eased back a little, and then a little more, until he was able to stick his head out to survey the ravine. Smoke curled from a smoldering tree branch and white ash scarred the rocks around it, but the fire hadn't descended to the bottom of the ravine. He retreated into the undercut once more. "Let's wait a few minutes for things to cool off a bit, but I think we're okay," he said. "How's Joy?"

"She's fine." She cradled the infant to her, tears streaming down her face. "I was so scared, but thanks to you, we're all okay."

"I didn't do anything," he said. "And for what it's worth, I was terrified, too."

She wrapped her arms around him. "I might have made it without you, but I'm glad I didn't have to try," she said.

They waited half an hour, then climbed out of the ravine, emerging streaked with soot and ash to a landscape filled with the blackened skeletons of trees and exploded rock. Smoke curled from the ground, and they walked carefully, trying to avoid hot spots. Walt moved in front of Hannah to break the trail, and she gasped.

He glanced over his shoulder at her. "What's wrong?"

"Your back!" She pointed, then covered her mouth with her hand. "It's burned."

He hadn't noticed anything until that moment, but when he reached around and felt along his ribs he winced at the sudden, searing pain. "Your shirt is almost burned away," she said. "You let that happen and you never said a thing."

"I had other things on my mind." He faced forward again. "It doesn't matter. We have to get out of here."

"But where are we going?" she asked.

"Away from the fire."

A droning sound overhead made them both look up. When Walt recognized the helicopter, he raised both hands to wave, ignoring the pain in his shoulders as he did so. Hannah took the blanket from around the baby and waved it also. The chopper dipped lower, and they could clearly see the pilot. He circled them, and then slowly descended to a spot about two hundred yards away.

By the time Walt and Hannah reached the helicopter, the pilot had shut down the engine and climbed out to meet them. "What are you two doing out here?" he asked.

"It's a long story," Walt said. "I'm Agent Walt Riley with the Ranger Brigade. Can you take us to Ranger headquarters?"

"Whoever you are, you need to get out of here. Climb in." The pilot walked around to the door of the chopper. "I'll radio this in once we're airborne. Headquarters is never going to believe this."

"I DON'T BELIEVE THIS." Commander Graham Ellison frowned as an EMT bandaged Walt's blistered back. "When Metwater's people told us you and Hannah had left, we suspected something was up, but not that you'd been trapped in that wildfire."

"Which the fire investigators now say was deliberately set." Carmen joined the group clustered around Walt, Hannah and the baby.

"When Metwater's goons didn't succeed in tracking us down yesterday, he probably thought the fire would be a good way to finish us off." Walt winced as the EMT tightened the bandage.

"That's crazy." Hannah looked up from feeding the baby. "They could have burned down their own camp."

"They were probably counting on the road and the creek to serve as a firebreak," Marco said. "And the prevailing winds were in their favor."

"Metwater is already claiming he knows nothing about anything," Graham said. "And he's telling anyone who will listen that you murdered Alan Saddler—aka Kiram—in cold blood."

"He was trying to kill us!" Hannah stood, unable to rein in her outrage.

"I'm sure the investigation will prove that," Graham said. He turned to Walt. "Until that plays out, you're probably going to take a beating in the press. Metwater has his lawyers working overtime, filing charges."

"But he'll have to submit to the paternity test the court ordered, right?" Hannah asked. Soon after they had arrived at Ranger headquarters, she had learned the court order for the DNA test to determine the baby's identity had come through.

"He will," Graham said. "We won't let him off the hook on that."

The EMT pressed the final bandage in place, then stepped back. "You need to have a doctor check that out ASAP, but I'm guessing you're going to need a couple of weeks off to heal," he said.

"Good idea," Graham said. "You lie low and let us handle Metwater."

"He assaulted me, kidnapped Hannah and he stole my bike," Walt said.

"I've got your bike in my garage," Michael Dance said.

Walt scowled at him. "What are you doing with my Harley?"

"When we showed up at Metwater's camp, looking for you, I spotted it tucked behind one of the shacks," Michael said. "I decided I'd better take it in for safe-keeping before it disappeared altogether."

"Don't let him fool you," Marco said. "He just wanted to ride it."

"It's a sweet ride," Michael said, grinning.

"Metwater didn't try to stop you?" Walt asked.

"He told us you had just left it there when you de-cided to take off," Marco said. "That's when we knew he was lying about what happened to you. You wouldn't abandon the Harley."

"What about Lucia Raton?" Hannah asked. "Have you found her?"

"Not yet," Carmen said. "But we found a witness who saw her after she supposedly left Metwater's camp, so that seems to let him off the hook."

"For now," Graham said. "As for the rest, the as-sault charges are going to be tough to make stick, es-pecially with Metwater making a stink about Kiram's death. And the kidnapping—" He looked at Hannah.

"He held me against my will," Hannah said. "But we'll probably have a hard time finding anyone except Walt who will testify to that."

"We'll see what we can do." Graham touched Walt's arm. "As of now, you're on medical leave. Get your back seen to, then go away somewhere and try to relax. Avoid the press."

"But I don't—" he started to protest, but Hannah took his other arm and he fell silent.

"Why don't you come to Texas?" she asked. "I could use some help settling in with Joy."

She didn't blame him for the doubt in his eyes. After all, she had wasted a lot of time protesting that things would never work out between them. But those moments in the fire, when they had been so close to death and he had been willing to risk everything to save her and Joy, had made her see how foolish her fears had been.

Aware of the others watching, she leaned closer to him and lowered her voice. "Please? I've decided I was right that first day I came in here—you really are the one I want to help me."

Her cheeks burned as he kissed her on the lips. His coworkers broke into applause and she pulled away, laughing. "Is that a yes?"

"It's a yes," he said. "Play your cards right and I might even stick around longer than two weeks."

"I always was a good card player," she said, a thrill running through her. She'd never been a big gambler, but right now she was willing to risk a lot to be with the man she loved.

Epilogue

Carmen Redhorse looked up from her computer terminal and smiled at the little family that had just walked into Ranger headquarters. Out of uniform and toting a baby carrier, Walt Riley was the picture of a suburban dad. The woman beside him, Hannah, had lost the pinched look that had haunted her before and now glowed with the happiness of a woman in love.

"I just stopped by to clean out my locker and my desk," Walt said, setting the carrier on a chair by the door.

"How's the back?" Carmen asked. She came over to admire the infant, who babbled and flailed her arms, chubby cheeks framing an adorable baby smile.

"It's fine," he said.

"He's got some scars," Hannah said. "But I think he's almost proud of them."

"Good for his macho cred," Carmen said.

"Where is everybody?" Walt asked.

"Marco and Ethan are at training, Michael and Lance are trying to track down a guy who's been stealing rare plants from the park, Simon is in court, the commander and Randall are at a meeting in Montrose, and I'm holding down the fort here."

"What's the latest on Metwater?" Walt asked.

"Not good," Carmen said. "The DA says we don't have enough evidence to prosecute him for anything. Lucia Raton is still missing, so the fact that her locket was found sort of near his compound doesn't mean much. Anything we have any proof for, like the assault on you, Metwater blames on Kiram, whom he says was acting without his authority or knowledge."

"Right." Walt looked like he wanted to punch someone.

"At least we proved he isn't Joy's father," Hannah said. "He has no claim on her."

"He probably contributed to your sister's death, though we'll never prove it," Walt said.

"Let it go," Hannah said. "I am."

"We're still watching him," Carmen said. "He's going to make a wrong move one day and when he does, we'll catch him."

Walt nodded. "You're right." He looked at Hannah. "And so are you. I'm going to move on."

"So you're really abandoning us for Texas," Carmen said.

"The Dallas County Sheriff's Department has an opening, so I'm going to give it a try."

Carmen turned to Hannah. "Are you sure you're ready for life with a Harley-riding cop?"

Hannah shook her head. "No more Harley," she said. "He sold it."

Carmen put a hand to her chest in a pantomime of shock. "You sold the Harley?"

Walt's cheeks reddened. "Yeah, well, you can't strap a car seat on the back of a motorcycle."

"This must be serious," Carmen said.

Hannah slipped her arm through Walt's, smiling at him with the indulgent look women in love shared. "Yes, it is."

Carmen caught the flash of the diamond on the third finger of Hannah's left hand. "How did I miss this?" She grabbed the hand for a closer l ook. "Nicely done, Agent Riley," she said. "Have you set a date?"

"We're thinking in the spring." He grinned.

"Congratulations," Carmen said. "You almost make me believe in true love."

"Hey, I was a skeptic, too," Hannah said.

"She just had to meet someone tough enough to call her bluff," Walt said.

"Someone who showed me I could trust myself." She squeezed his hand and Carmen felt the pressure around her heart. Why was it some people found love easily and some—like Hannah and Walt—had to fight for it?

The answer didn't really matter, she decided. In the end the prize was all that mattered, not how you came to win it.

* * * * *

Can't get enough of
THE RANGER BRIGADE: FAMILY SECRETS?
See where it all began in

MURDER IN BLACK CANYON,

and don't miss
THE MEN OF SEARCH TEAM SEVEN:

COLORADO CRIME SCENE
LAWMAN ON THE HUNT
CHRISTMAS KIDNAPPING
PHD PROTECTOR

Available now from Mills & Boon Intrigue!

"Shaye!"

"Cole?"

Her voice was weak, but relief hit him hard, a wave that almost took him to his knees. She was alive.

He rounded the second car and found her huddled near the back tire. The flat back tire, Cole realized. The gunman's final shot must have just missed her.

But relief was short-lived, because she was hit. There was a trail of blood alongside the car, as if she'd dragged herself here. He yanked his cell phone out, calling Monica directly. "Gunman ran east out of Roy's parking lot, on foot. Male, white, average height and build, wearing jeans and a dark hoodie, carrying at least one pistol. Send backup. And get me an ambulance to Roy's, right now."

He barely paused as he knelt next to Shaye, who was abnormally pale, her freckles standing out more than usual against her porcelain skin, her red hair tangled around her face and her pretty brown eyes huge. "Talk to me. Are you okay?"

POLICE PROTECTOR

BY,
ELIZABETH HEITER

MILLS & BOON

First Published in Great Britain 2017
By Mills & Boon, an imprint of HarperCollins*Publishers*
1 London Bridge Street, London, SE1 9GF

ISBN: 978-0-263-92900-3

46-0717

Our policy is to use papers that are natural, renewable and recyclable products and made from wood grown in sustainable forests. The logging and manufacturing processes conform to the legal environmental regulations of the country of origin.

Printed and bound in Spain
by CPI, Barcelona

Elizabeth Heiter likes her suspense to feature strong heroines, chilling villains, psychological twists and a little romance. Her research has taken her into the minds of serial killers, through murder investigations and onto the FBI Academy's shooting range. Elizabeth graduated from the University of Michigan with a degree in English literature. She's a member of International Thriller Writers and Romance Writers of America. Visit Elizabeth at www.elizabethheiter.com.

It's amazing to have friends who've been by your side since childhood. Robbie Terman, Jaime Pulliam, Julie Gabe and Esi Akaah—this one's for you!

Acknowledgments

Thank you to Paula Eykelhof, Kayla King, Denise Zaza and everyone involved in bringing *Police Protector* to readers. Thanks to my family and friends for their endless support, especially my "usual suspects": Kevan Lyon, Chris Heiter, Robbie Terman, Andrew Gulli, Kathryn Merhar, Caroline Heiter, Kristen Kobet, Ann Forsaith, Charles Shipps, Sasha Orr, Nora Smith and Mark Nalbach.

Chapter One

She'd made it.

Shaye Mallory smiled as she juggled two bags of groceries and headed toward her ten-year-old sedan at the far end of the grocery store parking lot. She'd been back to work at Maryland's Jannis County forensics lab for a full week now.

A full week where no one had shot at her.

It felt like a good reason for a celebration, so tonight's trip to the grocery store had included a big carton of chocolate-chunk ice cream. She tried not to feel too pathetic that she'd be having that celebration all by herself on a Friday night in her living room with an old movie and spoonful after spoonful of sugar.

But she'd lived in Maryland for only two years. She'd moved out here for the computer specialist job. She worked with police officers in her role, but bullets had seemed as foreign to her as living alone, far away from her big family. When she'd left the forensics lab last year after the shooting, most of those friendships had eventually lapsed. At the job she'd taken in tech support before returning to the lab, she'd kept mostly to herself. Although she had friends, there wasn't anyone close enough to tell she wanted to celebrate going a

week without being shot at or having a nervous breakdown. And celebrating with her family over video chat
seemed way too pathetic, not to mention that it would
get them worried about her all over again.

The truth was today was a milestone for her. A year
ago, when she'd quit the job, she'd sworn she'd never
return. Never walk back into the forensics lab parking
lot—one that was shared with the Jannis City Police
Department—where she'd watched three officers die.
Where she'd hit the pavement, panicking as shots rang
out, having no way to defend herself, knowing she was
going to be next.

The shiver of fear that bolted up her spine now was
just a memory, Shaye told herself, repositioning her
bags so she could dig out her car key. She'd worked late
tonight, but when she'd arrived at the store, the parking
lot had been relatively full. Apparently she'd spent too
long inside debating treats because now it was nearly
empty. She forced herself not to spin around, not to
check her surroundings, not to give in to the paranoia
that had caused her more than one moment of embarrassment over the past week.

But she'd done it. She'd conquered her fear and finally called the forensics lab back, finally accepted their
offers to return to her old job.

Every single time she'd walked into the parking lot
where the shooting had happened, she'd felt a near-
paralyzing fear. She'd frozen more than once before
stepping out of her car, but she'd done it. And each day
she'd paused for slightly less time before gathering the
courage to run for the lab.

But everything was getting back to normal now,

Shaye reminded herself. Soon—hopefully—she'd hardly even remember feeling afraid.

If only she could say that right now. She stopped ignoring the tingle at the back of her neck and glanced around the vacant lot, dimly lit with bulbs and two cars, barely keeping hold of her groceries as she slid her key into her door. She swore as one of the bags ripped and started sliding out of her hands.

She dropped to her knees, trying to catch the bag before eggs broke everywhere, and then a *boom* she'd recognize anywhere rang out. A gunshot.

She panicked, and her feet slid out from underneath her, sending groceries smashing to the ground. Then another gunshot split the night air, and pain exploded in her hip.

Dropping lower to the ground, Shaye looked around the parking lot, certain she'd see that same rusted-out sedan with the spinning rims from a year ago cruising to a stop, gang members leaning out the windows with semi-automatics. Instead she saw a lone figure running across the dark parking lot toward her, a weapon in his hands.

Shaye whimpered, her blood racing through her veins so fast her whole body started to shake as blood spread on the leg of her khakis. *Not again.* And this time she was all alone. No Cole Walker, heroic police detective and star in too many of her fantasies, to save her.

Fear overrode her ability to think clearly as her brain went back to that horrible evening when gang members had tried to get revenge on the police station for investigating them. She'd been dawdling as she'd left the lab, hanging out closer to the station than her own building, hoping for a chance to run into Cole, when the gunfire started. Shoving the memories back, she glanced up at the key in her car door. Could she get it unlocked, get inside and start the car fast enough?

She looked back toward the shooter, who'd made it halfway to her and stopped to line up another shot through the lot's dim lighting.

Pressing her feet hard against the concrete, Shaye launched herself toward the front of her car. She heard another bullet hit—probably her car—but didn't stop to check.

Adrenaline pumped so hard she couldn't feel the bullet wound on her leg, or the nasty scrapes she knew she'd made on her hands and knees when she'd shoved herself along the concrete. She kept going, her heart thudding in her eardrums as she scurried around to the other side of her car. It wouldn't be a barrier for long, but now he'd have to get closer to hit her.

There was another car ten feet away. If she could make a run for it, dart for new cover while he was trying to move closer, maybe it would give someone inside time to call the police. Or another vehicle would pull into the lot and scare him off. She scrambled to her knees and got ready to race for the other car, but the sound of footsteps pounded toward her too quickly, and she knew she'd never make it in time.

A sob lodged in her throat as she readied herself to make a run for it anyway, one last desperate effort to survive when she knew she was going to fail. She'd lived through the shooting at the lab, actually conquered her fears enough to return to that job, and now she was going to die in a supermarket parking lot.

"Shots fired at Roy's Grocery."

The call came in over his radio, and Cole Walker

scowled at it, then pressed the button and replied. "Detective Walker. I'm a minute out. Responding."

He punched the gas as Monica's voice came back to him, "Aren't you off duty, Detective?"

It was a rhetorical question, so he didn't bother answering. A cop was never really off duty.

"We believe there's a single gunman in the parking lot," Monica advised him. "Call came in from the owner, who thinks there's at least one customer out there, too. No other information at this time."

"Got it," he muttered, not bothering to key the radio. It didn't really matter what information they had; with shots fired, they always reacted as though there could be more gunmen. Ever since the shooting at the station last year, calls about gunfire spurred extra caution.

That thought instantly made an image of Shaye Mallory form in his head. He wouldn't have been anywhere near Roy's Grocery, except he'd been on his way—uninvited—to her house. And the store was only a few miles down the road from her. His gaze caught on the champagne bottle with a ribbon on it that rolled off his seat and smacked the floor as he whipped his truck into the grocery store parking lot.

The store had crappy lighting, but he zoned in on the shooter immediately. The man glanced back at him, a hoodie obscuring his face, and then darted around one of two cars in the lot, firing at something—or someone—behind it before sprinting around the corner.

Cole hit the gas, scanning the parking lot for any sign of additional shooters. But he saw no one as he raced past the first car. He was ready to continue past the second after the shooter when his mind registered the make and model of the first one—he recognized it.

He slammed on the brakes, yanked his truck into Park and had his weapon out of its holster before he'd even cleared the door.

"Shaye!"

"Cole?"

Her voice was weak, but relief hit him hard, a wave that almost took him to his knees. She was alive.

He rounded the second car and found her huddled near the back tire. The *flat* back tire, Cole realized. The gunman's final shot must have just missed her.

But relief was short-lived because she was hit. There was a trail of blood alongside the car, as if she'd dragged herself here. He yanked his cell phone out, calling Monica directly. "Gunman ran east out of Roy's parking lot on foot. Male, white, average height and build, wearing jeans and a dark hoodie, carrying at least one pistol. Send backup. And get me an ambulance to Roy's right now."

He barely paused as he knelt next to Shaye, who was abnormally pale, her freckles standing out more than usual against her porcelain skin, her red hair tangled around her face and her pretty brown eyes huge. "Talk to me. Are you okay?"

He didn't wait for an answer, but tucked his phone against his shoulder, holstered his weapon and found the source of all that blood. It was coming from her right leg, up near her hip. Finding where the bullet had entered, he grabbed the fabric of her khakis and ripped so he could see the wound.

"Hey," she complained, but her voice was even weaker, and she leaned her head against the car as he prodded carefully around her wound.

It was bleeding badly, but not as badly as it would

have been if the shooter had gotten a major artery. He slid his hand down into the leg of her pants around to the back of her thigh and found what he suspected. An exit wound. The bullet had gone straight through.

"How bad is it?" Shaye whispered, her eyelids dropping to half-mast.

"You're going to be fine," he promised.

"What's happening?" Monica asked in his ear. "Backup is close. Two minutes out."

He cursed inwardly, hoping the shooter wouldn't be long gone before officers arrived. Two minutes was too long. This guy had shot Shaye. Cole wanted him in handcuffs now.

Monica's voice sounded in his ear again. "I'm getting that ambulance now."

"Cancel it." Cole shifted his weight and warned Shaye, "This might hurt a little." Then he wiped the blood on his hands onto the leg of his pants and scooped her into his arms. "Shaye Mallory was hit," he said into his phone as Shaye's arms went around his neck and she tucked her head against his chest, almost before he saw her wince with pain and clamp her jaw closed.

"I'm driving her to the hospital myself," he told Monica as he hurried back to his truck, deposited her in the passenger seat and then ran around to the driver's side. "I'll call you when we get there. Send me updates as they come in," he said, then hung up the phone and hopped in the truck, yanking it back into Drive.

As he sped out of the parking lot, Shaye asked, "Were you on your way to a date?"

"What?" He frowned over at her, both at the oddity of her question and the way her voice sounded like she was in a daze.

She gestured to her feet, and he looked down, realizing she was talking about the bottle of champagne on his floorboard, which was still miraculously unbroken.

"That was for you," he replied, seeing her confusion before he yanked his attention back onto the road and drove as fast as he could through the surface streets toward the freeway.

"For me?"

"Put pressure on your wound," he said, instead of explaining that he'd gotten it to celebrate her returning to work.

He risked a glance at her as her head dropped forward. As if she'd just realized how much blood there was, she pressed both hands down frantically against her leg.

She was coming out of her shock. He'd seen enough shooting victims to know what was coming next: panic.

He tried to stave it off as he merged onto the freeway and punched it up to ninety. "We'll be at the hospital in three minutes," he promised, keeping his tone calm despite the fear he felt. "You're fine. It's a flesh wound. I know it looks like a lot, but the bullet went through and you haven't lost enough blood for it to be a problem."

He'd seen enough bullet wounds to know when they were life threatening. But he'd also seen enough to know that sometimes they surprised you. He'd seen people operate on adrenaline, actually getting up and running, when their injuries said they should already be dead. And he'd seen minor wounds turn fatal.

Not for Shaye, he promised himself, speeding off the freeway. A few more too-fast turns and then he made an illegal turn into the hospital parking lot and slammed to a stop. He tossed his key at the valet and ran around the other side to open Shaye's door.

An orderly was coming their way with a wheelchair, but Cole ignored him, reaching in to lift Shaye himself. If it was possible, she looked even more pale and terrified, reminding him of that day almost exactly a year ago and the drive-by at the station. Shaye had been caught in the middle of it all.

"Why does this keep happening?" she whispered, then promptly passed out.

Chapter Two

Shaye woke in a hospital bed, a warm blanket pulled up to her chin and a frowning nurse strapping a blood pressure cuff to her arm.

"How are you feeling?"

She'd recognize that voice anywhere. Shaye turned her head, and there was Cole, perched at the edge of a chair next to her bed, his reddish-blond hair rumpled and concern etched onto his normally laid-back expression.

Embarrassment heated her. Had she actually *fainted*?

Okay, yes, she was a lab rat, and gun battles—except for the gang shooting that still gave her nightmares—were *way* outside her experience. But she'd managed to make a run for that second car, hiding until Cole had magically arrived. She'd managed to stay relatively cool until they'd made it safely to the hospital.

Yet she'd fainted in front of Jannis's best detective, the guy who'd led the charge to bring down the entire gang's network after that shooting. Cole was one of the bravest people she knew.

And she was most definitely not.

"I'm okay," she said, surprised when her voice came out weak. She realized just how tired she was.

"We stitched up your wound," the nurse told her, jotting something down and then taking the blood pressure cuff off her arm. "You were lucky—it went straight through and didn't hit anything crucial. The doctor is going to want to watch your vitals for a few hours, but then we'll send you home. You should be feeling fine in a few days."

Shaye nodded, trying not to focus on the dread she'd felt as soon as the nurse mentioned leaving the hospital. Would she ever feel safe again? Or would everywhere she went become like the forensics lab, requiring her to psyche herself up to leave her house? Tears welled, and she shoved them back, refusing to show any more weakness in front of Cole.

Once she knew no tears were going to escape, she looked over at him, hopeful. "Did they get the shooter?"

He frowned, shaking his head. "Not yet. But we're already reaching out to the news stations. We'll be putting out a call for information on all the evening shows. Someone will know something. We'll find him."

She shivered, suddenly cold, pulling the blanket tighter around her. Would they really? The department was good. She'd seen firsthand how dedicated they were. But with nothing to go on but a vague description of a gunman? Especially one who'd managed to escape the police's net?

Cole must have sensed the direction of her thoughts, because he said, "We've got officers at the scene now, pulling the slugs from your car. The security camera at the grocery store was just for show, but we're canvassing the area, hoping someone saw the shooter running away. And we're checking nearby traffic cameras, too.

Unless he lives close by, he must have had a vehicle waiting. Once we find that, it's over."

There was a dark determination to his voice that told her he planned to be there to slap on the handcuffs himself.

And what he was saying made sense. Although her job was peripheral—she analyzed digital devices like laptops or cell phones that cops brought to her under the fluorescent lights in her lab—she'd seen how investigations worked.

Roy's Grocery was in a safe area. There were a lot of independent businesses there, and it was close to family neighborhoods. People watched out for one another. They would report someone running away after hearing gunshots. Logically, that would lead to a location where the shooter had a car waiting, and a license plate they could run through their system to get a name. She'd seen it happen before. She'd seen it work plenty of times.

But she'd also helped with cases where they'd come up empty no matter how hard they tried, and she couldn't shake the feeling that this was going to be one of those cases. Even worse, she hadn't been any help at all. All she could say about the shooter was that he was male, probably white, definitely determined to kill her.

"Do you think it was the same people from last year?" She spoke her deepest fear.

Gangs didn't give up. They didn't forgive, and they held grudges.

The police had rounded up the whole group, killing some at the scene, then getting the driver from her identification. After that, they'd worked tirelessly to bring down the leadership, being creative by going after them on racketeering charges, using the digital trail she'd found before the shooting, before she'd quit. But was everyone behind bars, or had they missed someone? Had someone gotten out?

With gangs anything was possible, including someone new making a play to bring the group back, to make a name for himself by taking out the key witness in the trial that had brought down the old leadership. Last year she'd worried that she'd never be safe again. There had actually been talk of the Witness Protection Program.

But Cole and his partner had kept at it, even working with local FBI agents in one of the biggest task forces their small department had ever seen. She'd been gone by then, but she'd heard the rumors. Cole had ignored death threats. He'd kept going until he was certain every member was behind bars.

She'd seen the news headlines later that year, too, proclaiming the demise of the Jannis Crew gang. Her fear of returning to the station hadn't gone away, but at the time, her logical brain had said there was no more reason for her to be scared.

"We're looking into it," Cole said, fury in the hard lines of his jaw. "But don't worry. Chances are this is totally unrelated. You were probably a random victim, just in the wrong parking lot when he happened to be looking for trouble."

"You think this guy was planning a mass shooting and the parking lot was emptier than he expected?" she asked. Or had Cole arrived before the shooter could head into the building to find more victims, she wondered, staring at the man who'd saved her life for the second time.

She flashed back to that moment when she'd flattened herself to the ground in a different parking lot, certain she was going to be killed. Back then, there'd been three other men in the lot with her, armed men, who'd each taken a bullet before they could unholster their weapons. She'd gotten as low as she could, with nowhere to run, bullets spraying over her head, and then Cole had run out the front door of the station, right into the line of fire.

"It's definitely a possibility," Cole said, and she refocused on their conversation.

Mass shooting. This was different from last year, she reminded herself. Except back then, she hadn't been an intended target, either. Just at the wrong place at the wrong time. How many chances would she get before she ran out of them, or Cole wasn't around to save her?

A shiver worked through her, and she spoke quickly to change the subject, knowing he'd seen it. "How long have I been here?"

He didn't even glance at his watch. "A few hours."

And he'd stayed beside her the whole time? She didn't need to ask. She could tell from the way the nurse had maneuvered around him when she'd left the room without even looking, as if she'd been doing it repeatedly.

She had an instant flashback to the day she'd arrived in Jannis, having accepted the job as a digital forensics examiner. She'd walked through the station doors, thinking it was connected to the laboratory she was supposed to report to, her palms slick with nerves and her stride quick with anticipation. She'd turned the corner toward security and walked smack into Cole Walker.

She was tall, and in the heels she'd worn that first day with her carefully tailored suit, she'd been close to his six feet. But even in heels, she didn't have slow or dainty strides. She walked with purpose, so she'd collided with him hard. Enough that the impact with his rock-hard chest had almost sent her to the ground.

The memory made her flush, warming her up, and Cole's lips turned up at the corners like he could tell what she was thinking. Before he could comment on it, she blurted, "I'm not quitting."

He looked surprised by her outburst, and, in truth, it had surprised her, too. She'd had no idea she was even thinking it until the words came out, but as soon as she spoke, she realized they were true.

A year ago she'd let the tragedy at the station derail her career. The fact was she'd let it derail her life.

She was scared. But how many times could she be this unlucky?

And she was tired of running from the things that scared her. She met Cole's gaze, momentarily distracted by the perfect sky blue of his eyes, then felt her shoulders square on the scratchy hospital pillow. "Whatever needs to be done to catch this guy, I want to be a part of it."

HAPPINESS BURST FORTH, then instantly warred with Cole's need to keep Shaye safe.

He'd been thrilled when she had returned to the lab. It had been part of his motivation when he'd called her a month ago, asking for some off-the-books help with a situation his foster brother Andre had been battling. When she'd provided key information to help them nail the guy who'd been coming after his brother's new girlfriend, he'd seen it boost her confidence again. Even more, he'd seen it remind her how much she loved the electronic chase.

He'd worked with enough forensics specialists in his years at the police department to know Shaye was special. She had a gift with computers, able to pull from them things no one else could find. And that kind of talent rarely came without passion.

When she'd left the job last year, he'd understood. A tiny part of him had even been glad, because it kept her out of the line of fire while they chased down the dangerous gang nervy enough to stage a drive-by at a police station. But he'd missed seeing her every day, those few moments each morning when they'd walk in from the parking lot together before she veered off to the county's forensics lab located behind the station. Those few moments each evening when she'd wait for him outside the station doors, and they'd stand and chat before going their separate ways.

Once he'd been confident they'd shut the gang down, he'd reached out a few times, tried to convince Shaye to return. He knew her director had, too. But each time she'd refused, seeming embarrassed by the fact that she was afraid to come under fire again. So he was shocked that she was standing her ground now.

"Are you sure?" he asked. Before she could argue, he continued. "Believe me—I want you to stay. I think this is where you belong. But we don't know who came after you today—and although I don't think you were the target, I want to be sure. Your safety is most important."

"I—"

"Hopefully, we'll catch him today and discover he's acting alone and picked you at random. But until we're certain, I think you should go into protective custody."

When she looked ready to argue, he held up a hand.

"Not WitSec. I'm not asking you to give up your life here. This is nothing like last year."

He hoped that was true. Nothing about this situation resembled the other—the shooter hadn't been wearing gang colors, and he'd gone after Shaye at a store, instead of attacking where the rest of the gang's presumed targets would be, back at the station. All logic pointed to this being random.

But he couldn't shake the fear that someone wanted Shaye dead. And he couldn't let anything happen to her.

"Just temporary police protection," he continued, trying to stop his morose thinking. "Then, once we're sure you're out of danger, you get back to work." He reached out and took her hand, which felt cold and tiny on top of the too-warm blanket. "Deal?"

"No."

He almost laughed at the stubborn tilt of her chin, the petulant look in her eyes. But this wasn't a joking matter. "No?" he repeated, in his best "bad cop" voice.

Staring at her now, looking so vulnerable in that hospital bed, made all his protective instincts fire to life. She might have belonged in forensics, but she could have gotten a job doing that anywhere. He'd been the one who'd lured her back to this department after she'd helped with his brother's case. So everything that was happening to her now was on him.

The idea that he'd had any part, no matter how small, in putting her back in danger left a sour taste in his mouth. He'd always been drawn to Shaye, from that first day she'd shown up at the station, looking nervous behind her determined posture.

She'd slammed into him, all lean muscle and surprisingly soft curves, and then her cheeks had gone such a deep red, he'd been immediately charmed. He'd sought out excuses to see her every day. But he'd never been able to bring himself to ask her out. She was shy and sweet and smart. She came from a close-knit family and he knew when she looked into her future, she saw someone solid and stable to share it with, someone with a normal job. She deserved far better than he'd ever be able to give her.

But when it came to this—when it came to her safety—he knew he was the best man for the job.

He could tell she was scared. It was there, behind the determination in her eyes, in the slight tremor in her hand. But she shook her head.

"I let a shooting scare me off once. I work in law enforcement. Maybe I'm just a lab rat and not a cop, but I'm not letting it force me out again."

"There's no shame in going into hiding for a short time," he told her, but she was already shaking her head again. "You know they'll hold your job for you."

"It doesn't matter." A smile quivered on her lips, fleeting and self-deprecating. "If I leave now, I'll never come back. And I want to do this job. I want this life. I'm not giving up on it."

Cole stared at her, not really sure what she meant by *this life*. But he could see it in her gaze—she wasn't going to back down. Which meant he'd have to keep her safe. It would be way more challenging than if she'd agree to go off the grid, but the more he thought about it, there were upsides, too.

With no evidence this was a targeted hit, he'd be hard-pressed to convince the brass to use resources to protect her. He knew he could talk them into it for a short time, but it wouldn't be easy. And if she went to a safe house, they'd assign a couple of patrol officers to watch her. If she kept working, he'd be on the case. He'd make sure of it. And that meant he'd also be personally in charge of her safety.

"Okay," he said, not pulling his hand away from hers even as her cheeks started to flush from the extended contact. "Have it your way. But you'd better get used to having me around, then, because I'm not letting you out of my sight until we catch this guy."

Chapter Three

He wasn't letting her out of his sight?

All sorts of inappropriate thoughts ran through Shaye's mind until she was sure Cole could see exactly what she was thinking, especially when his pupils dilated, staring back at her.

She dropped her gaze to her lap, her heart thudding way too hard after the day she'd had, and pulled her hand free from his. She'd had a massive crush on Cole from the moment she'd met him. But if she hadn't already known it, last year's shooting had quickly shown her that they'd never work. While she'd turned in her resignation the very next morning—over the phone because she was too afraid to return to the scene of the crime—he'd gone right back to work.

They would never be equals. He would always be the brave detective with the badge and the gun, and here she was again, the terrified forensics expert. It couldn't be more obvious, with her stuck in this hospital bed, in a hospital gown someone had changed her into—she hoped not in front of Cole—and him ready to dive right into solving the case.

But this time would be different, she vowed. Because she might be way too shy, way too awkward, way too boring for a man like Cole Walker, but she was tired of feeling like a coward. Two years ago she'd moved out to Maryland from Michigan, leaving behind her big, well-meaning family and the anonymity that came with being the middle child in a group of five. She'd dived into the unfamiliar, trying to break out of her comfort zone. She'd even bought a house, putting down roots right away, to force herself to stay if things got tough. And things had sure gotten tough.

She wasn't going to let herself be driven out of the job she loved and the place she'd come to consider home a second time.

She clenched her jaw and looked back up at Cole, praying her cheeks would cool. "What do we know so far about the forensics? What can I do?"

Her specialty was computers, but she had plenty of cross-training. There had to be some way she could help catch this guy. And once they caught him, maybe she could get back to the task of putting her life back on track.

Cole patted her hand. "Right now I just want you to focus on healing up."

"I'm fine." She knew he didn't mean to condescend to her, but if she wanted him to take her seriously as a professional—and not a victim he had to take care of— she needed to show him a reason. She shoved off the blanket and got to her feet, remembering too late she was hooked up to an IV.

The nurse ran in as her monitor went off, and Shaye clapped her hand over the crook of her elbow where she'd pulled out the line.

Cole stood, tried to steady her as she wobbled a little on her feet. "What are you doing?"

"Going home."

"You need to be under observation," the nurse stated, scowling as she slapped a piece of cotton over the blood on Shaye's arm and taped it down.

"I'm fine," Shaye said. "The wound on my leg is closed, right? My heart rate and blood pressure have been pretty normal the whole time I've been in here." She'd been peeking over at her monitor periodically as she and Cole talked. "You said you were going to release me today. I'm ready to go."

The nurse frowned at her, but it was nothing compared with Cole's expression, a mixture of worry, frustration and anger.

Shaye stood her ground. "Have the doctor look at me if you need to, but I feel okay. I want to go home."

The nurse muttered something under her breath, then looked her over. "All right. But if you start feeling dizzy or your wound opens up, I want you to come back here—understood?"

Nodding, Shaye hoped she wasn't making a mistake. But she couldn't stay here any longer. She needed answers about who had shot at her—and why. And she wasn't going to get them on her back in a hospital bed.

She was tired of letting things happen to her. It was time to fight back.

"EVERYTHING HAS BEEN quiet all night," Marcos Costa told Cole as soon as he drove up next to the car.

Cole's youngest brother may not have shared his blood—they'd met at a foster home as kids—but they'd formed a bond that went deeper than genetics. After Shaye had spent several hours in the forensics lab, Cole had driven her home and then promptly called his two brothers to see who was available to watch her house until he got off work. Their middle brother, Andre, was on a mission for the FBI, but Marcos had been free.

Now it was 3:00 a.m., and everything looked quiet on Shaye's street. Her house was situated on a corner lot in a cute little neighborhood that boasted its fair share of picket fences and young families. The kind of place where a stranger skulking about would be noticed.

Still, it was Shaye. He wasn't leaving anything to chance. And his youngest brother worked for the DEA, so he had plenty of experience spotting suspicious characters.

"Thanks," Cole said through his window as his car idled next to Marcos's.

"No problem. We all love Shaye." Marcos glanced past Cole at his partner, Luke, in the passenger seat and nodded hello. "Is there a reason we're doing this on the street instead of in her house?"

"She doesn't know you're here."

"Yeah, I got that," Marcos said with a dimpled smile. "I'm wondering why exactly."

"She refused police protection." Luke Hayes, Cole's partner on the force for the past three years, spoke up. "Officially we can't force her."

Marcos frowned. "But if someone's gunning for her—"

Cole didn't have to turn his head to feel Luke's glance as he replied. "No one is gunning for her. The shooting that happened earlier this evening looks random."

"Ah." Marcos nodded knowingly. "Got it."

"It's a precaution," Cole said, not bothering to hide his annoyance at what Marcos and Luke were clearly thinking. That he was overreacting because it was

Shaye. That no matter how far out of his league she was, he was still going to be there whenever she needed him.

"Don't worry," Marcos said, starting his engine. "I don't mind. But right now I'm going to head home and get a little sleep." He started to shift into Drive, then paused and asked, "Shouldn't you get some of that yourself?"

"That's why Luke is here."

Marcos grinned again. "You're going to nap while he keeps watch?" He peered at Luke and joked, "All that Marine training means you don't actually need sleep?"

Cole's partner had been in the Marines before becoming a police officer.

"Ha-ha," Cole said. "We're going to take turns getting a little shut-eye."

"Good luck," Marcos said. "Call me if you need anything, okay?"

"You got it." As Marcos pulled away, Cole eased into the spot his brother had chosen at the corner of the street. It was a perfect vantage point since it gave him a good angle on the two sides of Shaye's house that abutted streets. The remaining sides of her house were bordered by neighbors' yards, and they would be trickier for someone to approach.

Cole shut off his truck. It was a typical November night, hovering near forty degrees, but Cole didn't want the running engine to draw any attention from the neighbors, in case anyone was a night owl. Besides, he and Luke were used to working in uncomfortable conditions. Both of them had been patrol officers before being bumped up to detectives.

They sat in silence for a few minutes, checking the area, and then Luke asked, "Have we officially released her car yet?"

Shaye's car was still at Roy's Grocery, where the parking lot had been roped off so he and Luke, along with a handful of cops working with them on the case, could pull evidence. They'd finished an hour ago, but Cole figured he'd tell Shaye in the morning.

"Technically, yeah. I thought I'd take her to pick it up tomorrow."

"Or just have it towed," Luke suggested. "She'll need that bullet hole repaired."

The gunman had fired three shots. One had hit the driver's door of Shaye's car, another had hit the back tire of the grocery store owner's car and the third had gone into Shaye. He'd asked the forensics lab to put a rush on reviewing the bullets, but they'd looked insulted he'd even asked. Shaye was one of them. They were already rushing it.

"We hear anything yet about those security cameras?" Cole asked. Although the camera at the grocery store wasn't real, there were others nearby they were checking. He'd probably have heard if there was news, because he'd made sure everyone working the case knew they should call him at any hour with updates. But he'd also spent several hours this evening at the hospital while Luke headed up the investigation. It was possible he'd missed something.

"Not yet," Luke replied, but he dutifully pulled out his phone and tapped in a text, then shook his head a minute later. "They haven't found the guy on any cameras yet."

Cole wasn't surprised. The grocery store wasn't in a highly commercial area, and it didn't get much criminal activity, either. There weren't as many security cameras as there would have been if the shooting had happened in another area of town. He wondered if that had been the shooter's intent.

"Shaye's got bad luck."

"What?" Cole shifted in his seat to face Luke, who always looked serious, with his buzz cut leftover from the military and his intense greenish-blue eyes.

"That's all this was. We went over her timeline. She was at work until eight, and then she drove straight to the grocery store, which she said she hadn't originally planned to do. If someone was after her specifically, that means they would have had to watch the forensics lab from at least five and then followed her. And in three hours, sitting outside a police station, don't you think someone would have spotted him?"

Cole nodded. He knew it was true. All the evidence said this had nothing to do with Shaye. Still, ever since he'd shown up at that shooting, his instincts had been buzzing the way they always did on a case when he knew something was off. And it was telling him there was more going on here.

"If it was random, meant to be a spree shooting, then why did he wait until the place was almost empty?"

Luke frowned. "Yeah, that bothers me, too. But he ran into the parking lot. Maybe he'd been coming from committing a crime and Shaye was in his way."

"We didn't have any reports that would match up," Cole reminded him.

"Not yet. Or maybe he planned to keep going—run though the grocery store lot, taking out anyone there, then move on to the rest of the businesses on the street. There are a couple of restaurants that were pretty full."

It was one of the reasons they didn't have any witnesses yet. It seemed counterintuitive—the shooter had run toward businesses full of people—but on a Friday night, it meant the music was loud, the patrons were drinking and no one heard a thing. Except for Roy still inside the grocery store, who'd sheltered in place and called the police.

"That's possible," Cole agreed, but he still couldn't shake the dread gripping him, saying Shaye had a direct connection. Because Luke was right about one thing: how unlucky could one woman be? Two attempts on her life in a year?

"Today is almost a year to the day of the shooting at the station," Cole said, even though he knew Luke didn't need the reminder. Luke had been there, too; he'd run out right behind Cole, firing back at the gang members, completely outgunned with their service pistols against semiautomatics.

"Yeah, and that's why I'm sitting in this car with you instead of in bed at home," Luke replied. "Because I think we got everyone in that gang. But they've all got families, too."

Cole nodded. It hadn't occurred to him that a gang member's family member might be trying to get revenge on Shaye for speaking up as a witness in the trial earlier in the year. His thoughts had always been on the families of the three officers who'd died that day. But his and Luke's bullets had killed two gang members at the scene, and four more had died in subsequent raids, because they'd pulled weapons instead of throwing up their hands when police came to arrest them. Any one of those men—or the ones who'd landed in prison—could have family or friends desperate for revenge.

"That theory has the same problem, though," Luke said. "If Shaye was a specific target, someone followed her to that grocery store. And if we're talking about someone affiliated with a gang, yes, they wouldn't be afraid to stake out a police station, but I doubt they'd be subtle enough to get away with it."

"True. And if we're looking at that kind of revenge, wouldn't someone want us to know it was them?" Cole added. "Or go after the station too? Both of us instead of just Shaye? I don't like the timing, and it seems way too coincidental that she's targeted by gunmen twice—"

"She wasn't targeted before," Luke cut him off. "They had no idea she was involved in the digital analysis that got us the lead we needed on the gang leadership in the first place. They were there because we'd been investigating. She just happened to be on our side of the parking lot."

A fresh wave of guilt washed over Cole. He knew why she'd been by the station doors, when she should have been on the other side near the forensics lab, out of the line of fire. Most days they'd ended around the same time and stood outside chatting for ten or twenty minutes before going their separate ways. That day, he'd been late, caught up in paperwork. And she'd almost paid with her life.

"Well, still," Cole said, hoping Luke didn't notice the new tension in his voice, "she's been shot at twice in just over a year. I don't like it."

"Me, either," Luke said, then swore.

"What?"

"Here she comes."

"What?" Cole said, spinning back toward the direction of Shaye's house.

His partner was right. Shaye was storming their way, her injured leg dragging a little behind, her hands crossed over her chest and a furious look on her face. None of that stopped him from noticing she was heading toward them in a nightgown that was way too short and way too thin for this kind of weather.

His mouth dried up as he got out of his truck, rushing over to her side and slipping his arm behind her shoulders in case she was still off balance from her injury. Behind him he heard Luke step out of the vehicle a little more slowly.

Shaye shrugged his arm off. "What are you doing?"

"Keeping an eye on things," Cole said. "Just until we catch the shooter."

She scowled but didn't look at all intimidating in her nightgown. It was just cotton, basically a big T-shirt, but on Shaye it somehow looked sexy. Especially with her hair spilling around her shoulders, loose and rumpled.

"I told the chief I didn't need protection." Her words lost some of their anger as he continued to stare at her, trying to keep his gaze on her face. As if she suddenly realized what she was wearing, she tugged the hem of her nightgown farther down her legs, her gaze darting to Luke and back again.

Then she spun around. Just when he thought she was going to demand he leave and call the chief about his unauthorized stakeout, she called over her shoulder, "This is unnecessary. But if you're going to insist on being here, you shouldn't sleep in the truck. Come on. You can stay with me."

A million images rushed through his brain, most of them involving that nightgown on the floor, and Cole knew he should refuse and climb back into the truck with his partner. Instead he followed Shaye inside.

Chapter Four

Shaye tried not to feel self-conscious as she strode quickly back to her house, but she'd never been more aware of the swing of her hips as she walked, of her long, awkward limbs. She pulled at the hem of her nightgown, willing her cheeks to cool as she held the door open for Cole without turning around.

Mixed in with her embarrassment was annoyance. The chief had offered her protection, even though she could tell he thought it was unnecessary. She'd had only a moment's hesitation before she refused. And yet here Cole was anyway, deciding what was best for her.

She tried to shove back her frustration. Cole was just doing what he always did, what seemed to come naturally to him: protecting everyone around him, whether they needed it or not.

"I'll be right back," she said over her shoulder as she headed to her bedroom. Pushing the door shut behind her, she changed quickly into a pair of loose sweatpants and a T-shirt, cringing every time she moved her leg. The painkillers were starting to wear off.

She paused a minute in front of the mirror, combing her hands through her messy hair. There wasn't much she could do about the deep circles under her eyes, not without makeup, and she wasn't going to dress up for Cole. Not when he'd shown up uninvited, determined to look after her whether she wanted his help or not. And not when the sound of his car on the quiet street had woken her from an almost sleep.

When she returned to her living room, she found Luke settled on her couch, his legs stretched out in front of him and his hands tucked behind his head. Somehow he managed to look relaxed and totally alert at the same time. She nodded at him and continued looking around, until Luke pointed silently into her kitchen.

That was where she found Cole, checking the locks on her windows.

Shaye let out a heavy sigh. "I always leave those unlocked."

He spun toward her. "What?"

"The front door, too. I just let anyone in who asks."

He frowned, giving her the kind of stare she'd seen him use on hostile suspects. "That's not funny."

She planted her hands on her hips, subtly resting more of her weight on her left foot as her whole right leg started to throb. Apparently when the painkillers wore off, it wasn't a gradual thing. "I told the chief I was fine. *You* told me I had nothing to worry about, that this was an unlucky fluke. So why are you here? Were you lying to me?"

He leaned back slightly, and she could tell she'd caught him off guard. *Good.* She was tired of being scared all the time, tired of waiting for someone else to solve her problems. Tired of being in the dark about what was happening with cases that concerned her.

"No," he said slowly, looking her over as if he wondered what had happened to the nervous computer nerd he was used to.

She's gone, Shaye wanted to say, *and she's not coming back.* Except that wasn't the truth.

The truth was she *was* scared. But she needed to take charge of her life instead of letting things happen *to* her.

"Maybe you should sit down," Cole finally said.

Frustration built up in her chest, and she was humiliated to feel tears prick the backs of her eyes. But she'd been shot today, so maybe she had an excuse. Her hip felt like it was on fire.

"I'm fine," she lied. "And I really don't need a couple of babysitters."

"If I'm a babysitter, my rate is ten dollars an hour," Luke called from the other room.

A smile quirked her lips, and she tried to hide it as Cole rolled his eyes.

"I wasn't lying to you," Cole said, taking a step closer, his hand hovering near her elbow, as though he expected to need to catch her if she suddenly fell. "There's no reason to suspect this guy was specifically targeting you. Because if that were the case, how would he even know where you were at that exact time? It makes more sense that he'd come here, beat the pathetic lock on your front door and do it in the middle of the night when you were sleeping."

She must have gone pale, because he was quick to continue. "That's not what happened. You were at the wrong place at the wrong time—that's it."

"Then why are you here?"

"Because." His frown deepened, but instead of looking annoyed, he looked flustered.

She didn't think she'd ever seen him flustered. She

tilted her head, curious. "Why?" she insisted. "If this was a total fluke and no one was targeting me, then what were you doing sitting on my street in the dark, watching my house?"

They were keeping something from her. She stared up into his light blue eyes, trying to find answers there. "It's gang related, isn't it? You think this guy wants revenge for last year?"

"Probably not."

"Then what?" she snapped, leaning even more on her uninjured leg. She wanted to sit, but he already had a height advantage. Plus, he was properly dressed in dark jeans and a button-down while she was dressed like a slob. And she needed answers. Needed the truth about what danger she was really facing. "What is it?"

"I can't take the chance," he barked right back at her.

She swayed, and it had nothing to do with her injury. "It *is* connected to the shooting from last year?" She had an instant flashback to being in that parking lot, bullets flying over her head as she hugged the pavement. To the panic, the absolute certainty she was going to die, and all the things she hadn't accomplished yet in her life.

"It's not connected to anything. Everyone thinks I'm crazy. But it's you, so..."

Her lips parted and she tried to find words, but there were none. Because all of a sudden, she saw what was underneath the anger and worry and frustration in his gaze. He was attracted to her. And not just in a he'd-seen-her-in-her-nightgown kind of way, but genuine interest.

The realization slammed through her, shocking and empowering. The pain in her leg faded into the background as she took a small step forward, then leaned in.

For several long seconds, he stood immobile. Then something shifted in his eyes, and all she could see was desire.

Shaye's heart took off at a gallop as his hands came up slowly and feathered across her cheeks. His thumbs stroked her face, and then his fingers plunged into her hair and his mouth crashed down on hers.

I'm kissing Cole Walker. The stupefied thought blared in her head as he nipped at her lips with his mouth and tongue and teeth until a sigh broke free and her lips parted. Then his tongue was in her mouth, slick against hers, sending shivers up and down her entire body.

She leaned into him, and thankfully he dropped his hands from her hair to her waist, keeping her from falling. His big hands seemed to make a hot imprint through her T-shirt and for a second, she wished she'd worn something sexier. Then she couldn't think at all as he changed the angle of their kiss, and every nerve in her body came alive.

The scruff on his chin abraded her face, but it didn't stop her from pressing even harder, wanting more, wanting it now. Looping her hands around his neck, she pulled herself up on her tiptoes to eliminate any last space between them, and then yelped as pain shot down her leg.

Cole lifted his head, the fire that had been in his gaze doused with worry. "Did I hurt you?"

"No."

He held her at arm's length, still breathing hard. "I shouldn't have done that. I'm sorry."

Why not? she wanted to ask, but before she could

get the words out, he'd reached past her and dragged a chair forward, pushing her into it.

"Did your wound open up?"

"No."

"Are you sure?" He reached for the band of her sweatpants, and she scooted sideways.

"Yes, I'm sure. I'm fine. Why—"

He stood up, backing away from her. "We came here to make sure you were safe. That was...that wasn't part of the plan."

Heat raced up her cheeks, this time from embarrassment. He kissed her like *that* and then told her it wasn't part of some plan? If it weren't for his use of the word *we*, reminding her that Luke was in the other room and had surely heard exactly what they were doing, she would have kissed him again.

Instead she nodded silently and got to her feet, holding up her hand when he tried to help her.

"We're friends," he said quietly. "I don't want to mess that up."

Shaye gave him a halfhearted smile, hoping the fact that she wanted to cry didn't show on her face. Because she could tell he was lying.

"Shaye—"

"Good night, Cole."

HE WAS AN IDIOT.

It was something Luke had been all too quick to tell him when he'd joined his partner in the living room after Shaye had headed to bed. As if he didn't already know.

He'd had Shaye Mallory in his arms, and he'd pushed her away. That was about as stupid as a person could get.

Except while everything about that kiss had felt

right, he'd known it was all wrong, for a laundry list of reasons. He was here to protect her. She was injured. They were friends. But most of all, she wasn't the kind of woman you messed around with.

And there could never be anything long-term between them because they came from different worlds. She was smart and educated, with the kind of earning potential he'd never have. She might have picked law enforcement for now, but Cole knew that if they weren't already, private-sector companies would be seeking her out soon, with huge salaries and perks. And she deserved that sort of life, one far from the bullets and crooks he dealt with on a daily basis. She deserved a man who was just as smart and educated as she was, someone who could give her things Cole never could. And he wouldn't pretend otherwise.

He cared about her too much to lead her on.

But was that exactly what he'd been doing for the past year? He'd known she had a crush on him when they met, and instead of staying away, he'd sought her out. He'd hover by the door each day before work, waiting for her arrive to start his day off right by chatting with her. He'd let her wait for him each day after work, let her beautiful smile and soft voice soothe away some of the crap of his shift.

He needed to take a step back, try to treat her like any other civilian who might need police protection. But no matter how many times he told himself that, he couldn't get that kiss out of his head. Hours later he could still taste the mint of her toothpaste, still feel the imprint of her lips on his. For someone who was normally shy and reserved, she'd been a firecracker in his arms. And he wanted more.

Luke had claimed the couch after Shaye had disappeared, leaving Cole with the big recliner in the corner. He'd slept in far worse, but as the sun seeped through the curtains, he realized he hadn't slept at all.

"Get over it, or do something about it."

Luke's voice startled him, and Cole glanced over, seeing his partner had one eye open. Luke's ability to sense movement even with his eyes closed was an asset in stakeouts, and the way he seemed to read people's minds was great for interrogations. But right now it was pissing Cole off.

"What am I supposed to do?"

When Luke raised an eyebrow, Cole snapped, "Don't be crude. This is Shaye we're talking about. I can't…"

"What?" Luke prompted. "Sleep with her? Date her? Tell her you've been obsessed with her since the day she walked through those station doors? Why not?"

Cole shot a glance down the hallway that led to Shaye's bedroom. Her door was closed, and he hoped she was still out cold. "We're friends. Let it go."

Luke shrugged. "I will if you will."

Grumbling under his breath, Cole gave up on sleep and trudged into Shaye's cheery red-and-blue kitchen. He dug around until he found the coffee, then started up a large pot. Before he'd made it back into the living room with his first cup, he heard Shaye come into the room and prayed she hadn't overheard his conversation.

But one look at her face, her chin up high, her cheeks tinged with red, her gaze daring him to bring up any of it, and he knew she had. A thousand curse words lodged in his throat, and he held them in, instead handing her the cup of coffee as a peace offering.

She cradled it between her palms and drank half the

cup before she lowered it again, but he wasn't surprised. He'd heard her tossing and turning last night, probably the result of the painkillers not keeping up with the sting of her bullet wound. Or maybe the events of the night playing over and over again, all the possible outcomes racing through her mind the way they had in his. They were lucky she was alive.

"I'm going to get myself a cup of coffee—"

"And me," Luke interrupted, popping to his feet as though he'd slept ten hours.

"And then we're going to go through yesterday's timeline, make sure we're covering all of our bases," Cole finished.

Shaye nodded, but her hands shook around the coffee cup. "If this is going to turn into an interrogation, I need some breakfast first." She started to limp toward the kitchen, and Cole put a hand on her arm to stop her. She pulled it away fast, like his touch burned her.

Trying to pretend he hadn't noticed, Cole said, "I'll make breakfast. Just relax a little."

"There's nothing to make," she replied, pushing past him. "It's cereal and coffee. All my groceries are in Roy's parking lot. Unless you want frozen burritos for breakfast, that's what I've got."

He followed her into the kitchen more slowly, while Luke disappeared in the other direction, toward the bathroom.

She slowly set a few boxes of cereal on the counter, keeping her back turned to him, like she was waiting until her embarrassment fled. But when she finally turned, her cheeks were still flushed.

Shaye had never been good at hiding her emotions. After dealing with criminals day in and day out, he found it one of her most charming attributes, but he knew she hated it.

"About last night—"

"Don't." Her cheeks went from rose pink to fire-engine red.

"Shaye—"

"Just let it go."

Luke rejoined them at that moment, so Cole did. Instead of apologizing yet again—which probably wouldn't get him anywhere—he focused on her safety, and not the fact that he might have ruined their friendship. A ball of dread settled in his stomach, but he kept his mind on what he could do something about: eliminating the nagging feeling that this had been a hit.

"Let's go through your day yesterday, from the moment you woke up." Cole set down his spoon in cereal he'd barely touched. "Did you drive straight to work?"

"Yes."

"Your car was in the garage overnight, right? Did you step outside to get a paper, anything like that?"

"Yes, my car was in the garage, and, no, when I got in it to head to the lab it was the first time I'd left my house. And let me save you some time, because I've heard you talk to witnesses before. I didn't see anyone following me. Not yesterday, not in the past few weeks, not ever. And as far as I know, there's no one who has a reason to come after me, not with the Jannis Crew shut down."

"What about at work?" Luke asked. "Anything unusual there?"

Shaye frowned. "Like what?"

"Like anything. Coworkers acting strange around you, someone who's shown an interest in you even though you've turned him down or made it clear you're not interested?"

Shaye shook her head slowly. "No. There's been a little turnover since I left a year ago, but most of my colleagues are the same. And the ones who are new all seem fine. It's business as usual at the lab."

Cole stared at her, wondering what that meant. He'd visited her in the lab a few times, and his presence had always surprised her. Not just because it was him and he didn't tend to come over to the lab, but because she'd been so focused on whatever digital device she'd been analyzing that she hadn't even noticed he was there until he'd told her.

Was she that oblivious all the time? Would she even realize if someone had been stalking her, waiting for the right moment to get her alone?

He wished he knew. But the truth was even though they talked in the course of their jobs, and they had an unofficial agreement to meet up before and after work each day, he'd rarely seen her outside investigations. Even last month, when he'd asked for her help, it had been an off-the-books case. The realization momentarily surprised him, because she'd become such an important part of his life. And yet she was almost totally separate from it.

He wasn't sure if that said something about the strength of their friendship or just about his willingness to let people get close to him. Except he had plenty of friends, and to this day, he still tried to help kids coming out of the foster system because he knew how hard that transition was. So why? He wasn't sure, but he had a feeling if he probed that too deeply, he wouldn't like the answer.

"What about your job?" Cole asked when he realized the silence had dragged on a little too long. "What devices do you have right now?"

"I'm looking at computers from that corporate espionage case. And the girl who's being stalked, to see if her computer was hacked. I've only been back for a week." She shrugged. "That's all I've got right now."

Neither were likely connections to today's shootings, but he gave Luke a meaningful look, and his partner nodded. They'd check both out. The corporate espionage involved two local competing businesses, and both sides had been repeatedly fined for violating various laws, but he doubted they'd resort to violence. And the stalker was young; that kind of behavior always made him look twice, because it was often a gateway crime, but usually the ultimate target was the person being stalked, not someone connected to the investigation. Still, he planned to check every possibility.

"How about cases from last year?" Cole asked. "Anything you dealt with that's still in the courts?"

"Yeah, probably. I know there are a few that haven't gone to trial yet, but they're cases I worked peripherally. Nothing where I'm a witness. At least not yet. I guess I could still get subpoenaed."

Luke shook his head. "Probably not those. But let's make a list of all these cases—especially where you took the stand or your name would appear in the court documents—where someone went to jail."

Shaye glanced from him back to Cole. "Isn't this a waste of time? Shouldn't you be focused on witness statements or trying to track down this guy some other way?"

"We will," Cole assured her. "But no reason not to attack it from both directions."

She scooted her half-eaten bowl of cereal away from her and leaned on the counter. "But I'm not a direction at all, right? I'm just unlucky enough to have been shot at twice?"

Her words hung in the air. Cole wanted to nod, like he'd done last night, and tell her this had nothing to do with her. But the more he thought about it, the more he worried that Shaye was at the center of something dangerous. And he had no idea what it was.

Chapter Five

"Let's go." Shaye unlocked the door to the lab and held the door for Cole and Luke, trying to calm her nerves. There had been hardly any cars outside the lab, but they didn't work weekends unless a big case required a rush analysis. But across the parking lot, cops' vehicles were lined up in what should have been a reminder of her safety.

She'd come so close this past week to feeling normal again. But maybe it wasn't ever going to happen now. Maybe her parents and her four brothers and sisters were right. She wasn't cut out for a job where bullets were involved.

Luke was gazing around curiously, but Cole stared back at her, like he could read her mind, and she ducked her head. If she wasn't cut out for a lab job, she definitely wasn't cut out for dating a detective. Not that a detective had asked her out. Just given her the best kiss of her life.

Pulling the door until it clicked shut behind her, she led the way through the sterile hallways. Past locked doors with the labels Biology/DNA, Firearms/Toolmarks, Latent Prints and Toxicology. Down to the end, where a shiny new label marked "Digital Forensics," the most recent addition to the Jannis County Forensics Laboratory. Her territory.

Before she'd started—and last year when she'd taken the other job—digital devices had been sent off to the state lab. But it was one of the fastest-growing areas of forensics in Jannis, and Shaye was still surprised the job had been open a year later for her.

She used her key card to get into the room as Luke remarked, "Good security."

"Yeah, well, we take chain of command pretty seriously. And that includes making sure no one can access anything they shouldn't while it's in our possession. Everything gets logged. Even what I'm going to pull up for you will have a digital log that I accessed it, at what time and for how long." She'd helped set up some of those extra precautions last year as one of her first assignments on the job.

She glanced around her tiny space, jammed full of equipment—mostly computers. Her office was in the back with no windows, which often made her feel penned in, but today she appreciated it. And she was happy to have something to do besides sit around her house while Cole and Luke drove her crazy. They'd installed new locks on all her doors, exercised in her living room and called the station repeatedly for updates, and to assign leads. And that had all been before 10:00 a.m. So when they'd wanted to go through suspects, she'd suggested they come here.

"Let's get started," Cole said, dragging her empty whiteboard to the center of the room.

He was wearing the same jeans and button-down from yesterday, just a little more rumpled. The short beard he always had was a tiny bit longer, too, and she fixated on it, remembering it scraping against her chin. She could almost feel his arms going around her again, the breadth of his chest pressed against her, big enough to make her feel surrounded by him. She shook off the memories, hoping her thoughts weren't broadcast across her face. But Cole was focused, his detective face on.

He jotted the words *Possible Suspects*, *Unlikely* and *Ruled Out*, then carefully underlined each one. "Any case you testified in or were involved in, now or last year. Pull them up, and let's get to work."

He sounded determined, almost enthusiastic, and she supposed that was the kind of attitude you needed to be a detective, to slog through hours and hours of clues until you found the right answer.

She understood it because she could do the same with a digital device, dig and dig until it revealed all of its secrets. But hers was a totally different kind of quest, one fueled by years of shyness and feeling over-looked in her big, noisy family. Being the middle child in a family of seven meant you either had to demand attention or be content without it.

She loved her family. She *missed* her family, living so far away, when the rest of them had stayed in Michigan. But she'd needed to break out, make something of herself as *Shaye*, not just one of the Mallory siblings.

She settled into her well-worn chair. Time to see if the skill that had moved her past her sheltered, invisible life was threatening to destroy it, too.

"Let's start with the most obvious first," Luke suggested, snagging the only other chair in the room while Cole stood in the center of the small space, marker raised and ready.

"The Jannis Crew." Just saying the name made her

feel a little ill. Shaye nodded and opened a file. Because she'd been in the line of fire, her boss had sent the digital devices they'd recovered after the shooting—computers, phones and tablets—to the state lab, so there'd be no conflict of interest. But she'd been on the stand, because she'd found the original trail to the leadership. And she was the only living witness able to identify the shooter.

The three officers who might have seen him had died on the scene. Cole and Luke had run out the station doors as the car was driving past. Forensics later discovered that their bullets had killed the two men in the backseat, but not the shooter. So Shaye had gotten on the stand, ignored her thundering heart and pointed directly at him, sending him to prison for the rest of his life.

"Well, we know it's not Ed Bukowski," Cole said, writing his name under "Ruled Out." "He was killed in prison last week."

Shaye jerked, spinning her chair to face him as an instant picture of the driver, one tattoo-covered hand draped over the wheel and the other aiming a gold-plated pistol out the window, formed in her head. "He was?"

"Crazy Ed found someone who wasn't impressed with his crazy," Luke said, using his gang name. "But put relatives on the *Suspect* list. The timing could fit. Maybe someone wants revenge for Ed's death. They can't go after the drug lord who shanked him, so they're going after the woman who fingered him, put him behind bars in the first place."

A violent shudder passed through her, and Shaye

knew they'd both seen it. She spun to face her computer, sensing Luke and Cole sharing a look behind her back.

"Maybe we should do this part at the station," Cole said. "You provide us with the list, and we'll go through it."

"No. I want to help."

"There's no reason for you to relive—"

"I *said* I want to help." Shaye turned back, staring hard at Cole. "You don't need to protect me from this."

"That's my job, Shaye."

His job. Of course it was. It wasn't personal to him. But it was personal to her. "It's my job, too. So let's do this." She didn't give him more time to argue, just looked at her screen again and read off the next case.

Three hours later, the whiteboard was full. Most of the names were listed under "Unlikely" or "Ruled Out," but they had a handful of possible suspects that Cole and Luke were going to check out.

She stared at the list of names under "Possible Suspects," and the knot that had taken up residence in her rib cage eased for the first time since she'd walked out to Roy's parking lot. The only name that worried her was Crazy Ed, the man who'd been at the center of her nightmares over the past year. He may have been dead, but someone like that was bound to have attracted likeminded friends. Were there any left?

More important, were there any left who were willing to risk their own freedom for revenge? Because they couldn't have missed the massive cleanup Cole and his team had done after the station shooting. They'd have to expect any attempt to go after someone connected to that case would result in the same intense scrutiny.

Shaye let out a breath. "I don't think this had any-thing to do with me."

Cole and Luke looked from the board to her and back again, and then Luke was nodding. "I agree. We're just being thorough."

When Cole was silent too long, Shaye asked, "Cole? What do you think?"

"Chances were always slim that this was a targeted attack," he replied, but there was an edge to his voice that told her he was holding something back.

"But…" she prompted.

"But nothing. Luke's right."

She frowned, but before she could argue, the door to her lab burst open, smacking the wall and almost hit-ting Luke on the way.

He scowled at the petite woman with the pixie cut and wrinkled pantsuit who stood on the other side, and she fidgeted. "Sorry. Shaye, I'm glad you're here."

"What's up?" Shaye asked, hoping no one had no-ticed the way she'd jumped in her seat at the unex-pected noise.

The woman in the doorway, Jenna Dresden, was one of the lab's best firearms experts, and one of Shaye's closest friends here. Or at least she had been, until Shaye had left last year. Since she'd returned, things had been a little strained. Maybe because Shaye hadn't stayed in touch over the past year.

"I looked at the bullets we recovered at the scene yesterday."

Cole and Luke gave Jenna their full attention. "What did you find?" Cole asked.

"Well, I can tell you the bullet was a nine millimeter.

And I can tell you that it doesn't match up to anything shot from another gun we have on file."

Cole didn't have to say a word for Shaye to know exactly what that meant. Someone connected to Crazy Ed being involved just sank down to unlikely. Working other cases had taught her that gang members sold one another weapons, so they often ended up with guns that had been used in previous crimes.

"The gun's a virgin," Luke said. "So we won't know anything until we match the bullet to the gun it came from."

At that point, Jenna could compare the striations from the bullets they'd retrieved from the scene with those in the weapon's chamber and see if they lined up. If they did, they had their weapon. And whoever it belonged to was probably their shooter.

"Afraid not," Jenna agreed. "I wish I had better news. And now I'm going home, because I've been here since last night."

"Thanks," Shaye called as the brunette headed back the way she'd come. She looked questioningly at Cole.

"Back to square one."

"So, SOMEONE CONNECTED to Crazy Ed is out," Luke said.

Cole frowned. "I guess so."

After Jenna had given them the news about the bullet, that was practically a foregone conclusion anyway, but Cole wasn't leaving anything to chance. So he'd bribed a couple of his fellow officers coming off duty with a pair of basketball tickets to go home with Shaye and watch her until he and Cole were finished.

After hours in the stifling heat of the station—the air conditioner was on the fritz—they'd tracked down anyone even remotely connected to Crazy Ed, which wasn't a lot. It made Cole sad for the little boy Crazy Ed had once been: parents both killed in a drive-by when he was ten. He'd gone to live with an aunt, who'd overdosed a few years later, and then he'd ended up in the system.

Unlike Cole, who'd managed to form a brotherly bond with Andre and Marcos inside what felt like his fifteenth foster home in eight years, Crazy Ed had found gangs. The rest of his gang was now dead or in prison, and if he had any family left, Luke and Cole couldn't find it. So no one left to avenge his death.

"He shot up a police station," Luke reminded him, clearly able to read the direction of Cole's thoughts. "He chose his path. Nothing we can do about it now."

"Yeah." Cole shook off his thoughts about whether Crazy Ed had ever really had a chance before he started dwelling on all the other kids he'd seen in homes over the years, kids he hadn't kept track of. Kids he hadn't taken on two jobs to provide them with a real home and ease their transition out of the system, like he had for Andre and Marcos. Because it sure hadn't been easy for him, suddenly totally on his own, not even a roof over his head when he hit eighteen.

The truth was, Marcos and Andre had saved *him*. By then they'd been his brothers, and Cole hadn't been about to lose the only family he'd ever had. So, he'd walked out the door of that final foster home on the day he'd turned eighteen, determined to do whatever it took to build a home for the three of them. It had kept him out of gangs, out of any kind of criminal enterprises. It had led him straight to the police force, somewhere he could make a difference.

"Shaye's current cases are also out," Luke said, crossing off those names on the whiteboard they'd brought from Shaye's lab and bringing Cole's attention back where it needed to be. "The business owners both have alibis. And so does stalker boy."

"And I haven't been able to find anyone else connected to the Jannis Crew with the means or opportunity to pull something like this off," Cole said. Every name on the "Possible Suspects" list had a line through it, so he stared at the few names left on the "Unlikely" list. "What about Ken Tobek?"

"Ah, the engineer. Well, he did his bit and got out. He's alibied, too—he was drinking beer with a friend from work around the time of the shooting. The guy says Tobek was at his house until past midnight. And that jerk got lucky anyway. I'd hope he learned his lesson."

He and Luke had taken the call a year ago from Tobek's wife, Becca, who'd claimed her husband was plotting to kill her. She'd had some suspicious bruises and they'd found a judge with a particular hatred for domestic abuse and gotten lucky with a warrant. They'd been about to give up on finding anything when Tobek's computer had gone to Shaye for one last try. She'd dug up searches on murder and body disposal he thought he'd deleted. When they'd gone to execute another warrant, they'd found him in the process of trying to kill Becca.

In court, he'd been cleared of attempted murder and found guilty of only assault. Tobek had spent thirty days in jail and as far as Cole knew, he'd kept far away from his now ex-wife ever since.

Cole crossed him off and moved to the final name on the Possible list. "Derek Winters?" He'd been paroled for good behavior just last week, and his original prison sentence had been reduced for time already served by the time the case had finally made it through trial. Initially they'd thought he was going to go free, but Shaye had pulled apart the GPS in his car and proved his location during the kidnapping of a young girl for ransom.

Cole and Luke had been on the team to bring that girl home three years ago, and when he'd handed her back to her parents, he'd promised them they'd find the person who'd taken her. It had taken eight long months, but they'd finally arrested him, only to have some of the evidence deemed inadmissible before they even hit trial. Then Shaye had started at the lab, their first local digital expert, and the computer had been handed off to her for one last-ditch effort. Shaye's find had been exactly what they'd needed. It was actually less damning than what they'd originally had on him that they couldn't take to court because of a technicality, but it had put him away.

Cole would love to see him go back. "He's the right size and he's definitely bold enough to try something like this."

Luke shook his head. "Shaye said the shooter was white. Winters is light-skinned, but you think she'd mistake him for white in the dark? I don't know."

"Shaye wasn't the one who described the shooter," Cole said. "That was me. But I saw a blur of movement—a hoodie and jeans. Definitely a guy, but skin color? I basically saw his neck. My impression was white, but I could be wrong. Let's just check him out."

"Okay," Luke said, lifting his phone.

"What are you doing?"

"Starting with his parole officer."

Ten minutes later, Luke was shaking his head again. "His parole officer actually *saw* him that night."

"That late?"

"Apparently, Winters is paranoid. Calls and asks for meetings all the time, wants to talk about the FBI agents following him."

Cole's eyebrows lifted. "Is the FBI looking at him for something?"

"Nope. Guy's jumping at shadows. His parole officer is ready to pass him off to someone else. But he's alibied." Luke stood and took the marker from Cole, crossing the final name off their list.

"I was so sure this was about Shaye…" Cole muttered.

"You ready to tackle this the right way?" Luke asked.

Cole scowled at his partner, and anxiety took up residence in his chest at the idea that he was screwing up the case.

"Look, we're doing this investigation a disservice by assuming Shaye was the target," Luke insisted, looking convincing with his ramrod posture drilled into him by the military and the intensity on his face. "We're letting valuable time pass when we need to be approaching this like any other case, without presumptions. Start with what we know for sure and look at all the possible avenues."

Cole knew guilt was going to keep him up tonight as he nodded. His partner was right. He'd been so blinded by fear for Shaye that he'd let it impact the case, something he'd never done in all his years as a police officer. It was time to start thinking like the professional detective he was.

"Jeez," Luke said. "Nobody died. Wipe that despair

off your face. She's one of us. We had to be sure. But let's start over and find this guy. Make him pay, whether Shaye was his intended target or just the result, okay?"

"I'm on board with that," Cole agreed just as his cell phone rang.

He would have ignored it, except it was one of the officers watching Shaye. Putting the call on speaker, he asked, "Hiroshi, what's up?"

"We're coming back in." The intensity of Hiroshi's tone made even Luke freeze.

Cole grabbed his weapon instinctively. "Why? What's happening?"

"We've got a tail. Rusted-out old Taurus, used to be blue, a real junker. He picked us up after we stopped at the store to get Shaye some groceries, and he's been with us ever since. We quit heading for her house and turned around, but I don't know how long until he realizes he's been made."

"Any way you can flank him and get a plate?" Luke asked.

There was a pause; then Hiroshi replied tightly, "I'm in Maryland traffic. This isn't a military op, man." He read off his location and direction. "See if you can go the other way and get behind him. Meantime, in case this is a shooter, I'm not taking chances. We're coming in."

"We're on our way," Cole said, putting himself on Mute but keeping Hiroshi on the line as he looked at Luke.

His partner grabbed his keys and swore like the Marine he'd once been as they raced for the front of the station. "I was wrong."

Cole glanced at him, eyebrow raised.

Someone *is* after Shaye."

Chapter Six

"Stay down," the officer in the front passenger seat—
Hiroshi something—told her.

Shaye crouched even lower in the backseat of the
police vehicle, behind the cage like a criminal. Panic
danced in her chest as the car slowed to a near stop. The
doors didn't open from the inside. She was trapped in
this tiny space, just her and the groceries she'd grabbed
from Roy's, determined to return there to prove to herself she could do it.

What had she been thinking? Had he been staking
the place out, waiting for her?

A sob caught in her throat, and she swallowed it
down. Who wanted her dead? And why?

The car started moving again, and then Hiroshi's
partner, Wes, swore, speaking into his partner's cell
phone. "He realized we made him. He just turned off,
hopped the curb and headed for the freeway."

"He must have figured out where we were leading
him," Hiroshi said softly.

Shaye was relieved. She knew she should have hoped
he kept following, gave the police a chance to pull him
over or even just find a way to get a license plate num-

ber. But she also knew that bullets weren't going to be flying again, and right now that was what mattered.

"What's the plan?" Wes asked.

"Bring her in," Cole's voice came over the speaker, calming Shaye's nerves. "I'm going to talk to the chief, see if we can get a helicopter up, try to spot the car from the air."

"Unlikely," Wes replied. "From that freeway, he can get onto—"

"Yeah, I know," Cole cut him off. "Just bring Shaye in."

"On our way," Wes replied tightly and hung up.

He started to say something else, but Hiroshi interrupted him. "Relax. You know what this is about."

What's it about? Shaye wanted to ask, but she was suddenly too exhausted to follow the conversation. Instead she asked, "Can I get up now?"

"Stay down," Hiroshi replied, shooting her an apologetic smile. "Just in case."

So she did, feeling foolish instead of terrified now as she kept her face pressed close to the vinyl seats, easy for wiping down after suspects left blood or puke or whatever else in here. She could practically smell the forensic material all over the backseat now that she wasn't busy bracing herself for the sound of gunshots.

Hiroshi and Wes were sitting straight, only the metal of the cage protecting them, even as they'd taken precautions for her safety. Hiroshi had recently married, and she'd seen the pictures Wes kept tucked inside his hat, two curly-headed boys that looked just like him.

Here they were, putting themselves on the line for her, and she couldn't even give them something to go on. Except for the cases she'd worked that Cole and

Luke were running down now, she didn't really have enemies. Did she?

Who hated her enough to try to kill her twice in two days?

Sooner than she'd expected, the door was wrenched open and Cole was reaching inside, unhooking her belt and helping her out. Her feet were embarrassingly unsteady as he and Luke rushed her into the station.

"My groceries are still—"

"We'll get them," Luke cut her off.

"Thank you," she called behind her to Hiroshi and Wes as Cole and Luke continued to help her past the secure doorway and into the inner sanctum of the station, until she was in the center of the bullpen. She found herself settled in a surprisingly comfortable chair at Cole's desk, and then the two of them were off again, warning her to stay put.

The bullpen was quieter than she would have expected, even on a weekend. A pair of officers stood at the other end of the room, drinking coffee and talking quietly, but the rest of the room was empty. She'd been in the station before, but she suddenly realized she'd never been back here, where Cole worked every day.

Curious, she glanced around, taking in the bulletin board on one wall, a watercooler beside it. The door to a tiny break room was next to that, and the bullpen itself was filled with desks, broken up into little groupings. It actually looked like a lot of offices, until you got down to the little details. The Wanted posters on the bulletin board and the case timeline on another wall. The handcuffs tossed over a stack of case files on one desk, the gruesome crime scene photos tacked up on a half-built cubicle wall, the labels by type of crime on the huge file cabinet behind Cole's desk.

Cole's space was organized, which was no surprise. *He* was organized, always on top of everything. It was all job focused, a computer on one side and a notepad in the center, all his case files locked up like they should be. On the other end of his desk was a photo, and Shaye couldn't help herself. She picked it up.

It was obviously him and his brothers as kids. Cole had the same reddish-blond hair, the same intense gaze. On either side of him, she recognized Andre's darker skin and the cleft in his chin, and Marcos's almost-black hair and dimples. Cole must have been about fifteen, which would have made Andre fourteen and Marcos twelve. Now, nineteen years later, the men were all in law enforcement, and they looked it, with muscles earned taking down suspects in the police force, the FBI and the DEA. Back then they'd been scrawny, three lonely boys who'd found a family together.

She didn't know a lot about Cole's history, except that he'd met Andre and Marcos when he'd moved into one of his many foster homes. They'd bonded instantly, and in the few times she'd met his brothers, she knew it was a bond that would never break.

She thought of her own family back in Michigan. They could be too rambunctious, and they could overlook her because she hid in the background, but they loved her. It didn't matter how far she traveled. If she asked, any of them would be by her side in an instant. It was something she'd taken for granted, part of her close-knit Midwestern heritage that had always been assumed.

What had it been like for Cole, alone at two years

old, tossed from one family to the next until he made his own?

She didn't know how long she sat there, imagining Cole as a baby, then as a little boy, never knowing that sense of security and love she never really thought twice about. But suddenly Cole and Luke were back. Cole looked questioningly at her hands, making her realize she was still holding the picture.

"Sorry." She set it back on the desk.

"That's fine. It's me and Marcos and Andre."

She nodded. "I know. From when you met?"

"No, right before they sent us all to different foster homes."

She jerked in her seat, surprised. She'd thought they'd stayed together once they'd met—she never realized they'd been separated. There was so much she didn't know about him.

She'd been half in love with him for two years, and all of a sudden she wasn't sure she knew him at all.

He was staring at her quizzically, and she tried to wipe whatever emotions were showing off her face. "What did you find out? Do we have any idea who was in that car? Is it possible it was a fluke? Maybe he wasn't really following us?" she asked hopefully, even though she knew the answer before Cole spoke.

"No, Hiroshi said he saw the vehicle at the back of the grocery's parking lot. He thought it was empty, but the driver could have just been slouched below the windshield, waiting for you to come out."

"Why would he risk following me in a police car?"

"Best guess is he hoped they'd drop you off and leave," Luke replied.

"Which would suggest he doesn't know where you live," Cole added.

"So, what? Could this be random, like he picked me out at the grocery store, and that's the only place he knows to look for me?" The idea of being the focus of some psychopath was even more unsettling than someone coming after her because of a case.

"Those guys tend to stalk their victims first," Luke said. "It'd be a little weird if it was a wacko who just didn't know where you live. It's possible, but given the fact that he's managed to pick up your trail twice and get away from us, I doubt it."

"More likely someone followed you from the station, and that's the only place he knows to look for you besides work," Cole said, but he didn't sound totally convinced. "It makes sense if the reason he knows you is connected to your job."

"Okay, then it's probably about one of my cases, right? What did you discover about the suspects?" Shaye asked, trying to focus on the fact that she had the city's best detectives on the case and not that someone was tracking her again this soon after being run off by the police.

Luke shook his head. "Nothing promising."

"We need to start thinking about who else has a reason to hurt you. We'll start with connections you've made at the lab, outside of your cases," Cole added. "And until we figure it out, I don't care if this guy only seems to know about your lab and the store. You're not going home. You can stay with me."

"WHAT MADE YOU become a detective?"

"What?" Cole paused in fitting her groceries into his

surprisingly full refrigerator and stared back at her. "I don't know. I wanted to help people, I guess. Plus the pay was decent, and I didn't need an advanced degree to join the force."

Was it her imagination or did he look embarrassed when he talked about not having gone to college? She thought about telling him that he was one of the smartest people she knew, but she figured that would make him more uncomfortable. Instead she asked, "How long have you lived here?"

She glanced around the galley kitchen. It was small but clean, with dark-wood cabinets and pots and pans hanging overhead that clearly saw regular use. She tried to imagine Cole cooking, and she liked the picture she conjured up. Especially when she imagined herself in the kitchen helping him. She pushed the image away. It was too domestic. It didn't matter how much she'd been drawn to this man since the moment she'd met him— they had a work relationship. And she knew he'd never cross that boundary—at least not more than the kiss they'd shared in her kitchen.

"Couple of years," Cole said, not reading the direction of her thoughts for a change. "Thank goodness my brothers are smart. They both got scholarships, so that cut down on the debt. But it was tiny apartments for years."

Shaye took a minute to digest that. "You supported them? Like a parent?"

She hadn't had even a part-time job during college. She'd gotten a small scholarship, too, which had helped, because her parents had five kids to put through school. But they'd been adamant that she focus on school and not worry about working until she was finished. They'd even let her move back home after graduate school while she applied to jobs, until she was on her feet and had a little nest egg.

She'd had it so easy compared to Cole. At every turn, he'd chosen the more difficult route simply to help others. He was doing it still, with his job.

The more she learned about Cole, the more obvious it became how different they were, how far out of her league he was. But it didn't stop her from wanting to know even more.

He shut the fridge and picked up the overnight bag he'd carried in for her. "What's with the third degree? You looking to switch jobs, become a detective, too?"

"No." She leaned against the counter, blocking his way. "But you called us friends earlier, right?" Back when he'd said kissing her was a bad idea.

He nodded slowly, like he thought he was walking into some kind of trap, and she tried not to notice how good he smelled, standing this close to her. An intoxicating mix of spices and musk.

He'd taken off his button-down when they'd walked in, and the T-shirt he wore underneath stretched tight against his chest, outlining muscles her hands itched to touch again. She clenched them at her sides. "So why don't I know this stuff about you already? I've never even been to your house."

"Neither have most of the guys at the station." He seemed to realize that was the wrong thing to say as soon as he blurted the words, because he backtracked. "It's not really set up for entertaining."

"Sure it is." She'd seen only the kitchen and the family room right off the entryway. It was cozy, the kind of place she could imagine tons of friends crammed in, eating Cole's barbecue and watching a game. It would probably be rowdy, sort of like a family gathering at her house. Cole might not have any blood relatives, but she wasn't the only one drawn to him. Everyone at the station respected him, treated him like a friend. She wondered why most of them had never been to his house.

He scooted past her, barely fitting between her and the counter, his body brushing hers in a way that had her replaying yesterday's kiss in her mind. From the flash of awareness in his eyes before he turned his head, so was he.

From the moment she'd met him, she'd put him up on a pedestal: her ideal, unattainable man. As a couple maybe they'd never make sense—she didn't know what kinds of women he dated, but she knew he wasn't shy. He went after what he wanted, and he'd never chased her. Not even close. But there was no question he was attracted to her.

She lived her life cautiously, always had. The biggest risk she'd ever taken was moving across the country for a job, but plenty of people did that without a second thought. Maybe for once she needed to stop thinking about all the consequences, stop worrying about the fact that there was no future for her with a man who ran into gunfire without hesitation. Maybe it was time to live for today.

Cole was heading into the family room, clearly expecting her to follow, probably planning to get back to work, tracking down anyone with a reason to hurt her.

The reminder strengthened her resolve. There was actually a gunman hunting for her. If he caught up to her, what would she regret not having done in her life?

Right now every answer she could think of involved Cole Walker.

She took a fortifying breath and followed him. It was time to stop having regrets.

Chapter Seven

Who was gunning for Shaye?

Luke wasn't wrong about serial criminals. Anyone savvy enough to have tracked Shaye twice in two days from a police station—if he'd spotted her in the regular course of her life—would have figured out where she lived by now. Except obviously this guy hadn't. Unless he was purposely trying to draw police attention. Cole frowned, liking that theory even less.

The police had stopped him. So far. Which meant he probably didn't know where she lived. Which told Cole that he'd first spotted Shaye at the lab. And if he and Luke were right, it wasn't connected to one of her cases. Maybe a colleague? But anyone employed at the county lab had extensive background checks. Had someone slipped through, someone with a vendetta against hard-working, easygoing Shaye?

He spun around, expecting to find Shaye seated on his couch, ready to brainstorm. "We need to find…" He trailed off as he discovered she wasn't anywhere near his couch.

She was inches away from him, so close she'd actually had to back up when he'd turned to face her. And she was staring up at him with determination.

How had she gotten that close without him realizing? All his senses kicked into overdrive as a crisp ocean-breeze scent he always associated with Shaye floated around him. He doubted she wore perfume, so he guessed it was her soap or maybe her laundry detergent, something that shouldn't have been a turn-on but on her was. He noticed the cluster of freckles across her nose and cheeks, so faint she could have hidden them with makeup, but she didn't. He realized what a gorgeous shade of brown her eyes were, like a bottle of expensive scotch. Then her pupils dilated until he could hardly see golden brown at all, and her arms slid slowly over his chest to hook around his neck.

His skin tingled through his T-shirt from the light touch, and it should have been a warning to back away. He'd just promised himself he was going to treat her like any other victim. But then hurt flashed in her eyes as he didn't take what she was offering, and he ignored all his good intentions and gave in to temptation.

She was only a few inches shorter than him, so he didn't have to lean far to claim her lips with his. The second they touched, she let out a sigh and tunneled her hands in his hair. She tasted like cinnamon.

And this was a mistake, because the taste of her was addictive, rapidly eliminating all sane thoughts from his head as his hands slid over her slim hips and up underneath the back of her T-shirt. Her skin was ridiculously soft, her waist insanely tiny. His fingers crept around to the front, playing over her rib cage as her grip on his head tightened and the pace of her kisses grew frantic.

He backed her against the wall, needing less space between them, and his whole body thrummed at the feel of her, but even that wasn't enough. His hands slid down, ready to grip her butt and lift her, let her wrap those amazing legs around him so he could take her to his bedroom. Then sanity hit. He yanked his hands away just before he hurt her injured leg and pulled back.

She stared up at him, her chest rising and falling too fast, her lips swollen and her eyes unfocused. She blinked, then took a step closer.

Cole held up a hand, trying to get control of his own breathing. If he didn't stop now, he was going to let her rock his world, and they'd probably both regret it later. Well, maybe he wouldn't, but she surely would when he told her they'd never be anything more than coworkers and friends.

Who was he kidding? he wondered as the desire in her eyes slowly turned to uncertainty. He'd never felt so out of control in his life. Every time he saw her, he lost all focus. And right now, this was about more than being distracted at his job. It was about her life.

The thought broke through his haze of need, and he backed away even more. "This isn't a good—"

"Don't say it," Shaye cut in. "Just…if things go wrong, I wanted to do that once more." She slipped sideways from the wall, away from him, then lifted her head, a completely different determination on her face now. "So I don't need a lecture about our friendship. I won't do it again. Let's catch this jerk so I can get on with my life."

She wouldn't do it again? That was exactly what he needed. But it only made him want to pull her toward him and change her mind.

He stepped back farther, trying to get his body in tune with his head. The sooner they solved this case, the sooner things could go back to normal. Except would he ever again be able to stand and chat idly with Shaye at the beginning and end of each workday, without imagining her body plastered to his? Without remembering the perfect fit of her lips, the softness of her hair through his fingers, the way her body melded to his like a puzzle piece?

He swore under his breath, and she gave him a perplexed look as she settled on his couch, straightening the shirt he'd twisted in his haste to feel her skin.

"That car was distinct."

"What?" He blew out a breath, trying to catch up.

"The car," she repeated, like he was slow. "It was a total piece of crap. It looked like it shouldn't have even been running. I only saw it for a second," she added quickly, "before Hiroshi made me duck. But there's got to be a way to track something like that, right? If he's a regular at the grocery store, maybe Roy knows who drives a car like that."

She was right. Tracking down suspects with a motive to hurt Shaye wasn't getting them anywhere. And even though the new incident pretty much guaranteed the shooting was no fluke, Luke was right, too. Cole needed to tackle this case like any other, by following the trail of evidence. Especially if they were wrong and they were dealing with a serial killer, maybe one who'd spotted her so recently he hadn't yet tracked her to her house. Someone like that wouldn't have any logical connection to Shaye—they often picked victims they didn't know. And a serial killer could definitely get so fixated on a particular target that nothing would deter him.

Cole's mind clicked back into detective mode, and he grabbed his phone. "I'm going to get officers to run that down right now."

He made a quick call, asking officers to talk to Roy again. He was probably driving them all crazy. He knew he was driving his chief crazy, especially after he'd fought so hard to have a helicopter go up after Hiroshi's car had been followed.

The chief had actually given in, but it hadn't done any good. He'd also announced that the police would officially offer Shaye protection, but Cole had shut that down for now. The better option was to hide her. And if this guy hadn't found Shaye's house yet, he definitely wouldn't have located Cole's. The fact was as much as Cole trusted his fellow officers, he knew no one had the same personal stake in her safety as he did. It would make it tougher to be out investigating, but as much as possible he wanted her in his line of sight.

"Okay, what now?" Shaye asked.

She was staring at him expectantly, but he was having a hard time focusing on the case with her cozied up on his couch, her feet tucked underneath her. It made his house look homey in a way it hadn't since his brothers had moved out years ago. Like she belonged there.

He cleared his throat and got his head in the game. "Did you get a look at the driver at all?"

Her lips scrunched. "No. Just the car, and then Hiroshi was yelling at me to put my head down."

Cole nodded, making a mental note to thank Hiroshi again when he saw the officer. Hiroshi and Wes hadn't gotten a good look at the driver, either. Hiroshi said he'd been wearing a hoodie again, which wouldn't look unusual in the cold. It had probably been intended to hide his face in case anyone spotted the car.

"Traffic cams," Cole blurted, and before Shaye could ask about it, he was dialing the station again, asking them to pull traffic cameras from around the area where they'd been followed. It was hard to avoid being caught on camera these days. All they needed was one good angle...

"Yeah, we're already on it," one of the other detectives told him; then suddenly Luke was on the phone.

"I've got more news."

"What are you still doing at the station?" Cole asked, glancing at his watch. It was almost midnight, and Cole was barely still standing. His partner had been up just as long—and while Cole had been parked in a chair beside Shaye's hospital bed last night, Luke had been handling the crime scene.

"The Taurus that was following Shaye today was bugging me," Luke replied. "I kept thinking that Crazy Ed had a really old one."

Cole sighed and settled into the chair across from Shaye, who was staring at him questioningly. "I don't know. He had a lot of cars, but I think most of them were newer."

"Yeah, well, I looked it up. He did have a Taurus."

"Where's that car now? Didn't most of his cars go up for auction?"

"Not this one. It wasn't worth anything. This car went to a woman named Rosa Elliard. And guess where Rosa was almost nine months to the day after Crazy Ed was arrested?"

"Tell me."

"Hospital. Having a baby boy."

Cole let that news sink in. "Crazy Ed has a son."

"I think so."

"But what does that mean? You think she found herself a babysitter and is running around in Ed's old

Taurus, hunting down people involved in the shooting? Because I may not be a hundred percent on skin color or age, but I'm pretty sure it was a man who was shooting in that parking lot."

"Maybe she's got family who doesn't like the fact that Ed Jr. will never meet his dad."

"All right," Cole agreed. "First thing tomorrow morning, let's pay Rosa Elliard a visit."

"NO CAR." COLE spoke the obvious the next morning as he and Luke walked up the short drive to Rosa Elliard's front door. Her yard was overgrown with weeds, the carport was empty and the houses to either side of her were boarded up.

"Not a great place to raise a baby," Luke said.

"Yeah, but shouldn't she be mad at Ed instead of Shaye?"

Luke shrugged. "She *should*, sure. But when we're talking about things she should have done, not having a baby with a gang member is probably on the list, too."

Cole didn't know much about Rosa. Her name hadn't surfaced when they'd swept up everyone connected to Ed's gang a year ago. Which meant she'd been on the periphery of his life—or people were trying to keep her out of it, trying to protect her from the hurt the police was bringing down on everyone involved in the gang's activities.

The details he and Luke had pulled up at the station this morning before making the drive to this dilapidated area of Jannis County said Rosa had grown up with a single father who worked three jobs. He'd apparently done his best to keep Rosa and her younger brother and older sister out of gang life. Rosa's sister had gotten out, gotten a degree, and made a life for herself. Apparently the same wasn't true of her brother, who'd dropped off the radar a couple of years ago. Or Rosa, who'd fallen in with Crazy Ed.

Cole stared at the flaking paint on the beaten-up front door and wondered what had gone wrong.

"Get your head in the game," Luke said, rapping his knuckles on the door. A minute later, he rapped harder.

"Maybe she's out," Cole said just as the door was whipped open.

The woman standing in the doorway with a baby cradled in one arm glared at them. Despite the neglect outside, Rosa and Ed Jr. were well dressed, and Rosa's gaze was clear, no sign of drug use like they'd seen with a lot of Crazy Ed's gang.

"What do you want?"

"Ma'am, I'm Detective Cole Wal—"

"Yeah, I know who you are," Rosa snapped, even as she rocked slowly side to side for Ed Jr., who blinked sleepily at them.

Cole forced himself not to look at his partner. Their names had been in the papers connected to Crazy Ed's arrest and trial, but that was the only way she'd know them. So why hadn't she been on their radar before now?

"We want to talk to you about the Taurus that used to belong to Ed Bukowski."

"Why? You want that, too?" she huffed.

"You still own the car, ma'am?" Luke asked.

Rosa's eyes narrowed. "You see a car here?"

"Who has the car now?" Cole asked, knowing she was lying from the way her rocking suddenly increased.

Before she could answer, a man strode up behind

her. Average height and build, light brown skin and angry brown eyes.

Wearing jeans and a hoodie, he matched their gunman. Cole's hand shifted a little closer to his weapon.

"Why are you hassling my sister?"

The man's eyes were also clear, no sign of drug use, but a lot of fury there. And peeking out the top of the long-sleeved T-shirt he wore were the edges of a tattoo on his chest. *A gang tattoo?* Cole wondered.

"Dominic Elliard?" Luke asked.

"That's right." Dominic elbowed Rosa back, stepping in front of her and trying to fill the doorway without quite the bulk to be able to pull it off.

"We'd like to talk to you about Ed's old Taurus. How long have you been driving it?" Cole asked.

"Are you messing with me, man? The police department doesn't pay you enough? You took all of Ed's nice cars, and now you're back for the junk?"

"No, sir," Luke replied calmly. "We just want to know who's driving it."

"It's sitting in a junkyard," Dominic said. "Now leave my sister alone."

Before Cole could get out his next question, Dominic slammed the door in their faces.

"He's been driving it," Cole told his partner.

Luke nodded. "Yeah, but where's the car now?"

Chapter Eight

"Do you recognize this guy?"

Shaye stared intently at the picture Cole held up of a man in his midtwenties with dark, close-cropped hair and square, masculine features. He might have been good-looking if he weren't scowling. And if the fury in his gaze didn't send chills through her.

She shook her head and looked up at him. "Who is it?"

"His name is Dominic Elliard. He's got a connection to Ed Bukowski. We're pretty sure he drives an old Taurus, and he looks like our shooter."

Fear started to creep back in when she heard Crazy Ed's name. They were back to the gang connection? But no matter how hard she stared at Dominic's picture, she didn't recognize him. "He doesn't look familiar."

She was still at Cole's house, restless after a morning stuck here. Sure, he'd sent his brother Andre to stay with her while Cole ran leads. And she liked Andre. But she felt like a burden. Even worse, she felt helpless again.

She wanted to be doing something. Even if there *was* a gang connection and she had no training, no weapon. She knew Cole would do everything in his power to make sure she was safe, but she was tired of being rescued.

Shaye pushed herself off the couch and faced Cole as Luke stood near the door, silent, arms crossed over his chest. The two of them had arrived a few minutes ago after being gone all morning, and she'd felt the difference in their energy level immediately. They'd spoken quietly with Andre, and then he'd disappeared into the kitchen to make coffee.

Shaye stared at Cole and tried not to let the fear in. Two days after the shooting, her hip hurt a little less, and she felt like she could move again. Or maybe that was because she'd just taken more of her pain medication. "How is this guy connected to Ed? And what does he want with me?"

"Crazy Ed has a baby. He must have gotten this woman pregnant pretty much the day he went away for good." Cole tapped the picture. "This is the woman's brother. They both knew exactly who Luke and I were without us needing to tell them, and there was a lot of anger there. The thing is I'm not sure why they'd be so fixated on you as opposed to the police."

He frowned. Shaye could tell he was mulling it over, that the pieces weren't quite fitting together.

"Maybe she's step one," Luke spoke up. "Because she's an easier target."

Cole glanced back at him, nodding thoughtfully. "So let's redirect his attention toward us."

"I don't think—" Shaye started.

"Bring him to us," Luke agreed, a hint of a smile curling his lips. "I'm up for it. Let's get him to stop thinking about Shaye. Remind him who arrested his nephew's father."

"Wouldn't—"

"Get him to come after us," Cole said darkly. "And then get him behind bars."

"Hey," Shaye said, taking an aggressive step forward that got both detectives to look at her. It was instinctive for cops—move toward them, and their attention snapped to you, regardless of whether you were a threat or not.

They were talking about purposely pissing off the friend of a crazy gang member just to move the target off her. The idea of him chasing after Cole and Luke instead of her didn't make her feel any better. Despite knowing they were armed and capable of protecting themselves, it made her feel worse.

"I don't want you putting yourselves in danger for me. It might be faster, but doesn't it make more sense to run down the car? Trace it to the crime scene and then lean on this guy?"

"We'll be careful," Cole promised as Andre came back into the room, holding out two mugs of coffee to her and Luke.

Luke took his, but Shaye shook her head, remembering from the last time she'd met Andre how he made his coffee. Cole looked amused her refusal, and he grabbed the cup when Andre offered it to him next.

After Andre disappeared back into the kitchen for a mug for himself, Cole whispered, "Wimp."

"It tastes like motor oil," Luke muttered.

"I can hear both of you," Andre called from the kitchen. But when he returned again, he was smiling, a crooked grin that lit up his deep brown eyes.

It was funny. Cole and his brothers looked nothing alike, but there was something about them that pegged them as family anyway. And it was more than just the easy camaraderie they shared, the good-natured ribbing.

Shaye was staring at Andre, trying to figure it out, when Cole nudged her with his elbow.

"You met his girlfriend, remember?"

Was Cole *jealous*? From the quick glance Andre and Luke shared, Shaye realized they thought so, too.

Cole took a small step back, redirecting his gaze to Andre. "How long are you available to hang here with Shaye? I think Luke and I should dig up some more information and then pay Dominic another visit."

Shaye put her hands on her hips. "Did you not hear me? If this guy is running around town with a gun, do you really want to put a target on yourselves? You hid me, but he knows where to find you whenever he wants. If he's anything like Bukowski, he's not afraid of firing a gun at a police station."

"We'll be ready for him," Cole promised, like her opinion didn't matter at all.

"And I don't get a say in this? This guy is after me."

"Yes, and we're trying to change that," Cole replied tightly, as though he was trying to be patient.

She turned to Luke. "If it was someone else being targeted by a shooter, is this how you'd handle it?"

He opened his mouth, but Cole spoke first. "Every case is different, Shaye. If Dominic is coming after you because of what happened to Ed, then logically he should have a vendetta against us, too. I want him to deal with that one first."

The scene from a year ago raced through her head: the smell of gunpowder in the air. The feel of someone else's blood under her hands as she dropped to the concrete. The sheer terror of knowing she was next.

The relief she'd felt when shots had fired from be-hind her—*toward* the shooters—had morphed quickly to an even greater terror when Cole had run past her, followed closely by Luke. She'd been positive she was going to die, and that feeling had seemed to go on for-ever as the officers around her had been hit and she'd been all alone. Cole and Luke's bullets had found their marks quickly, and her fear for their lives had been brief. But it had been even scarier than thinking it was her about to be shot.

She couldn't go through that again, knowing Cole was luring another gunman to him. "You use this plan and I'm going home."

"You can't go home. It's safer—"

She cut Cole off. "You can't force me to stay here. So you find another way to catch this guy or I'm leaving."

"Shaye's going to be pissed at you," Luke warned.

"We tried to trace the car," Cole said. "It wasn't hap-pening. Besides, even if we hadn't paid Elliard and his sister another visit, he was still mad from earlier. He might have switched his attention to us even if we hadn't gone back."

"Yeah, well, now we're definitely on his radar. Watch your six on your way home tonight. You don't want to get him fixated on you just to lead him right back to Shaye."

"I hear you," Cole agreed, even though they'd seen no sign of Dominic Elliard near the station this evening. The two of them had been back for hours, taking one last crack at finding the car. But Dominic had nothing in his name. Not an old Taurus, not a house, nothing. He hadn't for years, which told Cole he was into something. And the second tattoo he'd gotten a glimpse of on the man's arm when they'd gone back to his house that afternoon suggested it was a gang.

"He's not starting up the Jannis Crew again," Luke said.

Cole nodded. It looked like Dominic had fallen in with the Kings, another gang that had gained territory when he and Luke had shut down the Jannis Crew. It always seemed to work that way: knock down one criminal organization and another one was waiting in the wings to take its place. Sometimes the fight seemed endless; it was always the same battle, just new opponents. "But any gang connection tells us he's comfortable with violence."

"Yeah, well, let's just be careful he doesn't recruit other members to help him out. I'm with you on distracting him from Shaye, but I don't want to get him so mad he brings friends in on his personal revenge mission."

"I doubt it," Cole said. "If the Kings' leader knew Elliard was shooting at anyone without the group's say-so, it wouldn't bode well for him." The head of the Kings was notoriously paranoid and even more notoriously protective of his status. Any hint of a member running something on the side and that person ended up in the Jannis County morgue.

"True, but you never know with these guys. Anyway, I'm not afraid of whatever Dominic Elliard can bring down on us. I've been in worse firefights. But I don't want to lose another brother. You hear me?"

Luke was aiming what Cole thought of as his Marine stare at him. Cole nodded soberly. He definitely didn't want to put Luke in danger, and he didn't want

Andre and Marcos to have to deal with another loss if Cole got careless. "Yeah, I hear you. Whoever this threat is, I want him behind bars fast. I think getting him to do something stupid where we can control the area is our best bet."

"Well, you'd better make sure Shaye doesn't figure out what we're doing. Because I believe her when she says she'll take off on her own," Luke warned. "She's desperate to keep you out of harm's way, too."

"I'm a cop." Cole frowned. "I'll never be out of harm's way." Maybe he needed to remind her of that—remind her exactly why she shouldn't be looking at him like he was potential boyfriend material.

Remembering the way it had felt when she'd kissed him, his body disagreed. But his mind knew it was the right move. When this was all over, he would still be a cop, and Shaye would still be a forensics specialist—one who'd been through trauma twice working with the police department. He wasn't about to drag her further into his world, expose her to more of it, by dating her. When whatever was happening between them now burned out, where would that leave them? He couldn't imagine his days without their morning chats, without her smile to close out his shift at the station.

What if that smile was waiting for him at home? The thought filled his mind and refused to leave.

"...too bad."

"What?" Cole shook off thoughts of Shaye climbing into his car at the end of the workday and coming home with him and tried to figure out what Luke had been saying.

"I said, I wish the chief would let us run surveillance on this guy. It's too bad we don't have something more solid, so we could pull in additional resources, because Elliard's got just enough anger to be behind this. But I still can't figure out why he's targeting Shaye instead of us. He didn't react as strongly to her name as he did to our presence."

"Maybe he's doing exactly what we hoped, focusing on us instead of Shaye," Cole contributed. Truthfully, he was surprised by that, too. But maybe Dominic was a better liar than he seemed.

"I hope so. But for now I'm heading home. Otherwise I'll crash here again, and I'd rather sleep through a sandstorm than in a holding cell."

"Be careful."

"You're sticking around?"

Cole nodded. Andre had promised he was available as long as he was needed, and Cole was bothered by that car. Years of talking to suspects had honed his internal lie detector and there was no question Elliard had been lying about it being in a junkyard. But if it wasn't at his sister's place and Dominic didn't own property, then where was it?

"See you in the morning."

Cole waved absently, pulling up Elliard's record again, looking for any connection he'd missed—someone who might store a car for Elliard. Three hours later, he had no new leads. Elliard didn't seem to run outside Kings circles, and none of them would risk their leader's wrath.

Giving up for the evening, Cole yawned and dialed Andre as he headed out to the parking lot. When his brother picked up, Cole asked, "How's everything there?"

"Your girl isn't happy."

"Why not?" Cole asked, refraining from commenting on the obvious. Shaye wasn't his girl.

"She suspects what you're doing."

"What do you mean?"

"Don't play innocent with me," Andre replied. "I've known you too long. And it looks like Shaye knows you too well. She's sure you're trying to get a gang member to come after you. Is that really—"

The rest of his brother's words were cut off by automatic gunfire.

Cole hit the pavement, and the cell phone slid out of his hands as he went for the weapon holstered at his hip. His gaze darted around the parking lot, looking for the threat.

And there it was—someone in a hoodie running toward him holding something much bigger than a pistol.

Cole swore as he slid behind the cover of a parked patrol car, wishing he hadn't been the last one at the station. He yanked his Glock free of its holster, knowing it was a poor match for the weapon aimed at him.

But he was a trained police officer, and he was sure the man shooting was Dominic Elliard. Gang members tended to rely on firepower rather than accuracy, and Cole could use that to his advantage.

Heart pounding, Cole got to his knees beside the wheel, listening for the pounding of footsteps. He needed to pinpoint the shooter's location so he could aim fast.

Before he could do it, more gunshots rang out. Cole looked back at the door, wondering if he could make a run for it.

Dominic Elliard had brought friends.

Chapter Nine

"Give me a gun," Shaye demanded.

"What?" Andre looked over at her from where he was pacing in Cole's living room, a phone pressed to his ear and his free hand locked in a fist. "No."

"We need to go help him!"

"Shaye, this is going to be over before we get there. I called backup. They're on their way."

Tears pricked her eyes, and Shaye blinked them back. She knew Cole had been going ahead with his dangerous plan. She'd known it, and she'd fought him on it. But she should have actually followed through on her threat and walked out the door. It would have brought him back home. It would have pissed him off but kept him safe.

"This isn't your fault," Andre said softly.

His deep brown eyes were soft, filled with understanding, but underneath was his own fear. He and Cole were so close. If something happened to Cole, it *would* be her fault.

What would she do if he was hurt? If he was killed? The thought made her chest seem to cave in, made breathing difficult.

"Luke is driving back to the station right now,"

Andre said, his voice still calm, probably a result of constantly running into dangerous situations with the FBI. "They've got patrol cops close. And my brother is a fighter. Plus he's smart. I've seen him go up against tough odds before, and he's good at turning them in his favor."

"These are gang members," Shaye said, realizing she sounded hysterical but unable to calm down. The longer they went without news, the more it set in what Cole was up against, all alone.

She'd been sleeping—or at least trying to sleep—when Andre's panicked voice had woken her. She'd run into the living room to hear him demanding help at the police station. And then he'd said he'd heard multiple automatic weapons firing.

"Why haven't we heard anything?" Shaye demanded.

"Keeping us informed isn't their first priority," Andre replied, but his ear was still to the phone.

She didn't know who he had on the line until he said, "How close are you, Luke?"

"You should go," Shaye told Andre. She knew he had to be desperate to go help Cole, no matter what he was telling her. "I'll stay here. I won't leave, I promise."

"Can't do it," Andre said, barely looking at her as he listened to whatever Luke told him. Then he closed his eyes and let out a long breath.

"What is it? What happened?" A million horrible scenarios ran through her head until she really couldn't breathe. Then she could barely hear over a high-pitched ringing in her ears.

But she heard Andre's voice as he asked, "Is he dead?"

And then she was falling. The floor came up to greet her, and she couldn't hear anything more.

How MANY OF them were out there?

Cole's pulse ratcheted up way too high as he glanced at the exposed station doorway. No way he could make it and use his key card to dive inside without being shot.

He'd been so certain that Elliard wouldn't bring backup. It was a stupid mistake, underestimating him. It was a stupid mistake to rely on his gun and badge as if they made him invincible. And right after Luke had made Cole promise not to make anyone plan his funeral.

Bullets were still spraying, way too many of them. He'd fired a few shots, but was pretty sure they hadn't hit their marks. Someone—he thought it was Elliard—was screaming, but Cole couldn't make out the words. A bullet hit the tire beside Cole, and the patrol car shielding him dropped on the left side. The windshield shattered, too, and glass rained down around him.

He was trapped. And he didn't have much time before the gang members decided to run around the car and shoot him straight on. Cole glanced around again, trying to find any way to increase his chances of surviving until backup arrived.

There was no question Andre had called in help. He prayed his brother wasn't still on the line, that he wouldn't hear the shot that killed Cole when it happened.

Cole shook glass off himself, trying to watch both sides of the car. The car suddenly sank again, until the entire right side was higher than the left, and he realized a bullet must have hit the back tire, too. An idea formed—it wasn't much of an idea, but it was the best one he'd had so far.

Praying no one would choose that moment to round the front of the car, Cole peered underneath. Locating a pair of legs running his way, Cole aimed and fired. There was a scream, and the man dropped, his machine gun sliding out of his grasp and skidding away from him on the concrete.

Before the gang members could realize what he was up to and try to target him the same way, Cole lined up another pair of legs and took another shot. A second man hit the pavement, and then he heard the most glorious noise.

Sirens, a lot of them, and getting louder.

The direction of the gunfire shifted, and he heard footsteps pounding as the shooters tried to escape. A car started up, and then shotgun blasts joined the automatic gunfire.

Cole's backup had finally arrived.

The engine rumbled on what must have been the shooters' vehicle, and then another shotgun blast sounded, followed by a noise like an engine failing. "Hands up!" someone screamed. It sure sounded like Luke.

Then there were a lot more voices, all at once. "On the ground! Now! Get down!"

Carefully Cole peered around the side of the car to see a small group of Kings members dropping their guns and lying flat on the pavement. Two more lay moaning and bleeding where he'd shot them. And then, way off to the side, in a spot where he might have had an angle to shoot Cole, was another man, clutching his chest and drawing in the kind of loud, hacking breaths that said he'd been hit.

Cole ran toward him, not lowering his pistol, and kicked the MP5 out of reach. The man had one hand pressed hard against the bottom of his rib cage, and blood spread out over his dark hoodie. From the wheezing sounds he made with every breath, the bullet had collapsed his lung.

Reaching down, Cole pulled the hoodie away from his forehead. "Dominic Elliard."

"Help me," Elliard rasped.

"We're going to need an ambulance over here," Cole called.

"Already on its way," Luke yelled back. "You okay?"

"I'm not hit. But Dominic here is."

After he finished cuffing the two men Cole had shot, Luke hurried over to Cole's side.

"I guess our plan worked," Cole said weakly.

"Yeah, but we were wrong about Elliard bringing backup."

Cole frowned, glancing from Dominic to the other Kings members and then back again. "I don't think so."

"What do you mean?"

"I didn't shoot Elliard."

Luke looked over at the patrol car Cole had been hiding behind, which was covered in bullet holes, the entire left side pockmarked. He swept the two men with leg wounds lying halfway between the gang members' car and the patrol vehicle, then the two other men being cuffed at the far end of the parking lot. "If his own gang shot him, why'd they bring him here to do it? There's only one car."

"Unless Dominic parked somewhere else and walked."

"Or they were all in it together and someone turned on him. Or just hit him by accident—they did have semiautomatics and the Kings aren't exactly known for their marksmanship."

"I need help," Elliard rasped at their feet as an ambulance swung into the lot and one of the officers waved the EMT toward them.

"It's coming," Luke replied. "So what was the plan, Dominic? You do this yourself, or did someone above you order this hit?"

Elliard's eyes widened, and Cole knew he'd just realized what Luke was implying. Regardless of whether the others had come with him or come to hunt him down, if the Kings' leader *hadn't* ordered Cole's death, then Elliard had just guaranteed his own.

"Maybe you'd better talk to us," Cole recommended, holding back his anger that this man had just tried to kill him. "So we can protect you."

"My sister," Elliard wheezed. "My nephew. Please, don't let anyone hurt them."

Cole nodded at Luke, who stepped away and made a phone call, as the EMTs bent down to look at Elliard's wound.

"Tell me what happened here," Cole said, bending close. Realizing he still had his pistol in his hand, Cole tucked it into his holster. Adrenaline pumped through him, giving him energy now, but he knew he'd crash hard later.

Elliard's lips trembled, and Cole couldn't tell if it was anger or fear or pain—or maybe all three. "Rosa has nothing. Ed promised to take care of her and the baby. And then practically the day after he found out she was pregnant—the day after he swore he'd leave that life and take care of them—he went and got himself arrested. If that wasn't enough, then came the police, taking away every little thing he'd owned, every last dollar that should have been Rosa's."

"Sir, try to relax," the EMT said, shooting Cole an annoyed gaze. "Maybe you can do this another—"

"So you decided to make the same mistake as Ed, shoot up a police station and land yourself in jail so your sister has no one to help her," Cole spoke over the EMT.

"Maybe if you'd left us alone," Elliard snapped, then groaned, his eyes rolling back in his head as the EMT pressed down on his wound. "But you just kept coming, like having loved Ed made Rosa guilty, too."

"Sir," the EMT said, trying to nudge Cole out of the way as his partner lined up a backboard and they rolled Elliard onto it.

"How'd you convince your friends to do this with you? Or were they here for you, Dominic?"

Elliard's gaze latched on to Cole's, filled with pain and panic. He blinked a few times and then sucked in a deep breath before his eyes closed and didn't open again.

"Get him in the ambulance," the EMT said, and his partner loaded him on, then jumped in, too, doing compressions on Elliard's chest. The first EMT raced to the front and got behind the wheel. Then the ambulance raced off, sirens blaring.

"Pure luck I wasn't shot…automatic weapons…five of them…gang members."

Cole's voice filtered back to her, disjointed, sounding farther away than he really was. She'd heard him arrive home ten minutes ago. Or maybe it had been an hour. Shaye had lost all sense of time since Andre had carried her in here, put her in the center of Cole's big bed and told her to try to rest.

That felt like days ago, but when she glanced at the

clock on Cole's bedside table, she saw that it had been only a few hours. A few hours since he'd come in and told her Cole was okay. He was alive.

Just thinking about those moments when she'd thought he might have died made Shaye's heart rate pick up. She breathed in Cole's scent, still sensitive to it even though she should have stopped noticing by now. But it was all around her, rising up from his pillow. His room looked like what she would have expected—masculine and understated.

She didn't know if Andre had put her here because he thought it would be comforting or because he hadn't been thinking about it at all, just been desperate to get back on the phone for news of his brother. She couldn't believe she'd fainted twice in the past few days, when until this week she'd never fainted in her life.

From the living room, Marcos's voice joined Andre's, angry and worried. Marcos had arrived a couple of hours ago, too, shortly after they'd gotten the news that Cole was okay. He and Andre had both checked on her repeatedly, until she'd finally told them she wanted to sleep.

Sleep hadn't come, but she'd needed the reprieve from their worry, from the constant reminder that Cole had almost died tonight. The panicky feeling in her chest still hadn't left, and she had a sudden insight to what it must be like for the wives of police officers. Did they feel this way every day when their husbands were on the job, this nonstop fear? How did anyone live this way?

"You've got to stop trying to handle everything yourself for everyone you love!" she heard Marcos say, cutting into her thoughts.

Cole started to respond, but Andre interrupted him. "We're all in dangerous jobs, but you're making yours more dangerous."

They must have been close to yelling, because where the words had barely filtered through the walls before, now she was hearing them clearly. Shaye felt a little guilty and wondered if they remembered she was back here. Maybe she should go remind them. But she wasn't sure she could look at Cole right now without bursting into tears or racing into his arms. And she didn't think he'd appreciate either one.

"Just like the fire when we were kids," Andre said, his voice softer now.

Shaye frowned, sitting up in bed and straining to hear.

"I'm sorry," Cole said. "I didn't want to put you through that." His voice sounded choked up. "I'm never going to forget those minutes thinking Marcos wasn't going to make it out."

There was a long pause, and Shaye thought they were just speaking too softly for her to hear, until Andre's voice carried to her clearly: "And knowing that if you weren't holding me back, you'd have run right back in there for him."

A new kind of pain wound around Shaye's residual worry. She knew only bits and pieces about Cole's childhood, but she'd once heard him mention a fire that had destroyed the foster home where he'd lived. How old had he said he'd been? Fifteen? She'd had no idea they'd actually been *inside* the house when it happened.

She couldn't help it. She knew she shouldn't, knew that if she were thinking more clearly, she'd stay put until she had her emotions under control. But she shoved the covers off and climbed out of bed, a little unsteady on her feet.

Then she walked into the living room, right past Andre and Marcos, and threw herself into Cole's arms.

Chapter Ten

Cole hesitated a minute, and then his arms went around her, too, pulling her tight against him. If his head wasn't turned slightly away, she could have leaned up on her tiptoes and kissed him.

This close she could feel him take in a deep breath and knew tonight's firefight had scared him more than he was saying. She could have sworn he was breathing in the scent of her hair before he set her gently away from him.

"I'm okay, Shaye," he said softly.

She stared up into the perfect blue of his eyes, noticing the furrows between his eyebrows, the tension in his jaw. A million responses rushed to her lips—wanting to yell at him and kiss him and tell him everything was fine now—but she just nodded.

"Are you sure the threat is over?" Marcos asked. Cole's youngest brother looked more serious than Shaye had ever seen him, no sign of his ever-present grin.

"Positive. Dominic is still in critical condition, but Luke and I interviewed the other gang members. We're still not sure if they were with Dominic or against him—they're not saying much—but one thing is totally clear. This hit wasn't ordered. At least not on me."

"Not like they're going to admit that," Andre said, sounding skeptical.

"No, but the head of the Kings just isn't that stupid. He actually called the station, making all kinds of noise about being a concerned citizen, but it was clear he wanted me to know he had nothing to do with it. And I don't think he was just backtracking. None of these guys are asking for lawyers, and it's because they want to stay in the cell. Whether they were helping Dominic or trying to kill him, they don't want to deal with their boss's wrath for disobeying his orders—or failing them."

Marcos and Andre were nodding as Shaye studied all of them. "So, you're saying you're safe?"

"I'm saying *you're* safe," Cole replied. "Dominic was dressed practically the same way as the last shooting. Even if he pulls through, he's going away for a long time."

"So I can go home?" Shaye asked, even though it was the last thing she wanted to do right now. She knew Cole hadn't been hit; she could see with her own eyes that he was fine. But she also knew it wouldn't truly sink in for a while, and she'd feel better if he was near her.

"No." Cole's tone was firm. "You're sticking close until we confirm whether these guys were with Dominic or against him. My bet is against, but I want to be certain. And I want to make sure he doesn't have anyone else who'd help him with this vendetta. Because Luke sent a patrol car to pick up his sister and her son to keep them safe, and they were gone. No sign of a struggle."

"A gang would kill them there," Andre agreed.

"We think Dominic probably took the Taurus— which we're searching for now—so someone must have picked her up. Most likely for the same reason we were there, but I'm not taking chances."

At his words, Marcos and Andre gave him identical raised eyebrows—which Shaye interpreted to mean "except with your own life."

Cole held up his hands, suddenly looking beyond exhausted. "I promise I'm going to be more careful."

They didn't look appeased, but Andre said, "You're crashing. We'll get out of your way." He looked at Shaye. "Take care of him, will you?"

"I will," she replied, ignoring Cole's protest, and hoping his brothers hadn't told him about those embarrassing moments a few hours ago when she'd woken up to find Andre checking her head for signs of injury.

Then his brothers were gone, and it was just her and Cole, staring at each other. Energy sizzled between them, an awareness mixed with too many other emotions to untangle. On her side, anger and frustration and fear. She wasn't sure exactly what he was feeling besides the need to sleep.

"You should go to bed," she told him, and for one drawn-out minute, she thought he was going to suggest she come with him.

He said, "I can't sleep right now. I need to decompress a little. I'm going to wash the crime scene off me." He said it like it was any other case he'd been called to, instead of one where he'd been the intended victim.

Then he disappeared into his bedroom, leaving Shaye alone in his living room. She stood awkwardly, knowing the worry from tonight meant she should be crashing now, too. But she felt edgy, wired and anxious, and she wasn't sure why.

Was it really over this time? Was she truly safe? Or

would she go another year and find herself in someone else's crosshairs, some other person in Crazy Ed's life they'd never known about?

Somehow, it didn't feel like it was over. Maybe because Cole had almost died a few hours ago, or maybe because Dominic Elliard was in the hospital and they didn't have the full story yet. But what if it never ended?

She'd worried from the start that things would never go back to the way they'd been when she'd begun her job two years ago. Now she was sure of it. She was never again going to have that naive certainty that she'd just be unraveling puzzles in a lab. She'd never again be able to have that pure, simple joy without a little fear mixed in. She'd fought so hard for this life, but did she want it like this?

She honestly wasn't sure.

"Shaye?"

Cole's voice was soft. When she spun around, she found him standing close to her, his hair wet from a shower, wearing different clothes. How long had she been standing here?

He brushed a lock of hair out of her face. "I promise you I'm fine. It wasn't as bad as it sounded."

"You're lying." His face was so close to hers, the scruff on his chin heavier than it had been this morning, the shadows under his eyes deeper. And the look in his eyes… She lifted her hand, unable to stop herself, and slid it over his cheek.

He leaned into her palm. "I don't want you to worry."

"I can take it." Could she? She wasn't sure, but not knowing all the details of the shootout meant she was imagining every possible scenario. Maybe the truth would be even worse than she could imagine, but at least if he was honest with her, she could help him deal with it.

He stared at her for another long minute, then slowly turned his face into her palm and kissed her, and the light touch seemed to dance up her arm. Then his mouth was moving over her wrist, making her pulse jump and her heart race, and up to her elbow. His hand followed, and he tugged her toward him.

An instant before his lips would have met hers, she stumbled backward, pulling out of his arms. "Cole—"

"I'm sorry. You're right." He shoved his hands in his pockets. "I said we were just going to be friends. I'm trying to mean it."

The look he was giving her was anything but platonic. She tore her eyes away from his before she caved and tried not to sound breathy as she replied. "I don't want to be a distraction."

"You're not a distraction." He sounded insulted.

"What I mean is, I want to talk about this. I want to know what happened." And she wanted to know why his brothers—the people who knew him best in the world— thought he was putting himself in danger. She didn't say it out loud, but he seemed to hear her thoughts, because he frowned at her.

"Andre and Marcos are overreacting."

"Okay, then tell me about the fire."

"The fire?" He was scowling now, but it wasn't really aimed at her.

"You said you wanted to be my friend—"

"We are friends."

"Then *talk* to me. Tell me the truth about something, about what happened tonight, about your life."

"You think I'm lying to you?" He yanked his hands

out of his pockets, crossing them over his chest. "Honestly, Shaye, I spent the evening being shot at by gangsters with semiautomatic weapons to protect you! And you're accusing me of what exactly? Not being a good friend?"

"That's not what I'm saying." Wow, she was tired. It hit suddenly, draining her of all energy and making her doubt herself. Was she being unreasonable, pushing him because *she* was scared? Or was she right, knowing that to even begin to figure out how she felt about him, he had to really let her in?

It was probably a little bit of both, and right now, with emotions high, wasn't the best time to get into it. But frustration built in her chest, edging out the fear and confusion. "I just want you to trust me enough to treat me like your equal, instead of someone you have to constantly protect."

Her words came out defeated, and hung there between them until he shook his head and left the room.

"I WOKE UP and the house was on fire."

"What?" Shaye rolled over, looking groggy and way too tempting lying in the middle of his guest bed in another one of her oversize T-shirts.

"Back when I was fifteen," Cole clarified, sitting on the edge of the bed and trying not to let his gaze wander down to her bare legs. He should have waited until she'd woken up this morning, but he'd been up half the night thinking about how he'd ended their conversation.

This morning, after a few hours' rest and a little distance from the shooting, he felt bad about walking out on her. He still thought she was being unfair, but maybe if he laid it all out for her, she'd finally get it. They were way too different.

Her life was like one of those old-school sitcoms, with parents who were still married and a bunch of close-knit siblings. A comfortable life, a good degree and the chance to do the same thing when she married. That sort of world was so foreign to him, he didn't know where to begin.

He didn't really want to get into his past, or push her away, but maybe that was what he needed to do so both of them could move forward.

Tugging the sheet up her chest, Shaye scooted into a sitting position, suddenly looking wide-awake. Her hair was a mess, falling over her shoulders, rumpled on top of her head.

He'd never wanted to run his fingers through anything so badly.

"What happened?" Shaye asked softly.

Cole shrugged, his breath suddenly shallow like he was back in that smoke-filled hallway, desperate to get to his brothers before the ceiling caved in. "They ruled it an accident." But recently he and his brothers had had their doubts.

Shaye's fingers curled around his, and the light contact made his chest tighten.

From the moment he'd met them, Andre and Marcos had been there for him, but he was the oldest. He'd never had a real family before them, but he'd done his best to do the things a big brother should, which meant taking care of them as best he could. It was hard for him to lean on anyone else, maybe because he'd been tossed into foster care at two and never stayed in one place more than five years. It was a bad idea to rely on anyone, because you never knew when they'd be pulled away from you. His brothers had been different. Maybe Shaye was, too. Maybe she was right about him not trusting her.

"What are you thinking?" she whispered.

He squeezed her hand tighter. "I was taken away from my birth family when I was two because of neglect."

She jerked, like the change in topic had thrown her, but then scooted even closer, and man if she didn't somehow smell like the ocean again. Maybe it was her shampoo.

As a kid he'd never seen the ocean, despite living relatively close to it all his life. As an adult, it had represented freedom to him: the ability to do what he wanted without foster parents restricting him or social workers evaluating him. Shaye represented freedom to him, too. Except she was the kind of freedom he could never really have.

Although he'd been avoiding this conversation with her for days—if he was being honest with himself, maybe he'd been avoiding it for two years—he suddenly wanted her to know, to understand him. "I don't remember them. I've seen my file—apparently public safety officers found me locked in a closet and emaciated—but I don't remember that, either."

Tears filled her eyes, and her lips started trembling, trying to hold them back.

He gave her a small smile. "It's okay. I honestly have no memory of that time."

She clutched his hand tighter. "It doesn't matter," she said, sounding furious on his behalf. "It's still part of you, whether you consciously remember it or not. It's not okay."

"No. But I just—I never had a normal family. I don't know anything else. Until Andre and Marcos came along, it was just me. And—"

"And even then you wanted to take care of them."

"Yeah." The tightness in his chest loosened a little, knowing she understood.

"So then who looks after you?"

A smile quirked his lips. "Nobody needs to anymore. I got through that time. And now I'm an adult. I'm a cop."

"Right. So you can take care of even more people."

He'd never thought of it that way, but he supposed it was true. Still… "What's wrong with that?"

"Nothing." She smiled at him, but it was sad. "But everyone needs someone to look after them."

He didn't like the idea of her feeling sorry for him, and he shifted on the bed, pulling away from her a little. "I don't think—"

The ringing of his phone cut him off. Cole used his free hand to pull it out of his pocket, not wanting to completely sever the connection to Shaye yet. He glanced down. Luke.

Pressing the phone to his ear, he answered. "What's up?"

"We found the car."

"Good." Except why did Luke's voice sound dire?

"No, not good, Cole. We've confirmed that it's what Dominic drove to the station—he parked a few blocks away—but it's not right."

"Not right how?" Cole asked as a bad feeling came over him, suspecting what Luke was going to say next.

"It's not the same car. Dominic isn't the one who was shooting at Shaye. Whoever was trying to kill her is still out there."

Chapter Eleven

"Are we sure it's not Dominic?" Cole asked. "Maybe he just used a different car when he followed Shaye in the police vehicle. We never did find what he was driving when he hit Roy's Grocery."

Cole stared hopefully at his partner, but inside he was discouraged. He'd come to the station an hour ago after personally dropping Shaye at the lab next door and forbidding her to leave until he came to get her. It was midmorning on Monday, but he figured her boss would cut her a little slack after what she'd been through.

"Pretty sure," Luke replied, somehow looking wide-awake despite how little sleep Cole knew he'd had all weekend. His partner sat ramrod straight at his desk, managing to radiate authority despite the cargo pants and T-shirt their boss was always trying to get him to stop wearing. "The car is a really old Taurus, just like the one at Shaye's shooting, but it's the wrong color. And according to Hiroshi, it's way less of a rust bucket than the vehicle that was following his patrol car."

"And the one you found is definitely the car Crazy Ed left to Rosa?"

"Yep. The VIN matches."

"Do we know where Dominic was keeping it yet?

Because I'm not ready to drop this guy yet. He sure looked like the shooter, wearing another hoodie at the scene."

"A hoodie isn't exactly a smoking gun," Luke countered. "And Dominic had a semiautomatic, whereas Shaye's shooter was carrying a standard pistol. Why the difference?"

"I'm a cop. He'd expect me to be armed. I'm sure he figured Shaye would be an easy target." The idea made his whole body tense. He'd tried so hard last year to clean up the Jannis Crew—in large part because it was his job and they'd killed three of his coworkers. But also because he knew Shaye would never truly be safe if he didn't get all of them.

The fact that she was still dodging bullets made him wish he'd pushed harder for Witness Protection last year. Except then she'd be out of his life for good, and even thinking about that was painful.

"Maybe." Luke still didn't sound convinced. "Until Dominic wakes up—*if* he wakes up—all we've got is the car. And the other gang members, but they're not talking. They're clearly more afraid of their leader's wrath than doing serious jail time."

"Like he can't get to them in prison." Cole scowled, debating whether another interview was worthwhile.

"On the upside," Luke said, "we found Rosa and Ed Jr."

"Really?" Cole whirled his desk chair toward his partner. "Where?"

"They went to stay with her older sister out in the suburbs. It's not the best hiding place, but I talked to her on the phone right before you got in. She said her brother told her to take off last night. Claims she didn't know why, but she had a feeling he'd gotten wrapped up in something bad just like her ex used to, and so she did. She also says Dominic was trying to get out of the Kings. She thought that's why he wanted her gone."

"Hmm. If that's true, the other gang members coming after him might not be about him trying to kill a cop without permission. It might just be because he's trying to leave the group."

"Yeah. I'm not sure that should make Rosa feel any safer, but she claims Leonardo and Crazy Ed had an understanding, and that because of it, Leonardo would never come after her or the kid."

"Leonardo?"

Luke laughed. "Yeah, not exactly the kind of name you'd expect a gang leader to have, right?"

Cole nodded, trying to shake off thoughts of Shaye. Of course he knew the name of the Kings' leader. He needed to get his head in the game. "So you believe Rosa when she says she didn't know what Dominic planned to do last night? What did she say when you asked about him going after Shaye?"

"Well, I talked to her on the phone, so it's not like I could watch her body language. But yeah, I believe her. And she didn't even seem to know who Shaye was. Which makes me think Dominic wasn't the one trying to kill her."

Cole frowned. If Dominic had been looking for revenge on his sister's behalf, it didn't make a lot of sense that Rosa didn't know Shaye's name. Unless she was a good liar. Or Dominic's grudge went deeper than hers, which he could imagine. Because although he was furious about being shot at last night, he was more angry at himself for letting it happen than at the men who'd come after him. But when he thought about Andre coming under fire earlier this year by his girlfriend's ex, Cole sure had a lot of fury for that crook.

"I'm not ready to give up on Dominic yet. But you're right. We need to broaden our search again." Cole tapped his fingers on his desk, out of brilliant ideas. They'd gone through the list of people with possible grudges against Shaye. And they'd gone through the evidence from the shooting at Roy's Grocery. Neither had yielded anything.

"I'm not sure where—" Luke started when an idea bloomed and Cole cut him off.

"You said the Kings' leader was anxious to convince us he had nothing to do with this, right?"

Luke swore, long and creatively until Cole had to laugh. His partner knew him well enough to realize Cole was about to suggest something dangerous.

"Now you sound like a sailor," Cole joked.

Luke flipped him off with a smile that quickly turned serious. "I'm not going to like this, am I?"

"Probably not."

"Okay, lay it on me."

"I think we should go talk to the head of the Kings gang."

There was a long pause; then Luke finally demanded, "Are you crazy? Didn't we *just* talk about you trying to stay out of the line of fire?"

"Yeah, and I plan to."

"By scheduling a meet-up with a gang leader?"

"Look, you said it yourself. Leonardo was desperate to convince you that he had nothing to do with this. Let's see if we can get him to tell us what those other gang members were doing there."

Luke didn't budge from his seat, just crossed his arms over his chest. "You think he'd tell us if he ordered a hit on anyone?"

"No. But I think he's seen how dogged we can be, what we did with the Jannis Crew. I think he'll find a way to tell us what we need to know without admitting anything."

Luke scowled, but Cole could tell his argument was making sense to his partner. "Because then we'll know if we have to worry whether Dominic has any other friends willing to take up his cause."

"Yeah. And given the way things went down last night, if Leonardo suspects who they are, I think he'll hand those names over fast."

Luke swore again and opened his top drawer, pulling out his weapon and holstering it. "All right, but let's be really careful how we handle this. I don't want a repeat of last night."

"Believe me," Cole muttered as he followed Luke out to the car. "Neither do I."

"Hi, Shaye."

It took Shaye a minute to identify the voice on the phone, but then she realized. "Andre. Is Cole okay?"

Panic struck as she glanced in the direction of the police station, so close. Could something have happened without her hearing about it? She *was* pretty insulated, way in the back by herself in her closet of a lab. She jumped to her feet.

"Yeah, he's fine."

Shaye let out a long breath. "Good."

"Sorry. I didn't mean to worry you. I was just checking in with you."

In the background, she heard a strange *whomp whomp whomp* she couldn't identify. "What is that? Where are you?"

"Quantico. Just came down from a helicopter and I had a sec, so I wanted to make sure everything was all right there. Nothing out of the ordinary at the lab?"

"No." Just a handful of new digital devices she needed to analyze, and then hope the results wouldn't send a criminal after her. Shaking off the negativity, she asked, "Did Cole tell you to call?"

"No. But I know he doesn't like having you out of eyesight, and my brother's worry tends to rub off on me, even when it's unnecessary." He laughed, and she could tell it was for her benefit. "Inside a forensics lab fifty yards away from a police station is pretty safe."

Except for last year. Or last night.

Of course, both of those incidents had taken place in the parking lot, so she should be fine as long as she stayed in here. The lab required a key card to get in, not just at the front door but also at each lab. And no one had the card to access her room except for her and the director.

She'd been jumpy all day—she didn't like being away from Cole, either, and it was from worrying about his safety as much as her own—but she forced her voice to sound unconcerned. "Everything is fine here."

"Great," Andre said, sounding rushed now. "Listen, I've got to go back up and rappel out of the copter again. But be safe and tell Cole I'll talk to him tonight."

Andre was gone before she could say goodbye. Shaye stared down at the phone for a minute, bemused and touched. Cole might not have had a traditional family—or any family—for too many years, but he sure did now. He cared about her, so his brothers did, too.

She almost laughed when her phone rang again and it was Marcos. "Hi, Marcos. I just got off a call with your brother."

"What's Cole up to right now? Any new leads?"

"Your other brother."

"Oh." Marcos laughed. "Guess we think alike. I suppose you already told him everything is fine there, right? You're safe?"

"I'm good." She paused, biting her lip, wondering if she could talk to Marcos about what had kept her distracted all morning.

"Out with it," Marcos said. "What's worrying you? Because I promise you Cole is going to keep you safe."

"No, it's not that." She absolutely believed Cole would do everything in his power to make certain nothing happened to her. The question was whether something would happen to *him* in the process. "I just... Cole told me a little bit about the fire that happened when you were kids, but we got interrupted and he never said how you all managed to make it out of there." A terrible thought occurred to her. "Did someone get stuck inside?"

There was a long pause, and Shaye realized she'd probably just crossed a boundary, asking Cole's brother for personal details he hadn't yet shared with her himself. "I'm sorry. I—"

"That's okay." Marcos sounded more subdued than usual. "I guess I shouldn't be surprised he told you about the fire, but Cole keeps stuff to himself. Honestly, I'm not sure he's really talked about it to anyone besides us and Luke."

Oh, Cole. Sadness slumped her shoulders, thinking how few people Cole let into his world. And it was such an incredible world.

"We all got out. The fire started downstairs, and the kids were all upstairs. Well, almost all of us," he amended and she could tell there was a story there, but he kept going. "I woke up and it was like being blind from the smoke. I couldn't breathe, couldn't see, didn't know what was happening or what to do. I was twelve."

There was another pause, and Shaye knew she was making Marcos relive it. She opened her mouth to tell him it was okay, that he didn't have to tell her, when he continued.

"Then Cole was there, waking up Andre, making us hold on to each other as we went down the stairs. I don't know what happened, but I tripped and then they were gone." He let out a loud breath. "Scariest moment of my life. But I managed to make it out. And by the time I got outside, it was clear the whole place was about to go up. Cole was holding Andre back, but if he hadn't…I guarantee you, they both would have run back in for me. And it would have been a bad idea. I had to go another way."

Shaye took a shaky breath, realizing she'd been holding it while Marcos spoke, even though she knew they'd all lived through the fire. "And after that you were all separated?"

"Yeah. Those foster parents had to rebuild, so they didn't have a place for us anymore. It was hard not having Andre and Cole around all the time, although we tried to find ways to talk, to see each other if we could. But let me tell you, the minute I turned eighteen, Cole was there, waiting on the doorstep." Marcos's voice sounded teary as he finished. "He had a home waiting for me."

"He's a great guy," Shaye said, her own voice watery. She knew he'd supported Andre and Marcos when they'd gotten out of foster care; he'd accidentally shared as much with her a few days ago. It shouldn't have surprised her that he'd literally been standing outside to drive Marcos home when he hit eighteen and the foster system kicked him out to make it on his own.

"Yeah, he is. And I know he can be hard to reach sometimes—or at least it might seem that way—but he's worth sticking it out for, Shaye."

"I…" What could she say to that? That Cole didn't want her in his life, at least not that way? That she was scared even if he did, she wasn't cut out to date someone who put his life on the line as part of his job description?

"Just don't give up on him," Marcos said softly. "I've got to go, Shaye. I've got an undercover meet in less than an hour, and I'm going to be late."

"I'm sorry. I—"

"Stay safe. Tell Cole I'll call him."

"Okay," Shaye promised, but he was already gone.

And then she was staring at the wall in her lab, covered with cartoons only someone with a deep understanding of digital analysis would find funny, but not really seeing any of them. She'd known it all along, but Marcos's words had just driven it home. Cole deserved someone in his life, someone who would look after him as much as he looked after everyone around him. And he deserved someone much, much braver than she could ever hope to be.

Chapter Twelve

The second Cole parked his car alongside the curb, six men wearing gang colors and shirts loose enough to cover weapons started ambling his way.

"Maybe we should rethink this," Luke muttered from the passenger seat, his hand hovering near his own weapon on his hip. His gaze scanned the area.

Before Cole could reconsider, there was a yell, and the men all stopped, glanced over their shoulders and then walked back the way they'd come. Then just one man was walking toward them, his hands out at his sides, to show he wasn't holding.

"Leonardo," Luke muttered, opening his door.

Cole followed, walking around the front of the car as he inspected the leader of the Kings. Leonardo Carrera was a big guy, at least 250 and only five-ten. He was covered in tattoos, with a seemingly permanent scowl on his face. He'd had a handful of run-ins with the law, but despite having a reputation as a man not to cross in the gang world, he tended not to mess around with law enforcement, especially since the Jannis Crew had been shut down.

"Detectives," he greeted them now, as if he were an upstanding citizen welcoming them into his home instead of a gangster who'd ordered hits on men—if only they could prove it.

"Leonardo." Cole's gaze assessed the other Kings members. "Can we have a little chat in private?"

Leonardo glanced over his shoulder and nodded, and the other men scattered, some heading inside the house behind them and others striding down the street. "Of course. What can I do for you?"

Talking to the head of the Kings always threw Cole, and he remembered that Leonardo had actually gotten a business degree before returning to his old neighborhood and taking over the gang his older brother had run before his death a few years earlier. It was probably why the Kings were so good at making money—and had been so successful at evading law enforcement. That would eventually change. Just not today.

Today Cole had other concerns on his mind.

"I need some information about Dominic Elliard," Cole told Leonardo.

"He's not a part of my social circle anymore," Leonardo said.

Normally Leonardo's euphemisms would make Cole smile, but today he just scowled. "And when did that happen?"

Leonardo shrugged. "It's been coming for a while. I knew he wanted out, and that's just not cool with me. Let one guy leave and others think they can do the same if they feel like it. But I was gonna make an exception and let him go, seeing how he's looking after his sister and all."

"You and Ed have some kind of agreement?" Luke asked.

Leonardo gave a smile that was somehow far more

creepy than happy. "Let's just say we understood each other. We grew up together. He chose the wrong side. Obviously. But we were good friends once." The smile dropped off. "A long time ago. So, yeah, I was giving Dominic a little leeway, for Ed's sake. But then he started talking about revenge on cops, and I'm not having any part of that. I'm a businessman, you know."

Cole nodded, knowing Leonardo actually thought that. "When did this come up, Dominic's plan to get revenge on cops?"

"Yesterday."

"Yesterday?" Cole glanced over at Luke, who was frowning. They'd visited Dominic for the first time yesterday, but Shaye had been shot at before that. "What about shooting lab employees?"

"Lab?" Leonardo shook his head, looking perplexed. "What kind of lab?"

"County forensics," Luke said.

"Didn't come up. It was cops. He said they visited Rosa's place, talking smack about taking her car, and it brought up all this old anger." Leonardo paused, glanced from him to Luke. "Guess that was you two, huh? Dominic thought he was going to get all of Ed's money when he went to jail or after he died, like it wouldn't get caught up in the system. Fool. He never got over that. It's been stewing inside of him for a year."

"What about the others who were at the police station last night?" Luke asked, taking a step toward Leonardo that made the gangster raise an eyebrow. He shifted slightly backward at the force of Luke's glare. Leonardo might have had a solid seventy pounds on Luke and probably more than one pistol hidden on his massive body, but Luke had seen some serious combat as a Marine that still showed when he wanted it to.

"Shouldn't have happened where it did," Leonardo said, speaking slowly, like he was choosing every word carefully.

Which he surely was, since any obvious admission to participation in a crime would land him in a jail cell. And knowledge of it before it happened could land him in cuffs, too.

"So, they were interested in Dominic?" Luke pressed.

"Yeah. They were supposed to…talk him out of whatever he planned to do." He gave a toothy smile. "I don't stand for people who step out of line, you know."

"We've heard that," Cole said. He believed the man. "Thanks for your time."

As he and Luke turned to go back to their car, Leonardo called, "I heard about that shooting at the grocery store. Papers said a county employee was hit. That what you're interested in?"

Cole spun back. "You know anything about it?"

Leonardo held up his hands. "All I can tell you is it wasn't anyone from my social group. Not my, uh, chess opponents, either."

Cole stared at him, knowing he was referring to members of other area gangs. "How sure are you?"

"About my own? Positive. About the others? Pretty sure. If it was them, I'd have heard about it by now. Someone would have bragged. Word always gets out about that kind of thing."

Cole nodded and returned to the car. Instead of starting it up, he looked over at Luke as his partner climbed in and slammed the door. "You believe him?"

"That no gang member was behind this? Yeah. If it

was gang related, someone went way off the reserva-
tion."

Cole ground his teeth together as he started the engine, resisting the urge to repeat some of the creative
cursing Luke had done earlier. If it wasn't a gang member, then they were down to zero suspects in the attempt
on Shaye's life, and she was still in danger.

Cole was in a bad mood when he met Shaye in her lab
at the end of her workday.

Actually, it was two hours past the end of her workday, but she didn't mind. She knew he was trying to
confirm Dominic Elliard was the one who'd shot at
her, and she had plenty to catch up on anyway. Being
away from the lab for a year—even though they'd sent
digital devices to the state lab in the meantime—meant
there had been a lot waiting for her when she returned.
They'd tried to ease her back in with just a few assignments, but today, she'd asked for everything.

"What's wrong?" Shaye asked Cole, nerves rising
up because she knew before he spoke that the investigation wasn't closed.

Cole's shoulders slumped. "I'm sorry, but it doesn't
look like Dominic Elliard is our shooter."

"What?" That didn't make any sense. "I thought you
arrested him at the scene?"

"No, I mean, yes, we did. He's *my* shooter, but he's
not the one who was coming after you. We'll still talk
to him when he wakes up, but I think there's someone
else out there."

"Then why was Dominic shooting at you if it's not
connected? I thought you talked to him about the attempt on me, and that's why he came after you?"

"Sort of." Cole sighed. "Turns out, Dominic was pissed about Ed's money and belongings being confiscated."

"But he earned them illegally—"

"Yeah, I know, but Dominic thought it all should have gone to his sister—or directly to him, for some reason. When we asked about the car, I guess that was the last straw. He snapped."

Shaye tried to wrap her mind around that. "Are you serious? He shot up a police station over a rusted-out, decade-old car?"

"Seems so."

She shifted from one foot to the other, wrapping her arms around herself to ward off a sudden chill. "What does this mean for me?" Before he could speak, she added, "Please don't say Witness Protection."

She might not see her family as often as she'd like to since she'd moved here, but never seeing them again? She couldn't even imagine it. And the thought of never seeing Cole again hurt just as badly. Whatever the threat was, she couldn't give up the people she loved to stop it. Not even if it meant her own life was in danger.

Loved. The word rolled around in her brain as she realized she'd put Cole in the same category as her family. But she couldn't dwell on that now, because she had bigger concerns than falling for a detective who'd never feel the same.

This was never going to end. The fear. Never knowing if she was safe or if she'd walk outside and face a barrage of bullets. Was this what Cole felt like every day as a detective? "How do you do this?"

"Do what?" he asked, peeling her hands off her arms and holding them in his. "Listen, I'm sorry it's not over.

I wanted this to be the end of it. But we're not giving up until whoever did this is in handcuffs. Until then I'm going to keep you safe. I promise you, Shaye."

"How do you deal with this without going crazy, without being too paralyzed to live?"

"The danger?" he asked softly, something in his eyes shifting, though she wasn't sure if it was worry or pity for her or just Cole closing himself off.

"Yeah. Because you just seem to run into it like it's nothing. I don't know how to do that. I don't know how—"

"You don't *have* to do that. I don't want you doing that. I'm going to get this guy, Shaye, whoever he is, and then things can go back to normal."

She didn't want them to go back to normal. Frustration filled her, almost overtaking the fear. She wanted to learn how to manage the fear. She wanted to understand the risks that Cole faced, so she could stop feeling so terrified whenever he was out of her sight.

Shaye sank into her chair, not letting go of Cole's hands. When had this happened? When had her worry about Cole become greater than her concerns about the threat facing her? She dropped her head on top of their hands.

When had she gone from halfway in love with him to totally, madly, completely in love? And what the heck was she going to do about it?

"I STILL DON'T like this," Cole said an hour later as he opened the door and tucked her under his arm, practically running her to the hospital entrance.

"Maybe if I see him, it'll spark something."

"And maybe if he sees her, it will be obvious he recognizes her," Luke added as he met them in the lobby.

"All right," Cole grumbled. "Let's get this over with. I want Shaye back in a controlled location. There are too many people here."

"This guy would have to be pretty desperate to try and shoot up a hospital," Luke said.

"Yeah, well, Elliard shot up a police station," Cole reminded him.

Luke gave Shaye a look she interpreted as "my partner is seriously overreacting," and she gave a hesitant smile in return.

Since her realization in the lab, she'd felt completely distracted and way too self-conscious, like Cole would read her mind. It wasn't totally unreasonable—she'd seen him pick up on things people were thinking plenty of times. It must have been part of his detective skill set. She didn't want him using it on her. Not today.

He'd definitely known something was wrong that she wasn't sharing, though, because he'd asked her about it the entire ride over here after Luke had called to tell them Dominic Elliard had woken up. Thankfully, he'd seemed to think it was just fear of not having her shooter in custody. She was perfectly happy to let him keep thinking that until she figured out what she was going to do about her feelings for him.

"Come on," Luke said, leading the way over to the elevator. "He's been moved out of ICU. But I didn't give him a heads-up we'd be coming, and given that he just regained consciousness, we'd better be careful if we ask him anything we expect to need in a courtroom."

"We've got him on the police station shooting no matter what," Cole said. "Our cameras caught him pretty clearly, plus my testimony. But we'll need to be careful how we approach Shaye's shooting. If he actually did do that, I want him going away for it, too."

Luke nodded. "Agreed. Though the reality is that unless someone majorly screws up here, this guy shouldn't ever get out."

The elevator reached the third floor, and the three of them headed down the hall. An officer stood outside a room that had to be Dominic's. Cole and Luke exchanged a few words with the officer, and then Shaye took a deep breath as they opened the hospital door.

She didn't think she'd seen the shooter's face at the scene, but she knew that sometimes witnesses recalled more than they thought they did when faced with a lineup. Would she recognize Dominic?

She followed Cole and Luke into the room and stared at the man in the hospital room. He was unnaturally pale, with a bandage covering the right half of his chest, his arm in a sling and a bunch of tubes and wires connected to him.

He turned his head slowly, wincing, and his lips turned up into a snarl when he spotted them.

Shaye studied him, her heart thudding too rapidly, taking in the exaggerated cupid's bow of his lips, the small eyes with the heavy eyebrows, the thin nose that had clearly been broken at least once. His focus shifted off Cole and Luke over to her, and he met her gaze.

He had dark brown eyes. They looked angry and a little confused. But she didn't recognize them. She didn't recognize him. She let out a nervous breath, then glanced over at Cole and shook her head.

"Let me guess," Dominic said, obviously going for a sarcastic tone but failing when it came out weak. "You came here to get my car keys."

"Actually, Dominic, we found your car already," Luke said. "We came here to talk to you about Shaye."

"Who?"

"Shaye." Cole gestured to her, and Dominic's gaze bounced back to her.

"I don't know who that is. You plan to give her my car?"

"It's not your car, Dominic. And you're probably not going to have much use for one in prison," Cole snapped. "So I'd cut the sarcasm and try to cooperate."

He rolled his eyes. "Cooperate with what? You said you already took my car."

"Forget the car," Luke said. "We want to talk to you about a shooting that happened three days ago."

Dominic let out a string of curses, his voice gaining strength with each one. "Oh, no. You're not pinning some random shooting on me. What's this? That gangbanger over on 109? That wasn't me. Why would I shoot him?"

"That's not who we're talking about, Dominic," Luke said. "We're talking about Shaye."

He looked confused for a minute. "She ain't shot."

Luke shook his head just as Dominic went into another rant about being framed. "Thanks for your time, Dominic," Luke said, gesturing for them to follow as he left the room.

"He didn't recognize her," Luke said.

"Yeah, and he definitely couldn't hide his anger toward us," Cole agreed, "but he seemed indifferent to Shaye. He's not our guy."

"So who is?" Shaye asked as they headed back to the elevator.

Dominic's cursing followed them the whole way.

Chapter Thirteen

"You've been acting weird all evening," Cole said, studying Shaye and trying to figure out what was going on with her. He knew she was worried about still being in danger, but all his detective instincts were screaming that there was more to it than that. "What's going on?"

Shaye fidgeted on his couch, still wearing the conservative gray slacks and emerald green blouse she'd worn to work. She'd knotted her hair up into a bun on top of her head, and it had loosened, looking like all it needed was a little tug from his fingers to send her hair cascading down.

He sat on the edge of the chair, keeping his distance, and stared at her. They were back at his house, where she was going to stay until this case was conclusively solved. The desire to have her here even longer nagged at him, but he needed to continue to remind himself to keep things professional. He hoped he could manage to do it.

"Nothing." She shrugged, her fingers twitching on the couch as she avoided his gaze. "It's just been a long day. Maybe we should order a pizza."

"Sure, but you honestly expect me to believe that?"

He couldn't stop his grin. "I'm a detective, and you might just be the worst liar I've ever met."

Her gaze snapped to his, her lips parting at the insult, and he couldn't help but follow the move with his eyes. She didn't seem to wear lipstick, just swiped some pink gloss on her lips periodically that he desperately wanted to kiss right off.

Professional, he reminded himself.

"It's been a tough day," she said. "I'm just trying to…figure things out."

He instantly got serious. "I told you I'd protect you, Shaye, and I meant it."

"I know. It's not that. But…"

"What?"

"Who's going to keep *you* safe?"

He suddenly realized she looked truly worried. Her lips were actually trembling a little, and there was a sheen of tears over her whiskey-brown eyes.

"Hey." He got up from the chair and joined her on the couch, sitting far closer than he knew was wise. "Shaye, I had to go through a lot of training to be a cop. I might have joined because it would provide a good income without a real degree, but—"

"Bull."

"What?"

"You joined to keep people safe."

"Well, sure, that was part of the appeal, but I'm serious about the income. There aren't a lot of jobs that give you decent benefits *and* a decent salary with nothing but a high school degree, and being a cop is one of them." He felt himself flush, because he knew how smart she was, but he was mad at himself for doing it. He had a good job and he'd done what he needed to do to take care of the people he loved. He shouldn't feel ashamed about that.

"And you needed *that* because you were planning to take care of Marcos and Andre," Shaye said, sounding pleased with herself.

"Sure." He shrugged. "So? What does this have to do with anything? Look, the city gives us solid training, and I have one of the best partners on the force. You know Luke always has my back."

"Marcos told me about the fire, about how you got them both out," Shaye said, biting her lip as she stared up at him.

"He did?" She nodded, and he wasn't sure if it surprised him or not. His brothers were more open about their past than he tended to be. But how had the conversation come back to this? "Okay. And you're bringing that up because?"

"Because I want to know about you. I want to understand how you keep safe in your job, and I want to know about your past. I want…"

She was silent for so long that he finally prompted, "What? What do you want, Shaye?"

"You."

His heart picked up speed, like he'd gotten a sudden jolt of adrenaline the way he did when a case came together. Only this was much more potent.

Shaye Mallory wanted *him*. He stared at her, at the hopeful, nervous expression on her face, and gripped the couch cushion to keep from grabbing her and yanking her to him. Because he didn't think he'd ever wanted anything as badly as he wanted her right now.

He cared about her. A lot. And he knew Shaye. She wasn't the fling sort. She hadn't dated anyone—not even casually—during the entire time she'd worked at the lab. And it wasn't like she hadn't had opportunities. He'd heard colleagues ask her out, watched her blush and stammer and try to let them down easy. Shaye wasn't the kind of woman you messed around with, and he sure wasn't going to be the one to break her heart.

He was always going to be a blue-collar guy, a first responder who ran toward all the things she should stay far away from. He tried to calm his pulse and let her down as easy as she had all those other guys. "Shaye—"

"I know you're attracted to me."

He let out a heavy breath. "Yeah, of course I am, but—"

"And I know you like me as a person. You'd be good for me, Cole. And you know what? I think I'd be good for you."

His heart pinched at the idea of rejecting her. She looked so nervous and so determined. But in the long run, he was doing her a favor. Probably himself, too. How did anyone get over Shaye Mallory?

"Shaye, we're really different."

"Who cares?" He tried to talk, but she kept going, speaking fast so he couldn't break in without talking over her. She leaned even closer, challenging his resolve as she said, "You have a high school degree. I have a bachelor's and a master's. Who cares?"

She had multiple degrees? That shouldn't surprise him.

"You grew up in foster care, and I grew up with a big Irish Catholic family that drives me crazy because they're so loud and busy and outgoing, and I'm just not. Who cares? You're a cop, and I sit in front of computers all day. Who cares? All that really matters is that I…"

She took a deep breath, blew it out and looked at her shoes before staring up at him. "Cole, I—"

He cut her off before she said anything she'd really regret, before she said anything that made him either put someone else on her protection detail or drag her into his arms and never let go. "*I* care, Shaye—that's who. Those differences matter to me. We're not a good fit. We never will be. I'm sorry."

SHAYE WAS DREADING seeing Cole this morning. She'd mumbled something about being tired last night after he'd rejected her like he didn't even need to give it any thought and then she'd run off to his guest room.

The relative solitude hadn't helped, because the room looked like Cole, all masculine and practical. Somehow it smelled like him, too. Maybe she was just imagining his scent, conjuring it up to torture herself.

She'd put herself on the line, been about to admit she loved him—which surely he'd realized—and he'd said no so easily. Her cheeks flushed just thinking about how badly she'd embarrassed herself. The worst part was she didn't understand it. He was attracted to her; that had been obvious not just in the kisses they'd shared but in the way he looked at her when he thought she wouldn't notice. And he liked her—they'd become friends almost instantly. It should have been enough. Enough at least to give something more a *chance*.

But apparently not for Cole.

And now she had to go sit across the kitchen table from him and eat breakfast, then let him drive her to the lab. Then he'd pick her up at the end of the day and drive her back here for another awkward evening together. And there was no end in sight, no real suspects in her case now that they'd ruled out Elliard.

She needed to do something. Review the cases she'd worked on herself, double-check everything, then make a list of anyone in her life. She couldn't imagine any of her colleagues doing this, but working in law enforcement had taught her that people could surprise you. Maybe if she ran down leads, too, this would end sooner. She'd be able to go back home, and go back to her old life. Problem was she didn't want her old life anymore.

She wanted something better. She wanted to get the joy in her job back, sure, but she wanted to have a life outside the lab, too. Most of all she wanted Cole. But she couldn't have him, so she needed to take charge of the things she could control. And this was a good place to start.

"Shaye?" Cole's voice was more tentative than she'd ever heard it. It was followed by a few taps on the bedroom door. "You ready to go?"

"Yep." She grabbed her purse, straightened her shoulders and pulled open the door.

There wasn't much she could do about the blush she felt making her whole face hot, but she tilted her chin up and strode toward his front door. "Let's go."

He followed, wisely not saying a word until he dropped her off at the lab and promised to pick her up at the end of the day.

As the lab door swung closed behind her, she tried not to dwell on the heaviness in her heart. Despite the fact that they'd never really interacted socially, Cole had become one of the best friends she had. Her declaration last night had ruined that.

She was going to miss what they'd had. But she still couldn't bring herself to regret trying for more. It was time to start doing that in all aspects of her life.

If she didn't get what she wanted, at least she'd go down with a fight.

"GET YOUR HEAD in the game." Luke slapped a rolled-up stack of papers against his arm, and Cole scowled back.

"Focus, man. You've been distracted all day."

"Sorry." He tried for the millionth time to shake off thoughts of last night. Had Shaye really been about to say what he'd thought? He'd gone over it in his head again and again and decided he was crazy. She couldn't possibly love him—or think she loved him. If that *had* been what she was going to say, it was probably just a result of their close proximity. Having your life in danger made you think and say all kinds of crazy things.

"I think we need to focus on the car again," Luke announced. From the way he said it, Cole suspected he'd been repeating it.

Cole straightened in his chair, let the sounds of the bullpen filter back in: the ridiculously old coffeepot gurgling in the corner, the old pipes rattling, a group of officers talking about traffic-stop safety in the corner. It helped him focus, but he still didn't have any brilliant new ideas. "Without a license plate, I'm not sure how far an old, rusty Taurus is going to get us."

"Let's go back to that list of suspects you made, of people connected to Shaye's case. I don't care if the person has an alibi—let's run them all and see what they drive. Because Dominic isn't the only one who could be on a vengeance mission for someone else."

New energy filled Cole. "You're right. But wouldn't the person drive their own car?"

"Yeah," Luke agreed. "So we're going to be looking at a lot of names, but unless you have another idea..."

"Nope. Let's do it. And while we're at it, let's just see what her colleagues are driving. I doubt any of them have a grudge no one knows about, but stalkers are usually in the person's life, even if they're way in the periphery, so let's check."

Two hours later, Cole looked up from the records he'd been cross-referencing on his computer and rubbed eyes that had long since gone blurry.

"Here."

He looked up and found Luke holding out a cup of coffee. "Thanks." Cole took a big sip, hoping to erase some of the fog from not sleeping last night. Or the night before. Or any night, really, since Shaye had been shot at in a parking lot.

"You want to tell me what's eating at you?" Luke asked, leaning against the edge of Cole's desk and effectively preventing him from diving right back into the search.

"You know what's bothering me. It's this whole case. I don't like seeing Shaye in danger."

"Nah." Luke sipped his coffee leisurely and settled in more comfortably against Cole's desk. "We've been partners long enough. We've been *friends* long enough. I know there's more to it. And I know you're not big on sharing your feelings, and I get it, but come on. You look like you could use a sounding board."

Was he really that bad? Cole frowned at his partner, weighing the things Shaye had said to him over the past few days about not letting anyone close to him. "Shaye's said some things lately. Do I really keep everyone at arm's length?"

"Yeah." There wasn't even a brief pause while Luke considered it. "But, look, we're all like that at least a little. It's a cop's nature, I think. We spend so much time investigating all the horrible things people do to each other, all the ways they betray one another." He shrugged. "We're bound to get a little jaded."

But Cole had always been this way. And he might have had reason, but that didn't mean it was a good way to live.

He set down the coffee and leaned back in his chair, thinking about all the times Shaye had tried to get to know him better the past few days and all the ways he'd tried to push her away. Maybe they were too different to ever make something last. But if she was crazy enough to want to give someone like him a chance, then how much crazier was he not to take it?

Maybe it was time to make some real changes in his life. And maybe he needed to start with Shaye Mallory.

Chapter Fourteen

"Shaye." Cole let out a string of swearwords as she walked toward him.

Shaye kept her head up and tried not to let the sight of him hurt but failed miserably. She had no idea how she was going to get over this man, but solving this case so she wasn't under his roof was probably a good start.

"What are you doing here? What's wrong? Why didn't you call me? I would have come and gotten you."

"I walked across the parking lot," Shaye cut in before Cole could continue his barrage of questions. "I'm fine. There were four officers standing outside the whole time."

His lips pinched together, and she could tell he was letting it go even though he wasn't appeased. "What's wrong?"

"Nothing's wrong. I had some information I thought you might want." She'd been digging up information all day on her tablet—thank goodness she'd brought her personal one so she didn't have to do this on her work computer. She was now behind on what she *should* have been doing at work today, but she just might be one step closer to figuring out who was after her.

"Okay, let's hear it," Cole said, standing up and offering her his chair as Luke rolled his chair around the desk to join them.

Shaye settled into the seat, still warm from Cole's body, and dang it, even the chair smelled like him. She scooted forward a little, trying to focus and glanced up, catching his gaze. And then everything—her breathing, her thoughts, her very heartbeat—seemed to jerk to a stop, then start up again in double time.

Cole was staring at her with a look she'd never seen before. He'd looked at her with desire in the past, but usually it was tempered, like he was trying to hide it. Right now it was like he was intentionally broadcasting that he wanted her. His gaze drifted slowly over her, then back up, with lingering eye contact that made her squirm.

What was happening?

"Ahem." Luke coughed.

Cole gave her a slow smile, then blinked, and his serious detective face was back, and Shaye tried to decide if she'd just imagined the whole thing. Because those were some serious mixed signals, less than twenty-four hours after he'd told her they were too different to be together.

"What's the information?" Luke's voice seemed to come from far away. She must have taken a really long time to respond, because he added, "Shaye?"

"Um, right." She fussed with the hem of her shirt, pretending to straighten it as she tried to make her face blank as easily as Cole had done. Sure she was failing completely, but knowing she could only stall so long, she cleared her throat and said, "I want you guys to take a closer look at Ken Tobek."

"The engineer who tried to kill his wife?" Luke frowned. "He was alibied at the time of the shooting."

"By a friend, right?"

"Yeah, why?" Cole leaned toward her. "You have some new reason to suspect him? Did you remember something more from the day of the shooting?"

"No, but his brother-in-law owns a really old Taurus, along with a couple other vehicles. And the day of the shooting, he blew through a red light about five minutes away from Roy's Grocery. It was earlier in the day," she rushed on, "so it doesn't ruin his alibi, but maybe he was casing the place, knowing I usually get my groceries before the weekend starts."

"And you know this how exactly?" Luke asked.

"We don't want to know," Cole said quickly, glancing around like he was making sure no one had overheard.

He knew her hacking capabilities very well, because she'd used them for Andre when his girlfriend had been in danger. She smiled, trying to look innocent.

"Okay, we'll look into it," Cole promised. "But I want you to stay away from this case."

"I—"

"And if you're not locked in that lab, I want you in my sight." His tone was firm, almost angry, and intense. "No exceptions, and I don't care how many police officers are nearby—you got it? If they're not me or Luke, they don't count."

Luke laughed into the silence that followed. "Don't worry, Shaye. This is just Cole's way of saying you're important to him."

She expected Cole to scowl at his partner and walk her back to the lab. Instead he leaned close to her and whispered in her ear, his breath feathering across her skin. "He's right."

"PLEASE TELL ME Shaye hasn't been using her hacking skills to help us in investigations," Luke said.

Cole looked over at his partner and smiled. Most of their colleagues would probably assume Luke—the former Marine with the deadly stare who refused to wear anything but cargos and T-shirts to work—would be the rule bender. The reality was, of the two of them, Cole was more likely to use...unconventional methods. "No. But I knew she could do it. I asked her to help me out with a personal matter before, so I wasn't surprised."

"And by personal matter, you mean the hit men out to get Andre's girlfriend?" Luke asked, pulling their car to a stop at the curb in front of Ken Tobek's house.

"We weren't really worried about the chain of evidence," Cole replied, "so much as saving her life."

Luke nodded. "I hear you. But make sure Shaye watches her own trail. She should know better than anyone that if it's digital, it's traceable."

"Yeah, I know. I didn't ask her to do this one. I wouldn't have asked with Andre's case, but—"

"I get it. There were some strange circumstances there. But let's do this one by the book. We catch the person who's been coming after Shaye, and I want to be able to lock him up, not have him get out on an evidence technicality."

"Not a problem," Cole agreed, even though he didn't think he'd ever handled a case before this one where he honestly didn't care if the suspect ended up in handcuffs or a body bag.

He was way too emotionally invested. If he were really going by the book, he should recuse himself from the investigation because of a conflict of interest.

Cole grabbed Luke's arm as he started to open the

door. "Don't say anything about my relationship with Shaye, okay? I don't want it getting out until this is over."

"Couldn't even if I wanted to," Luke replied. "Until you gave her bedroom eyes in the bullpen, I thought you were still being an idiot about the whole thing."

"I am," Cole muttered under his breath as Luke got out of the car. He should probably have been embarrassed by his partner's description, but he wasn't. He'd made his decision, and he'd needed to act on it before he chickened out. Even if he didn't deserve her, maybe he could make her happy for a while. And then hopefully the ultimate fallout wouldn't destroy him.

It was ironic. He could run into gunfire, but he was scared to tell a woman how much he cared about her.

"You coming?" Luke called.

Cole climbed out of the car and followed his partner up the long drive to Tobek's house. The garage was shut, but there was a window. Cole took a quick detour to peer inside. "There's nothing in here but a Benz," he reported. "A new one."

"I just bought it."

The voice startled Cole, making his hand instinctively reach for his holster as he turned toward the voice.

"Why are you casing my place?" Tobek asked as he came around from the backyard, a pair of pruning shears in his hand. "Do I need to call the police?"

Luke flashed his badge. "We *are* the police. Could we come inside and talk to you for a few minutes, Mr. Tobek?"

The man stared at them a long minute, his lips pursed. He was the right build to be the shooter—average height and weight. He looked older than Cole remembered, his blond hair thinning, deep grooves under his eyes that a good night's sleep wasn't going to get rid of and horizontal lines from the corners of his lips downward, like he frowned often.

"You're the ones who arrested me and claimed I was trying to kill my wife." His voice was monotone, and Cole couldn't figure out if he'd just realized it or if he'd been pretending from the moment they'd showed up.

"Sir, we—" Luke started.

"I made a bad error in judgment that day. Got to drinking and let my anger get the best of me. She frustrates me so much, and she wouldn't stop—" He let out a long breath. "But I would never have truly hurt her."

Cole made a noncommittal noise. The words of a man who was still blaming his ex-wife for his violence didn't hold a lot of weight in his book. But would the guy have come after Shaye? It seemed like a stretch. A coward like that seemed unlikely to chase after the forensics expert on his case while she was in the back of a police car.

But Shaye thought there could be something here, so he couldn't discount it. "We just have a few quick questions, and then we'll be on our way."

Tobek hefted the pruning shears, grabbing the handle a little higher, and used the long blades to point toward the backyard. "We can sit out back. I'll answer your questions, I guess, but you're not welcome in my house. I did jail time, and you two were part of that."

Cole gave Luke a perplexed glance as they followed him. For someone with obvious rage issues, Tobek was oddly calm. He'd expected more anger, more resistance to a discussion, not this bizarre monotone. But maybe Tobek was medicated—it might explain some things.

Too bad Cole had no legitimate reason to go after that information.

A minute later, the three of them were settled at a huge wrought iron table that looked expensive and struck Cole as sort of sad, since the man now lived alone. But maybe he entertained a lot.

"We just want to ask you about last Friday night," Luke began.

"Are you kidding me?" Tobek snapped, then rolled his eyes. "Someone from the station already called about this. I mean, what exactly are you accusing me of?"

"We're not accusing you of anything," Cole said calmly, interested that this question had gotten a little emotion from the guy. "This is just a standard interview to knock you off a list."

Tobek's eyes narrowed. "What kind of list?"

"Someone came after a state employee, so we have to get alibis from anyone connected to her cases," Luke said. "So how about you help us out by giving us yours so we can move on?"

"I already did," Tobek said tightly, then settled back into his seat, as though he wanted them to think he didn't care they were questioning him again. "I had drinks with a guy from work, okay? I was at his place all evening. Check with him if you want."

"A friend of yours?" Cole asked.

Tobek shrugged. "Not really, no. But he's sort of new to the area, and he doesn't know a lot of people. He asked and I didn't want to be rude, so I said yes. To be honest, I think he asked a lot of people, but I guess I was the only one who agreed to go. It was a little last minute, and I happened to be free."

"What time did you get there? And what time did

you leave?" Luke asked. "And did anyone else see you that night?"

"Jeez," Tobek said. "What is this? I need to make sure I'm around people all the time now because of one little mistake over a year ago? No, no one else saw me. I drove home after work, got home...I don't know, maybe six fifteen? Then I ate a quick dinner and I was at his place by seven thirty. I got home late, after midnight. The guy's a talker."

"What did you talk about?"

"What didn't we talk about? Work, life, women."

"What did you drive to his place?" Cole asked.

Tobek made a face. "You were just ogling it. My Mercedes. How many cars do you think I own?"

"Not an old Taurus?" Cole persisted, watching Tobek closely.

He squinted, shook his head, then spoke purposely slowly. "Why would I drive an old Taurus when I just bought a Mercedes?" He glanced at Luke, then back at Cole, and stood up. "Listen, I don't know what this is about—I don't even know your *state employee*—and I'm finished answering your bizarre questions. If you're fishing around, trying to get something on me, don't bother. I made one mistake. One. I paid my debt. It's over."

He pointed toward the front of the house, using the sharp end of the pruning shears he had clutched in his hand tightly enough to make his knuckles white. "Now get out."

SHE SHOULDN'T BE doing this.

Shaye glanced at the door again, even though she knew it was tightly shut. She was back in Cole's guest bedroom, but instead of Cole outside the room, it was Marcos. Cole had dropped her at his house after work, waited for Marcos to come and babysit her while he and Luke ran down her theory.

She felt a little bad about leaving Marcos to entertain himself when he was here keeping her safe, but an idea had struck on the drive back and refused to let go. So she'd claimed a headache and told Marcos she wanted to lie down for a while. His eyes had narrowed a little, like he could tell she was lying, but he'd simply nodded and let her go.

Now here she was, on her trusty tablet again, pulling up files she had no business accessing. But at least most of these were public record. This time, it wasn't so much that she was breaking the law to get information, more that she might be breaking Cole's trust.

He hadn't asked her to help him. But the words he'd spoken yesterday morning, when she'd woken up to him sitting on the edge of her bed had been haunting her ever since. *"I woke up and the house was on fire."* Then later in the conversation, he'd told her the fire had been ruled an accident. But the way he'd said it…

He didn't believe it.

And if someone had purposely set a house on fire with Cole and his brothers inside, she didn't care how many years it had been. She wanted answers for them.

Newspaper reports about the incident were surprisingly low on details: a house had burned to the ground around dawn. No one had died, but eight people had been inside at the time, including two adults and six foster kids, ranging in age from seventeen to eleven.

The images that went along with one of those reports made Shaye's heart ache for Cole. There were two shots:

one where the fire was still in progress and firefighters were attempting to put it out, and another once the fire had been doused. The second one showed a shell of a home, burned out and totally unsalvageable. The first one showed flames seeming to shoot from the ground all the way up past the roof on the second story. She couldn't believe everyone had made it out of that fire.

She dug for information for another hour, then glanced at her closed door. If Marcos was anything like his older brother, he'd come check on her soon and make sure she was okay. Time to move on to less public records.

Thankfully, the fire department in the town where Cole had lived had digitized their old records, and their security was a joke. She pulled up the arson investigation report on the fire and read through it, frowning.

Point of origin had been a study on the first floor. Apparently candles had been left burning and melted onto the enormous amount of paperwork Cole's foster dad kept on his desk. From there, it had been a quick jump to the curtains, which had been homemade and not even close to fire retardant. The investigation determined that from the time the fire started until the house was completely engulfed had been less than twenty minutes.

Shaye swore again, louder this time, and Marcos's voice came through the door, "Shaye, is everything okay?"

"Yeah, sorry. Headache is actually feeling better. I'll be out soon."

There was a pause, then: "Whatever you're up to, just call me if you need help, okay?"

"Okay," she said weakly, embarrassed she was so

transparent. She heard his footsteps moving away, and she stared down at her tablet.

Twenty minutes. Twenty minutes for eight people to run out of that house, where any pause or delay could have cost them their lives. And Cole had stopped twice, once for each of his brothers.

The sob caught her unexpectedly, and Shaye took a deep breath. She looked up at the ceiling and said a quick prayer of thanks that she'd gotten to meet Cole at all.

And maybe she'd misunderstood his tone when he'd told her about the report. Because the arson investigation looked solid from what she knew about those things. There were no signs that the fire had been intentionally set. Except...

Shaye frowned and clicked on a linked file, an addendum that had been added only a week ago. Then her breath caught again as she read through the new information.

Cole was right. The fire that had been set all those years ago *hadn't* been an accident.

Chapter Fifteen

"How did it go?" Shaye met Cole anxiously at the door as soon as he walked in. Marcos stood more slowly behind her.

She tried to hide her nerves from both of them, but the way she was wringing her hands was probably a dead giveaway that something was wrong. Marcos had definitely noticed when she'd come out from the guest bedroom an hour ago. But she'd wanted to talk to Cole about what she'd found first, then let him be the one to tell his brothers.

She tried to focus on what he'd expect her to want to know. After he and Luke had dropped her off here a few hours ago, they'd taken off again to talk to Ken Tobek.

The more she'd thought about it, the more strongly she felt about him as a possible suspect. When she'd given her testimony in court, he'd sat impassively, probably trying to appear innocent and apologetic. But when she'd passed him in the hallway afterward, the way he'd narrowed his eyes at her, almost snarling…it still gave her chills.

Cole sidestepped her, closing and locking the door behind him. Then he took her hand and pulled her toward the couch, earning a raised eyebrow from Marcos.

Shaye's pulse started a crescendo. She'd been trying not to dwell on that lustful look Cole had given her back at the station, but it had been hard not to, even while she'd been distracting herself looking up information on the fire. But that didn't mean she wanted a repeat in front of someone else.

So, for now, she focused on her case. She'd worry about giving Cole the bad news about the fire later. "What did Tobek say? Did you see the Taurus?"

Cole settled on the couch, keeping his hand tucked in hers as Marcos sat back on the chair, looking curious but keeping quiet. "He denied it, of course. He still blames everyone else for what he did, but there's no sign of the Taurus. And his alibi looks solid. We spoke to the coworker who alibied him, too, after we saw Tobek. That guy seems to be generally nervous, so it's hard to tell what spooked him or didn't, but I can't see any reason for him to lie for Tobek."

"Maybe he's being paid," Shaye suggested.

"We laid into him pretty good, trying to scare him about what would happen about lying during a police investigation, but he stuck to his story. And his and Tobek's were consistent. Plus this guy is young—about fifteen years younger than Tobek. Jumps at his own shadow. I think he would have broken if Tobek had paid him off."

Cole's thumb started absently stroking her hand. "We'll keep digging, talk to the brother-in-law about the Taurus, but we need to check into other suspects. I don't like Tobek, but I'm not sure he'd risk trying to gun someone down in public. Honestly, he strikes me as the kind of guy who hits his wife behind closed doors and then goes out and chats up his neighbors. Following a police car to get to you? I don't know."

"Do any of the other suspects look promising?" Marcos spoke up.

Shaye had almost forgotten he was there, the way Cole's thumb was sliding over the sensitive skin on the back of her hand. She'd almost forgotten *everything* she needed to be thinking about right now.

Cole's shoulders slumped. "Not really. But we've broadened the list, trying to look at anyone remotely connected to Shaye. This guy holds a personal grudge, which means he's connected to a case or connected to her. We'll find him."

"Let me know if I can help," Marcos said, standing up and stretching his arms. His gaze dropped to their linked hands. "I'm going to head home and let you two be alone."

"Thanks," Cole said, dropping her hand to give his brother a hug and walk him to the door.

Then he was sliding the lock and leaning against the closed door, the expression on his face pure hunger. And 100 percent directed at her.

Shaye's breathing went shallow as two years' worth of daydreams about Cole Walker suddenly seemed possible. She tried to shake it off, tried to focus. She had something important she needed to tell him, but the longer he looked at her, the more her mind seemed to go fuzzy and her body took over.

"Shaye," Cole said, his voice huskier than usual as he pushed away from the door and headed toward her.

There was no doubt about it. He was going to kiss her.

But had anything really changed? Last night he'd

told her nothing could ever happen between them. So what was going on? Was this supposed to be a onetime thing? And if she had a fling with him, would she ever recover from the heartbreak? Could she even do anything without first coming clean about what she'd just discovered about his past?

He kept coming, slowly, purposefully, and she knew she had to make up her mind.

"Cole," she said, and her own voice didn't sound quite right, either. "I—"

He watched her carefully, waiting for whatever she was going to say.

And then she made up her mind.

COLE COULD SEE it the instant Shaye made a decision. If only he knew what choice she'd made. She was giving him mixed signals, still eyeing him like she wanted to swallow him whole, but with one hand up. Not that he could complain too much after the mixed signals he'd been giving her. Still, he hoped the whole eating-him-alive thing won out.

"I have to tell you something," Shaye said, her voice wobbly as she dropped her hand.

A satisfied smile threatened, because he knew why she was struggling to speak. But he held it in and asked, "Is it about us?"

Furrows appeared between her eyebrows. "Not exactly. It's about the past—"

"Unless it's about you and me and all the ways I'd like to show you how stupid I've been these past few days with my lips and my tongue, let's save it for later, okay?"

"Uh…" She gave a nervous laugh, and he took a step closer.

Cole let his gaze drop over her, from the top of those curls piled on her head, down over the simple blue blouse and black pants that hugged her in all the right places. He came back up just as slowly, lingering on the spots he was desperate to kiss, until he met her eyes.

She was staring back wide-eyed, desire and uncertainty battling.

He took another step; all he'd have to do was reach out his hand and he'd be touching her. But he resisted, waiting, hoping she'd give him the okay to do all the things he'd been dreaming about since the moment he'd first seen her. The longer he'd known her, those dreams had gotten more detailed and more intense.

"What happened?" she whispered, her voice suddenly scratchy. She licked her lips, and his eyes were glued to the movement.

"What do you mean?"

"Yesterday you said—"

"Yesterday I was being an idiot."

"You've changed your mind?" She reached out tentatively, let her hand glide over the buttons on his shirt, barely touching him, but sending desire zigzagging through his body.

He wanted to lie and say yes, because he sensed that one word was all it would take to get him to heaven. But he couldn't do that. "Depends what you mean."

She frowned. "I mean about you saying we were too different to make a relationship last."

"I still think that."

She dropped her hand away from his body.

"But I'm willing to try anyway."

"I don't understand." The desire in her gaze was starting to clear, replaced by confusion and wariness.

"I still think that long-term, our differences are going to get in the way." He took her hand, slid his fingers between hers. It was such a perfect fit. "But you were right, too, when you said we'd be good together. I think we would."

She pulled her hand free slowly. "Cole, I—I've never had a fling with anyone."

"That's—"

"Hear me out. I care about you a lot, and I know myself. As much as I may want you, I don't think I can go into a one-night—"

"That's not what I'm asking for," Cole cut her off, not wanting her to think for a second that he'd expect one night and nothing more. As if one taste of Shaye would be enough.

Would any amount of Shaye be enough? The thought made panic flutter briefly, but he pushed it down. "I'm in this for as long as you are. I promise you that."

She stared at him, and the seconds drew out as he tried to read her gaze. Then he didn't have to, because she launched herself into his arms.

COLE'S ARMS LOCKED around her waist. No sooner had she lifted up on her tiptoes than his mouth was crashing down on hers. He kissed her with desperation, like he'd been waiting to do it for years, nipping at her lips with his teeth, licking at them with his tongue, his soft beard rasping against her chin. The moment she sighed and opened her mouth, his tongue slipped inside, and Shaye's knees buckled.

He bent low, scooped one hand under her knees and

lifted her. Then they were moving, and Shaye didn't care where, just as long as it was somewhere horizontal so she could feel his whole body pressed to hers and ease the ache inside her. He kept kissing her as they walked, frantic, passionate kisses that matched exactly the need she felt. Only it still wasn't enough.

Sliding her hands through his hair, she got distracted by the softness of it, the contrast to the slick feel of his tongue exploring her mouth so thoroughly and the hardness of his chest against her side. Then he was laying her down, and she opened her eyes, realizing she was in his bedroom.

She gave herself a brief moment to glance around, curious, since she'd been too distracted by worry last time she'd been in here. She took in the framed family pictures on his dresser, the clothes stacked on a chair in the corner like he hadn't had time to put them away. The walls were a light blue, almost the color of Cole's eyes, and she looked back at him.

He was still standing beside the bed, a soft smile on his face unlike any smile she'd ever seen from him. There was desire in it, but something more, something tender.

And suddenly she knew what his words had meant.

She was in love with him, but yesterday she'd tried to convince herself she was strong enough to move on. And she would have been; she'd proven it to herself when she'd been about to turn down his offer, thinking it was for one night. His words in the living room had confused her at first. How could he be completely committed to a relationship if he was still sure they were too different to last? But now she understood. He'd said he was in it as long as she was—he was just certain *she'd* eventually get tired of *him*.

He hadn't rejected her yesterday because he'd been uninterested in a relationship with her; he'd rejected her because he'd been scared of one.

But right now, with him staring at her with that softness in his eyes, like he'd do anything for her, she realized something else. He loved her, too. He probably didn't even know it yet, but he did. She was suddenly certain of that fact.

Her heart started beating even faster, and then he was climbing onto the bed with her, carefully lowering himself on top of her. Her body arched up to meet him, and a low moan escaped at the first feel of him against her, at the sheer giddiness of knowing how deeply he cared for her.

He groaned in response. "Shaye," he whispered. "You're killing my self-control here."

The idea that she could have that effect on him made her feel powerful and intensely happy. She wiggled her hips a little, giving him a devious grin.

He smiled back at her, laughter in the quirk of his lips. Then his fingers were threading with hers, lifting them up over her head. She expected his mouth to dive back to hers, and she craned her neck, reaching for him, but he didn't meet her. Instead he bent his head to her neck, then her ear, making her squirm.

She tugged her hands free, needing to feel him, and then his hands were buried in her hair, yanking out the bun. He combed through it with his fingers, spreading her hair over the pillow behind her, all the while doing things to her earlobe with his tongue that made spots form in front of her eyes.

Sliding her hands down over his back, she tried to get underneath his button-down, to better feel all the muscles that had rippled under her touch. She couldn't quite reach, so she grabbed a handful of his shirt and tugged it upward.

Cole swore, then moved her hands and stood up. "Sorry, honey. You're making it hard to think straight." He unhooked the holster from his belt and stuck it in his bedside table, then he was getting back into bed, but this time he pulled her on top of him.

"Oh." Shaye twined her legs with his, liking the feel of him underneath her. She scooted up on her elbows, so she could undo the buttons on his shirt, and he used the opportunity to tackle hers. Before she had his half unbuttoned, he was sliding the sleeves down her arms, yanking them away from him. "Hey!"

"Mmm," Cole murmured, his gaze locked on the blue silk bra she was suddenly very happy she'd decided to put on this morning.

Then his hands were sliding around her waist, and she found herself being pulled upward. Shaye caught herself on the pillow, laughing. "What are you…" She trailed off on a moan as his tongue slid under the edge of her bra.

"You taste good," he mumbled against her skin, and her whole body seemed to heat up another couple of degrees.

Hooking her thighs around him, she pulled herself back downward, fusing her mouth to his, desperate for the feel of his lips against hers again. Then she was up on her knees, with him sitting under her. She rocked against him, fumbling to get her hands between them again to finish his buttons. Finally she had them undone, and she could slide her palms up and down his chest and abs.

Muscles contracted under her every touch, and then he was tugging her knees, pulling her tighter against him until she tipped her head back and moaned. His lips returned to her neck, then worked their way downward again. She felt cool air on the back of her thighs and realized he'd managed to undo the hooks on her pants and slip them down to her knees.

She could barely breathe as he slid one of her bra straps down, trailing his hand with his mouth, while the other hand cupped her butt, the imprint of him hot through her silk panties. She sank down on his lap and then his mouth was on hers again, the pace of his kisses increasing as his hands slid up and down her body. His hands moved slowly, like he was learning every inch of her—or just trying to drive her even crazier.

She was going to make love to Cole Walker. And wow, was the reality turning out to be even better than any of the thousands of fantasies she'd had about him over the past two years.

"Shaye," he breathed, like he was right in tune with her, feeling the same thing.

Then his phone rang, making her jump as it vibrated against her butt. He tugged her back down, ignoring it, his fingers slipping under the waistband of her panties as she reached for his belt.

It stopped ringing, then started up again almost immediately. Cole swore, lifted her off him like she weighed nothing and dug in his pocket, struggling to yank out his phone. "What?" he snapped as he answered it.

The volume must have been turned up high, because

Luke's voice came through clearly as he laughed. "Uh, sorry. Am I interrupting something? Because I've got a lot of news."

"Yes, you're interrupting something," Cole said tightly. "Is this a lot of news I have to hear right this second?"

"Yeah, I'm afraid so."

The desire slipped off Cole's face, replaced by what Shaye had come to think of as his detective expression. "What is it?"

"Well, first, Elliard escaped custody at the hospital."

"What?" Cole swiped his hand across his forehead, glancing at her. His gaze wandered downward and she realized the desire was still there; it was just hidden. "Do we have people looking for him?"

"Yeah, but there's more, and this is the main reason I called. Remember that anonymous tip we got the other day about a gun in the water near the Kings' territory?"

"What about it?"

"They ran it at the lab. Cole, it's the gun that was used to shoot at Shaye."

Chapter Sixteen

"Can we just hit Pause on this?" Cole asked, his eyes glued to her. "Maybe you could wait here, just like this, until I get back?"

Shaye was leaning up against his headboard, her hair loose around her shoulders and a mess from his fingers. Her shirt was gone, somewhere on his floor, and one of her bra straps dangled down her shoulder. She'd tugged her pants back up but hadn't bothered to button them, and he could still see a hint of the underwear he'd been about to slide down when Luke had called.

A thousand swearwords lodged in his throat at the idea of leaving, but this was big news. The gun being found in Kings territory meant that Leonardo was probably lying. Either he *had* okayed Elliard going after Shaye, or he'd okayed the rest of his gang helping Elliard get revenge on the station. On him.

All of *that* meant that Cole wanted every last Kings member rounded up and at the station immediately.

"How long do you plan to be gone?" Shaye asked, her voice suggestive, like she was actually considering waiting in his bed for him in her underwear until he returned.

Cole's body reacted immediately, and he seriously

considered calling Luke back and saying he'd be at the station in an hour. But half an hour with Shaye wasn't going to be nearly good enough, and especially not the first time. "I wish I was serious about you waiting right here," he said. "But this will probably take all night."

Her shoulders slumped, and he climbed into bed, crawling toward her, then planting a long kiss on her lips. "But this is almost over now. We have the gun. We're going to bring everyone in and keep them there until someone talks." He lifted her hand to his lips, pressed a kiss to her palm. "And then I'm going to lock the door, turn off the phone and stay in bed with you for an entire day. What do you think?"

"I like it," she replied, a little breathless. "Now hurry."

Cole laughed. "Yes, ma'am." He got out of bed, already missing her, and redid his belt. Forgoing the shirt she'd tossed on the floor, he grabbed a clean one and buttoned it up, then looked at his watch and frowned. "I'm going to see which of my brothers can head back over here."

"Just go," Shaye said. "Leave your poor brothers alone. This guy doesn't know where you live, or he would have already been here."

"Yeah, well, Elliard is on the run, so I'm not taking any chances."

"If Elliard was the shooter, he couldn't even figure out where *I* live, and my personal information is easier to find than yours," Shaye said.

It wouldn't surprise him if she had looked, given her computer skills.

"Well, I'm calling them anyway," Cole said, grabbing his cell and trying Andre first. When Andre picked up, he told Cole he'd just been called out for a mission. "Stay safe," Cole told him, then called Marcos.

"Sorry to ask you to turn right back around," Cole said.

"No problem," Marcos replied, sounding tired. "Be there in twenty."

Cole hung up, then sat back down on the bed with Shaye. "How do you feel about some good old-fashioned necking while we wait for Marcos?" he teased her, wiggling his eyebrows.

But Shaye looked serious all of a sudden.

"Don't worry. I'll be careful, and we're close. I can feel it," he told her.

"It's not that," Shaye said, scooting closer and taking his hand. "I need to tell you something."

"What?" Nerves overtook him. What had she said before? "Something about the past?"

"Yeah. I know I didn't ask you first, and I hope you're not going to be upset, but I looked up information about the fire."

A jolt went through him. Shaye had always been able to pull things from digital devices, from the vastness of the internet, that no one else he knew could find.

His throat went dry. "What did you discover?"

She squeezed his hand. "It wasn't an accident."

"Are you sure? How do you know?" Before she could answer, he sighed and dropped his head. "It was Andre who brought it up, during his girlfriend's case you helped us with. He had this dream and—" Cole broke off, swearing. "He remembered that our foster dad and one of the foster kids came from the back office, where the fire started. It was the middle of the night—well, nearing dawn, I guess, but it felt like the middle of the night. Everyone should have been up-stairs asleep."

"But they weren't," Shaye said, and he wasn't sure if it was a statement or a question.

"No. It actually wasn't the fire that woke me exactly. It was the noise. My foster mom yelling, then I saw her run past my room, out of her bedroom at the end of the hall. And then the other two foster brothers we lived with—I can't even remember their names anymore, but I shared a room with them. They were falling out of bed and running. And I got up and..."

He let out a heavy breath as the memories overtook him, the sheer panic, the unbearable heat, the smoke that made it hard to breathe. Then desperation to get to Andre and Marcos in the bedroom down the hall.

"You did it," Shaye said softly, somehow even closer than she'd been before, although he hadn't felt her move. "You got them out."

"Sort of," he said. "We lost Marcos on the way down the stairs. I thought he was behind us still, but—"

"But he made it," she reminded him, stroking his arm. "They're both okay."

"Yeah." His jaw tightened. "But it could have turned out different. Who set the fire? My foster dad?"

"No." Shaye shook her head. "Another foster kid. Brenna Hartwell. There was a juvenile record attached to the old arson report that had just been unsealed this week. It says she set it for kicks, and it got out of hand."

Cole frowned, angry and sad at the same time. "Brenna was eleven. We considered that she set it, that maybe something bad was happening with our foster dad we didn't know about, since they were back there together, but she did it for fun?" He sighed heavily as the doorbell rang. "Marcos isn't going to take this well. She was his first crush."

"I'm sorry," Shaye said.

He kissed her forehead. "Thanks for caring about me enough to look into this. I don't like the answers, but at least I know."

Then he stood. "Now I'm going to go and get some answers for you."

SHAYE PACED BACK and forth in Cole's bedroom. She'd been unable to sit still waiting with Marcos in the living room, but she hadn't wanted to show him just how nervous she was. She'd claimed exhaustion and headed for the bedroom.

She'd debated a minute in the hallway whether to return to the guest room or just wait in Cole's, and she'd finally decided on his room. He'd suggested she stay here anyway, and even though he'd been half joking, she knew he wouldn't mind. Besides, this way Marcos would have somewhere to sleep besides the couch if Cole was at the station late. Which she suspected he would be, since he was literally bringing in an entire gang.

She couldn't believe she was back here again, with a gang threat over her head. *Another day, another gang.* She let out a choked laugh at the thought, but the reality was the fear she'd been trying so hard to battle was returning with a vengeance.

It was like a year ago in replay: she was hiding again while Cole was out there putting himself in danger, trying to keep her safe. She prayed he could pull off the same miracle twice.

"You okay in there, Shaye?" Marcos's voice came through the door.

"Yeah, sorry. I'm a little stressed out. I'm going to go to bed."

"Don't worry," Marcos said. "Do what you need to do. If you need company, I'm here, okay?"

"Thanks." The word came out garbled as she choked up a little. Cole's brothers had treated her like family since the moment Cole had first introduced her to them.

His footsteps echoed as he walked back to the living room and Shaye locked the door just so he wouldn't come back and check on her while she was changing. She stripped out of her clothes, grabbed a T-shirt off the pile on Cole's chair and slipped it over her head, breathing in the scent of his laundry detergent.

Then she crawled into his bed and closed her eyes, hoping when she opened them again, he'd be climbing in beside her.

The *creak* pulled her partway out of sleep, and she rolled over, still groggy, her hand reaching for the other side of the bed. But it was cold and empty.

Sleep pulled at her again, a dream where Cole was home and safe and all the threats facing him in his job every day no longer existed. But why did he smell like he'd been drinking? Shaye sniffed and frowned.

Then there was another *creak*, and she realized it was coming from the wrong direction to be Marcos.

She opened her eyes, shooting up in bed, her hand reaching out instinctively for something to grab as a weapon, searching for a lamp on the bedside table. She struck a mug, and it slipped off, hitting the floor and shattering.

She blinked in the darkness, thinking she'd been

imagining a threat, when she was yanked out of bed and a hand clamped down over her mouth. The scent of liquor seemed to surround her, acrid in her nostrils.

Shaye flailed, kicking, trying to elbow her assailant as she heard Marcos's footsteps pounding toward the room.

Then something cold and sharp pressed against her neck, and a deep voice whispered in her ear. "Make him walk away or I slice you open right here."

Going completely still was her only option as she identified the object at her throat. A knife. A very big, very sharp knife. Every breath made it push into her skin, threatening to break through.

"Shaye! You okay?" Marcos called.

"Do it," the voice whispered, sending shivers down her arms.

"I'm fine," Shaye called, but her voice came out weak and shaky, because with each word she could feel the knife's edge more.

The man behind her—someone not much taller than her but with a lot more strength than his size suggested—moved the knife to give her a little space.

The doorknob started to turn, then caught because she'd locked it.

"He leaves or you're not the only one to die," the man growled in her ear, his mouth moving against her skin in a way that was making her desperate to squirm away from him.

His arm shifted alongside her. When she looked down, she saw a pistol in his gloved hand, pointing at the door.

The handle stopped moving, and Shaye knew what

was coming next. Marcos would kick it down. And Marcos would die.

She'd always been a bad liar. Shaye closed her eyes and risked precious seconds taking a calming breath. "Sorry about that," she called out, her voice clear and calm. "I had a bad dream and knocked over Cole's coffee mug."

There was a pause. "Why's the door locked?"

"I, um—" She tried to sound embarrassed. "I got hot and went to bed in my underwear."

There was low laughter in the hallway, and relief slumped Shaye's shoulders. "You're going to make my brother really happy. He's on his way back."

"In case I'm asleep when he gets in," Shaye said quickly as the knife pressed hard against her neck again, "tell him…"

She paused so long that Marcos just said softly, "He knows, Shaye."

"Tell him I was right," she rushed on quickly, as the voice in her ear suddenly clicked into place and she thought she recognized it. *Maybe.*

"Right about what?" Marcos asked, a hint of concern creeping back in.

"His bed is more comfortable than mine," she said, and the knife eased up again.

There was more soft laughter from the hall. "I'll let him know. Good night, Shaye."

"Good night."

The footsteps headed away again. The voice whispered in her ear. "Good job. Now keep following directions, and I won't have to kill him *or* your boyfriend."

He spun her around and she realized what the noises she'd heard earlier were: he'd cut a hole in the window and then opened it, climbing inside that way. Now he pushed her toward it, in her bare feet and Cole's T-shirt. "You're going first. And remember—I have a gun. So I wouldn't try making a run for it."

Shaye swallowed hard, her gaze darting to the closed door, the scent of alcohol—was it whiskey?—so strong it was making her gag. But she still couldn't make out the face of her abductor, only pray that she was right about his voice sounding familiar. Because otherwise, if Marcos and Cole managed to decipher her clue, she'd be sending them in the wrong direction.

The knife jabbed her in the back, pricking through the T-shirt and into her skin. She muffled a yelp, then climbed carefully out the window.

He was outside behind her before she could even consider making a run for it, and then he was shoving her along to a sedan parked at the curb. He popped the trunk. "Get in."

She started to turn toward him, and that knife jabbed her again, sending tears to her eyes. There was no question: if she climbed into this trunk right now, she was going to die.

She hesitated briefly, then climbed inside.

Chapter Seventeen

"How'd it go?" Marcos greeted Cole when he came home.

Cole sighed, kicking off his shoes and sinking onto the couch beside his brother. "Not great. We rounded up the whole gang and put them all into holding or interrogation rooms. Luke and I leaned on them pretty hard, but they're more scared of Leonardo than us."

"That's not surprising," Marcos said. "That guy has a reputation."

"Yeah, I know, but I was hoping that someone would be scared enough of *us* after what we did to their competition to talk. Honestly, I thought we had a shot with Leonardo himself handing over the shooter."

"Where are they now?" Marcos asked. "You have to let them all go?"

Cole gave a halfhearted grin. "Nope. We figured out a way to hang on to them all for now. We'll see if a night in jail makes them realize we're not giving up until the Kings go the way of the Jannis Crew if they don't give us some answers."

"Your girl has been in bed for a while."

"Good. I figured as much when she didn't greet me at the door. She's a worrier."

"It can't be easy, dating someone in law enforcement," Marcos said.

"Yeah, I guess not." It was something he'd worried about from the start with Shaye; it wasn't fair to drag her into that kind of life. Cole rested his head on the back of the couch, still anxious to go join Shaye, but wanting to decompress a little first. He knew she'd wake up and he'd need to reassure her he was fine.

"Especially after what she went through last year."

Cole lifted his head, looking at his brother. "Did she say something to you?"

"No. But she was a ball of nerves all evening. She finally went and hid in your room so she could pace in there without me seeing."

A small smile lifted the corners of his lips. "That sounds like Shaye."

"By the way, she told me to tell you she was right about your bed being more comfortable than hers."

"What?" Cole shook his head, perplexed. Had she ever said something like that? He didn't think so, but then he'd been so focused on getting his lips and hands on her, maybe he'd missed it.

"I should go," Marcos said, standing. "Let you go reassure her you're okay."

"You're welcome to stay," Cole said. "Save the drive for the morning."

"Nah. I'll let you two have some privacy. A word of advice though, big brother? Hang on to that one. For a computer nerd, she's pretty special." He grinned.

Cole swore.

"I'm just kidding about the computer nerd thing."

"No, it's not that. Sit down for a second, would you?"

Marcos sat, looking wary. "Why? What's going on?"

Cole shifted to face his brother, knowing he needed to tell Marcos now, instead of delaying things. "Shaye did some digging into our past."

There was a long pause, and then Marcos tensed and shook his head, surely realizing why Cole looked so grim right now. They'd talked about the possibility that Brenna was involved when Andre had first realized the fire might not be accidental. "I don't believe it."

"There was an unsealed juvie record, Marcos. She admitted she did it."

"She must have had a reason. Maybe—"

"She said she did it for fun, and things got out of hand."

"Then why was our foster father down there? No, I don't buy it."

"He probably heard something and caught her doing it," Cole said. "I'm sorry. I know you had a crush on her when we were kids."

"She was so alone. So sad," Marcos said, looking sad himself. "I can't believe—"

"I'm sorry," Cole repeated. "I just wanted you to know."

"Have you told Andre yet?"

"No, but I'll give him a call tomorrow."

Marcos clapped a hand on his shoulder and stood again. "You have enough on your plate. I can do it."

"That's not—"

"It's fine," Marcos said, but his usual nothing-gets-me-down expression was gone, looking like someone had given it a solid kick. "Say good-night to Shaye for me."

Cole walked him to the door, his heart heavy as he closed it behind Marcos. Then he headed for the bedroom, anxious to curl up beside Shaye and get a little sleep.

Never let anyone lock you in the trunk.

Shaye was pretty sure that was safety rule number one. When she'd gotten inside, she hadn't seen any other options. There was nowhere to run that her abductor wouldn't be able to shoot her. And then Marcos would run outside, and what if he got shot, too?

If it had been just her, she might have risked it over whatever this guy had planned for her whenever they got where they were going. But she couldn't risk Cole's brother.

But now she wished she'd tried *something*. What exactly she could have tried, she still wasn't sure.

The car bounced over something at a speed high enough she knew they must have been on a freeway. Shaye bounced with it, her head banging against the trunk even as she tried to brace herself. Then she rolled, slamming into one side and then the other. Tears stung her eyes, but at least there was nothing else in the trunk to hit. Of course, if there had been, maybe she could have armed herself for when the vehicle eventually stopped.

Even thinking about what might be coming made her panic, and she started to hyperventilate. Shaye closed her eyes, bracing her feet and hands on either end of the trunk as she focused on taking deep breaths. It was awkward and hard to get a good angle the way she was folded in here, but the next time he ran over something—what the heck was on this freeway?—she didn't move as much.

Her hands and feet started to ache, and the places he'd pricked her with the knife stung. It was pitch-black, so she had no idea how badly she was hurt. Before he'd gotten moving so fast, she'd probed at the wounds, trying to find out. She was definitely bleeding, but as much as they hurt, she didn't think it was bad. It wouldn't be those injuries that would kill her.

Calm down, Shaye reminded herself, trying to think. She had no weapons. No idea where she was going. And she was in bare feet and Cole's T-shirt, which kept riding up past her underwear as she was tossed around the trunk. A thousand new worst-case scenarios ran through her mind.

Kick out the taillights.

The idea flashed through her mind out of nowhere, and she remembered a case she'd read about in graduate school where a girl who'd been kidnapped had done that. She'd still been killed by her captor, but her DNA on the broken taillight he'd later had fixed had landed him in jail.

Shaye shifted, trying to reposition herself as she searched for the taillights. But all she felt was carpeting. Except…

She pried at a seam with her fingernails and it peeled away. Part of one fingernail broke off and the forensic specialist in her thought about how, as long as he didn't vacuum too carefully, that piece of her could convict him if she wasn't around to do it.

Stop it, Shaye silently yelled at herself, but it was hard not to think about her death. She didn't know why he hadn't simply killed her at Cole's house—except maybe that would make it too difficult to get away. But she had no doubt that was his intention.

"The taillight," Shaye muttered. She was so panicked, she wasn't thinking right. She felt around behind the cover she'd broken off and there it was: the back of the taillight! Excitement filled her and Shaye tried to shove the light out with her hands, but it didn't budge.

She blinked back the tears that filled her eyes, then scooted around again until her feet were positioned over the taillight. Knowing it was going to be painful with her bare feet, she closed her eyes, braced herself and then kicked with all her might.

The taillight snapped free, shooting out of the car, and Shaye's right foot slammed the metal edge while her left one went partially through it, bending her toes at an impossible angle. She screamed at the pain that raced up her leg, but didn't waste any time before spinning around again.

Ignoring the throbbing, she put her eye up to the hole. If she could stick her hand out and wave, maybe another car on the freeway would see her and call the police.

But when she peered outside, all she saw was darkness, and she realized that she'd been so focused on her plan she hadn't noticed the car slowing. They were no longer on the freeway.

The car made a turn, then came to a stop and the engine turned off.

Shaye made one last desperate search for a weapon, her hands tracing over the whole trunk. They grasped the cover of the taillight. It was pathetic and flimsy, but it was all she had.

Holding in tears, she gripped it in both hands as the trunk slowly opened.

Chapter Eighteen

"Shaye?" Cole tried not to panic. She'd undoubtedly been exhausted, so maybe she'd fallen into an especially heavy sleep.

But he'd been knocking on the door for more than a minute, and he was practically yelling her name now. He took a deep breath and hoped she'd forgive him, then stepped back and leveled a hard kick at the door, right beside the doorknob, like he'd do if he had to break down a door at a suspect's house.

It splintered, and a quick jab with his shoulder pushed it the rest of the way in. It hung off the frame, revealing an empty room.

Shaye was gone.

Now the panic had free rein as he took in his bedroom. His covers were rumpled, the comforter half on the floor. There was a broken mug beside his bed. Had there been a struggle? But if so, why hadn't his brother heard anything?

His blood pressure rising by the second, Cole grabbed his cell phone and texted Marcos a quick message: Get back here now.

Then he went to the window, noticing the glass on the ground, along with a little bit of blood. The window was closed, and there was a neat circle cut into the glass, made by the type of tool a professional would have.

Cole unholstered his weapon and ran to the front door. He whipped it open and was just clearing his porch when Marcos's car screeched to a stop at his curb. Then his brother was running toward him.

"What is it?" Marcos asked, drawing his own weapon.

"Shaye is gone."

"What?" Marcos shook his head. "I talked to her less than an hour ago. She was in your room. She sounded…"

"What?" Cole spun to face his brother.

"She sounded odd at first. I almost broke down the door, and then she said everything was fine. We had a conversation through the door." He swore. "You think someone was in there with her?"

"I don't know." Cole checked the immediate area for any unfamiliar cars. "Follow me. Let's check the back. She went out the window. Someone definitely came in from outside. If we don't see anything there, we get Luke and the rest of my department down here."

"I've got your back," Marcos said as the two of them rounded the corner of the house, making their way quickly to the window outside Cole's bedroom.

Cole used his phone to shine a light at the ground. "More glass, but just a little." He shook his head as he glanced around. His house backed up to his neighbors' yards. An unlikely route for a kidnapper. "He must have had a car waiting. She could be anywhere by now."

"I'm so sorry," Marcos said. "I can't believe I didn't—"

"It's not your fault," Cole said, and he meant it. His

brother was good at his job, and if he hadn't realized someone had come into the house, the guy must have been silent and quick. And it wasn't as if Cole had told Marcos not to take his eyes off her. Cole had thought she'd be safe in his house. Having his brother there had just been a precaution.

Marcos was fiddling with his phone, and a second later, he had it to his ear. "Luke? It's Marcos. Shaye is missing. We need your help." There was a pause, then Marcos said, "Yeah, bring the cavalry."

"We have to find her," Cole said. His voice sounded broken and scared. He should have realized this threat was too big as soon as the gangs got involved again. He should have disregarded his own selfish need to keep her in his life and insisted she go into Witness Protection. Better he never see her again, if it meant she'd have been safe.

What if he never saw her again?

Marcos's words broke through his frenzied thoughts. "We'll find her."

"How? This guy could have taken her anywhere by now." He couldn't bring himself to say the words out loud, but he also couldn't turn his law enforcement brain off. Because years as a cop had taught him the awful reality: Shaye could already be dead by now.

"LISTEN UP," LUKE SAID, sounding like a drill instructor as his voice cut through the noise, quieting the cluster of cops in Cole's living room.

Cole knocked the handful of items off his coffee table and spread a map there. "Shaye disappeared within the last hour and a half out of this house." If her abductor had gotten on the freeway, she could be quite a distance away by now. Heck, she could be in another state. But most perpetrators stuck to what they knew, because it was easier to control the variables. Which meant places the police could track—Cole hoped.

"We still have all the Kings members locked up," Hiroshi said. "And we have a pretty good handle on that group, right? Could there be someone in the gang we don't know about? Someone who could pull this off?"

"Unlikely, but we're not taking any chances. We've got Dawson and Pietrich back at the station laying into the gangsters again," Luke said.

And there were a pair of lab techs in Cole's bedroom, searching for prints, though Cole figured that was unlikely to yield anything. Someone who'd managed to stay one step ahead of them for this long would have worn gloves to break into a police detective's house.

"Meanwhile, our best bet is that Elliard took her," Cole said. "He's still not accounted for, and the timing fits."

"He was in pretty bad shape still, wasn't he?" one of the officers asked. "I mean, the hospital wasn't even ready to discharge him when he snuck out. Would he have the strength to abduct someone?"

"He escaped custody at the hospital," Luke reminded them. "Which means he managed to get out of the cuffs tethering him to the bed and past his guard and then out of the hospital without being spotted. So, he must have been in better shape than he was letting on. Plus, we're assuming he's managed to acquire a weapon since then, and if that's the case, he wouldn't really need to rely on muscle when he took Shaye, just firepower."

"But we're not ruling out anyone," Cole added. He pointed at two officers in the corner. "I want you two to pay Ken Tobek a visit. His alibi seems pretty solid for the shooting, but apparently his brother-in-law owns an old Taurus. Make Tobek call the brother-in-law. Get the location of that Taurus."

"Cole and I are going to run down Elliard's haunts," Luke said.

"I thought he didn't own anything," Hiroshi spoke up.

"He doesn't. We've got his sisters' houses and we've got known Kings hideouts to check, so we'll take some help covering those," Cole said, trying to sound confident. But inside the dread he'd been feeling since he'd broken down his bedroom door just kept growing. Elliard probably *did* have somewhere that was his own, even if his name didn't appear on any papers they could find. It was why he and Luke were going to talk to Rosa, because she was the person most likely to know where that was.

"We also want a pair of you to start making phone calls to everyone at the lab. See if any of them noticed someone watching Shaye. They might have a different perspective on it than she did. If you get anything, call us right away," Luke said.

Cole prayed they'd get something from that; it was actually one of his strongest hopes for new information if Elliard wasn't behind this, because when Shaye got to work, she got so focused. She could have missed someone at the lab who had an unnatural fixation on her, but he bet her coworkers wouldn't. And someone at the lab would have a much easier time identifying where Shaye had been tonight than Elliard or another gang member.

"Meanwhile, all the officers out on patrol right now are watching for a car that fits the description of the one used during Shaye's shooting," Cole added, shaking off his contemplation. "If one is spotted, they'll tail it and call for backup. Don't approach this guy alone. Whoever he is, expect him to be armed and dangerous."

Cole looked around the room, thankful that all these officers were willing to drop everything and come here. He hadn't even questioned that they would, but it was touching. The brotherhood in blue ran deep.

He nodded at Marcos, who'd been standing silently in the corner the whole time. He knew Marcos still blamed himself, no matter what Cole had said, and he wasn't going to feel better until Shaye was back home and safe.

Cole's train of thought stuttered on the idea that when he imagined Shaye home safe, it wasn't her home, it was *his*. His throat tightened. When had he gone from an infatuation with this woman to being in love with her? Had it been a slow development, happening a little at a time so he never even noticed? Or had he been fooling himself from the start, thinking he could ever just be friends with her or have something short-term?

Realizing Luke was staring at him expectantly, Cole cleared his throat and said, "Marcos is going to be staying here, coordinating everything. If you need anything, if you hear anything, call him. He'll get the word out."

Marcos would also be here in case Shaye managed to escape; meanwhile, he'd talk to Cole's neighbors to find out if any of them had heard or seen anything.

"Any questions?" Luke asked.

There was silence, until Hiroshi spoke up. "We're going to find her. We won't stop until we do."

Cole nodded his thanks, praying they'd find her alive. "Let's do this. Let's find Shaye."

SHAYE READIED HER pathetic weapon, her heart thundering against her chest so hard it actually hurt. She tried to position her legs so she could pop up as soon as the trunk opened a little farther, but she was stiff and there wasn't a lot of space to get leverage.

Then it was happening. The trunk jolted open the rest of the way.

Before she could move, a bright light shone into her eyes and she instinctively shut them. The taillight cover was slapped out of her hands and she was wrenched out of the trunk, hard enough to send pain through her shoulders, like he'd pulled them out of their sockets. Her bare legs scraped the edge of the trunk and then she was on the cold ground, her T-shirt up around her waist.

She frantically yanked it down, simultaneously trying to get to her feet, when her captor warned her, "Get up slowly. I've still got a gun, and while it isn't my plan to shoot you right now, if you make me, I'll do it." A nasty edge suddenly came into his voice as he added, "Though I might just shoot you in the kneecaps to start. Not kill you straight out, but let you die slowly for wrecking my plan."

Shaye shivered. She tried not to, but she knew he'd seen it. If he wasn't planning to shoot her, what was his plan?

He had the flashlight aimed at her face again, so he just looked like a big man-shaped blur, but that voice was familiar. Was she right? And if she was, had Marcos even told Cole what she'd said? Had Cole understood? It hadn't been much of a hint, but she'd had to think fast, while trying not to let on anything was wrong to Marcos or let on to her abductor that she was trying to give away his identity.

The flashlight darted right. "Get up. Start walking."

She squinted, trying to see around the spots in front of her eyes to study his face, but the flashlight moved back to her too quickly. Why didn't he want her to see him? A tiny glimmer of hope surfaced. Could it be because he planned to let her live?

But if so, then what did he intend to do to her? Or was she simply bait, a way to lure Cole to him?

She needed to figure out an escape plan. Because from the little she could see, wherever she was right now was rural. As in, nowhere to run for help. And no one to hear her scream. And for someone who'd had enough liquor that it was practically seeping from his pores, her captor didn't seem to have lost any of his co-ordination or strength.

"Get up!"

Shaye scrambled, pushing to her feet and biting down on her tongue to keep from screaming at the pain that jolted through her shoulders. When she took a step, her left leg almost gave out on her, and she realized she'd broken some toes kicking out that taillight. And all for nothing.

"Go." The flashlight shifted again, aiming off to her right, and this time, instead of trying to see her captor, she followed it. Down a dirt trail was a dilapidated old barn, with red paint peeling and a roof that looked like it could collapse at any minute. If the barn was part of property that also had a house, she didn't see it.

How was anyone going to find her here?

Shoving down the panic, Shaye limped toward the barn, and her abductor followed, close enough that if she slowed down at all, he'd walk right into her. She went a little faster, holding down the edges of her

T-shirt. Pebbles dug into her bare feet, and the spots he'd nicked her with the knife were throbbing.

"What is this about?" Shaye asked, hoping he'd tell her what he had planned for her. Maybe that way she'd know what she should do.

"What is this about?" he snapped, grabbing her arm and spinning her around. "You ruined my life and you don't even remember doing it?"

The more he spoke, the louder he was screaming, that whiskey scent shooting at her face, and still holding that flashlight on her, like he didn't want her to see him.

Why didn't he want her to see him?

"I don't…I can't—" Shaye stammered.

"Get in there." He shoved her forward.

She went down, landing on her knees. Shaye tried to get back up, but he put a boot in her side.

She yelped, clutching the spot as he reached past her and pulled open the door.

"Crawl," he growled at her.

Blinking back tears, she did, as pebbles scraped the cut on her leg. She made it just inside the doorway, before shock made her pause.

Tied up inside the barn was Dominic Elliard.

Chapter Nineteen

"Where is Dominic?" Cole demanded, jamming his shoulder against the door when Rosa's older sister tried to slam it in his face.

"I don't know!" she yelled at him, still struggling to push the door closed. "I haven't talked to him in years."

"But Rosa has," Luke said from slightly behind him on the stoop in the middle-class neighborhood out in the suburbs where Rosa's older sister lived.

"You can't do this," the woman grunted, leaning into the door harder. "This is my house."

"Your brother shot at a police station, then escaped custody and kidnapped a forensic lab employee," Cole replied, tensing his shoulder muscles. This woman was tiny but strong.

At his words, she slumped and let go of the door so suddenly, he almost fell inside. "Come in," she told them. Then she yelled up the stairs, "Rosa! Get down here! Now!"

Cole kept his hand close to his side, unsnapping his holster in case he needed to make a quick grab for his weapon. He doubted Dominic was in the house, but he didn't want to find out he was wrong the hard way.

Luke followed behind him, and Cole knew he was

keeping an eye on their surroundings as they followed Rosa and Dominic's sister into a brightly colored kitchen with sparkling appliances and kids' pictures on the refrigerator.

"You're lucky my husband took the kids to visit his parents this week," she said. Then she muttered, "I should have gone with them."

She gestured to the chairs at the kitchen table, but Cole shook his head. "We're in a hurry. We'd like to stop your brother from killing anyone today."

Her shoulders slumped and she sank into one of the chairs herself. "I thought he was finally going to get out of that life. Rosa said—"

"I said what?" Rosa asked, appearing in the doorway, scowling in a bathrobe, her hair hastily tied up on her head. She noticed Cole and Luke, and her lips turned up in a snarl. "Thanks for waking up the baby."

Cole tilted his head and realized that off in the distance, he could hear crying from upstairs. "We're sorry. We're in a rush. Your brother has kidnapped someone, and we don't have long before he kills her."

Rosa jerked, then shook her head. "No way."

"Have you seen him since he escaped custody, Rosa?" Luke asked softly.

"No." She shook her head. "No."

"Don't lie to us. You want your sister raising that baby because you're in jail as an accomplice?" Cole snapped, tired of messing around. Every second they wasted was more time for Dominic to kill Shaye.

He tried to push the thought from his mind, to focus the way he did for any other case, because if he couldn't, he knew he was useless to Shaye. But the thought of waking up tomorrow knowing that Shaye was gone for good, of going through the rest of his life without her, made his chest tighten until breathing hurt.

"What's wrong with him?"

The words seemed to come from a distance, then Luke's voice, closer, saying, "Nothing."

Then Luke was pushing him into a chair, pushing his head down, telling him to breathe.

Cole got a hold of himself, got the air back into his lungs. "Sorry, man."

"What just happened?" Rosa asked, sounding confused and afraid.

"It's his girlfriend your brother kidnapped. And he's not kidding when he says Dominic will kill her. He's already tried once, right before he came after Cole here at the police station." Rosa started to interrupt, and Luke said, "A whole station full of cops came when the call went out. We all saw him, Rosa."

"It's that stupid car." She sighed as her older sister glared at her, giving Rosa a silent "tell them everything" look.

"The car?" Luke pressed.

"Yeah, the car. He went crazy when you showed up that day. I honestly didn't think he'd go after you like that, but…he was so mad about what happened after Ed went away. I had nothing, me and the baby. I got canned from my job, because the manager found out I was Ed's girl, and he said he didn't want anything to do with the gangs. Then the pregnancy got rough, and I had to go on bed rest and I didn't know what to do. Dominic tried to help me, but he blamed the cops for taking everything Ed had, everything that should have been mine. When you came back for that car, it was the last straw."

"We weren't there to confiscate it," Cole said tightly.

"We were confirming whether it was used in the commission of a crime. Another shooting."

"No," Rosa said, shaking her head. "He was getting out of the life. I know you think I'm lying, but he was. Until you came about the car, he was doing really good. And whoever it was you were asking about, the state employee who was shot at? He didn't know what you were talking about. I can tell when my brother is lying. He wasn't lying about that."

Cole and Luke shared a look. "Where is he now, Rosa?"

She shrugged. "I honestly don't know. Look, I knew he was going to try to escape. You're right. But I haven't seen him." She glanced at her sister. "And anyway, he wouldn't come here."

Her older sister nodded at them. "Rosa's right about that. He knows I'd turn him in."

"Where would he go?" Cole asked, even as a thousand curse words filled his mind. Maybe Dominic Elliard wasn't even who they were looking for.

"I don't know. He had some places, but they were in Kings territory. When he told Leonardo he wanted out, begged him for Ed Jr.'s sake, Leonardo was going to let him go. But it meant Dominic wasn't welcome there anymore. He wouldn't go there."

"Thanks for your time," Luke said, handing over his card. "Please call us if you think of anything else, or if you hear from Dominic."

Then he and Luke headed outside. After Rosa closed the door behind him, Cole looked at his partner. "What do you think?"

"I believe her. I don't think Dominic took Shaye."

"Then who did?"

"KEN TOBEK," SHAYE said softly, turning away from Dominic, gagged and tied up with rope, his head resting against his chest on the far side of the barn.

The flashlight slowly lowered, and her abductor smiled. "So, you *do* remember."

She was right.

Please, please understand my desperate attempt to leave a clue, Cole, she willed him. *Talk to your brother.*

Shaye blinked and blinked, until the spots in front of her eyes cleared and she could get a good look at Tobek. He'd aged a lot since she'd last seen him in that courtroom, but the easy-to-overlook exterior didn't hide the fury behind his eyes.

He was going to kill her. The knowledge hit her instantly, with certainty, but instead of making her panic, a strange calm came over her.

There had to be a reason Tobek would bring her all the way out here, instead of pulling that car over as soon as they hit the boonies, shooting her and leaving her in a field. And there had to be a reason Elliard was here.

The voice in her head sounded like Cole, and Shaye glanced back at Elliard, suddenly realizing. "He's your patsy, isn't he? You're planning to frame my death on him?"

Tobek laughed, and it was part amused, part nasty. "Maybe. It was so easy. Once he shot up that police station, it was like he was handing me an out, even better than the alibi I'd cooked up. And especially after you got away from me that first time and I'd needed to set up another alibi. And then your boyfriend came to visit me… I knew I was right to have adjusted my original plan."

"You left the gun used to shoot at me at Roy's Grocery in Kings territory, then called in the anonymous tip," Shaye said, leaning her weight on her right foot. Her broken toes throbbed, sending pain all the way up to her hip, which seemed to remind her leg it had recently had a bullet in it, because that was throbbing now, too.

"You're smarter than you look," Tobek said, sing-songy.

"Why?" Shaye asked. "You spent a month in jail. You can move on. Why come after me now, after all this time?"

"A month in jail?" he echoed. "Like that's no big deal?" His voice raised until he was yelling. "You told a courtroom full of people that I tried to kill my wife!"

He had. Shaye had no doubt about it. If Cole and Luke hadn't shown up at the Tobek residence when they had, Becca Tobek would be dead. Ken had only been convicted of assault, and shouldn't he feel lucky he'd gotten off so easy? Shouldn't he be moving on, thankful the justice system had gotten it wrong?

He shrugged, his voice going back to the odd monotone she'd heard in the courtroom a year ago, the monotone that had jiggled free a memory when he'd broken into Cole's house. "I can't let you get away with that. Besides…" He grinned, and it was scarier than his yelling. "You're only part of my plan."

Please, please don't go after Cole, Shaye thought, glancing around the barn again, wondering if there was anything she could get her hands on to use as a weapon. But it was hard to see well, just shafts of moonlight filtering down through the broken roof and Tobek's flashlight beam. There might have been a workbench behind Elliard, but that was way too far away to be useful to her.

"But this is all falling into place even better than I could have ever planned," Tobek continued, sounding gleeful. "Because Elliard over there is a violent, violent felon. A gang member. They're pretty indiscriminate about who they kill."

Shaye frowned. What was he talking about? Framing Elliard for her murder wouldn't look indiscriminate; Elliard had a known grudge. What was she missing?

"Now move," Tobek said, suddenly all business. He gestured with his gun toward Elliard, and when she glanced back, she saw something she'd missed before.

A second set of ropes beside Elliard.

Shaye put her hands up. "Ken—"

"Don't try to sweet-talk me." He made a disgusted noise. "Women. You're all the same. You think you can convince me this isn't all your fault? Not going to happen. Now move."

Breath caught in Shaye's throat as she realized the rest of Tobek's plan. "You're going to try to kill your wife again, aren't you?"

Tobek gave a forced laugh. "Not me. Elliard. And he's going to succeed. But you? You're feistier than you look." His gaze dropped over her, and her hands fell to her sides, yanking down her T-shirt as far as she could.

"It's true actually. I didn't expect you to knock out my taillight. I'm going to have to fix that. But Elliard didn't expect it, either." Tobek shrugged. "Because after he killed Becca, you almost got the upper hand. You actually managed to stab him before he shot you."

A jolt went through Shaye as he laid out his plan so casually. He was going to shoot her. Panic threatened at the instant reminder of how it had felt when the bullet had gone into her leg at Roy's Grocery.

Tobek shrugged again. "Too bad you both died from your wounds." He glanced around. "And by the time police found you way out here in Elliard's hiding spot, your bodies were in pretty bad shape. So, forensics aren't going to help you much this time, are they?"

He pointed at the ropes next to Elliard. "Now move. I've got to work in the morning."

Chapter Twenty

"I need updates now," Cole said as soon as Marcos picked up his call. "I'm not so sure Elliard is behind this anymore. We need a new lead."

Where was Shaye? *Hang on, honey*, he tried to will her.

"Okay," Marcos said, his voice all business, but Cole could tell anyway. There was nothing promising.

Cole's shoulders slumped, and Luke took his hand off the wheel for a second and clamped it on Cole's shoulder. "We'll find her," he mouthed as Marcos's voice came over the speaker again.

"The lab guys didn't find any prints besides yours and Shaye's in the bedroom or on the window."

"Not surprising. What about the neighbors? Did they hear anything? Did anyone see a car on the street that didn't belong? Maybe an old Taurus?"

"No. And no one was answering at Tobek's house, but officers paid his brother-in-law a visit. He said Tobek *has* borrowed his cars before, but that everything is in storage now."

"Cars?" Luke asked. "How many does he have?"

"Five. Two he keeps at the house and three at a garage he rents downtown."

"And Tobek has the keys?"

"Well, he's not supposed to, but the brother-in-law thinks he swiped a set of his keys."

"Is he sure everything is in storage?" Cole asked, as the new information made his detective's instinct buzz. He glanced at Luke. "But Tobek's alibi was good."

Luke nodded, and from the furrow between his eyebrows, Cole could tell he was having the same internal debate.

"As far as he knows, yeah."

"Get the plate numbers on them anyway," Luke suggested. "Put them out on the wire."

"Already did," Marcos replied. "I gave them to Hiroshi. He's on it. Meanwhile, we don't have any sightings of a car that fits the description from the shooting at Roy's Grocery. And so far, the Kings' hideouts you all know about are clean—well, empty. But they're still checking."

"What about Kings members? Any of them talking?" Luke asked.

"Just demanding lawyers. But Leonardo did say— hang on." There was some paper rustling; then Marcos continued, like he was reading from something he'd written down. "Elliard is going to have some explaining to do. And if he thinks I don't know about his place in the country, he's wrong."

"What does that mean? We have an address?" Cole frowned over at Luke. Elliard had a place in the country?

"He's refusing to say any more, although officers did say they heard him muttering later about it being a stupid plan, how Dominic would never have the money or skills to build there anyway, so I don't know what kind of place it is. Your officers think he's keeping the location to himself, planning to go after Elliard when we let him go."

"Maybe we should let him go," Luke said.

"What?" Cole's and Marcos's voices overlapped.

"I know right now we don't think it's Elliard. But we still can't account for him, and the timing is suspicious. What if we let Leonardo go and follow him to Elliard's hiding spot?"

Cole's pulse picked up at the suggestion, and he nodded, liking the idea. "Except he's not likely to lead us right there. He's too smart to go right there."

"Unless we piss him off enough," Marcos suggested. "Make him believe Elliard was trying to pin the shooting on Leonardo by leaving the gun in his territory."

Cole frowned, shaking his head. "We got that anonymous call while Elliard was still in the hospital, under guard. If he made a call on a hospital phone, we could have traced it. It didn't come from there. It came from a burner phone."

"His sister visited," Luke said. "Maybe she brought him one. Do we have a better lead right now?"

"What about Shaye's coworkers?" Cole asked, still troubled by Rosa's certainty that her brother wasn't involved in Shaye's shooting.

"None of them thought Shaye had any enemies, and the only secret admirer they mentioned was you," Marcos said, a little amusement slipping into his tone at the end.

"Great," Cole muttered.

"But one of them did say something about a rusted-out Taurus they'd seen a few times parked on the street behind the lab."

"Away from the station," Luke said. "Where the cops would be less likely to see it."

"He did track her from the lab," Cole said. "So how

did he follow her to my house? You think he followed me, and I didn't see him?" The idea made guilt join the fear and anger rolling in his gut.

"Let's just worry about finding her now," Luke said. "What's our next move?"

"I agree with Luke. Let's try letting Leonardo go—" Marcos started, but Cole cut him off as realization struck.

"Marcos, what did Shaye say to you last night?" His heart rate started to pick up, knowing he was onto something.

"What do you mean?"

"You almost broke down the door. You said she sounded weird. What were her exact words, about the bed?" The comment he'd brushed off that had made no sense to him. Maybe it had been Shaye's way of sending him a message.

There was a long pause, and Cole knew his brother was trying to remember precisely.

"She said, 'Tell him I was right. His bed is more comfortable than mine.'"

"That's it," Cole said, his pulse skyrocketing.

"What?" Luke asked, giving him a confused glance as he continued to drive toward Rosa's house, where they'd originally talked to Elliard.

"Turn around," Cole said. "The part about the bed was just to make it sound like it wasn't a hint to her abductor. Shaye was telling me she was right. It was Ken Tobek."

"WAIT," SHAYE SAID, desperate to keep Tobek talking, to figure out a plan. Once she was tied up, her chances of survival—slim as they looked right now—dropped even lower.

"Come on now," Tobek said, wiggling the gun. "Don't make this difficult. Because I'm still willing to shoot you in the kneecaps if I have to, but that's going to make everything so messy."

"Look, I just—I deserve to know the rest of this. Come on. How do you think you're going to get away with killing your wife? You don't think the police will find that suspicious? That Elliard here broke out of the hospital just to kill me and your wife? How many times do you think you can pay your coworker to lie for you?"

Tobek frowned. "I didn't pay him. And believe me—he's not giving me up. Not unless he wants to go to jail himself."

"I'm sure the police would give him some leniency for helping—"

"Not that. He's doing me this little favor because I caught him with the boss's daughter after work one evening." Tobek laughed. "In the boss's office. And she's seventeen. Trust me. I told him all about how seventeen is still a child in the eyes of the law…and other prisoners. We all know what happens to child rapists in prison."

Shaye shook her head, trying not to look as disgusted—by both of them—as she felt. "I'm sure—"

"Oh, he believes me. Doesn't matter whether she's secretly dating him or not. The guy's a nervous nimrod. And anyway, I don't need an alibi for the middle of the night. I was at home asleep. Where else would I be?" He pointed the gun. "Now stop stalling, because I'm on a timeline here."

Shaye turned slowly, limping toward Elliard, who still hadn't moved. Her breath caught. "Is he already dead?" she asked, not sure she wanted to know the answer.

"Nah, he's not dead. Trust me—I learned a thing or two from the last time. I'm going to be real careful, so everything lines up, just in case. Though I'm sure that by the time police find you, you'll be so decayed that figuring out exactly when you died will be a miracle."

Shaye shivered, trying not to imagine it but unable to help herself. She worked in a forensics lab. She'd seen those kinds of pictures. She clasped a hand to her heart. Cole would see those pictures of her. Tears pricked her eyes, knowing what it would do to him. He'd blame himself.

For all the times she'd accused him of not opening up to her, the truth was, she knew him better than she'd ever realized. Because she knew, without a doubt, that he'd never recover from this.

"You'd be surprised what we can do in that lab. For example, they're going to be able to tell that this whole thing is staged." She took a breath, leaning on all the knowledge she'd learned outside her own specialty over that year she'd spent in the lab.

"They'll recover the marks on Elliard's wrists showing he was tied up before he died. Those go deeper than you think. They'll reconstruct the scene, realize that the knife marks on him are too deep or the wrong angle or had to have been made by someone taller, heavier. My prints will be in the wrong place because I didn't actually hold it in the way you would if you were stabbing someone. The—"

"Stop it!" Tobek moved forward quickly, getting in her face and making her stumble backward.

She tripped, landing on her butt, her T-shirt riding up again. His gaze followed, and Shaye quickly yanked it down.

"I guess it's a good thing I kidnapped a forensics expert, then, isn't it?" Tobek said, leaning toward her.

If she'd been stronger—if her left leg wasn't in serious pain, her shoulders weak—she might have tried looping her legs around his, pulling him down when he was off balance. But she knew it was a losing move, and she wasn't quite at the point of trying something she knew had no chance of succeeding. Not yet. But she was quickly getting there.

"Because you're going to help me get it right," Tobek said.

"Why would I help you?" Shaye spat, trying to sound brave despite her terror. "You're going to kill me anyway. Shooting my kneecaps first isn't going to make me help you get away with it."

"Really?" Tobek grinned, and it was so full of menace and glee, she shrank into the ground a little. "Don't forget I know where your boyfriend lives. You do what I tell you, or when I'm finished here, I'm making a trip back to see him."

THE GARAGE DOOR rolled up at the storage unit with frustrating slowness.

Cole bent down, trying to see inside before it was finished opening.

"They're all here," the man standing between him and Luke said with exasperation.

And they were. Three cars, the rusty Taurus Cole couldn't believe was still running right in the middle.

"Now can I go back to bed?" Tobek's brother-in-law demanded.

They'd woken him in the middle of the night, pressuring him to drive with them out to the storage unit where he kept his extra cars. Cole had been so certain they'd find the Taurus missing—or possibly one of the other vehicles.

He looked at his partner. "What now?"

Luke's gaze was still on the brother-in-law. "Where might Ken go if he wasn't at home?"

"I don't know," the brother-in-law said. "Jeez. We're not even that close. Honestly, I only put up with him for my wife. The guy is kind of a tool."

"He doesn't own any other places? Doesn't go anywhere particular, like a hunting cabin or something?"

"No. Tobek doesn't hunt. He drinks. Look, I don't know what you suspect him of now—"

"What do you mean by *now*?" Cole asked.

Tobek's brother-in-law rolled his eyes. "He went to jail before for assaulting his wife. Poor Becca. Now her, I did like."

"Right. Okay, well—"

"I don't know where he'd go. Honest. And yeah, he's been a little, I don't know, moodier than usual lately, but I hardly think he's using my car to commit crimes."

"Well, we'd still like your permission for our lab to take a look at it," Luke said.

The man threw up his hands. "Fine. Can I go home and go back to bed now?"

"Yeah."

He yanked the door down, which closed a lot faster than it had opened, then stomped back to his vehicle, while Cole and Luke stood in the deserted storage area, staring at each other.

"Has anyone talked to Tobek's ex-wife?" Luke asked.

"Yeah. Hiroshi and Wes just called and woke her up a few minutes ago. I got the update on the drive here while you were riding with Tobek's brother-in-law. She says she hasn't heard from him since he got out of jail. But Hiroshi says it's pretty clear she's still scared of him."

"Okay. Well, let's check in with Marcos again," Luke suggested, and Cole prayed his brother would have a new lead for them.

He dialed Marcos's cell, and his brother picked up before the first ring finished. "Any news?"

"I was hoping you'd have some," Marcos replied. "But look, I'm on my way to Tobek's house right now."

"What? Why?"

"Take me off speaker."

Cole glanced at Luke, who turned away, glancing around the storage unit, as Cole hit the speaker button and pressed the phone to his ear. "Okay, it's just us. What is it?"

"I know you wanted Hiroshi to go back and check the garage for Tobek's Benz, but I'm having him wait at the house instead. Hiroshi can't go inside the house without risking his job."

"I wasn't asking—"

"Yeah, but if you don't know anywhere else he might be, we need to check. It would be stupid of him, but what if Shaye's in his house?"

Cole's hand clenched the phone too tight. "If she's in there, we go in with the cavalry."

"I hear you. I don't think she is, but we need to check."

"Hiroshi's not the only one who'd be risking his job doing that without a warrant," Cole warned, swearing inwardly. He should be there, doing what Marcos thought was his responsibility since Shaye had been taken while he was at the house.

"Don't worry," Marcos said, his tone upbeat. "I won't get caught. I'll call you back once I've cleared it."

"Be careful."

"What are you going to do?"

Cole glanced at Luke. "Right now the only move I can think of is the one we talked about earlier. Let Leonardo go, and see if he can lead us to Elliard."

Chapter Twenty-One

"I should have killed Becca first," Tobek muttered, gesturing with the gun and walking toward her so she scooted back until she bumped something.

Shaye turned around and realized it was the legs of a workbench. Why was it here in this old barn? She couldn't see what was on it from this angle, but she wondered if Tobek had left anything up there she could use as a weapon.

"It's going to mess up your plan of how this whole thing is going to be interpreted," Shaye said.

Tobek scowled at her. "I knew I should have grabbed her first. But Elliard here just fell into my lap. I went to the hospital, hoping to snatch something of his I could leave at her house, and what did I find? This idiot sneaking out a service entrance." He kicked Elliard's leg with his shoe, then shrugged when Elliard didn't move.

"What's wrong with him?" Shaye asked.

"He didn't want to come with me. I had to use a little persuasion."

"What does that mean?"

Tobek stuck the gun in her face, inches from her nose, his face right behind it, breathing whiskey on her again. "It means I knocked him out. For a gang member, he's not so tough."

He'd also been recovering from a serious gunshot wound, Shaye wanted to say, but she didn't. She just nodded, then risked, "That will show up on an autopsy."

He gave her a mocking smile. "That's okay. *You* did that. Probably right before you stabbed him. The gun went off in the struggle and—oops." Tobek shrugged. "You got hit and didn't survive."

Shaye shivered. This man was crazy. She'd known he was guilty when she'd taken the stand, known in her heart that if he wasn't convicted, he'd go after his wife again someday—she'd even warned Becca Tobek of it when he'd been convicted of only assault. But she never expected he'd take such joy in the whole process, be willing to take out so many other people, too.

"All right, you've asked enough questions." He stood again, took a step back and leveled the gun on her. "Do I have to go and kill Becca first, then come back for you two?"

Shaye swallowed. The truth was he did. The medical examiner was good. And she didn't believe that she'd lie here rotting so long they wouldn't be able to tell. Cole would find her. In her heart she believed that. Whether it took days or weeks, he'd find her. And then the autopsy and the labs would show the truth. But Becca Tobek thought she was safe. It had been a year since she'd divorced Ken. She didn't have a detective watching over her.

As much as Shaye wanted Tobek to leave so she could try to escape, even if she managed to get free, she doubted she'd find help faster than Tobek could find and kill Becca. They were in the middle of nowhere. And it wasn't like she had a cell phone.

"No," she whispered, hoping she hadn't just signed her own death warrant.

"Good." He sounded gleeful. "Because I really want to save the best for last. No offense, but you're just the appetizer." His gaze dropped down her bare legs. "Although you're a tasty-looking appetizer."

Bile rose in Shaye's throat, and she tried to scoot backward more, but there was nowhere to go. Tobek was standing in front of her, slightly to her right, so she shifted left, bumping Elliard and making his head fall on her shoulder. She jumped, and Tobek laughed.

"Don't worry," he said, sounding slightly disappointed. "I'm not planning to leave my DNA on you." He glanced at his watch as Shaye felt something against her hip.

What was it? She leaned into Elliard a little more, realizing he had something hard in his jacket pocket. *A phone?* Her pulse jumped, and she wondered if she should backtrack on her claim that he didn't need to worry about the order of the deaths, but then she realized it wasn't a phone. It was too small for that.

"Time's wasting," Tobek said. "I have a lot to do tonight. We'd better get moving. So let's talk forensics."

Shaye nodded, only half paying attention to him now. Could it be possible? Did Elliard have a pocketknife that Tobek hadn't found?

It could make sense. Elliard had slipped away from his guard, gotten out of his cuffs. Someone could have helped him, brought him something to pick the lock with. A pocketknife had all kinds of tools in it. One of them might fit in the lock on a pair of handcuffs.

But how did she get it out of Elliard's pocket, open it and attack before Tobek shot her?

"SHAYE'S BEEN MISSING for hours." Cole knew he was stating the obvious, but he couldn't help it, just like he couldn't help the panic pressing down on his chest. "What if this is another dead end?"

"This is something proactive we can do now," Luke said. "Your brother is checking into Tobek at his house. You've got officers searching for any other places he could be. We're covering all our bases."

Cole knew his partner was right. They were doing everything they would be if this were any other kidnapping case. The problem was this wasn't any other kidnapping case. This was Shaye, the woman he wanted to spend the rest of his life with.

How had he been so blind about this? Everyone else had seen it. His brothers had been teasing him mercilessly about Shaye for two years, trying to get him to ask her out. Even Luke had joined in a time or two. They'd all known what he'd been trying to deny. His feelings for her weren't a solid friendship mixed with a too-strong attraction. They were flat-out love. And now he might never get to tell her.

"You'll get the chance to tell her how you feel," Luke said, and, for a second, Cole thought he'd spoken the words out loud.

Then he realized Luke just knew him that well. "I messed up," he told his partner.

"Well, let's see if he can help us remedy things," Luke replied, nodding toward the front of the station, where the head of the Kings was sauntering down the steps.

"Looks like they did a good job of making Leonardo

think he was intimidating them enough to let him go," Cole said. He could practically see Leonardo's smirk from here.

"Yeah." Luke slouched low in his seat, even though they were parked out in the street, far enough away that Leonardo would have a hard time seeing them.

Cole did the same, watching over the edge of the dashboard. "Please, please go straight to Elliard's hiding place," Cole willed him.

Leonardo did a mock salute to the officers who'd walked out behind him, then climbed into a car someone had dropped off for him and revved the engine. He spun the wheels, leaving behind a plume of smoke as he gunned it out of the station parking lot.

"This is going to be interesting," Luke said, flipping on the headlights, switching into Drive and following.

Luckily, even this late at night, there was some traffic. When Leonardo hopped onto the freeway, Luke visibly relaxed and dropped back a few more car lengths.

"Where's he going?" Cole wondered aloud ten minutes later.

"Leonardo did say Elliard's secret hiding place was somewhere in the country," Luke reminded him just as Cole's phone rang.

"Marcos," Cole answered, putting the call on speaker. "What did you find?"

"No sign of Tobek," his brother said. "His Benz isn't here, either. But I had Hiroshi put it out and we actually got a hit. Patrol officers driving by the storage place you visited earlier spotted it parked nearby."

Luke glanced at the phone, frowning. "But his brother-in-law said he wasn't missing any cars. And the right number of vehicles were there."

"What if he stole someone else's?" Cole asked. "A lot of people store their summer vehicles there, stuff they don't drive when it gets cold. He could easily figure someone wouldn't miss it for the night, return it before morning." As he said the words, he recognized the truth in them, but also what that meant for Shaye.

Dawn was coming fast now. If Tobek's plan was to be back home by morning, Shaye didn't have much time left.

"We need to get the manager there, see if any units have been tampered with," Cole said.

"What about security?" Luke asked. "Wouldn't they have noticed if someone drove out of there with a car?"

"Not if they expected him," Cole said. "Tobek has been there before. He could have gone in with his brother-in-law's key, then driven out with a different car. The security guys probably don't match vehicles to people, just access."

"But then his name will show up on a log," Luke said.

"Yeah, but that doesn't mean much if we can't tie him to a crime. He probably wasn't too worried about that."

"I'm on it," Marcos said. "I'll call security and find out what car he drove out of there, then get them to figure out whose it was and run license plates so we can put a BOLO on it."

By then, would it be way too late?

"He's getting off," Luke said, drawing Cole's attention back to Leonardo, who was indeed taking the exit ahead of them.

"That doesn't lead anywhere. It's all farmland," Cole said.

"Exactly," Luke agreed.

"Marcos, I'm going to have to call you back. But let

me know the second you have something. We'll let you know if we need backup."

"Be careful."

"I will," Cole promised, his fists opening and closing on his lap. He didn't plan to need backup. Wherever Leonardo was leading them, if Shaye was there, Cole planned to take Elliard down with his bare hands if he had to.

"He's slowing down," Luke said, swearing and dropping way back.

Cole prayed the Kings' leader was so focused on his mission, he wasn't bothering to check his rearview mirror. Because if he did, there'd be no missing them.

There was no way for Luke to stay far enough back not to be seen, not out here in the middle of nowhere.

"There aren't even any houses here," Luke said. "I think he might have made us. He could be leading us on a wild-goose chase."

"What's that?" Cole asked as Leonardo suddenly pulled off the road.

Luke slowed the car down some more. "Looks like a barn? But I don't see anything else. Do you think this is some kind of trap?" He reached for his phone. "Maybe we should call for backup."

Cole yanked a pair of binoculars out of the glove compartment and focused them on Leonardo as he climbed out of the car, parked down a little path from the barn. "There's another car there, sort of hidden in those bushes."

"This could definitely be an ambush."

"No, I don't think so." Cole's pulse picked up as Leonardo lifted his trunk and pulled out a shotgun. "Not for us anyway. He's got a shotgun."

Leonardo slammed the trunk and started walking toward the barn.

"This is it!" Cole said. "This must be Elliard's place. Shaye could be in there. Go!"

Luke hit the gas, and Cole's head slammed back against his seat as he wrestled for the pistol in his holster.

Ahead of them, Leonardo glanced back, spotted them and then started running for the barn.

IT WAS NOW or never, Shaye thought as Tobek stuffed the gun in the back of his waistband and bent down, wrapping the rope around her wrists.

"Ouch," she yelped. "Remember what I said about the ropes leaving marks?"

He squinted at her, like he wasn't sure if she was helping him to avoid being shot in the kneecaps or trying to play him for a fool.

She tried to look innocent, sure she just looked terrified.

Tobek grunted at her, easing up on the rope, and Shaye braced herself, getting ready to leap for Elliard, praying what was in his pocket was what she thought it was.

Before she could act, Elliard let out a low moan; then his head rolled back before he straightened it. He glanced around as Tobek leaped away from her, reaching for his gun.

Now or never, Shaye reminded herself, and she shoved her hands into Elliard's pocket.

Then he was squirming, spitting the gag out of his mouth, yanking at his ropes, pushing at her.

Shaye got her hands free as Tobek frantically tried

to bring his gun back around. He dropped it when Elliard let out a huge roar of pain or anger and heaved himself to his feet.

As Tobek dived for his gun, Shaye glanced down at the object in her hand. She was right! Panicked, she fumbled to open the pocketknife and get to her feet as Tobek got his hands around the gun and Elliard launched himself at Tobek.

A gunshot blasted, and Shaye flinched but managed to open the knife. It was tiny, and the idea of bringing a knife to a gunfight hit her hard. She glanced at Elliard, sure he'd been shot, but he hadn't realized his feet were bound and he'd tripped. Tobek's shot had gone wide, but he was aiming again, swinging the gun back at Elliard.

Shaye rushed forward, unable to believe she was risking her life for a gangster. She led with the knife, hoping to reach Tobek before he could readjust.

His gaze jumped to her; then his gun swung for her, but Elliard got to his knees, batting Tobek's hand aside with his bound ones and sending the gun flying.

Tobek responded with an uppercut, and Elliard flew backward, smacking his head on the workbench legs.

Shaye jabbed, but somehow Tobek grabbed her wrist, twisting until she dropped the knife, yelping at the pain. He took a swing at her, and she jerked out of the way, falling to her side.

Then he was moving toward her, holding the pocketknife she'd dropped in one hand and the knife he'd pressed to her throat in Cole's house in the other. She didn't know where he'd had it, but he was grinning, something pure evil in his eyes, as she shoved herself back to her feet.

She moved away from him, her hands up, reminding him, "This will never pass for a fight between me and Elliard." Her back bumped the workbench and then there was nowhere else to go.

COLE LEAPED OUT of the car before Luke even had it in Park. "Get the shotgun from the trunk," Cole yelled at his partner as he cleared his pistol from his holster and ran after Leonardo.

Leonardo swung around and fired. Cole ducked, wasting precious seconds glancing at Luke, but his partner's head popped back up over the steering wheel and he gave a thumbs-up.

Then Leonardo was racing for the barn again, and Cole hurried after him, even as a gunshot fired inside the structure—this one from a pistol. Fear spiked in Cole's veins, and he prayed he hadn't found Shaye only to have her killed seconds before he made it to her side.

"Stop!" Cole screamed, but Leonardo ignored him, darting inside the barn.

Cole pushed his strides, going as fast as he could, and skidding to a stop when he made it through the doors.

In front of him, Leonardo was lifting his shotgun to fire again. He was aiming at Elliard, who was groaning on the ground, but then Tobek spun toward him, dropped to the ground and grabbed a pistol. Leonardo moved the shotgun toward him.

Behind Tobek was Shaye, her hands up, backed against a workbench. She was *directly* behind Tobek. A blast from a shotgun could go through Tobek and into Shaye.

Tobek lifted his pistol, and Cole lined up his weapon as Leonardo's finger started to drop under the trigger guard.

It felt like it was all happening in slow motion and Cole could see it all playing out in his head. Luke was coming, but he wouldn't get here with the shotgun before three bullets were fired. Cole was going for Leonardo, but Tobek saw what he was doing and was starting to shift his weapon toward Cole.

Cole clenched his teeth. If he could stop Leonardo, Tobek could shoot him. Cole knew his partner would get in there and take out Tobek before he could kill Shaye. And that was all that mattered.

Time sped up again, as Cole heard himself screaming, saw Shaye twisting backward and saw Tobek snarling. Cole pulled the trigger, and Leonardo dropped, falling on top of his shotgun milliseconds before his finger cleared the guard and a shot went off.

Cole turned to Tobek, even though he knew he wouldn't make it.

Tobek knew it, too. He was actually grinning as his finger started to press the trigger. Then his eyes widened, and he crumpled.

Behind him Shaye was breathing heavily, holding what looked like a metal C-clamp in her hand that she'd grabbed off the workbench and slammed into Tobek's head.

"Shaye," Cole breathed. She was alive. He'd made it in time. His vision blurred, and Cole realized tears of relief had clouded his eyes. He blinked them back, and then she was limping toward him, still holding that C-clamp.

"Seriously? I missed it?"

Cole turned and Luke was in the doorway, brandishing the shotgun. "We could have used that a second ago," he teased his partner. "But luckily Shaye's got good aim, too."

Luke's gaze dropped to her makeshift weapon and he nodded, setting down the shotgun and pulling out his cuffs. He checked Leonardo's pulse, then shook his head and moved on to Tobek as Cole covered him with his pistol and Shaye kept coming toward him.

"Out cold," Luke said after checking Tobek. He cuffed the guy anyway, adding, "Nice job, Shaye." Then he checked Elliard, stood up and shook his head. "He's passed out, too. I'll call for reinforcements to transport these two back to the station and the coroner for Leonardo."

"Thanks," Cole told his partner, holstering his weapon and striding toward Shaye, who fell forward, letting him catch her. "Are you okay?"

She smiled shakily up at him. "Some cuts and bruises. A couple of nicks from that knife, and some broken toes. I'll live." Her smile shifted, changing into something serious. "I knew you'd find me. I'm so glad you found me before—"

"Me, too," Cole said, not wanting to think about the alternative. He bent, then carefully scooped her into his arms. "Shaye, I don't know what I would have done—"

She pressed a finger to his lips. "I'm okay." She gave him another trembling smile. "And now we can think about getting back to what we started before you got that darn call about Elliard."

Had that been today? It felt like a lifetime ago.

And speaking of a lifetime...

Cole kissed her hand, then kissed her lips, then spoke fast before he lost his nerve and waited until they were somewhere besides a barn in the middle of nowhere with his partner keeping watch over three violent criminals, two wounded and one dead. It wasn't the most romantic spot in the world, but he didn't want to wait another minute to tell Shaye how he felt.

"I do want to get back to that. I want to get back to dating you, and I want to work every day to deserve you. I want you to move in with me." When she opened her mouth, he hurried on quickly. "Or I can move in with you. I want to marry you and have babies together and live a long, happy life together."

Shaye's eyes widened, her lips moving but no words coming out. Then she laughed shakily. "Cole, we've barely started dating yet."

"I know. And I know it's fast, but—"

"But I like that plan," she cut him off. "Let's take it one step at a time. Because I love you. And I want that future with you."

He smiled at her, and he could tell by the way she was looking up at him that what he was thinking was plain on his face. But he said it anyway, because she deserved to hear it. "I love you, too, Shaye. Now let's get out of here."

He glanced back at Luke. "You got this?"

"Cavalry is on the way," Luke said, giving him a thumbs-up. "Keys are in the car."

"Good." Cole shifted Shaye in his arms and started walking. "Because I'm ready to start that future right now."

Epilogue

What did the chief of police want?

Shaye straightened her blouse and shoved down her nerves as she crossed the parking lot from the forensics lab to the police station. Funny how the walk didn't seem so scary anymore. But getting called to the chief of police's office? A little nerve-racking.

It had been three weeks since Tobek had taken her hostage in that barn. And while she'd wanted to drive out of there and straight back to Cole's house, he'd taken her to the hospital instead. They'd taped up her toes, inspected her cuts and told her to take it easy. By the time they were back in the car, her adrenaline had faded and she'd fallen asleep.

She'd woken to him carrying her inside his house, then he'd helped her clean up in the shower and tucked her into bed. The next morning, she'd learned Tobek and Elliard had been processed and were both heading to jail. She was dreading Tobek's trial, but Cole had assured her there was no way he was ever getting out again.

Since then things had fallen into a rhythm with Cole, like they'd been dating for years instead of weeks. She still had to pinch herself thinking about the things he'd said in that barn about their future. It wasn't that long ago she'd been daydreaming about him, thinking it would never be real.

Pulling open the door to the station, Shaye had a sudden flashback to the first day she'd arrived on the job and mistaken this building for the one she'd be reporting to. A smile quirked her lips, remembering how she'd turned a corner and slammed right into Cole. She'd stared up at him, turning beet red, knowing even then he was her fantasy man. And the reality was so much better than anything she could have imagined.

Confidence picked up her steps as she headed for that same turn she'd taken two years ago toward the chief's office. The hallway was emptier than usual, and Shaye wondered for an instant where everyone was. Then she rounded the corner and stopped in her tracks.

The hallway was filled with officers, and they were all staring at her. And was that… Shaye squinted through the crowd. It was. Andre and Marcos were here. What was going on?

She glanced around, looking for Cole, and then the crowd parted a little and he was walking through it. He strode up to her, then dropped to one knee, and her hands clasped over her mouth, smothering her gasp.

His hands were shaking a little as he opened a box, revealing a ring that seemed to catch the light from every angle. "Shaye, two years ago, right on this very spot, you changed my entire world. I didn't know it then, not really, though I probably should have, because you were on my mind every moment from then on."

"Cole," she whispered, dropping her hands from her lips. Her heart was thundering in her eardrums, and if it could burst from happiness, she was in some serious danger right now.

"I know being married to a cop might not be what you had in mind for your future, but—"

She dropped to her knees, too, taking his hands in hers, that gorgeous ring in the middle. "Oh, but it is. I'll tell you what. You teach me how to handle the worry that comes along with being married to a guy who runs into danger all the time, and I'll teach you how to open up more and value in yourself all the things I love about you. Deal?"

He grinned back at her. "Is that your way of saying yes?"

A smile trembled on her lips in response. "Did you ask me a question?" she teased.

He got serious, and, wow, did she love serious Cole, with his sky blue eyes laser focused on her. "Shaye Mallory, I'm looking for something a little different in my life."

The smile burst free as she remembered how not that long ago, he'd thought their differences would keep them apart. But the truth was she knew their differences would keep them going, make them stronger together.

"Will you marry me?"

"Yes," she whispered. "Oh, yes."

"We can't hear you!" someone called from the crowd. She was pretty sure it was Marcos.

Cole grinned as he slipped the ring on her finger and she yelled out, "Yes!"

Then the entire police station burst into applause, and Cole pulled her into his arms, kissing her the way he did in all her dreams. The way he was going to do for the rest of her life.

* * * * *

717/46

"I have a seriou[s] ... you."

God, even after all these years of mutual dislike and loathing, even after he'd married another model, a woman a few years older than she was, whom she'd nevertheless considered her mentor and close friend, whom he'd had a child with, even after he'd blamed her for helping his marriage to Jacqueline combust, how could she still feel this giddy anticipation? When was she going to get over this...ridiculous fascination with Nasir?

"How interesting," Yana said, pouring her excitement on thick even as her belly twisted into a knot. Leaning toward him, she mock-whispered, "But my kind of propositions are not usually your... *forte*."

Billion-Dollar Fairy Tales

Once upon a temptation...

Meet the Reddy sisters—Nush, Mira and Yana. As the granddaughters of tech tycoon Rao Reddy, their lives have been full of glitz and glamour. Until tragedy strikes and their beloved grandfather passes away. Amid their devastation, each girl finds a note, Rao's last gift for them to help them live out their dreams. But chasing their happiness won't be a smooth ride!

Nush has been in love with her longtime family friend and billionaire boss, Caio, for longer than she can remember. She's ready to move on... but then he proposes they have a convenient marriage!

Read Nush and Caio's story in
Marriage Bargain with Her Brazilian Boss

Mira and Aristos's marriage was purely for convenience, but Mira fled their powerfully real connection. Now...she's back with not one but two surprises!

Read Mira and Aristos's story in
The Reason for His Wife's Return

Yana and Nasir avoided the temptation of their connection once before, but now that they're bound together by a mutually beneficial deal, will the heat between them become too hot to ignore—or resist?

Read Yana and Nasir's story in
An Innocent's Deal with the Devil

All available now!

Tara Pammi

AN INNOCENT'S DEAL
WITH THE DEVIL

PRESENTS

Recycling programs
for this product may
not exist in your area.

ISBN-13: 978-1-335-59324-5

An Innocent's Deal with the Devil

Copyright © 2024 by Tara Pammi

For questions and comments about the quality of this book,
please contact us at CustomerService@Harlequin.com.

Harlequin Enterprises ULC
22 Adelaide St. West, 41st Floor
Toronto, Ontario M5H 4E3, Canada
www.Harlequin.com

Printed in U.S.A.

Tara Pammi can't remember a moment when she wasn't lost in a book—especially a romance, which was much more exciting than a mathematics textbook at school. Years later, Tara's wild imagination and love for the written word revealed what she really wanted to do. Now she pairs alpha males who think they know everything with strong women who knock that theory and them off their feet!

Books by Tara Pammi

Harlequin Presents

Returning for His Unknown Son

Billion-Dollar Fairy Tales

Marriage Bargain with Her Brazilian Boss
The Reason for His Wife's Return

Born into Bollywood

Claiming His Bollywood Cinderella
The Surprise Bollywood Baby
The Secret She Kept in Bollywood

Once Upon a Temptation

The Flaw in His Marriage Plan

Signed, Sealed...Seduced

The Playboy's "I Do" Deal

Visit the Author Profile page
at Harlequin.com for more titles.

CHAPTER ONE

SHE WAS NOT just broke. She was in a mountain of debt. And now that she was finally ready to admit her blunders and bawl her eyes out and beg him for help, the one man who'd loved her was gone.

Yana Reddy walked through the quiet, dark halls of her grandparents' house like a night wraith wandering through the dark woods from one of her favorite fantasy stories.

While her younger half sister, Nush, had always proclaimed her love of fairy tales, it was the much darker fantasy tales populated with demons and ghouls and djinns that drew Yana's interest. Especially one particular author she'd fallen in love with at a young age. Even then, her tastes had been drawn to the forbidden.

Now her grandfather leaving notes for his three granddaughters from beyond the grave appealed to her. She pulled the crisp folded letter out of its envelope and pushed it back in again without reading it, like she'd done a hundred times that day—the day they'd officially said goodbye to him.

Unlike both her half sisters, Mira and Nush, who'd

burst into happy tears at one last note from their beloved Thaata, she knew the moment she'd seen her name written in that beautiful cursive script, that she wasn't going to read it.

Not yet.

Maybe not ever.

That would be her punishment. Plus, the possibility of a forever unclaimed present appealed to the contrarian in her. One last ploy to annoy Thaata.

A few hours ago the house had been full of extended family, friends and people who'd loved and respected her grandfather, who'd started a software company called OneTech, which his protege Caio Oliveira had turned into a billion-dollar venture.

Thaata had believed in second chances. Only Yana had never been able to use one to prove herself worthy like her sisters had done. To make him look at her with respect and love. Not frustrated resignation and the pain that he couldn't reach her.

Their alcoholic father had clearly preferred variety in his sexual partners for none of the sisters shared a mother, so Yana's grandparents had been the only responsible adults in their lives, and had essentially raised the three girls.

But all through her childhood and adolescence, Yana had resented them for it. Had chosen, in her early teens, to go and live with her flighty, unreliable, beautiful mother, Diana, instead of what she'd considered to be the much stricter regime of her grandparents.

By the time she'd realized the irreparable damage Diana had done to her, it had been too late. She'd trusted a woman who had, in return, emptied out all of Yana's bank accounts to pay for a cleverly disguised gambling habit.

Worse, in the last few months, Diana had ruined Yana's credit by borrowing off her credit cards when she'd refused to carry on funding her extravagant spending.

Closing the door to her grandparents' bedroom behind her, Yana fought the grief that had kept bubbling up like lava. If she let it out, it would burn her through, leaving nothing but ashes. She walked around, trailing her fingers over Thaata's things—a worn-out leather diary on his nightstand, a biography title on his desk and a picture of her, Mira and Nush with him.

It had been taken during one glorious summer where Yana hadn't fought with him or her grandmother, when Diana had gone to live with her brand-new second husband.

How could you have made such a wrong choice? she wanted to scream at her teenage self. How could she have chosen to live with her mother, who'd shown her nothing but neglect and abuse, over the grandparents who'd only wanted the best for her?

A woman who'd eagerly asked Yana about the *assets* that Thaata might have left her only a day after his death. Yana didn't have to wait for the reading of the will to tell Diana that whatever assets Thaata might have left her would be all tied up so that she couldn't touch them for a very long time. A witness to Yana and her grandfather's arguments more than once, Diana had believed it.

She'd left instantly, leaving Yana with a crippling debt. Just…breezed out of her life with barely a goodbye.

Almost nearing thirty now, Yana's modeling contracts were coming few and far between. As she didn't want to be a model for the rest of her life, she'd already given up on most of the networking necessary to stay current. She thought again about the new career—a work in progress for some years—she'd hoped would take shape before her life had fractured into tiny fragments.

For a second she considered asking Mira or Nush to help her sort out the mess her life had become. But she couldn't. And not just because they were finally moving forward in their own lives with men they loved.

Hitting rock bottom had cleared up one thing for Yana—she'd fix her life by herself. It was the only way to restore her own faith in herself.

Grabbing the keys of Thaata's vintage car and one of his cigars from a secret compartment in his dresser, she tiptoed back to her room.

Rummaging through her closet, she grabbed a black leather corset top and skinny jeans and got dressed. Pushing her feet into stilettos, she tied her hair into a high ponytail, slapped on mascara and lip gloss without looking at the mirror and rushed to the garage.

The crisp night made goose bumps rise up on her skin as she drove with the windows rolled down. With the engine humming sweetly and the scent of the cigar smoke filling her nostrils, she felt a measure of peace, for the first time in weeks.

Running away again, a voice very much like Thaata's

taunted, but Yana refused to listen to it now just as she'd done when he'd been alive.

Yana knew who the man was the moment the double doors of the secluded VIP lounge of the night club opened. He stood framed by the archway bathed in beams of purple lighting.

She knew even though it was dark and quiet.

She knew before that distinctive gait brought him to the chaise longue over which she'd draped herself, having fought off three different men who'd wanted to take her home.

She knew because she'd always possessed a weird extra sense when it came to *him*.

A Yana's stupid-for-this-man sense.

A basic, lizard-brain *wanting* that screamed she was prey even though he'd never played predator. A let's-ditch-any-self-respect-and-make-a-play-for-him urge.

Nasir Hadeed.

World-famous fantasy author, current political strategist and retired investigative journalist, reclusive billionaire and most important of all—her stepbrother for just four years.

They'd only ever spent a few months under the same roof out of the four years his father had been married to Diana. During the time when she'd transformed from a gangly, awkward fifteen to a leggy, brazen, stupidly confident nineteen, who'd imagined herself to be a tempting seductress.

Already, Nasir had been successful, renowned and

respected in literary circles and the political world as a just-retired war-zone correspondent.

Twelve years older than she was, he'd not only been incisively brilliant in ways Yana couldn't comprehend, but also effortlessly suave and stunning with a roguish glint in his eyes that the world didn't see. His brilliant, award-winning tracts on war zones and world issues hadn't captured her heart, though.

It had been the fantasy novels he'd written, garnering worldwide acclaim that had thoroughly captivated her. Those brief months she'd spent with him had been in a different universe in which he hadn't loathed her. An alternate, upside-down timeline.

He'd indulged her overlong, extravagant breakfasts at the palatial mansion that had been his father's house in Monaco—when she'd demanded to know why a loathed character had to be redeemed or a favorite one had met her demise—with a dispassionate fondness and that dark smile. As if she were a stray dog he'd pat on the head and throw a few morsels of affection at.

But thanks to her behavior on her nineteenth birthday, when he'd returned from the incident overseas that had given him all those scars, he'd written her off forever.

How Yana wished she possessed one of those time stones he'd written about in one of his novels. So many wrong and questionable and self-defeating decisions she could erase with one turn of the stone. Especially when it came to Thaata and him.

Two men—two of the most important men in her life who'd influenced her, made her want to be more than who she was. One of them, her grandfather, was forever gone now thinking the worst of her, and one was determined to think the worst of her forever. She wiped at a stray tear that flew into her hair, donning the superficial persona that had become like a second skin now.

Because if Nasir pitied her, she'd just fall apart.

One signal from Nasir to the nearly invisible bartender and bright lights illuminated the dark corner. Immediately, he moved to block the glare that made Yana blink gritty eyes.

Shards of light traced the blade-sharp cheekbones, the hollows beneath and the wide, thin-lipped mouth. And the scar that bisected his upper lip and zigzagged through his left cheek—the remnant of a near-fatal knife wound that had changed the trajectory of his life. And hers, in a way.

Awareness pressed down on her as he took her in with that quiet intensity. She'd never understood how there could be such intense energy between them when they detested each other.

"Hello, Yana."

A full body shiver overtook her and still, she lay there, stupidly gaping at him, gathering her armor, which had already been battered by grief and loss. "Am I in hell, then?"

In response, he shrugged off his jacket and draped it over her mostly exposed chest and bare shoulders. She'd always marveled at how cruel and dispassionate Nasir's kindness could be. Still, she couldn't sit up. Couldn't get her heart to stop thundering away in her ears. "Go away, Nasir. I'm in full party-girl mode and as we both know, you're lethally allergic to that."

It was like craving the warmth of the sun but spending years trying to figure out how to ignore its existence in the sky.

Of course, the hateful man sat down on the coffee table, cornering her. Despite the dark, even with her stomach hurting because she'd barely eaten anything the whole day, even with her head in a weird limbo of grief and self-directed rage, warmth unspooled low in her belly at the familiar scent of him.

Bergamot and sandalwood—it was as if a chemist had experimented and figured out the perfect combination of scents that provoked all of her sexual fantasies and then doused Nasir Hadeed in it.

Two minutes in his company and Yana wanted to kiss the man senseless and curse him to whatever hell would torment him the most. The only constants in her life were her abiding love for her sisters and this mad obsession…for Nasir.

She took a puff on her cigar, blew out a ring like a photographer friend of hers had taught her. Not her fault that Nasir chose to sit right in that space.

Shadows created by the interplay of darkness and light gave his face a saturnine cast. As if those stark features needed to be tarred with any more harshness. Light, amber-colored eyes, deep-set and invasively perceptive, met hers. The large beak of his nose—which should have rendered him ugly but instead made him look intellectual—made it effortlessly easy for him to look down on her.

"How are you, Yana?"

She took another puff of the cigar. "How did you know where to find me?"

"One of your staff followed you here and called me."

Raising a brow, she went for insouciance that she didn't feel in the least. "Keeping tabs on your favorite supermodel, you naughty man?"

Something flitted in and out of those thickly fringed eyes, too fast for her to catch it. "I was nearby when you tore out of the garage as if a demon was chasing you."

"I didn't realize I was so important to you that you'd come all this way to pay your respects to my grandfather," she said, going on the offensive.

There was no other way to act around him. Shields up one hundred percent and donning titanium armor, like the prickly heroine in her favorite sci-fi show. Also based on a novel this very man had written.

Seriously, her obsession with him had no chance of petering out when she gorged herself on every word he'd ever written—novels and articles and newsletters and political treatises—like a wanton glutton.

"Clearly, it was a self-indulgent fantasy to imagine I'd find you behaving like a responsible, normal adult in the throes of grief." The cigar that she'd barely taken two puffs of was roughly yanked away from her lips and put out with a pinch of fingers that should have burned him but drew not even a quiet hiss. "That's a disgusting habit and a lethal one, too."

"Did you miss me so much that you came all this way to harass me, Nasir? No one else to look down on and feel better about yourself?"

"I came here because I need you."

Yana sat up with the force of a coiled spring that had been stretched too far back, for far too long. Her head swam, the reason anything from starvation to the special kind of dizziness only he could cause. "Huh! The world is upside down today, I guess. Or I'm traveling through parallel universes like Uzma does," she said, mentioning the intrepid heroine of his latest novel. Plucking her phone from her jeweled designer clutch, she opened the camera app and thrust it in his face. "Care to repeat that so that I can record it?"

Silence lingered, full of his infinite patience and her childish taunts.

"Fine." She straightened her posture on the chaise, tucking her knees away from his. They were both tall people and in the tight space of his legs, her awareness was on steroids.

She tried to not linger on the way his black trousers bunched at his thighs, or the way the white shirt open to his chest drew her gaze to the swirls of hair on dark olive skin. Or the large platinum-faced dial of his watch on a corded wrist. Or the long, bare fingers that had once—only once—lingered on her jaw with something almost bordering on tenderness.

"I have a serious proposition for you."

God, even after all these years of mutual dislike and loathing, even after he'd married another model, a woman a few years older than she was, whom she'd nevertheless considered her mentor and close friend, whom he'd had a child with, even after he'd blamed her for helping his marriage to Jacqueline combust, how could she still feel this giddy anticipation? When was she going to get over this…ridiculous fascination with him?

"How interesting," she said, pouring her excitement on thick even as her belly twisted into a knot. Leaning toward him, she mock-whispered, "But my kind of propositions are not usually your…*forte*."

A muscle jumped in his jaw, the scar twisting with the action. He thrust a hand through that thick, wavy hair he usually kept military short. "Oh, believe me. Having found you in a nightclub two days after your grandfather's death, smoking a cigar, looking like you do… I'm questioning my common sense in even being here."

"Ahh…now, that's the guy I know and love to loathe." A tinkling laugh escaped her. "Come, Nasir. You might be a diplomat in the biggest political circles and the hottest bachelor on the planet but it's the lowest denominator of you I get, no? Let's not try something new today, of all days. I've had enough shocks, thank you very much."

Remorse flashed through those usually inscrutable eyes. "I'm sorry for your loss, Yana. I know that grief takes different forms—"

"You don't know anything about my relationship with Thaata."

"Fair enough."

Irritation and hunger and something more danced across Yana's skin as she studied him.

"It's about Zara."

His daughter. Her facade fell away like snakeskin.

She reached for his hands but pulled away at the last minute. "Why the hell couldn't you have opened with that instead of insulting me?"

"Your worry about her is real." He sounded stunned.

"And you're an ass."

Feeling caged, her breaths coming shallow, she stood up. Her foot had fallen asleep on her, forcing her to grab him to keep her balance.

His white linen shirt proved no barrier to the firm muscles underneath and the heat coming off him. Under her fingers, his abdomen clenched.

The sensation of his hot, hard body under her touch stung her palm. His grip on her tightened as she tried to yank herself away. "Damn it, Yana! Stay still." The tips of his fingers pressed into her bare arm; one corded arm wrapped around her waist. It was too much contact and hyperventilation wasn't far away. "Or you'll ruin that pretty face and any hope of—"

"What's wrong with Zara?"

Now that she'd managed her overreaction to his proximity, she could see the exhaustion beneath his calm. It made the light, slightly raised tissue of his scar stand out in stark contrast to the rest of his skin. Worry and fatigue carved deep grooves around his wide mouth.

An answering pang vibrated within her chest.

"She's fine, physically. But losing her mother at that young age, even one as mostly absent as Jacqueline was…the doctors are saying she's not adjusting well to the loss." His Adam's apple moved up and down as he swallowed. "We've tried everything. It has been…

painful to see a bubbly, extroverted child like her with-draw to that extent. I'm at a loss as to how to help her."

"Children are much more resilient than we give them credit for. With support, Zara will get over losing Jac-queline."

"Have you gotten over your mom's neglectful, bor-dering on abusive behavior toward you?"

Something hot and oily bellowed under her skin. "That's none of your business."

"I'm just saying Zara shouldn't have to go through this alone."

"How is she alone when she has you?"

"I've tried my damnedest to get close to her. Don't pretend as if you don't know how things are between us. How Jacqueline messed everything up. How she tried to cut me off from my own daughter."

"I don't want to talk about Jacqueline."

"I don't, either." He rubbed a hand over his face. "This is about Zara. Not you, not me and definitely not her mother. She lights up when you text her or video call her. She talks for hours about your chats, your emails, the cards you send her from all over the world. That col-lection of keychains you've given her over the years… Every single one is worn down for how much she plays with them." A shuddering sigh made his chest rise and fall. "She keeps asking for you, Yana."

Yana jerked away from him, wobbled again and braced herself against the back of a dark leather sofa. Shame coiled tight in her chest. "I'm sorry I haven't been to visit her recently."

Damn it, how could she have forgotten all the promises she'd made to Zara when Jacqueline had fallen ill? Why had she gotten involved when she had such an abysmal record at handling expectations? What about being the child of two absent, neglectful, narcissistic parents equipped her to handle a fragile child? "Between losing my grandparents only months apart and work—" and keeping her head afloat while her mother robbed her blind "—I... I've been scattered."

"Nothing new in how you live your life, then, huh?"

His criticism stung hard and deep.

She loved Zara. Loved her despite the fact that Jacqueline had used Yana's tumultuous feelings for Nasir to feel better about her crumbling marriage. Despite the fact that he loathed the very sight of Yana.

Under the guise of fixing her hair, she dabbed at the tears prickling behind her eyes. Her failure rubbed her hollow.

She had failed Zara. After vowing to herself that she wouldn't let the little girl feel alone in the world like she'd once felt.

The vague headache that had been hunting her all day returned with a vengeance, making her lightheaded. Or was it the fact that she'd skipped lunch and dinner and her sugar levels were falling fast? "No, nothing new."

A soft curse escaped his mouth.

Nasir never cursed and if she was feeling normal, she'd have recognized it for the win it was. Suddenly, she became aware of the heat of his body at her back and her dizziness intensified. His fingers landed on her shoulders, the rough pads deliciously abrasive against her bare skin.

"I'm sorry. I came to ask you for help. For a favor. To…beg you if I need to. And yet, I can't seem to stop insulting you."

"Nothing new in how you talk to me either, then, huh?" Yana glared at him and sighed. "I want to see her. I do. Zara's important to me, one of the few important people in my life. But…" She rubbed at her pounding temples. "Right now things are impossible to get away from."

"That's where the proposition part comes in."

"Not necessary. I love Zara as if she were…" She bit her lip, heat flooding her cheeks.

My own, she'd been about to say. Which was laughable even in thought because she was the last person who should be responsible for a young girl. She couldn't even manage her own life without sinking into debt and self-rage.

Nasir's amber-colored eyes gleamed. "And yet, you don't act like she is. She's seen you once since Jacqueline died."

"I just told you I've been busy with shoots and—"

"I've heard whispers that you're completely broke. If that's true, I really don't care how it happened. I'll pay all your debts and pay you whatever sum you demand on top if you come spend the next three months with Zara."

"No."

Her answer reverberated in the quiet around them, the darkness amplifying it.

No, I don't want to be anywhere near you.

No, I don't want to spend three months under the same roof as you.

No, I finally have enough self-preservation to not cut myself down just because you hate me. No, no, no.

Even if that meant breaking her promise to Zara.

"I know you have no way out of the financial hole you've dug yourself—"

"No."

"Because your modeling contracts are drying up—"

"No."

"So my bet is that any assets you have will be seized soon and—"

"No."

"Damn it, Yana! You need this as much as Zara needs you."

"No," Yana repeated, even as the word continued to ring in her ears and her vision was blurring and fading and she felt nauseated and dizzy and...

"Yana...look at me. Yana! What the hell have you done to yourself now, you..."

He's really beautiful. The errant thought dropped into Yana's fading consciousness.

Nasir grabbed her and pulled her to him, and she could finally see the amber flecks in his eyes and the long, curved lashes casting shadows onto razor-sharp cheekbones. He was looking at her as if he didn't loathe her. As if he was actually worried about her. As if he...

No, she couldn't spend three months with the man she'd loved for half her life.

Not that she loved him anymore. *Not at all.* The

tightness in her chest was only an echo of what she'd once felt for him.

Yana fainted and in the flash of a second before she lost consciousness, she had the disturbingly pitiful thought that Nasir had caught her. That he hadn't let her fall to the ground.

CHAPTER TWO

NASIR HADEED WALKED the perimeter of the VIP lounge like a caged predator as the young doctor that had been dragged from the exotic restaurant downstairs examined Yana. He glanced at his watch for the hundredth time in the last half hour, a powerless ire simmering under his skin.

She'd remained unconscious for three and a half minutes. It had, however, felt like a hundred eternities. His heart hadn't yet calmed down from its rapid pounding rhythm.

Despite his long career in war-torn zones and some of the most dangerous places in the world, despite having tasted the loss of a woman he'd loved once that had forever calcified his heart, he'd never been so terrified as when Yana had folded into his arms like a cardboard doll. Amidst her litany of *nos*.

The saving grace had been that he'd shouted for his bodyguard/assistant. Ahmed had had the presence of mind to immediately commandeer a doctor.

Nasir had rubbed her arms up and down as soon as he'd carried her to the chaise longue. Even with her light brown hair hanging in a limp, messy ponytail, her lips chapped and even bleeding in a couple of places for she had the habit of worrying her lips with her teeth, her face a sickly sheen of white, she was still the most stunningly beautiful woman he'd ever seen.

Worse, not an hour in her company and he was cursing her recklessness, his own decisions that had led him to need her, and the universe all in one go.

And his weakness when it came to her, too, for he hadn't been able to stop running his fingers over the jut of those legendary cheekbones and the sharp, elongated tip of her signature nose that had skyrocketed her to fame at the tender age of sixteen.

Once she'd recovered consciousness, he'd moved to the far end of the cavernous lounge. To give her privacy and to get himself under control. *Ya, Allah*, what was wrong with him?

He'd chased her halfway around the world to this damned nightclub because he needed her for his daughter. And yet, all he'd done was insult her, over and over again.

Where was the diplomat the world lauded? Where was the responsible father of a five-year-old?

I always get the lowest denominator of you...

If only she knew how close to the vulgar truth she was. How she inspired and invoked and ignited his basest instincts. When she taunted him. When those gorgeous brown eyes landed near his mouth and skidded away. When she simply fluttered about in the locus of his own existence.

Her soft whispers as she spoke to the young doctor,

the quiet but husky chuckle, the trembling shoulders… everything about her called to him.

If only he could see the beautiful, vapid, vain teen she'd suddenly turned into one summer, he'd have no problem dealing with her.

His disastrous marriage to Jacqueline Yusuf—a sophisticated model and businesswoman he'd once considered his equal in every way—had completely cured him of the stupidity of trusting his judgment when it came to women.

But Yana…had always been indefinably stubborn and refused to be slotted into any one box.

He couldn't look at her and not remember the fifteen-year-old who'd shyly hero-worshipped him the first time he'd visited his father and his new wife. Or the one who'd begged for his autograph on a first edition. Or the passionate, sweet teenager who'd yelled and cried when he'd killed off her favorite character, or the hug she'd given him with an endearing smile on her suddenly stunning face when he'd brought that favorite character of hers back to life in the next novel.

He couldn't not see the nineteen-year-old who'd shocked him by walking through his room ditching pieces of clothing on the way to his bed, boldly declaring that she loved him with all of her heart, body and soul.

Or the girl who'd lied to her mother that Nasir had kissed her. Or the woman who'd looked as if she'd been dealt a staggering blow when Jacqueline, her friend and mentor, had introduced him as her fiancé. Or the woman who'd barely met his eyes when she'd stood by Jacqueline's side when they'd gotten married.

Or the woman who'd lied more than once to help hide Jacqueline's many affairs from him. Or the woman who'd stayed by Jacqueline's bedside for the last few weeks during her battle with cancer.

Or the woman who had miraculously managed to carve a place for herself in his young daughter's heart. Or the woman he'd touched in tenderness after Jacqueline had died, not a few minutes before his lawyers had discovered that Jacqueline had been preparing to sue him for solo custody of Zara, and Yana would have been the character witness to prove his negligence toward his daughter.

And yet, he'd learned, only after Jacqueline had died, how Yana had spent hours entertaining Zara, watching her, cooking for her, reading to her while Jacqueline was supposed to have been looking after her, how much attention she'd bestowed on his daughter when it should have been her mother doing that, how many times Jacqueline had dropped her off with Yana.

Yana Auntie this, Yana Auntie that... It was all his five-year-old girl would speak of. Just when Nasir had written Yana off entirely, the blasted woman revealed a new, complex dimension to herself that had dragged him back under her spell.

She loathed him and yet, she was capable of genuinely loving his child. What was he supposed to make of her? If only this ridiculous attraction he'd fought for so long would fade.

But he needed her and damn it, he needed Yana well again and ready to spar with him.

He needed her to not look like a lost waif, one hard breath away from falling apart. He needed her to fight him tooth and nail so that he didn't have to feel guilty about how he'd talked to her tonight.

She *had* just lost her grandparents—the only responsible adults she'd known in her life. And he'd done nothing but insult her and minimize her very real grief.

He'd never met another woman who provoked such extreme reactions in him. Not even Fatima—the woman he'd loved a lifetime ago—had tied him up in knots like Yana did.

From the tendrils of tenderness that had swamped him as he'd held her, to the rage that she didn't care enough about her own health. Even back then, he'd only learned of her diabetes when she'd gone into shock due to low sugar levels. It had been reckless and naive and foolish at sixteen. Now, almost thirteen years later... Had she still no sense of self-preservation?

What if he hadn't been there to catch her when she'd fainted and force feed her the bar of chocolate when she'd recovered consciousness? What if no one knew her whereabouts and she'd lain there for hours, going into shock? What if he'd had to inform his child that her Yana Auntie had taken seriously ill, too?

And he was inviting this...train wreck, this selfish, infuriatingly stubborn woman into his precious little girl's life.

Into his own life.

Into his space——his haven, which he allowed no one into.

It was like issuing an invitation to chaos and mayhem and sheer madness to reside in his house, in his head, in his heart.

"Here, sir," said Ahmed, stalling his walk, a bottle of water in his hand.

Nasir shook his head, too tired to reprimand the older man for addressing him using the honorific.

"Is Ms. Reddy okay, do you think?"

On cue, Yana laughed, leaning toward the young doctor.

He *wasn't* jealous of her attention toward the damned doctor, or her laughter or whatever it was she was saying to him. *He wasn't.*

"It was a miracle you caught her, Inshallah," Ahmed continued, unaware of his employer's roiling emotions. "Or she might have really hurt herself."

Nasir grunted and restarted his perambulations of the lounge, cutting closer and closer to where the doctor was now entering her phone number into his own cell phone. If he gritted his teeth any tighter, he was going to need dental work.

"Did the doctor say what caused the faint?" Ahmed asked.

"She probably forgot to eat." Nasir cleared his throat. "She's diabetic."

"I remember. Anything else you need from me?"

"No, get some sleep. We'll leave for London first thing tomorrow morning."

"Ms. Reddy has agreed to spend time with Zara baby, then?" Ahmed inquired, all polite affability.

Yana's multiple *nos* echoed inside Nasir's head like a chant. She hadn't simply refused him. No, she'd looked horrified—as if he'd invited her to sacrifice herself at some demon's altar.

He usually encouraged that impression of himself in most people, including his extended family and friends. That she saw him as some kind of autocratic, unfeeling beast grated, though.

"Sir?"

"No, she hasn't agreed." He bit out the words. "But she will. Even if it means I have to—"

"I know that you and Ms. Reddy don't see eye to eye, but I will not support kidnapping the young woman, sir. Even for Zara baby's sake."

Nasir laughed, the tension in his muscles relaxing for the first time in days. His bodyguard's strait-laced morality and hero complex never ceased to amaze him. "Things are going to be hard enough dealing with her, Ahmed. She doesn't need you as her champion."

"Beg your pardon, sir, but your father taught me that everyone deserves a champion. Ms. Reddy does, too. Especially since I've never seen you treat anyone with the kind of…" Ahmed broke off, then cast him an arch look that communicated everything he didn't say. "Have you forgotten how much your mother loathes Ms. Reddy?"

"She'll understand that Zara needs her," Nasir said, but even he didn't believe it. His mother's reaction to his bringing Yana home was a bridge he'd cross when he came to it.

"I just think bringing Zara baby to her could've been easier," Ahmed added with infinite patience.

"And let her drag Zara around like unwanted luggage just like Jacqueline did? Let my five-year-old daughter be exposed to alcohol and drugs and parties and toxic behaviors like her mother did? Should I also expose her to all the lurid gossip about her mother and her lovers that's still flying around even after all these months?"

"You're holding your wife's past mistakes against Ms. Reddy. I've never known you to be so...cruel." Ahmed sighed. "It *is* a hard situation. But if Ms. Reddy says she cannot make it, then she must have a good reason. I have seen her with Zara baby and she adores her, just as much as the little girl adores Ms. Reddy."

The conviction in Ahmed's voice only fortified his own. "Don't worry, Ahmed. I won't make you a party to this. You can catch a different flight." His jaw tight, Nasir stared at the woman who was sure to cause him untold problems once he was in his house. "But by kidnapping or some other way, she's coming home with me."

"Who's kidnapping whom?" Yana asked behind him.

Nasir turned around to find the young doctor glancing up adoringly at her, his arm propping her up. "Everything okay, Doc?" he asked, wishing he could laser the man's arm off with his vision.

"I'm fine," muttered the irritated voice next to him. Whatever the doctor saw in Nasir's face, he replied hurriedly, "Ms. Reddy's vitals are all good. Just exhaustion brought on by weakness."

"Glucose levels?"

"Normal. The chocolate bar you fed her helped stabilize her. She just needs lots of rest, hydration and proper meals."

"Ahmed," Nasir said, somehow holding on to the last thread of his patience.

His bodyguard escorted the reluctant, dazed doctor out the door while he was still shaking his cell phone in Yana's direction in the universal sign of "call me."

Finally, Nasir turned his attention to her.

Yana stood leaning against another high-backed lounger, her fingers fiddling with the jacket he'd draped over her. *His* jacket.

It hung on her shoulders, the thick collar drawing his gaze to the smooth skin between her small breasts and the one button holding it closed farther down. The tie holding her hair together had fallen off and now the golden-brown waves fell past her shoulders, the edges curling up.

"Don't treat me like an idiot," she bit out, all huskiness gone.

She still looked pale to him, but at least the fight was back in her. "Don't act like one, then."

"Just because you've caught me out at a bad time doesn't mean you get to look down that arrogant beak of a nose at me."

"You fainted, Yana," he said, gritting his teeth again. "And didn't respond for three and a half minutes."

Even the obvious fright in his tone had no effect on her.

"It's been a horrible few weeks. No, months. Seeing you just made it worse. I told you but you didn't listen."

When she wobbled, Nasir caught her at the waist. She fell into him with a soft thud, a quiet, enraged growl escaping her mouth. He felt her anger, her grief, her resignation, as if they were his own. Felt the force of her aversion to him.

"I hate you," she whispered, almost to herself. "I hate that you're the one who found me when I'm at my lowest."

Nasir let them wash over him, hoping the venom and rage in her words would dilute his own awareness. Her face close to his, her warm breath feathered over his jaw. Then there was the prick of her fingernails into his forearm. The wildcat was doing that on purpose and yet, the sensation only made his arousal sharper.

This was how it would be every minute between them—she cursing at him and he…would be in a constant state of arousal. It was funny, really, how they'd come full circle. She loathed him now and he couldn't be near her without his body betraying him like a damned teenager.

For a man who'd seen that heaven and hell could exist side by side on this very earth, maybe this was just punishment for his cruelty toward her. When she'd been nineteen and had needed firm handling and kind words and not his blistering wrath. When she'd been his bride's maid of honor at their wedding, Jacki's nurse at her bedside, a grief-stricken best friend with his child sobbing in her arms.

For a second he indulged the idea of telling her what her nearness did to him. Of shocking her as she constantly did him.

Would she be disgusted by his near-constant desire for her? Would she call him a roaring hypocrite as he deserved? Or would she simply count him as one among the scores of lecherous men that hit on her?

Slowly, feeling as if he'd run a marathon with no victory at the end, he tugged the neckline of her jacket higher.

"Can you please stop manhandling me? I'm all sweaty and gross. And why the hell did you cut open my top?"

"You were hyperventilating even before you fainted." He'd thanked the dim lighting of the lounge as the leather of her corset top had splayed open under the sharpness of his penknife. He didn't need more pictures of her naked perfection in his head. "That damned thing was so tight it's a miracle you could breathe."

Earlier she'd been too cold. Now her skin was warm as he held her up. The indent of her tiny waist, the slight flare of her hips, the jut of her hip bone, the smooth warmth of her skin…everything about her was fragile in his fingers.

"Let me go," she demanded.

"You'll kiss the floor the second I do," he said, holding himself rigid and stiff. Even with the aroma of cigar and the leather of the nightclub clinging to her, she smelled good.

It had been too long since he'd held a woman like this. Since he'd had sex. Since he'd worked out the pent-up frustrations of his body instead of engaging his mind.

Learning of Jacqueline's affairs had put him off relationships. Swiping left or right or whatever the hell side he was supposed to, casual dating or sex with strangers…he hadn't been fond of it in his twenties. At forty-two, the very idea of taking some strange woman to his bed made him want to hurl. And yet, every inch of his body was buzzing with an electric hum now.

Ironic that the one woman who made him react this way at the most innocent of contacts was someone he could never have. Even for a casual fling.

"Escort me to a cab, then."

"No."

"Have Ahmed drive me home, then."

"No. And for God's sake, stop arguing with me just for the heck of it."

"Or what?" she said, thrusting her face into his with a belligerence that got his blood pumping.

"Don't push me, Yana. We'll go to my hotel suite, where you'll eat, sleep for however many hours your body needs and then, in the morning, we'll finish our discussion."

"I don't want to spend another minute around you." She stepped back from him, palms raised. "If I have a heart attack next, it will all be your fault, Nasir."

He'd had enough. "You can screech and scream like a banshee for all I care. I'm not letting you out of my sight anytime soon."

Without batting an eyelid, he picked her up and threw her over his shoulder, fireman style. God, she weighed so little that he didn't even breathe hard, though it had been a while since his job demanded something so physical.

To his eternal surprise, she fell quiet. And he knew it was because she was on the last reserves of her energy. The chocolate bar would only prop her up for a while. Her quiet resignation rid him of any guilt that he was railroading her when she was feeling this weak.

She needed looking after as much as his five-year-old did, at least for a little while. Resolve renewed, he forged through the screaming throes of the nightclub.

Barely a few minutes later he crossed the foyer, then pushed the button for the elevator with Ahmed at his back. Thank God he'd booked a full suite at the same hotel. Still, they'd caught more than one curious hotel guest's attention. More than one eager paparazzo's prurient gaze.

But at least he had her now.

CHAPTER THREE

THE UNIVERSE WAS really cruel, Yana thought, as the man she'd taught herself to hate—and, oh, how easy he made it for her—placed her on his bed with a tenderness that stemmed from all the wrong reasons.

She rolled away from him using energy she didn't have and instantly regretted the impulse. It was *his* bed she was rolling in; his suite he'd brought her to. That heady cocktail of clean sweat and his signature scent clung to the sheets.

If she closed her eyes, she could still feel the hard dig of his shoulder over her belly, his muscled back smushing her breasts, his corded forearm at the tops of her thighs, holding her in place. Even more shocking was his sudden devolution from the veneer of the starchy, uptight, no-public-display gentleman he'd always shown the world.

Who was this Nasir who had no control over his words or his actions?

Slowly, she sat up, cataloging the exhaustion sweeping through her. She was hungry. Tired. Her mouth felt dry and gritty. But she hadn't had a fainting spell in years. Not that Nasir would believe her.

The stress of the past few weeks, her new medication and the fact that she hadn't eaten all day…they were excuses, however valid. She'd let herself drift into chaos again.

But better Nasir who found her than Mira or Nush or God forbid Caio—who took protective instincts to a whole other level. Her sisters would've been very upset at how close to burnout she'd edged. They'd have blamed themselves and that was a vicious cycle she'd never enter again with loved ones.

At least with Nasir, she'd had a lifetime of dealing with his contempt.

But if there was one thing they had in common, it was the stubborn tenacity once they decided on a course.

She saw it in his face now, in the tight set of his jaw. In the edgy energy that imbued his usually elegant movements. He'd decided that Zara needed her and he was determined to drag her with him. But as much as she adored Zara, how could she be a stabilizing influence on her when her own life was only two streets away from utter mayhem?

Brow furrowed, Nasir approached the bed as if she were a wild animal he hoped to not provoke. Yana splayed her arms over the thick headboard behind her and straightened. "I won't bite, Nasir." When his jaw tightened, she grinned. "I mean, I know you're much too conventional to enjoy something so…outside the box."

"Good to see your usual…spark back. As for what I enjoy…" His gaze skidded toward her mouth and away so fast that she wasn't sure if she'd imagined it. "Just because I don't advertise my desires for all the world to see doesn't mean they're all vanilla."

A shiver of pleasure ran down her spine—keenly felt after the miserable past few months. Damn, but the man could play.

With each step he took toward her, fantasies she'd buried years ago roared back to life. Done in pale pinks and warm yellows, the luxury suite amplified the stark, forbidding sensuality of the man. There had always been something almost ascetic about him. And like in the stories of celestial women who seduced sages, Yana had always imagined herself to be the one who broke through his reserve.

Coming to a stop at the foot of the bed, he rolled a bottle of water toward her on the silk sheets. She emptied it in a matter of seconds, wiping the water that dripped down her chin with the back of her hand. All the while, his gaze seared like a physical touch.

"One would think you'd take better care of your body seeing how it's your only livelihood."

She held her automatic response by the last frayed thread of self-control. Her dreams for the future, her hopes for a different career… He hadn't won the privilege of hearing about them. On the contrary, she wouldn't be surprised if he mocked her for having them in the first place. Curling her lip, she said, "One would think you'd have more capacity for empathy and understanding given you've seen the worst of the world."

His mouth flinched.

Had she wounded him? Was that even possible for a mere mortal like her?

"You're right. I have been overly judgmental when it comes to you. But that shouldn't preclude you from—"

"Please, Nasir. Try to understand. I cannot come with you." She let him hear her frustration, let him see her powerlessness in granting him this wish.

Amber-brown eyes searched hers. "Of course, you can. It's a choice you make to put someone else's needs, a child's needs, before your own." Hands tucked into his trouser pockets, he studied her with dispassionate intensity. "Tell me what I can do to sweeten the pot."

She raised a brow, calling on all the haughtiness cameras had taught her to fake most of her life. "How pedestrian and predictable of you, Nasir. Like every other man, you think you can buy me. Even my grandfather couldn't rise above bribes to make me behave."

"We both know you're in a financial hole. I'm giving you an easy way out." He rubbed a finger over his brow. "I admit I'm surprised you're not running toward me to snatch my hand off."

"Or you underestimate my loathing for sharing a roof with you."

Their gazes met and held. Memories swirled across the distance between them.

Long, dark nights spent in Jacqueline's Paris apartment watching over her as her death drew nearer. In those few weeks she'd spent at her friend's side, an intimacy of sorts had developed between Nasir and her. A byproduct of being so close to mortality, no doubt.

It had been more insidious than physical attraction, more dangerous. An intense curiosity in his eyes—as if he meant to peel away her armor and see beneath. As if, for the first time in their history, he found her interesting.

She'd even seen a flash of admiration in his eyes, and if she wasn't careful, she'd begin chasing it all over again. Like her mother was forever chasing the impossible win at the gambling tables. Like her dad with his alcoholic binges.

Addiction was in her genes. Only her drug of choice was this man's approval. And desire. And respect. And want. And her own need to bring him to his distinguished knees.

Not a week after Jacqueline's death, he'd turned on her. Accused her of conspiring with his late wife to separate Zara from him permanently. Accused her of cozying up to him even as she'd planned to betray him again. He'd consigned the worst motives to her actions and written her off as a backstabbing bitch, without giving her a single chance to defend herself.

His consequent cruelty was a shield Yana couldn't let go of.

"If I was wrong about you—"

"If?" she bit out. "Is it any wonder that I find rotting in penury more appealing than being saved by you?" She let out a huff, breaking eye contact and adjusting the oversize jacket around her shoulders. As if all of this was nothing but a nuisance she could shrug off. "Why couldn't you have just brought Zara to me?"

"Because she's already gone through too much upheaval in the last few months."

"Fine. You can oversee our visit together, looking down your beaky nose and holding me up to your impossible standards. I'd love to spend time with her here."

"Or you could be smart and just accept my help. It's not like you have a thousand other offers."

"Arrogant of you to assume that I don't have people who'd dig me out of my financial hole as you call it. All I have to do is ask."

"Like who?"

"Like my sisters, who are both independently wealthy," she blurted out, hating his arrogant assumption that she'd been abandoned by one and all. That no one found her worthy just because he didn't. "Like Caio, who's my grandfather's right-hand man and my brother-in-law, and the new CEO of OneTech. Like Aristos, my other billionaire brother-in-law."

"And yet, you haven't confided in any of them, have you? Why is that, I wonder?"

Every minute with him was a danger to her persona of shallow supermodel. "How do you know you haven't caught me right before I did that? As tacky as I can be, even I know not to ask for handouts just two days after my grandfather passed away."

"I don't believe you. I think you hate the thought of asking them for help. Of letting them see how spectacularly you've failed in managing your life. Especially when one of your sisters is a doctor and the other's a… coding genius. After all, you have that stubborn pride to contend with."

Dismay filled her at how clearly he could see through to her deepest wound. But then, no one else knew her flaws as well as he did.

She was saved from responding when his phone gave a series of loud pings. His frown went into scowl territory with each swipe of his fingers.

She pushed onto her knees. "Is it Zara? What's wrong?"

"Some imbecile snapped a pic of us going into the elevator." A pithy curse flew from his mouth. "It's clear it's you and me." His scowl changed direction. "You don't care?"

She shrugged, examining his reaction. His privacy was sacrosanct to him. No one even knew where his permanent residence was. "That cute doctor, can we make sure he doesn't leak that I fainted?"

A shrewd glint dawned in his eyes. "You don't care about being linked with me but you don't want anyone to know you fainted?"

She blurted out before she thought better, "I don't want my sisters to know."

"A hint of a rumor about you and me just months after Jacqueline's death…"

"Everything that mattered to me is…already gone. So please, keep your threats of destruction to yourself."

It was not some dramatic threat or a bait for pity.

The resignation in her eyes burned Nasir with its honest edge. And for a second, he felt the most overwhelming urge to save her. From herself, if required.

God, he was as arrogant and egotistical as she called

him. "Not even if Zara were to hear of that kind of gossip about her Yana Auntie and her father?"

"She's only five." She jerked her head up, her golden hair spreading around her face as if she were a lioness shaking out her mane. "She wouldn't hear such… lurid gossip."

"And yet, she knows the name of every one of her *uncles* who visited her mama on photoshoots at work. She's aware that her mama was fobbing her off on you even before she was gone. She's confused and heartbroken, Yana."

Her curse rattled in the silence between them. She looked stricken and yet she rallied. "I'm not an easy fix you can use when you're overwhelmed and then throw away like some dirty Band-Aid when you're done. You threw me out of her life, Nasir. You told me to never return."

"So you'll punish Zara for my mistakes?"

"I'm not." She pressed a hand to her chest as if it physically hurt. "There's bad blood between us. It won't be long before she catches on to it. That's more confusion you're dumping on her."

"Then we'll start afresh with a clean slate."

She laughed then and it wasn't just mockery. The glint of tears in her eyes, the bitter twist to her mouth, spoke eloquently. "Hell has more chance of freezing over before you'll see me as anything more than—"

"So this is about your ego, then?" Frustration and a powerless feeling burst out of Nasir. That he was being a beast to Yana was unforgivable. But that his past actions should now so adversely affect Zara, too, made him sick to his stomach. That he had forever calcified his heart as an unhealthy coping mechanism for an early loss in life, resulting in his worry that he wouldn't be able to connect with his own daughter, was a constant niggle at the back of his head.

"That I rejected your seduction attempt all those years ago? That I lost my temper over your continued lies about Jacqueline's affairs? That I'm telling you to your face that you're reckless and irresponsible and that you should get your life under control after you fainted in my arms?" he said, unraveling under the onslaught of a perfect storm of worries. "You're so insecure about one rejection ten years ago that you would abandon a child you claim to love when she needs you the most? Are you still just as desperate as you were back then for my approval?"

He couldn't bear to look at Yana's stricken face at his harsh words. He couldn't swallow the bitter lump in his throat that said he was no better a parent for Zara than Jacqueline had ever been.

"I don't want anything from you." Her whisper could have been a shout.

"Whether you accept my incentives or not is moot now. I know how to get you on the plane."

Large brown eyes searched his.

"I'll leak news of your debt to your sisters."

"You wouldn't."

"I will do anything to make Zara smile again," he said, grabbing the jacket he'd discarded earlier. "To not repeat the mistakes I've already made. So yes, I would tell the world that the incomparable Yana Reddy is so deep in debt that she can't even afford her own medication. That her team has jumped ship. Your sisters will pity you and—"

"You're a bastard."

"You know I am. So why sound so surprised?"

"And how do you know I won't fill Zara's mind with lies against you?" He didn't miss the cornered look on her face. A bitter smile pinched her mouth. "You've given me enough material over the years."

Some uncivilized part of him only she brought out wanted to growl like some wild animal at the threat. He was still fixing all the damage Jacqueline had caused by filling his daughter's tender heart with horrible lies about his apathy as a father. Still fixing his own blunders. For Yana to threaten him...

Nasir made himself take a deep breath. Forced himself to go with his instinct, to listen to his heart and his gut, instead of the more rational facts and fears. "I don't know that for certain," he said, the words coming more easily than he'd have imagined. Coming from some place he'd shut down a long time ago. "But I do know that however much you loathe me, you care deeply about Zara."

It was the dig about her wanting approval from Nasir that stuck like a craw in Yana's throat.

His words had cut her open as if he'd taken a scalpel to her skin. But examined again, out of his infuriating and overwhelming presence, as the blistering-hot water pounded out the soreness in her muscles that always accompanied her fainting spells, Yana acknowledged that it was the very truth that she'd spent years running from.

She'd always chased approval and validation—from her mother, from her grandparents, from her career, from Jacqueline. And she'd sought it in the most harmful, chaotic, childish ways possible.

For years, she'd wished she'd been smart and self-sufficient and self-composed like her older sister Mira. Then Nush had come into their lives and she'd wished she were full of hope and love and magic like her little sister was. Not forgetting that genius brain of hers.

Yana had always wished she were someone else. Someone more grounded, someone cleverer, someone more easygoing, someone less chaotic, someone healthier… The list of things she wasn't yet wanted to be was as long as the number of thugs Diana owed money to.

Even as Yana desperately wanted to be seen and appreciated and loved for herself at the same time.

Talk about confusing her little brain.

What Nasir was wrong about, though—and how she'd have liked to tell him that to his face—was that she'd sought his approval all those years ago with her pathetic seduction attempt. Or that she'd offered herself as some kind of cheap bargain. Or that she'd wreaked some sort of petty revenge afterward because he'd dented her ego.

As the hot water restored her sense and composure, she saw the root of her obsession with the blasted man.

Nasir was one of three people—her sisters Mira and Nush being the other two—who'd given her approval without her having to earn it with good behavior or better grades or by making restitutions because she'd ruined her mother's career simply by being born.

He hadn't judged her for being her mother's daughter or criticized her for being her chaotic, messy self, or mocked her for following him around with puppy-dog eyes anytime he'd visited. The four years she'd spent under the same roof as his father, the few months Nasir had joined them in between assignments and visits to his mother, he'd been unflinchingly kind to her.

Already making her name in modeling, Yana had been exposed to men and women wanting things from her. Her mother wanted the fame and fortune she'd lost by giving birth to Yana at a young age. Her alcoholic, mostly absent father wanted forgiveness in his rare moments of sobriety. How could she forgive someone who held no significance in her life except as a sperm donor?

The simple acceptance she'd received from an experienced, worldly man like Nasir had been like standing in sunbeams. Giving her the thing she'd craved most, he'd made her feel worthy of it.

There was magic in such unconditional acceptance.

She'd fallen for him with all the passion and intensity of first love, ready to sacrifice everything at his feet, follow him around the world with her heart in her eyes. Hence her pathetic seduction attempt. Just thinking of it now made her cringe in the shower.

And when he'd inevitably rejected her, with such brutal, cutting words that she'd forever lost not only her self-esteem but also his trust, she'd shattered. When her mother had found her running back to her room, tears running down her cheeks, Yana had lied to her that he'd kissed her.

Letting out a feral groan, Yana pressed her forehead to the pristine tile of the wall. It had been the stupidest trick she'd ever played in her life. In one stroke, with one foolish lie told out of the fear of making Diana angry, she'd made Nasir loathe her.

It was the same way she'd behaved with Thaata, too. The more she'd wanted her grandfather's approval, the more she'd acted against her own self-interests, against her own well-being.

Never again. Never again would she let her self-worth be decided by anyone else. Not her mother. Not her grandfather. And definitely not Nasir.

Stepping out of the shower, Yana wiped the moisture from the large mirror and stared at her reflection. A smile broke through the worried twist of her mouth. She'd been in that chaotic, self-damaging place before and she'd clawed her way out of it. This time there was the added motivation of ensuring a five-year-old's well-being and happiness.

A girl just like her, wanting nothing but love from the adults around her. A chance for Yana to make sure Zara's life was different from what her own had been. She'd give the little girl all the attention and affection she'd always craved from Jacqueline, like Yana had craved from Diana.

And just maybe this three-month stint with Nasir and Zara was the universe throwing her a bone. She needed a place to recoup the loss she'd sustained, recover from her mother's betrayal and plan how to get her life back on the right path. On a different path. A path chosen by her and her alone.

She'd do it all without letting herself be swallowed up by the man who'd made her believe in herself a long time ago.

CHAPTER FOUR

It was a month later that Yana found herself aboard Nasir's private jet on the way to one of the tiny islands that made up Bali, after her last modeling shoot for a while. She hadn't wanted to keep him waiting once she'd agreed to his proposition, but it was impossible for her to just check out of her world for three months at a moment's notice, just because he demanded it. When she'd presented him with the various demands on her schedule, he'd agreed that she couldn't leave with him readily enough. But of course, she should've known that he wouldn't simply take her at her word.

As if things weren't confusing enough, he'd stayed with her, followed her wherever work took her, staying at the same penthouse suite at the same luxury hotel when she'd returned for Nush and Caio's wedding. The picture of them together in that elevator had run in an online gossip rag, which had eventually come to Mira's notice.

Yana had given her sister a sanitized version of their fight and their subsequent agreement. Ever the practical and strategic Reddy sister, Mira had given Yana the best advice.

Treat it as a job. Be professional.

While Yana could see the simple yet profound wisdom in it, barely an hour since they'd taken off, she'd found it hard to implement.

Tapping her fingers on the armrest of her seat now, she studied the understated elegance of the aircraft's interior. Thanks to her modeling career, she'd traveled all over the world, to exotic destinations, no less. But her mode of transport hadn't always been this luxurious. Still, she could catalog the minor differences from when she'd traveled in such a cocoon of luxury.

The aircraft was state-of-the-art, but like Nasir, there was a quiet, industrial-type elegance to it rather than the flashy extravagance that most rich men she knew exemplified. Neither did she doubt that it was an efficient mode of transport for a man who traveled all over the Middle East and South Asia, instead of being a status symbol.

She'd had a month of him trailing her like a shadow, showing up at her shoots and events and even at her meetings with all manner of people, but Yana was still nowhere near used to his presence.

For the first time since she'd known him, she was going to get an exclusive glimpse into his very private life. When he and Jacqueline had been married, all the parties and gatherings that Jacqueline had hosted, even as a couple, had been at her apartment in Paris, or in New York.

Yana had even overheard a fight between them when he'd refused to open up his estate—wherever it was—

for one of Jacqueline's "outrageous, drunken soirees" as he'd called them.

"You're jumpy and fidgety. Is there something you require?"

Straightening her pink satin jacket with exaggerated care, Yana counted to twenty before she turned to face him. For the past hour, she'd tried to treat him as part of the very elegant, luxurious background. It shouldn't have been hard with his long nose buried in the documents in front of him.

"Is the fidgeting and jumpiness bothering you?" she asked, with a saccharine sweetness that made even her teeth ache.

If only she could continue to ignore his magnetic presence. But it was like ignoring the sun while orbiting him in the sky.

"No." His answer came so reluctantly that Yana laughed.

"Lies."

"Okay, fine, yes. It bothers me. Do you need something?"

"No."

He returned his attention to putting away the documents in front of him.

Yana studied his profile, drawn as ever to it. His hair had grown long enough to curl thickly over his brow and reach past the nape of his neck. Dark circles hugged his eyes and there was a gauntness to his features that made his cheekbones stand out.

As she watched, he shrugged off his jacket, undid the platinum links at his cuffs and rolled back the sleeves of the white shirt, revealing strong forearms covered in dark hair. Her gaze leaped to his fingers undoing the buttons at his throat, eager anticipation fizzing through her.

The plain, platinum face of his watch—Jacqueline's gift on their second anniversary—was a much-required reminder to stop mooning over him.

Pulling off the glasses that gave him a serious, sexy professor vibe, he let that perceptive gaze rest on her. He didn't do an inventory of her. But she knew that he had noted every little detail about her, from her dyed strawberry blond hair to the deep V of her top.

A shiver ran down her spine. Suddenly, she wished she'd tried to nap, or at least pretended to have fallen asleep for the duration of the flight. "You didn't have to wait for me to join you."

"I promised Zara I'd bring you back with me, no matter when I returned this time. I couldn't take any more chances of disappointing her."

His tone was, for once, affable. And yet, whether it was habit or some other defensive instinct, she felt the prick of his distrust. Took long, deep breaths through her nose, reminding herself that one of her own ground rules for this trip was that she'd be polite. No losing her temper, no riling him up and definitely no staring at him like a lost puppy, salivating with her tongue out and begging for a cuddle.

"I promised you I'd be there. I don't break my commitments."

"As that is something I'm not aware of, it made sense to stay and make sure."

"Do you have to turn everything into a character

assassination?" she said, instantly regretting the combative words.

Why couldn't she just let it be? He was trying to be polite, trying to put that whole clean-slate nonsense into play. Acting as if they were nothing more than two strangers who'd shared and lost a common friend.

His long, rattling sigh told her she'd completely missed the mark. "The stakes are very high for me. Can we agree on that?"

She nodded, heat streaking her cheeks at his gentle tone.

"Good. Let's say it has nothing to do with you and your character and everything to do with my own shortcomings."

Picking at a loose thread on her cuff, she gave him another nod.

He was worried about how to reconnect with Zara after all the damage his marriage, and Jacqueline's lies and his own aversion to engage in a fight, had caused the little girl. It was etched into his features.

"I have some conditions," she said, deciding to steer the conversation to a necessary topic. Maybe that was even the best way to act, moving forward. Ignore the little blips of her temper, the squeaks her heart made whenever he was near.

He raised a brow at the sudden shift away from their argument. "Conditions? Isn't that something you should've discussed with me before you got on the plane?"

"You might have no faith in me, but I decided to show some in you. Even though…" She shook her head, cutting off that line of thought. "I just believed that you would be amenable to whatever I asked for so that these three months with Zara, *for Zara*, can pass with the least amount of aggression between us."

A long finger rubbed over his temple, even as one side of his mouth curled up. "You have given this a lot of thought."

"I've decided to treat this like any other contract. Professionally. I mean, I *have* had a lot of experience dealing with arrogant, egotistical, petulant men, who think they are a gift to the world. So why not draw from my almost fourteen years of experience?"

His reluctant smile turned into a full-fledged one. The sudden flash of his even white teeth and the deep groove it dug on one side of his face… She barely buried the sigh that wanted to leave her lips. God, the man's gorgeousness was lethal when he smiled like that.

"So what are they?"

"What are what?" she said, stuck in that sticky place.

His smile deepened. "The conditions you have for me?"

"Oh, yeah," she said, making a big show of pulling out her notepad from her giant clutch and opening to the right page. She had no doubt that a full-blown blush was painting her cheeks and lowered her head to hide the evidence. "You already took care of my debts. That was my first condition."

"Ahmed dealt with all that mess. He decided it wouldn't do for me to know all the gory details."

She looked up, surprise and relief rushing through her. Though she had a feeling it hadn't been Ahmed's decision so much as Nasir's. Which meant his belief that *she* had accrued that immense debt was being propagated further. And she needed that barrier between them, needed him to think she was reckless with every area of her life. "Remind me to thank Ahmed."

She looked down at her list and hesitated. A month ago she'd wanted to never set eyes on her mother again. To completely wash her hands of her. After this last betrayal, she'd thought herself incapable of caring the smallest amount about Diana.

And yet, over the past few weeks of having a clear goal and vision for her own life, of talking to Zara over video calls, of watching her sisters move on in their lives, she'd realized it wasn't in her to just walk away. To close her heart off. To abandon her mother when gambling was a mental illness.

What if Diana needed a fresh chance like Yana was getting from Nasir, albeit at a high price? Would she ever be happy if Diana wasn't also in a good place?

Her decision was driven not just by common sense but compassion and a sense of duty, too. Breaking away from toxic patterns, suddenly felt like it was within her reach. She could move forward with her own life then. But of course, she needed help. First, to gain a spot in that clinic she'd researched; second, to be able to pay for it; and third, to convince Diana to give it a try.

She'd decided to add the first two to Nasir's list.

"I need a recommendation for a rehab clinic. I've done my research and found one that's nestled in the Swiss Alps, but it's expensive and very exclusive. They usually only take people based on recommendations. From big shots like you."

His gaze immediately latched on to hers. "Rehab?"

"Yep. I've decided to tackle the bull by the horns, so to speak. For my gambling," she added, her throat dry over the lie.

Instead of seeing relief or even the self-righteous "I knew it" that she'd expected, a thoughtful look entered his eyes. "I'm glad you decided to seek professional help. Is it that bad, though?"

There was a tenderness to his voice that her brain wanted to cling to. Or was it her stupid heart? "How about we leave it to me to be the judge of that," she said tersely, because she didn't want him to probe.

"Of course, you're the judge," he added in a kind tone.

She sighed. Every dialog between them felt charged. Or perhaps she was making it so. "Some of us develop unhealthy, damaging coping mechanisms to deal with life." She wasn't addicted to gambling but she was addicted to something else, all right. "Not all of us are perfect with iron-clad control like you."

His mouth twisted with bitterness. "Not only am I far from perfect, but I'm only realizing now how *my* unhealthy coping mechanisms have hurt others. At least you're self-aware. I have been deliriously, arrogantly oblivious of my own failings."

Now it was she who wanted to probe. That wanted to dig and dig until he was fully revealed and unraveled in front of her. That he'd hurt Jacqueline with his inability to love her was common knowledge between them. And yet, he'd never seemed to mind much before. She'd never seen a single hole in his convictions and beliefs about how he'd conducted his life.

Instead of giving full rein to that fascinated part of her, she forced herself to look down at her notepad.

"I will personally speak to someone on the board of administration," he said into the building silence. "Just let me know the timeline."

She nodded, running her finger down her scribbled list. "The next few things are not that big of a deal. I'm charging you twenty million euros for the three months. I'd prefer a bunch of chaperones as a buffer while I spend time with Zara and…"

His laughter was loud, booming around in the intimate space, pinging all over her skin. She looked up and lost her breath.

Head thrown back, muscles of his neck clenched tight, he was a study in masculine beauty. Attraction and desire tugged at her, a hook under her belly button pulling her closer, urging her to touch that smile, to taste that smile. Damn, she had it bad.

"What's so funny?" She went for irritation to hide her helpless attraction.

It was several minutes before he sobered up. "You are one expensive nanny, aren't you?"

A smile twitched at the corner of her lips. "Well, I guess I am. And please, before you come out with insults that I should be doing this out of the goodness of my heart, out of my love for Zara, don't. That's the price of me spending time under the same roof with you. Knowing that you will be overseeing everything

I say, judging me, and…" It was hard to stay detached or antagonistic toward him when he looked at her with that smile stretching his sensuous lips.

"Fine. Agreed. You will have enough money at the end of three months. And believe me, we will have chaperones galore."

She turned a page on her notepad, gathering the courage to ask the most important question.

"Is that it?"

"I want Zara to spend one month out of every year with me going forward. It could be two periods of two weeks or four different weeks. I want that written into a contract."

"No."

Neither of them was surprised by his instant, biting answer.

The surge of rage and something else—a sharp helplessness, in her expression—told Nasir he'd given her the answer based on the rules and rationale that drove him. Had he been too quick to reply without thinking it over?

She tapped a pink nail incessantly over the table. "That one condition is non-negotiable. If you don't agree, I'll turn around and leave the second this plane lands." Every word was enunciated with a staggering conviction behind it.

"You're springing this on me at the last minute," he said, pushing for time.

Her brown gaze was pure challenge. "My relationship with Zara needs to exist outside of my relationship or lack thereof with you, Nasir. That's what adults should do. Put their differences, their egos, aside, for the sake of a child. I don't know what the future or the aftermath of these three months—" she said, laughing, with no actual humor in the sound "—is going to look like. This way, I'm ensuring that regardless of what happens between you and me, Zara always has me in her life. And not just as some patch-up you bring in when things get bad."

For the first time in his life, Nasir was speechless. Golden hair flying around her face as she bit out each word, Yana looked like a lioness defending her cub. "You're a natural at this, despite the fact both your parents neglected you."

She tilted her chin. Whatever fragility he had seen that first evening at the nightclub was all gone now. "It makes me even more empathetic to Zara's plight. She's just a child. No child should have to starve for attention or affection. Or get lost in adults' mind games." She played with the ends of her hair, her thrust delivered with an efficient, but impersonal bluntness he was coming to appreciate about her. He couldn't even get mad because she was right; Zara had gotten lost among his and Jacqueline's conflicts. "As for Diana messing up…" Her throat moved hard. "I've realized there have been good things in my life, too. It's on me whether I move forward with gratitude or bitterness."

"You sound very wise," he said.

"You sound shocked," she retorted with a cutting smile.

Clearly, in the past month she had returned to some sort of routine. He hadn't missed the fact, seeing he'd shadowed her wherever she went. Meals, regular exercise and medication on time, he could see the changes in her face. That gaunt, lost waif look was gone, leaving her effervescently beautiful.

He liked her like this—full of passion and conviction. Suddenly, he realized he had seen her like this before. Before she'd entered the modeling world as a far too naive and impressionable girl with only her mother's greedy, grasping behavior as a guide. Forced to grow up too fast. Acting out in the form of reckless, paparazzi-attracting, almost orchestrated publicity stunts.

There was a contentment to her now that he found extremely satisfying and that in turn was disconcerting, to say the least. He didn't want to be invested in Yana's happiness or well-being. Or only so far as it affected her relationship with Zara. God, that made him sound like an utter bastard.

"You look different," he said, unable to help himself.

She scrunched her nose, and even that twitch was sexy. "Good different?"

"Good different, yes." He didn't miss the hungry expectation in her eyes for more, but refused to cater to it. It was better if they behaved like polite strangers.

"Maybe the fact that—" she giggled, moving her hands in an arc toward him, encompassing the aircraft and the notepad, and everything else, her gestures getting wilder and more expansive with each passing second "—I'm making you pay through the nose is the cause of the change?"

"A small price to pay, then. Your happiness is quite the halo around you."

She gave him a regal nod in response. Then she studied her fingernails, going for that casual vibe that she never could quite pull off. "I think sometimes we have to hit our lowest point to see that things aren't as bad as we thought, that they can still be fixed."

He returned her somber nod, marveling at how deeply her words reached inside him. He'd been at that lowest point once. But unlike dreaming on a different vision as Yana was doing or moving forward, he'd simply shut the world out. Had stopped caring about anyone. Had withdrawn into his mind, into his books, into his career. Even when he'd met and married Jacqueline, he'd designed his marriage to fit around his life. And of course, it had fallen apart in a spectacular fashion.

Because somewhere in the past fifteen years, he'd stored away his heart outside himself. And then, suddenly, he didn't know how to forge a connection with his own child.

"I know a little about being in dark places, feeling like you'll never crawl out of them." The words flew out of his mouth. "Or feeling as if you deserve to be there."

"Don't tell me the great Nasir Hadeed hit points of low confidence in his esteemed life."

"I will save you from the gory details, then," he said, trying to inject humor back into his voice. "It is not a good feeling when our idols turn out to be hollow, no?"

"I didn't idolize you," she said with a fake outrage he didn't buy.

He worried that she'd probe. It was unfounded.

It was becoming more and more apparent that Yana

wasn't anything like the flimsy illusion she weaved for the entire world.

"So, are you in agreement about me having Zara for a month?"

"If I insist on being present while you do?"

"Because you don't trust me to look after her?" she asked with big eyes. In that moment she looked as beguilingly naive and full of insecurities as his five-year-old. "I'd never put Zara at risk."

That it was a promise and not some outraged declaration made his chest ache. "No. I want Zara to see that we're not at each other's throats."

She nodded, taking his lies for the truth.

He had no intention of spending time with her on a regular basis, no intention of seeing her again after these three months were up.

And still, he wasn't able to help himself from prodding her. From poking at her sudden composure.

Suddenly, it felt as if he was standing behind a wall she'd erected. He shouldn't miss the messy, volatile Yana he'd once known, but he had a sudden feeling that this defensive barrier was a fundamental part of her.

"If that's a problem for you—"

"You keep thinking I'm still hung up on you. I'm not. Haven't been for a very long time. It might even be the right thing for all of us, because who knows how much time you actually give Zara. This way, you'll be forced to take time off from your work."

And there was the truth, putting him in his place in the perfect way. As only she could. "Yes, fine, you can spend time with Zara every year. But we don't have to put it in a contract."

"We do. I don't trust your good opinion of me will last forever."

And that was, apparently, that.

Pushing out her long legs, she reclined her seat and closed her eyes. Her arms were folded around her midriff, thrusting her small breasts up.

It took him seventeen long seconds to look away from the enticing picture she made even in repose, from her shiny hair to the deep cleavage at the V of her blouse to the long legs bared in pink shorts.

She was right.

He had no idea how the aftermath of these three months was going to look. Because the truth he'd refused to accept until now was that this woman had always threatened his control. Had always pushed and prodded at all the rules he'd lived his life by. She made him want to risk everything again all over. She made him forget the excruciating pain of loving and losing.

CHAPTER FIVE

"YANA? WAKE UP."

Yana tightened her arms around the solid warmth that enveloped her, needing to sleep for another thousand hours. "Get off. Leave me alone."

A soft tap on her cheek, followed by a chuckle, tickled the blurry edges of her consciousness. "We're here. Let's go, sleepyhead."

She was warm, and cozy and so tired, and the voice sounded so good against her temple. Like a deep bass reverberating through her, weaving a web of comfort she'd rarely known. "That's not how you wake up someone," she mumbled, snuggling closer and pouting.

A sigh and a hiss disrupted her pleasant state.

"Ahh… Would you like me to try the Sleeping Beauty method? I don't know my fairy tales properly but I think it involved a kiss."

A kiss? That deep, husky voice was offering a kiss to wake me up? Would it be as delicious as he sounded?

It wasn't a bad way to wake up, even though she'd always found the idea of someone kissing her to save her a bit problematic.

"Come on, Yana. Unless you want me to act on that threat."

Slowly, she blinked her eyes open and found amber-colored eyes gleaming back at her in the dark interior of the car. They were like warm, deep pools, inviting her to sink into them. She frowned. Something was wrong with the cozy picture, in and out of her head. In the past ten years, she'd only ever seen those eyes staring at her with contempt or anger.

It was Nasir. But why was Nasir offering to wake her up with a kiss? Was she dreaming again?

The car came to a sudden stop, forcing her to take stock of the surroundings. Through the tinted windows of the chauffeured car, she spotted a dark gray twilight sky, punctured by thick, tall trees that seemed to stand to attention, watching their arrival.

Her eyes widened as she realized she was in the car with Nasir and that they'd finally arrived at their destination. When he handed her a tissue, she stared at it blankly. A sigh left him before he gently wiped at the corners of her mouth.

Yana sprung back from him as if he were a viper flicking his forked tongue at her. Slowly, she pulled her limbs away from around him, even as her body bemoaned the loss of his solid warmth.

"It's okay. You're okay, Yana," he said so softly that the incongruence of it froze her. He'd never spoken to her with that tenderness. Not in ages. "You fell into an exhausted sleep," he added.

She wiped the corners of her mouth with the back of her hand and repeated the same to gritty-feeling eyes.

"Why am I not surprised that you are such an aggressive cuddler when you're asleep?" he said, a hint of humor peeking through his tone.

"It's information you shouldn't have at all," she quipped, feeling irrationally resentful. Though she knew he'd said it to put her at ease.

"No?"

"No. It's intimate information that's reserved for a lover or a boyfriend or a…"

With a groan, she closed her mouth. Why had he let her wrap herself around him like a clinging vine? Why not be cruel in action as with words and push her away? Then she wouldn't feel this discombobulated around him.

She straightened her shorts and her satin top, which was so badly wrinkled that it looked like she'd writhed on the ground.

No, just in his lap, a wicked voice she'd thought she'd left behind piped up.

With the guise of fixing her hair, Yana tugged at the roots roughly, to restore a measure of sanity to herself. "Where's my jacket?"

One long finger carefully held her unwrinkled pink jacket aloft. "You kept saying you were too hot."

"You should've woken me up or pushed me aside."

"You really think me an unfeeling beast."

"Yes. And I'd like to keep thinking that."

"And why is that?" The soft query came with a silky, but nonetheless dangerous, undertone.

Yana took the jacket from him and pushed her arms through the sleeves, ignoring him. Gathering the messy mass of her hair, she quickly braided it away from her face. Only when she felt a semblance of composure return to her did she turn to face him. "I'm sorry for—" she moved her hand between them, her cheeks heating up "—climbing all over you."

He exhaled in a sibilant hiss, pressing his fingers to his temple. "It's no big deal."

"It *is* a big deal. You're my employer, and I'd like to keep those boundaries clear."

A flicker of irritation danced in his eyes. "Pity you didn't have that rule all those years ago, huh?"

And just like that, the truce that had lasted the whole flight fell apart. Grabbing his wrist, she pulled it up to thrust the platinum dial in his face. "Wow, you lasted a whole nine hours without insulting me. That's got to be a record."

His long fingers grabbed hers. "Wait, that's not how I meant to say it."

"Let me go, Nasir."

"Not until you hear me out."

Of course she knew who he was talking about— Gregor Ilyavich, a sixty-six-year-old infamous painter of celebrated nudes. When he'd approached Diana, who'd also been her manager and coach back then, about painting Yana nude, her mother had been ecstatic. Just as she'd guessed, his nude portraits of Yana had instantly shot her into a new stratosphere of fame. All the big designers had wanted her face on their brand, were willing to pay whatever she wanted.

But the true price for her starry fame had come later—when Gregor had made his move on her. Something Yana chose to believe to this day that Diana hadn't known about. She herself had been a naive idiot who hadn't seen the power play until it was too late.

Thank God the portraits were now out of circulation as a private collector had bought them for millions. Not that Yana hadn't loved them. They had been gorgeous, otherworldly, elevating her to something more than the symmetry and perfection of her face and body. Gregor had pinpointed and then extrapolated things she'd chosen to hide from the world in those portraits—her insecurity and her vulnerability.

But the lurid gossip about her affair with Gregor, the over-the-top speculation that *she* had trapped him for his money, and her tattered reputation as some kind of backstabbing gold digger had left a bitter taste in her mouth.

Her justly deserved humiliation at Nasir's hands two years prior and then the flaming mess that had been her association with Gregor had been enough to confirm her belief that she was never going to get it right with men. Just like Diana.

"Are you forever going to dig up skeletons from my past and dangle them in my face? Is that the plan for the next three months?" A scornful laugh escaped her. "Because we both know there's enough material."

"No. Of course not. I brought it up the wrong way. I just…"

"Just what, Nasir?"

"I introduced you to Gregor at that release party for my novel. I felt responsible." A muscle jumped in his cheek. "I *feel* responsible, to this day."

Her righteous fury leeched out of her, leaving a void in its place. A void that would fill with dangerous things like hope if she wasn't careful. And even with that warning, she couldn't help but say, "What does that mean?"

"You were a very gullible twenty-one-year-old. He was notorious for charming and seducing women who were decades younger than him with the promise of fame and fortune. I was responsible for bringing you to his notice. For letting him enter your life. I hate that he…took advantage of you. That I didn't protect you."

"I was twenty-one. And Gregor coerced me in no way to pose for him. So there, I absolve you of all blame." She raised her palms, forestalling the distressing topic.

"Yes. But I should have looked out for you, should have made sure you knew his background. Abba took me to task for it enough times."

The mention of his dad was enough to make a lump rise in Yana's throat.

Izaz Hadeed had been one of the kindest men she'd ever known. Enough that she'd loved living in his home when Diana had been married to him. Enough that she'd known whatever had brought them together wouldn't last long because Diana didn't know what to do when good things came into her life and so she destroyed them.

Something Yana thought she'd inherited from her mother, in her lowest points, along with good skin and thick hair.

Enough to know that his son—while grumpy and

caustic on the outside—had inherited that very same kindness. God, the stupid dreams she'd weaved, imagining them all together as one big, forever family.

Even after he and Diana had separated, even after Yana's own horrible shenanigans and false claims about Nasir kissing her, Izaz had always kept in touch with her. Calling her on her birthday, sending her gifts wherever she was in the world, asking her if she was okay after Nasir and Jacqueline's wedding…he'd made her feel like a cherished daughter.

He'd loved her like one.

She bit her lower lip with her teeth hard enough that the pain held back the tears that threatened to spill. "Ahh, so that's what this is about. Izaz Uncle finding fault with you. That's why it still rankles after all this time."

"It wasn't just Abba's criticism that got to me…" His chest rose with the deep breath he took. She knew it was raw grief at mentioning his father, who had passed not a year ago. Only Izaz's affair and subsequent marriage to Diana had been the biggest divide between father and son—conquered and forgiven years later when he'd reconciled with Nasir's mom. And yet, she remembered Izaz being heartbroken that Nasir hadn't forgiven him completely, that his son had become a hardened man in the subsequent years.

"It rankles, still, because it's true."

In a sudden move she didn't expect, he clasped her cheek with a gentleness that shocked her. When she'd have pulled away, he held firm. Something about the expression in his eyes threatened to break her into so many pieces. His second hand joined the first one, in this assault of kindness.

She felt locked, pinned, splayed wide open.

"The world only saw your confidence, your success, your brazenness. But I know now, as I should've known then, that you were young, naive, so unused to the vipers and Gregors of the world. I should have warned you that he was a predator."

The genuine regret in his eyes forced out an answer. "He didn't…do anything I didn't want him to, Nasir. And if mistakes were made, I was twenty-one and so I'm allowed them."

She didn't know why she was propagating yet another lie between them when she could instead choose to clear the air and admit that she'd refused all Gregor's advances. Especially since it seemed Nasir's main regret, that he hadn't interfered, persisted after all these years.

"That mistake shouldn't have happened in the first place. You should've been—"

She slapped his hands away, his gentleness nothing but a hidden strike. "I think I prefer the version of you that blamed me for my impulsive, lazy, ruinous tendencies rather than this…patronizing one that invalidates my very existence. How dare you feel sorry for me? Or is it disgust over my actions and how you should have saved me from myself that keeps that massive ego of yours boosted?"

"Yana, you misunderstand me."

Without waiting for his clarification, she pushed the car door open and stepped out into the dark night.

She was so very exhausted—all the way down to the marrow of her soul. Just when she hoped that he saw her, *actually saw her*, and was beginning to respect her, he set her back to square one. And however many times she promised herself never again, it didn't seem to stick.

Her legs felt like they were made of that JELL-O that Zara adored as Yana stepped out of the car without falling face-first into the rough gravel. Not that she'd have managed even that without Nasir's steadying arm around her shoulders.

Once she could trust her legs, she quickly moved out of his reach. His scowl told her he hadn't missed her instinctual rejection.

She rubbed her eyes again, all the different time zones playing havoc with her body's rhythms. There was a chill in the air that nipped at her bare legs and chest. She inhaled deeply anyway, loving the scent of pine and something old in the air. Tugging the lapels of her jacket closer, she raised her head.

It was a big castle—no, strike that—a humongous castle that greeted her. Rather, it was the shadows and outlines of one, since twilight had now given way to thick, dark night. The castle looked like it had sprung right out of one of Nasir's stories. The stories that were situated perfectly at the periphery of dark woods, the ones that housed all kinds of scary and outcast creatures. The ones she'd always liked the best because she'd felt like she'd belonged in them.

Once he straightened, she reached to take her heavy shoulder bag from him. He held it away from her.

She ran a circle around his body, trying to reach for it, bumping into him. "It's fine. I can carry it inside."

"You're being ridiculous, you know that?" When she jumped for it, he circled a hand around her neck with a gentleness that made her pulse leap. The gesture was so unlike him, so much bordering on possessiveness, that she stilled. Every atom in her body stilled. "It's just a damned bag, Yana. Let it go."

Yana raised her hands in surrender, an unholy humor coursing through her at his cursing. There was nothing better than seeing him devolve to her level—whether in vocabulary or gestures or actions. Suddenly, power and something else between them felt more fluid than she'd ever assumed.

"Where are we?" she asked, following him as he began an upward trek from a gigantic courtyard where the chauffeur had dropped them off.

Small, hidden lights dotted across the land illuminated a gravel pathway toward the looming castle. All the tension she'd felt while imagining them together melted away as she took in the fresh air and the beautifully dark setting.

God, she and Zara would have so much fun here. And yet, she didn't miss the fact that it was also quite the deserted location for a five-year-old. Zara would need other kids and activities to engage with. But she couldn't bring that up now. She'd love to never bring it up and not give him a chance to put her in her place but that wasn't an option.

Zara was, and would always be, a priority, even if

that meant courting Nasir's special kind of disapproval. She made a mental note for later.

Apparently, they weren't going to walk in through the main entrance, which boasted two solid iron doors with knockers the size of her head. She felt like she was entering a fantasy world.

"It's a small village near Bavaria," he finally answered. "Close to the Alps. You'll see the view tomorrow."

The remoteness of the location was exactly how she'd imagined he lived. Had Jacqueline played queen of the castle?

Jacqueline had been quite the party animal, and their relationship had never made sense to Yana. But she'd put it down to her own conflicted past with him.

Now she knew that she'd been right in her intuition.

The closer they got, the larger the castle loomed with dark gray stone, and tall turrets and, oh, my God, a tower at the back that seemed to look down on the rest of the castle. "There's a tower in your castle?"

"Yes." His laughter at her enthusiasm reverberated in that single word.

"Please tell me you're renting it or I don't know... housesitting it?"

It was all a little too close to one of her fantasies. Fantasies involving castles and Nasir and dark, fairy-tale-esque romance had been the staple of her teenage years. Fantasies she needed to keep convincing herself she'd grown out of.

It was as if all her darkest dreams were taking shape in reality—she and Nasir in a castle, she and Nasir with a lovely little girl, she and Nasir finally meeting under one roof as equals. But there was no danger of that, she reminded herself bitterly.

When Nasir didn't loathe her, apparently he was busy feeling sorry for her.

She sensed his reluctance before he answered her. "No. I bought it. Recently."

"How recently?"

"Right after Jacqueline died," he said, meeting her gaze. Letting her know that he knew what she was doing. "We moved here from her Paris apartment once I took care of the legalities."

She took a shot in the dark. "You bought it to impress Zara?"

The moonlight didn't hide his grimace. "She wouldn't stop talking about castles and fairy tales and dark creatures. You'd left us—" he raised his hand, forestalling her protest and shook his head. "You're right. I shouldn't rewrite history. *I* made you leave. Jacqueline was gone. All Zara would talk about was living in a huge castle with three monstrous dogs and with a forest in the back and…" A long sigh seemed to emerge from the very depths of him. "It was the only bridge I had to build toward her."

"Oh."

He nudged her shoulder with his. The playful gesture stunned her. As did his teasing tone when he said, "I know where she gets that fixation from."

"I just shared everything that fascinated me at her age," she whispered, her mind scattering in a thousand directions.

What had changed in how he saw her? Had he finally understood that she'd always had Zara's best interests at heart? Was that enough to redeem her multitude of sins? And what happened when they didn't agree on something regarding Zara? Would his approval vanish?

"Stories saved me when I was a little girl. *Your stories* helped me escape my own life."

"I'm glad, then, that I got something right with you. Even if it was done unknowingly." His gruff tone hit her low in her belly, the soft underside she sometimes forgot existed.

Something built in the silence between them as he opened the relatively small but actually giant side door, and ushered her toward a dark staircase. And it seemed to stretch and stretch and stretch upward. Endlessly.

Without rancor or contempt or anger or intense mutual dislike coloring and cluttering the space between them, they were unmoored suddenly. As if anything was possible in that space now. As if they were any other couple who were trying to do their best for a little girl they both adored.

"I... I wanted Zara to have the same anchor during a hard time in her own life," she said, clearing her suddenly thick throat. "I didn't mean to create an obsession you'd have to deal with."

"No. I'm grateful for the spark of the obsession you planted. It became a lifesaver for us both."

He rubbed a hand over his face, and suddenly, in the dark corridor, Yana saw his own exhaustion, the emotional toll the past few years must have taken on him. Jacqueline's infidelities, her long battle with cancer, then her death and the full responsibility of Zara's well-being. Then suddenly, he'd lost his beloved father.

It was a lot for one man to take.

Even someone like Nasir, who was fully in control of himself and his emotions and the people around him and even his own circumstances. He was judgmental, ruthless, exacting in his standards for himself and others. And yet, now, beneath all of that, she saw something else, too. Something like regret.

Even just within the past month, he'd followed her wherever she went around the globe, all the while giving time to his own work and returning to see Zara every weekend so that she didn't feel abandoned yet again. It annoyed her how her heart ached for a man she needed to hate.

"Nasir, I'm—"

"You were a better parent to Zara than Jacqueline or I have ever been. For that, you have my eternal gratitude."

Stunned beyond words, she stared at him. That arch of electricity, that taut tug of connection, came again. This time it built faster and louder and stronger.

She nodded and walked on up the stairs, his words sitting like rigid boulders on her chest. Of course, he'd recognized that she loved Zara. And being the man he was, he'd immediately thank her for it, would give her the place she wanted in Zara's life. It was more than she'd expected when she'd said yes to this…contract, the best outcome she could've hoped for.

Relief should have come. Or at least some kind of vindication. All she felt, however, was a confusion, an ache.

"I feel like Maria from *The Sound of Music*," she

said, forcing a giggle into her tone. The last thing she wanted was to have an emotional breakdown in front of him, for him to see the wretched confusion in her soul. "Please tell me you don't have several children waiting for me to look after."

"That's a nice fantasy," he said, a thread of some deep, dark, cavernous thing dancing in his words.

Yana stumbled so hard that she almost fell on her face.

His fast reflexes meant his hand on her jacket held her upright just as they reached the landing on the second floor.

"What? Lording over me and Zara like Captain Von Trapp with his whistle? Finding fault with everything I do? Because let me tell you that particular fantasy's already come true."

He opened the door, a grin on his face. There was something really different about him, here in this place. Or was it simply relief that he finally had her where he needed her? "Why do you always assume that I want to think the worst of you?"

"My dear stepbrother," she said, using the term she knew he loathed, placing her palm on his chest in an exaggerated pout, pouring on her fake charm thick, to dissipate the fizzy bubbles in her own chest more than anything else, "it's our history that says that."

His long fingers wrapped around her wrist but he didn't drag her touch away. Her pulse raced under his fingertips, playing a symphony for his favor. "I don't remember it always being quite like that."

"Weren't you the one who taught me that history always has another version? Probably from the one who didn't originally have a voice?"

"What is your version, then, Yana?"

"Does it matter anymore?"

"It clearly does. To both of us."

She shook her head, telling herself it was a lie. "I made a ghastly, horrible mistake, no doubt about it. I knew I'd done something wrong the minute I told Diana you kissed me. I want you to know that I did eventually tell Izaz the truth. I was… I own my part in that, even though I'd like to say I was also a product of insecurity and codependency and…" She sighed and blew out a long breath. "You meted out a rather cruel punishment that would've lasted a lifetime if not for the fact that I came into Zara's life, quite by accident, which ended up, *luckily* for me, perhaps redeeming me a little bit in your eyes."

If she thought he'd dig into the very painful past and pick at the scabs of her *ghastly, horrible mistake*, Yana was proved wrong. If she thought he'd jump at the truth she'd just revealed that his punishment to cut her out of his life had hurt her, she was safe from that, too.

He simply stared at her for a long time, as if weighing her words. "You are right. And you're a better person than I am, clearly, for not holding it over my head."

A humorless snort escaped her. "That's what you expected when you came to see me, wasn't it? Me to hold your own behavior over your head? That's why you were so fast to use all the leverage you had on me."

"And you refused me, again and again, even though I know you want to be here for Zara. Don't think it escaped me that the possibility of being here with me was so distasteful to you that it sent you into a faint."

"Nasir—"

"Don't think I forget for one minute that my beastly behavior toward you might have cost Zara the stability she needs, the love of the one person she desperately craves. I might have failed my daughter all over again."

There was such a note of anguish in those words that Yana found herself reaching for him automatically. In that moment Yana remembered why she'd once admired him so much. There was a quiet dignity to him, even in defeat. "I didn't mean—"

"My relationship with my daughter is a mess I created. I let my unhappiness with Jacqueline, my distaste for her drama, create a divide between Zara and me. I assumed she was better off with her mother than being used as a pawn in a power play between us."

"A little girl would only see it as apathy," she said, unable to help herself.

His throat moved on a hard swallow and his mouth curved in a bitter smile. "I realized that too late. I got so good at keeping people out of my life that I succeeded with my daughter, too."

It was as natural as breathing to want to comfort him. "You and she will get through this, Nasir. I promise you. Things will be better soon."

With his hand at the small of her back guiding her through the darkness, and the tight corridor they were navigating, their gazes held. "You don't know that."

"You're doing everything you can to fix it. Including kidnapping me, blackmailing me, letting me drool all over your Armani jacket in my sleep. Just to make her happy. Just to give her a sense of security. She'll realize all the effort you're putting in soon enough. Zara's a very clever girl."

It was what she'd have done for anyone in such a situation. She'd always been a very touchy-feely person. But when her upper body pressed against Nasir in a tight, warm squeeze, she realized too late that she'd gone too far.

Too far with him, that was.

Because even a little was always too far with this man.

Suddenly, it was impossible to ignore her nipples pebbling against the muscled wall of his side. Her breasts aching and heavy. His hard, denim-clad leg nestled between her thighs, against the place where she'd dreamed of him being so many times. Her spine and her curves melting and molding around him to get a better fit, a tighter squeeze, a harder push.

She closed her eyes, and it was a mistake because the sensations multiplied by a million. Her breath came in soft, shallow pants as she searched in the darkness with her fingers. A liquid ache pulsed through her when she found purchase on his face. His soft, warm mouth that could be so hard with anger at her fingertips. The rough, pebbled texture of his scar. His breath on the back of her hand, heating her up even more.

And without her permission, without her knowing, without her will involved, her body bowed toward him. Offering itself up as some kind of ritual sacrifice at the very altar of the beast she should run from.

Forehead pressed against his shoulder, she breathed in long gasps, willing herself to let go. To step back.

His fingers around the nape of her neck were like bands of heat, brands of possession. Lingering at that sensitive place. Playing through the little wisps of hair there.

"Yana," he said, his own voice a husky whisper, echoing around the walls. "We can't… I can't do this. There's too much at stake."

She jerked back from him so fast and with such force that the hard stone banged into her head, evoking a pained gasp. Hot tears pooled in her eyes at the impact but he was already there. His fingers gently probing and prodding at the back of her head.

She took a tentative step away, putting herself out of his reach. "I'm okay. Let's just—"

"Yana, we can't—"

"No idea what you're talking about," she said, focusing her gaze over his shoulder. "All I did was offer comfort. Maybe even that's not palatable to you when it comes from me."

He searched her gaze in the dim light and nodded. But the truth of their almost-encounter shimmered in the amber depths, and her own senses, whipped into a frenzy of need, taunted her for her lies.

CHAPTER SIX

"WAKE UP, YANA AUNTIE! Auntie, wake up!"

Yana found herself tickled by small hands, but this time she knew who was wrapped around her like a baby koala. Her eyes opened to shafts of pure golden sunlight sliding in through the high windows, bathing her face in a warm light. For a second she lay with her open gaze focused on the high, vaulted ceilings, and yet another gleaming chandelier that reminded her of the castle and her and Nasir's almost-encounter.

Nope, not thinking of the thing that he claimed he couldn't give in to and that had never even happened. Although, the fact that he'd said that he couldn't take the chance…meant he wanted to do it, whatever it was that hadn't happened, right?

"Yana Auntie!"

Smiling, Yana trailed her fingers to her stomach where itty-bitty fingers were digging into her ribs, and caught them with her own. "Gotcha, Zuzu!" As she expected, Zara gave a loud squeal and burst into giggles when Yana shouted, "Tickle monster!" and went for the little belly. Like earthworms in mud—another favorite of Zara's—they rolled together on the bed, giggling for God knew how long.

Her chest burned as if a fire had cleansed away all the loss and grief, leaving fertile ground again. There was nothing like laughing and goofing around with Zara, who gave as good as she got. Eventually, they both ran out of breath.

Sitting up, she pulled Zara into her lap. Tiny arms immediately wound around her neck, with her face buried in Yana's chest. An almost clawlike hold of those little fingers raised a lump in her throat. Yana buried her face in Zara's thick curls. The little girl smelled of sunshine and dirt and strawberries, and it tugged at instincts Yana hadn't known she had.

She'd never given much thought to marriage or children, to stability and putting down roots. Planning her life was Mira's forte, and believing that it would turn out wonderfully was Nush's, whereas hers had been drifting from one mess to the other. And yet, ever since she'd been a chubby, charming baby, Zara had sunk her hooks into Yana's heart and they only seemed to dig in deeper with time.

"You pwomised you'd visit soon." The complaint came in a small, muffled voice as if Zara wasn't sure she had a right to even complain.

In response, Yana grabbed Zara's huge stuffed toy, and spoke to Lila the llama. She told the stuffed toy about how both her grandparents had passed away in the past year, and how much Yana had needed to be around her sisters and why she'd not been able to visit Zara sooner.

Pulling back, Zara stared with a seriousness that belied her tender age. "Your thaata died?"

Yana nodded.

"Like Mama?"

Hand shaking, Yana tucked a springy curl behind the girl's ear and planted a soft kiss on her chubby cheek. "Yes. But—" she trailed her fingers over the little girl's face and neck, straightening her pajamas, slowly tickling her again, forcing an easy cheer into her voice "—I'm not sad anymore. Now that I can hold my Zuzu girl again."

Explanation accepted, Zara sneak-attacked her, and they burst into another bout of giggles, made plans for picnics and walks and movie nights and ice-cream parties. The number of promises the girl elicited from Yana restored her faith in her decision to come.

Suddenly, three huge, excited dogs burst into the bedroom and began to sniff and bark and generally make mayhem around the bed. "And who is this?" Yana asked, eyeing the two shepherds and the pug.

One castle and three dogs... He really had gone all the way in making Zara's fantasy come true. Yana shouldn't really be surprised after his ruthless determination to get her here. How much further would he go to make Zara happy?

"That's Leo and Scorpio. And that one," Zara said, pointing to the cutest among the three, "is Diablo."

As if he knew how extra adorable he was, Diablo the pug lifted his front paws up onto the edge of the bed. Yana patted the sheets and immediately, the three dogs jumped up and went for their faces, licking them.

Zara suddenly fell quiet.

"What's wrong?" Yana asked.

"We're in twouble." Resolve tightened the little girl's features. "Don't worry. I'll tell Papa I let them on his bed."

Belly dipping, Yana noted the austere navy-blue furnishings, the starkly functional furniture and an entire wall full of bookshelves that shrank the vast bedroom significantly. The bed was a vast king bed with two night stands—one full of Zara's pictures in frames and the other held a pile of books and a pair of reading glasses.

This was Nasir's bed. This was his bedroom. Yana sighed.

Why did all roads seem to lead her to Nasir's bed?

"I let the dogs on the bed, Papa. Not Yana Auntie."

Nasir stood still at the entrance to the room, wondering if his heart could rip out of its shallow shell at the entreaty in his daughter's words. The doubts in her eyes tore him apart, reminding him yet again how badly he'd messed up with Zara.

"Don't send her away."

Hands on Zara's shoulders, Yana pulled his daughter into her body, as if she meant to protect her from everything, including him.

As if she were my own... He hadn't missed Yana's almost slip of the tongue that evening at the nightclub. The picture of them together like that on his bed—one achingly adorable with jet-black curls and the other, glowingly beautiful with dark golden waves spilling over her shoulders, packed an invisible punch to his sternum. With the sunlight limning their similar golden-brown coloring, they looked like they belonged together.

They looked right, real in a way he hadn't known in so long.

Shaking his head at the fantastical thought, Nasir moved toward the bed. With each step he took, Yana's mouth flattened.

Did she truly think him such a beast as to upset his own daughter over something so small? That although he'd unknowingly made Zara doubt his affection, it made him feel any less awful? Or like Zara, had he only shown Yana the grumpy, grouchy outer shell he'd adopted long ago?

Going to his knees, he gazed into his daughter's eyes. His hand shook as he straightened the collar of her pajamas. "It's true Papa doesn't like dogs in his bed. Because Papa's a grouchy old man who's used to things a certain way. But sweetheart, you'll never be in trouble with me over such a small thing. And definitely not your wonderful Yana Auntie, either." His five-year-old's lower lip jutted out in disbelief. "I pinkie promise that I'll never send her away again, yeah?" He extended his pinkie toward her and he wondered if his heart had moved into that digit now.

That trembling lower lip calmed and Zara tangled their pinkies. Her smile was a wide beam of sunshine. "Next time I'll close the door so they don't follow me."

He laughed and buried his face in her belly. "You're not promising that *you* won't sneak into your auntie's bed every morning, are you?"

She threw her arms around him again and with the sweet scent of her in his lungs, his pulse calmed. He bopped the tip of her nose before getting to his feet.

His gaze shifted to Yana, and in an instant, a full body flush claimed him as he took in her disheveled state. Her face free of makeup, her wild hair tangled around her shoulders, she looked incredibly young and vulnerable. As if she'd put away the mask she wore for the world. Something almost like approval glinted in her eyes.

"I'm sorry she woke you. I held her off for two hours."

"It's fine. Clearly," she said, waving her hand around the bright sunlight in one of those expansive gestures he was coming to recognize she made when she wanted to hide, "I overslept."

She asked him something in fragmented Arabic while trying to protect Lila the llama from the dogs so that Nasir had to move closer to hear her. When she repeated it, he laughed. Apparently, it was a morning of shocks. Or the month of Nasir pulling his head out of his backside. "You just asked me why you're standing in my bed."

Pink dusted her cheeks and she grabbed the duvet as if she needed a lifeline.

Seating himself next to her, he ignored how stiff she went. There was a wicked joy in making her brazen act falter. "When did you learn Arabic?"

Her sharp profile softened as a gentle smile wreathed her mouth. "When I lived with your dad. He practiced…" Her eyes shimmered with an aching fondness as she swallowed and corrected herself. "He used to practice with me all the time. He taught me a lot of bad words and said I needed to use them against you."

"He always liked you."

"He *loved* me." Her conviction shone so bright and clear that Nasir was taken aback. "He loved me as if I were his own daughter. He'd call me and text me and send me little gifts. Even though you forbade him to have any contact with me."

The profound ache in her tone made Nasir swallow hard. "You kept in touch?"

Her smile grew bittersweet. "Usually me venting about how the world was unfair and he'd remind me that the world didn't understand how wonderful I was." The love in her eyes made him feel like he was lost in a sea of emotions he'd willingly turned off inside him.

It *had* been his condition when his father had reconciled with his mother that he never have any more contact with Diana or her daughter. On an intellectual level, he knew why he'd insisted on that. Diana was destruction itself. And yet, he hadn't given a moment's thought to the fact that Yana had gotten caught in the crossfire. He hadn't wanted to punish her, even though she'd lied about him kissing her. He simply hadn't considered the effect on her of taking away his father's love.

"I did a lot of things wrong by you. I won't shame myself further by offering excuses."

"You thought I was beneath your notice. But he…"

"He what?"

She cast a quick look at Zara and the dogs, who were now playing on the terrace attached to the bedroom.

"Izaz Uncle wondered if you never forgave him fully for leaving your mother. He thought the bond between you two never…recovered fully." She held his gaze. "I believe he missed you. *The real you*, he'd say."

Standing up and moving away from the bed, Nasir rubbed shaking hands over his face. Regrets coated his throat like thorny prickles. "Of course I forgave him. My mother wasn't easy to love," he said on a wave of grief. "I… I wish he had just asked me. I'd have told him that it was all to do with me. Not him. He was a wonderful father whatever went on between him and Ammee." He turned to her, feeling caught between the sterile world he'd locked himself into and this new one where pain and loss ruled. "What else, Yana? What else did he say?"

"I'd console him by calling you all kinds of names." Her mouth twitched. "And he'd defend you, say you'd just lost your way. That his warm, loving son was buried somewhere beneath the cold, hard one you'd become."

And here was the proof—that the man who'd loved him with such depth, who'd believed in second chances, had thought Nasir had just lost his way. His father hadn't approved of his lifestyle, or his marriage to Jacqueline, but he'd never interfered because he'd believed that everyone had a right to make their own mistakes. Unlike his mother, though, Abba's concern had been about Nasir's happiness.

Nasir had not just lost his way, he'd actively distanced himself from all the good things in his life. Because losing Fatima had been so painful that he hadn't wanted to feel anything again.

A sympathetic murmur had him unclenching his jaw. He turned to find Yana looking at him with regrets in her eyes. That she could feel his pain when he'd been anything but kind to her...humbled him. "I didn't say it to hurt you."

"I know that."

They stared at each other, she from her cozy position on the bed, he standing under the archway leading to the terrace, as if at a crossroads.

She'd always been an incredible temptation. Easy to resist because she'd always embodied the very drama and loss of control he'd abhorred. And yet now, in revealing his own flaws to him, she was revealing herself to him. Bit by tantalizing bit. Anything between them could only be temporary, yet she was here for his kid and he shouldn't even indulge the mad idea in his head. But it was there, growing every second. He wasn't even sure if he could walk away from her again, like he'd done last night.

"I'm glad you and he kept in touch," he said, forcing his thoughts back. "That he could talk to you about... me."

She nodded. And he could see questions fluttering on her lips, her curiosity in the arch of her brows. He waited. And waited. And waited. The Yana he'd known once wouldn't have half the control she seemed to possess now. Even that felt like a loss to him.

Turning away to look at Zara, she said to him, "Why did you bring me to your bedroom?"

"I was as exhausted as you were." He thrust a hand through his hair as she slowly untangled herself from the mess Zara and the dogs had made of the sheets. A toned thigh, the flash of her pink thong and the shadow of her nipples—the artless show she gave him was sinfully arousing. He cleared his throat. "I think I automatically brought you here because it's the bedroom that's attached to Zara's."

Distaste filled her eyes as she jumped from the bed as if it might take a bite of that delectable bottom. "Wait, this is the room you shared with Jacqueline?"

"No, I told you last night, remember, that I bought this castle for Zara after Jacqueline died. You know as well as I do that she'd never have moved out of Paris for anyone or anything."

She kept moving until she was standing directly in front of shafts of sunlight. As if they couldn't resist her, either, light beams drenched her, delineating every rise and dip for his pleasure. Golden dust motes created a crown around her stunning face. Her legs...went on for miles, and it was only the background noise that Zara and the dogs created that stopped his thoughts from crossing over to forbidden territory.

"If you can have the staff show me to a new room—" Yana stepped back as he approached, a frown tying her feathery brows. "What?"

He grabbed a colorful throw from the foot of the bed and wrapped it around her, tugging her closer until the edges met in front of her chest. But he didn't let go. He didn't want to. There was something incredibly arousing about arresting her in his embrace, in having her face him like this. Gathering her messy hair, he pulled it back so that the throw could sit snugly around her shoulders. The brush of his knuckles over her nape, her rough exhale coasting his lips, every moment was pungent with an arching awareness.

Tying the edges of the soft throw to hold it together, he backed away.

Licking her lips, she stared at him.

"Your T-shirt is practically transparent."

Yana's belly did a slow, tantalizing roll. Her mouth dried up as if she'd spent hours in a desert. Which she had once for an underwear ad. But this was a delicious burn that seemed to taper off and arrow straight down to her pelvis. She tugged at the T-shirt she'd put on last night, far too exhausted to unpack properly. No bra and a thong with most of her legs bared.

In contrast to her disheveled state, Nasir was dressed in dark jeans and a white T-shirt that made his olive skin gleam. His wet hair was piled high on top, with gray streaking his temples.

But neither the casual clothes nor the gray in his hair or the fact that he looked like he hadn't gotten any sleep last night diminished the sexual appeal of the man one bit. It was too much. Her own skin felt too tight to contain the pleasure and anticipation sparking through her.

It wasn't just the magnetism of his good looks, though. This morning the strain around his mouth had lessened. He looked dreamy, carefree, even, approachable. And that it was because of her presence, even if only indirectly, made delight dance inside.

God, she was such a pushover, and the realization prodded her to brazen it out.

With one wriggle of her shoulders, she dislodged the throw he'd so gently wrapped around her, wishing she could shrug off the warmth of his body just as easily. Nakedness was nothing new to her. Her body, for so long, had been just a tool, another costume, that she put on to please the world. She wasn't going to feel shy or modest about it now.

She cocked a hip and straightened her shoulders in a move she could do in her sleep. "My transparent sleepwear is not my problem." The throw settled like a warm wrap around her cold feet. "Since you're the one who barged in here."

He grinned, and she had a sense of a passionate, almost violent, energy being contained in his body. "Right! The closed door means the dogs and I are forbidden to enter."

"You've got it wrong. Unlike you, the dogs *are* welcome. Even in my bed, Nasir," she retorted, incapable of keeping her mouth shut.

Palm pressed to his chest, he let out an exaggerated sigh that said it was his loss.

It was such a dramatic, outrageous gesture for him to make that she laughed out loud. A pang of nostalgia ran through her. He'd been like this once—playful, witty, as ready to mock himself as he'd mocked her.

And even this felt like madness, to laugh with him like this, to see him try so hard for Zara's sake, to see his eyes travel over *her* with that devouring intensity. The near chant in her head that he was just one of millions of men who derived pleasure at the symmetry of her face, at a body she'd achieved through hours and hours in the gym and nearly starving herself at the beginning of her career, didn't help one bit. It was impossible to see Nasir as just any man, even in her head.

"Anyway, I can't just take your room, Nasir—"

A new voice piped up, interrupting her. "No, she can't. It's bad enough that we have to see her making pretty eyes at you all over again. Didn't you learn a lesson with your wife, Nasir? Yana will only teach Zara more awful things about you."

Yana froze, recognizing that voice. Around her, a deafening silence fell. She felt Zara's little body tucking up against her bare leg and picked her up. Even the dogs seemed to know instinctively that they needed to be wary of Nasir's mother.

It took all she had to bite back a hysterical laugh because she didn't want to scare Zara. Already, she was stiff in Yana's arms. When she saw Ahmed fluttering behind Amina, Yana walked Zara over to him. "How about a picnic as soon as we get ready, Zuzu?"

Her head tucked into the crook of Yana's shoulder and neck, Zara gave her a doubting look. "Pwomise?"

"Yes, baby. It's a lovely day and we'll spend the entirety of it outside. Once you finish breakfast, grab your boots and your scrapbook, yeah? You live right in the middle of a forest. So we have to look for fairies, okay?"

"Fairies!" Zara beamed. "Don't be late, Yana Auntie," Zara said, leaning across into Ahmed's arms. No one could miss the worried frown wreathing her forehead when she cast a glance at her grandmother.

Another thought struck Yana and she rounded on Nasir as soon as Zara was out of earshot. "You've got

Zara stuck here, miles away from civilization, with only *your mother* for company? She hated Jacqueline even more than she hates me, Nasir. Is it wise to expose Zara to her brand of cutting honesty?"

"I'd never hurt Zara by showing my dislike for her mother," Amina spoke up.

"And yet, here you are, pouring vitriol in my face the first morning I'm here." Yana's voice shook. "Are you so wrapped up in yourself that you can't see that Zara can sense your feelings?"

Refusing to give Amina another chance to attack her, Yana closed the massive doors to the bedroom right in her face and pressed her back to it. Now she knew what Nasir had meant when he'd said they'd have chaperones galore.

If it was possible that there was a person who hated her more than Nasir did, it was his mother. The woman who blamed Yana's mother, probably justly so, for destroying her marriage. The woman who loathed Yana for being *that woman's* daughter and the one who'd made up a fake kiss from her son.

To trap him just like her mother had trapped his father.

Yana grabbed her bag from the closet and turned to Nasir. "Please book a hotel suite for Zara and me."

"No."

"I'm not staying here with *her.*"

"Yana, listen to me."

"And you call me manipulative."

"I never called you that. Not even when you lied

about kissing me all those years ago. You're far too reckless and destructively honest to be manipulative."

"You're just saying those things to try and calm me down."

She walked through the vast closet, feeling betrayed. No one could spew vicious truths like Nasir's mom. And she was already defenseless, having barely recovered from her own mom's betrayal, and from the void her thaata had left with his death.

"You should've told me she'd be here."

"Then you wouldn't have come."

"Can you blame me?"

"Only Zara matters, Yana. Ammi knows that." He raised his palms in surrender when she glared at him, his jaw so tight that she could see a vein bulging there. "I promise, I won't let her near you."

"You *can't* ensure that, Nasir, unless you stick to me like last night's gum." A strange tsunami of emotions built inside her, and Yana couldn't grasp it back under control. That Amina might be right, that she'd lose herself all over again over Nasir... "You can't control Amina...her grief, her loss, her...hatred. Not when they're all so raw after losing your dad just last year." She pushed her fingers through her hair roughly. "I get enough of this drama from my mom, and I've already had enough lashes about the past from you. I can't take it from her, too. Not even for Zara. Not when I'm trying to start a new chapter in my own life. Not when you both tried to make sure I lost your dad a long time ago."

Something about how still he stood arrested her frenzy. Yana knew she was losing it, betraying all the anger and resentment she'd tried hard to bury when Nasir had attempted to cut her out of his Dad's life, but she couldn't seem to stop. Not when he looked at her as if he was seeing her for the first time.

The real, messy, vulnerable, hurt-as-hell her. The girl no one had looked out for. The woman who'd thought she didn't deserve that kind of looking after. That kind of love.

"When I was growing up, I didn't know how deep words like that could wound. How toxic they could make me behave in turn. But not anymore. I can't keep getting battered by you and her, and my mom and all the shadows of my past mistakes. I'll fall apart and where will that leave Zara then?"

His fingers came around her nape in a firm, yet tender grip, stilling her. "Shh…breathe, *habibi*. Breathe for me, baby. You're okay."

"I—"

And then his arms were tugging her to him, and Yana sank into the embrace. It was a gift. As necessary as breathing. She'd been starved for touch for so long. Starved for understanding as she'd tried to hold her life from imploding. Starved for a lifetime of being held like this by him.

"You're safe here, *habibi*," he kept crooning at her temple, holding her as if she was the most fragile, most precious, thing in the world. Her breath came in shallow pants and she was trembling, and he kept whispering endearments as if he meant them. That bergamot and sandalwood scent dug deep into her roots, making a home there. Centering her. His large hands stroked all over her back, soothing her.

He'd been like this once before. A long time ago. He'd been kind and patient and… And he was only being so now because she was very near a breakdown and he needed her to not fall apart. He was a good father and would do whatever was required to keep her here for Zara.

She was in his life just because Nasir loved his daughter—she couldn't forget that.

"No lies," she said quietly, pulling away from him. "You decided it was okay for me to be exposed to your mother's vitriol. You're fine with treating me however you please because I'm an eternal car crash anyway, right? But no more. At least for Zara's sake, ask Amina to keep her mouth shut about Jacqueline." She wrapped her arms around herself, reminding herself that she was steel and ice. "I'll stay but you don't deserve it because you've broken my trust again."

After walking into the en-suite bathroom and closing the door behind her, she leaned against it. Yes, seeing Amina had thrown her. But she was stronger than an angry, bitter old woman, stronger this time than her childish attraction to Nasir. She'd be stronger for herself and for Zara.

CHAPTER SEVEN

NASIR STOPPED PRETENDING that he was getting any work done—even though it was a chapter he'd already plotted multiple times, minutes after he saw Yana walk to the pool with Zara's little hand tucked in hers. As he walked through the myriad corridors of the castle, their laughter floated upward from the multiple open terraces.

For over two weeks now, he'd told himself that work was more important, especially after the forced break while he followed Yana all over the world. But it was a fruitless exercise when all he wanted was to join them both and play happy family in a way Zara had never experienced with him and Jacqueline. Even that startling thought didn't stop his progress.

Every day, after walking the dogs, Yana and Zara promptly arrived at the pool. When Zara went down for a nap under the supervision of her actual nanny, Yana disappeared back inside the castle. Then the two of them would show up in the cozy library in the evenings, either reading or drawing or listening to rhymes. Yana even ate dinner with Zara. He didn't doubt one bit that Yana's day was precisely planned to have minimum intersection with his. Even during that early dinner, she retreated halfway through it to give him time with Zara.

It was exactly the kind of experience he'd wanted for Zara, with a few structured activities and free play-time, but had been unable to achieve with any of the myriad staff he'd hired. In only a couple of weeks of Yana's being here, Zara laughed, played naughty tricks and was more open and demanding with them—everything that a healthy, thriving five-year-old should be. Even his mother had to agree that Yana had an innate ability to love Zara like a mother.

With him, though, she was an ice queen extraordinaire. A thorn under his skin. The flicker of anguish when she'd said her pain was an acceptable price to him haunted him, day and night. The flash of grief when she'd said that she'd lost his dad, too, showed he'd become a villain in her life.

He knew he'd compounded his mistreatment of her by throwing her out after he'd learned that Yana was supposedly Jacqueline's character witness to enable her to gain solo custody of Zara. Having seen her open love for his daughter, he more than doubted his accusations now. Yana wouldn't have done that to Zara. Jacqueline must have instructed her lawyers to name Yana without telling her.

All of his distrust of her just because she'd claimed he'd kissed her when he'd never even touched her. It had been a stupid, juvenile impulse she'd given in to when she was only nineteen. Had he really behaved any better—a man twelve years older than she was? Had he shown any more maturity than she had?

Now she'd shut him out so thoroughly that Nasir felt as if he had been robbed of something he'd never even realized he had. He'd made peace with his attraction to her. But where did this need to be acknowledged by her come from? To be forgiven for all his multitude of sins?

Wherever it came from, it was so not a good idea. Especially when she'd always be a part of his little girl's life *and his life*. And still, he kept moving, instead of turning back.

Yana sat at the edge of the pool, praising Zara for everything she did right and for things she tried under the swimming instructor's tutelage. When Yana stood up, Nasir's breath left his body.

Her skin gleamed with a golden-brown sheen that came out of no bottle. The bright orange bikini she wore was basically three triangles that should come with a libido overload warning. Every movement sensuality in motion, she looked like a Bond girl from the eighties, all wild and free and innately sensual.

The swimming instructor and Yana struck up a relaxed conversation. Then she bent and lifted Zara out of the pool and wrapped her in one big towel, tying a turban-esque smaller one around her hair before the nanny came over to fetch the little girl for her nap.

"Do you see how she flirts with that boy? Is this the kind of behavior you want around Zara?"

Nasir's irritation leaped into dangerous territory at his mother's open insults. Of course, he saw the casual flirting, the laughter, the swat on the arm and how her body inevitably bowed toward the younger guy as she chatted to him, how she naturally made him open up and smile back at her.

What he hadn't understood until now was how that effervescence, that wildness, was an intrinsic part of her. Like lightning, she either illuminated or burned everything she touched. And just the idea of burning with her made arousal flood his body.

He cast his mother a quelling look. "Don't, Ammi."

"You will regret—"

"Stop, please."

In just a few minutes Yana had pinned down his mother's inconsolable grief and the outlet of bitter rage she used to channel it. The past year he had given in to his mother's demands to stay with Zara because he understood the sheer magnitude of her loss. He'd lost a woman he'd loved once. While Fatima's face was nothing but a distorted memory now, the hollow loss of it remained.

But now his mother's words were directly harming his own motherless child. That he hadn't seen Zara's reticence with her until Yana had pointed it out…made his very foundation flounder. "If you cannot be civil to Yana, I'll send you away."

"I'm Zara's grandmother. I've helped you look after her all these months."

"And for that," he said, "I'm forever grateful. I want Zara to know you, to love you. Jacqueline's parents are long gone anyway. But everything you say, everything you don't say, about her mother, and now about her precious Auntie Yana… Zara processes all this."

"She is only—"

"You can't have missed that any time Zara spends with you has to be overseen by me at her request, that it's out of obligation."

He could see her heart breaking at his harsh words but the truth had to be said. If she didn't fix her behavior, the damage would soon be irrevocable.

"You're choosing that woman who's a liar and cheater and…whose mother ruined my marriage over me?"

And there was the crux of the matter. "The only one I'm choosing here is Zara. I'm doing what I should've done from the moment Jacqueline told me she was expecting. If you can set your grief aside for one moment—" he raised his palms to hold her protest off "—you'll acknowledge that Zara flourishes when Yana is around. Yana's going to be a permanent part of our life, and I want you there, too. That means you have to let the past go. Yana was only a child herself when Abba and Diana met."

"What about the lies she told about you?"

"She was young and naive, and the only one she had to teach her right from wrong was Diana, who we both know has no moral compass. And I had just dealt her a brutal rejection." He'd never been able to get her stricken face out of his head. He'd turned on her, when he could have dealt the same rejection with a little grace and a lot more kindness.

Instead, mindless with grief and guilt over losing Fatima, he'd shredded Yana to bits. He saw the truth finally, clearly now. Yana had loved him with all the urgency and naiveté and fierceness of a nineteen-year-old.

"If I can let it go, then you can. And Yana's not responsible for Abba leaving you."

"You are attracted to her," his mother whispered in a shaken voice. "How just like a man!"

He didn't dignify that with a response.

"She is not right for you."

Nasir laughed. "I chose Jacqueline but she cheated on me again and again. And believe me, I was no great husband, so I very possibly drove her to it. Yana's suitability is moot because she loathes the very sight of me."

"That's impossible."

"No wonder my ego has always flourished, Ammi."

"If she's that important to Zara," she said, having to have the last word before she walked off, "then you'd better keep your distance."

Having been celibate for more than three years, Nasir wondered if part of what was driving him might just simply be sexual frustration. But he knew it wasn't just a need for release.

Yana's ice-queen act was rattling things he didn't want to delve into. It was time to take not quite a sledgehammer to it, because Yana was far more fragile than he had ever thought her, and not just in body. The most shocking thing, however, was this…strange energy between them. He understood now how much of her natural passionate nature went into hating him. And hating, he knew from his own experience from his marriage to Jacqueline, was not apathy.

He relaxed into the lounger while Yana took her own swim. Let the bright afternoon sun soak into his skin.

When was the last time he had taken a moment for himself like this? The last time he had found this pleasurable fizz run through all of him at the mere idea of a conversation with a woman?

In a smooth, single movement, Yana pulled herself out of the pool. Water glistened over golden-brown skin in shimmering drips, licking at toned muscles and lush valleys and hollowed dips that he wanted to chase with his own tongue.

Yana walked past him, as if he was no more than one of the statues littered around the estate.

Nasir wondered what his life might have been like if he hadn't dictated her life from afar, deciding rights and wrongs for her, and he'd never quite loathed himself more than he did then.

And like a statue brought to life by a sorceress's hand, he suddenly felt all these things he had shut off long ago, when Fatima, the woman he should've protected with his life, had died in his arms.

If she was disconcerted by the fact that he was waiting for her by the pool in the middle of the day when they hadn't even made eye contact for more than two weeks, Yana didn't show it by the flicker of an eyelid. Having toweled herself down briskly, she grabbed a tube of sunscreen and began to apply it to her belly and legs liberally.

Nasir saw all of this out of his periphery, and it was as if she had stripped naked in front of him. Just for him.

The shimmery white gel soaked into her skin like

magic dust, not that she needed it. Slightly angling her torso, she lifted her bikini top and took her breasts in her bare hands with a brisk efficiency that came from parading in front of strangers with a power only a few could own. Once the bikini top was back in place, she reached around her back, twisting herself like a gymnast.

He stood up and grabbed the tube of sunscreen. "Let me help."

She didn't even look up. *Ice queen indeed.* "I can manage, thank you."

He was damned if he walked away now. "Right, it makes you uncomfortable if I touch you. Forgive me."

The slender line of her shoulders stiffened. He'd have missed it if he wasn't entirely too fascinated by her body language. Tension drew a line down her back and spine, giving him a map to her emotions.

"And why would I be uncomfortable if you touched me casually?"

"I wondered that, too." He managed a shrug, somehow keeping his lips from twitching. "But it's a fair assumption based on how you keep jerking away from me."

She snorted and somehow even that was elegant, too. "My body is a tool. I've sold clothes, shoes, hairstyles, cosmetics, jeans and most of all, sex. I've had hundreds of photographers and designers and camera boys and tailors maul me about like I was a mannequin."

Nasir wished he could see her face, the bloom of pink on her cheeks, the little sparks that made her brown eyes glitter when she was aroused. Take her in as she was right now, instead of the icy wraith that had been walking through his castle recently.

But he forced himself to stand there, just a little behind her.

After exactly thirty seconds, she looked up at him. Determination written into every line of that achingly lovely face, she nodded at the plastic tube he was holding. He dropped to his knees by her thigh.

Awareness jolted into him at the aching beauty of her up close. Like an exquisite painting that bestowed some new boon every time he looked upon it.

Chin tilted up defiantly, she presented him with her back. He pushed up the messy tendrils from the nape of her neck, while tugging at the two fragile strings holding the bikini top there with the other. And then the one below.

Her forearms rose to hold the loose top in place, thrusting those perfect breasts into a cleavage that he could unwittingly see perfectly from his vantage point. He didn't know if he should feel like a voyeur or be glad that his libido was back with vengeance. Shuttling those thoughts aside, he poured the sunscreen liberally into his palms and began to rub it down her back.

Smooth golden skin and toned muscles under his palms—he shouldn't have felt such sensual, sensory pleasure in the simple action, and yet Nasir could feel himself getting harder by the second. The contact was innocent and nonsexual, and yet heat seem to arc between his fingers and her flesh, something he could tell she tried her best to hide, but failed.

"As long as I have your attention," she started, and

Nasir smiled, because he knew she was trying to distract herself. Was it all simply want on his part and hate on hers? Or was there more?

"If I had known you were looking for my attention, I would've insisted that you stay on for dinner after Zara goes to bed."

She shivered under his hands. "I'm taking the evening off."

"When?"

"Tonight."

On an upward sweep of his hands, he found tight knots at her shoulders. "For what?"

"I need a night off."

"Has Zara worn you out?" When she stiffened, he quickly added, "Quite the prickly thing, aren't you? Anyone would be worn out and begging for adult company when one spends most of their waking hours endlessly running around after a five-year-old."

He pressed his fingertips gently into one stubborn knot and heard her soft moan. The sound went straight to his groin. Thank God she couldn't see him because at this point, he must look obscene.

"I have castle fever," she finally said.

Somehow, he infused humor into his words when all he felt was a tsunami of inappropriate wild urges. "I thought you loved castles."

"As a fanciful teenager, Nasir. Castles are all well and good, especially when you think a charming prince lives in them but—"

"I'm the devil. Is that it?"

"More like a beast." Her answer was immediate.

He grabbed the bottom ends of the bikini top by reaching around to the front and almost grazed the underside of her breasts. Breath shallowing, he tied the strings at the bottom, and then took hold of the ones at the top. His fingers lingered on her neck, as he tried to keep the damp tendrils of her hair from getting into the knot. Her shoulders trembled as he touched the jut of her clavicle, marveling at how much passion was contained in such a fragile body.

Shooting to her feet all of a sudden, Yana jerked back. And he saw it then—the pink flush that shimmered under all of that golden-brown skin. And not just her cheeks or neck, but dusting the tops of her breasts. Her throat moved in a hard swallow that rippled down her chest.

"I apologize for hurting you," he said, transfixed by the sight.

Gears turned in his head, mostly driven by the molten desire in his blood. Truth dawned and held him in thrall—she definitely wanted him.

"I'm not going to break apart because you caused a little pain."

"But I should not cause it in the first place," he said, coming back to himself.

Knowing one of the most beautiful women in the world wanted him was a trip all on its own. But it was also a sop to his masculine ego that had taken enough dents with a partner who'd cheated on him as if she was picking a different weekly flavor of her frou-frou coffees.

But knowing that someone like Yana—vulnerable

and innocent and full of heart and fragile—wanted him…was a honey-coated thrust to his insides. "Yana, I should like to talk to you about what you said the other day."

Grabbing a sheer white robe, she tied it at her waist with a fierce tug.

He had the most insane urge to pull those ends with his hands until she fell into him and he could burn the edge out of them both in the best way he knew.

"It's not necessary. As I've proved to you over the last two weeks or so, I'm very much capable of having a polite relationship with you, Nasir. Please, let's not dig back into the past and play the blame game again."

"Even if it's only so I can admit to you that I've been inexcusably wrong?" he slipped in.

For a second, just a second, it looked like she would give him a chance to talk. Something almost like longing flashed in her eyes.

But then she was shaking her head, and her messy bun fell apart, and long, wavy dark gold strands of hair framed her face. In that moment she looked very much like a beautiful, naive prize that had been grabbed up by the beast. He was beginning to hate that damned fairy tale.

"A friend of mine will be here to pick me up around five this evening. I've already prepped Zara so you don't have to worry. She knows I'll be back tomorrow morning by the time her Arabic lessons are done. If you'll just inform security to let him through the electronic gates—"

"No."

"What do you mean, *no*?"

"I mean my security won't let him in."

He turned around and started walking away. That was not the end of it, he knew. But he'd had enough of kidding himself that he didn't want to explore this thing between Yana and him. Enough of his own lies that somehow he'd keep away from her.

Right now he simply wanted her company. Her forgiveness. Her wild laughter. Her eyes on him.

She grabbed him by the shoulder and turned him and thrust her face close to his, all warm, golden skin and exploding temper. "Is old age affecting your brain cells? Because I wasn't asking for permission."

He laughed.

That lovely, lush lower lip fell open as she watched him, drinking him in. Warmth crested his cheeks at the open, artless way her eyes stared up at him, as if he was exactly the tall, cold drink she needed after a swim in the afternoon heat.

"Oh, believe me, every faculty, even those I thought were faulty or dead, are now functioning at peak capacity. Thanks to you, *habibi*."

Her mouth opened, closed and then opened again. Curiosity danced across her face and he willed her to give in, to ask him what he meant. But he lost. "Are you saying no to my friend coming here to pick me up or are you saying no to my going out?" Tiny lines pinched at the corners of her eyes. "What gives you the right to say no to me for anything?"

"No to both. For one, I don't want some random friend of yours finding out where I live. And second—"

"Have Ahmed drop me at the nearest village, then."

"You never asked for a day off when we were talking terms." There was no way he was going to let her go off and see some male *friend*. He didn't care to examine his motivations just then. Maybe never. Maybe there was a freedom in going all in into becoming this ruthless, arrogant, uncaring beast she thought him to be anyway. "If it's not in the contract, Yana, it's not happening."

She pushed at him with her hand on his chest, but he didn't budge. And he saw now how volatile and touchy she got when her temper was riled.

Raising his hands, he gave her a sweet smile that he knew would only push her closer toward the edge. He wanted to see the explosion, the thundering temper, the impulsive, self-destructive step she might take.

And then he wondered what it would be like to be in the path of all that destruction she wreaked, to let himself be devoured by the storm that was this woman.

She stomped her foot, much like Zara did when she didn't get to eat her dessert before dinner. "Oh, how I hate you sometimes!"

"I prefer hatred to what you've been serving me up this past fortnight or so."

She colored. "I'm keeping my end of the bargain. I spend most of my time with Zara. I love spending that time with her. It's only for an hour or so during her nap, and then again after she has her dinner and goes to bed that I leave her. So why are you—"

He stepped closer to her, determined to not let her run out without giving him an answer. "Where is it that you disappear to? And what do you do? Don't tell me the party girl, supermodel extraordinaire, retires to bed at only seven in the evening?"

"That's none of your business." She shut him down so hard that it only made Nasir more curious. "As you've just mentioned, I'm not used to being tied down to one place for too long. I need a night out on the town."

"Where do you want to go?"

Her response was the cutest twitch of her nose in distaste. Something in his chest melted and he wondered how much of him had been frozen over the years to be constantly melting at each taunt and expression that she threw at him. And what would eventually happen to him if he didn't stop her?

"A nightclub. I want to go dancing... I have all this energy I want to get rid of." There was something so sensuous and yet, unpracticed in that little wiggle of hers that all Nasir wanted to do was see her do it again. And do it because she wanted his eyes on him. Do it because she wanted to please him.

"Give me a few days and I'll take you."

She laughed and it was like watching a sunrise captured in one of those time-lag videos. It was beautiful, and breathtaking and made his breath falter in his throat.

"You at a nightclub?"

"You sound more scared than excited at the prospect. What are you so afraid might happen?"

She swallowed and didn't meet his eyes. "If you come, it will become a big thing. I don't want to be photographed with you again."

"I thought you didn't care about being photographed with me. Your sisters know where you are, right?"

"It's not my sisters that I'm hiding from."

"Nobody can get to you here. I promise you that. You don't have to be scared, *habibi*." The endearment fell from his lips as easily as if he'd said it a thousand times.

"It's not what you think," she said. "It's just… I don't want Diana to know where I am."

He wanted to probe the source of the argument between them. Not that he was surprised at her wanting to hide. Diana had never been a good parental figure. For now he let Yana be.

Soon, though, he would have all her secrets. He'd lay her bare, see through to the real Yana she hid under the party-girl persona. Maybe that was the way to break this fascination with every facet of her. Maybe then he could go back to viewing her from afar with a mild interest at best.

"Have dinner with me in a few days. We'll have guests over, since you're scared of being alone with me."

"I… Who?" Suspicion marked that single word.

"A few good friends of mine. You'll have good conversation and dancing choices other than me."

Her eyes widened. "Really? You're going to let your friends see me here at your forbidden castle? Has hell frozen over?"

"You're the one making all the assumptions here, Yana. And you won't give me a chance to dispel any of them. One might wonder why you need to retain them. Almost like armor, one could say."

He left her standing there, with her mouth open, incredibly frustrated with her and even more so with himself. But he'd brought temptation into his life, into his house, into his very bed even, and he had nothing left in him to resist her.

CHAPTER EIGHT

YANA WAS SEARCHING through her wardrobe for something to wear to Nasir's dinner party when she heard a knock on her door.

For a second she wondered if it was one of the staff to tell her that Nasir had rescinded the invitation. Because nearly a week later, she still couldn't process his change of heart.

Tolerating her for Zara's sake was one thing. Actively seeking her company was another. Although, she didn't doubt that he thought he was being all protective and honorable by keeping her out of trouble. Whatever his motive, though, she was far too tempted by this chance at a glimpse into his life to refuse.

She opened the door to find an army of people. Surprise made her gasp as Ahmed and a younger woman rolled in a dress stand, followed by Zara, her hand tucked into her grandmother's bigger one.

Yana followed Ahmed and the colorful display of dresses on the stand. "What's going on?"

"Nasir Sir thought you might need help with getting ready for tonight."

"Did he?" Yana asked, somehow keeping her bitterness to herself. "Does he think I'd embarrass his highbrow friends, Ahmed?" she hissed in a whisper so the others couldn't hear.

He shook his head. "This is my daughter, Huma," Ahmed said, beckoning the younger woman closer. "If it's okay with you, she wishes to dress you for the party."

"I was just going to wear something from my wardrobe," Yana added, wary of Nasir's new behavior. But the crestfallen expression on the younger woman's face made her feel horrible. "Of course, I didn't pack for one of Nasir's fabulous dinner parties. I'd love a chance to try one of your creations." She ran her fingers over a couple of evening gowns made of frothy chiffon and cut in simple, classic lines. Nearly a decade and a half in the industry had given her a discerning eye when it came to fashion. "These are gorgeous. Did you design these yourself, Huma?"

Pride and joy shone in Huma's eyes. "Yes, I'm studying fashion."

Ahmed gave his daughter a nudge. "Nasir Sir has already paid for her education. But she refuses to leave because she thinks her old papa cannot take care of himself."

Yana's heart warmed at the obvious affection between these two. Suddenly, she could see why Nasir might have suggested to them that Yana needed help. It wasn't a big surprise that he was a wonderful human being when it came to other people. It was only her he held in such low esteem.

Even if it's only so I can admit to you that I've been inexcusably wrong...?

His question had been haunting her. Did he truly want to apologize to her? To begin a different sort of relationship? Could she bear that? Or was she letting him mess with her head again?

"I'd love to wear one of your creations, Huma, as long as you let me pay you for it."

Huma shook her head. "Not at all. It's a dream come true to see you wear one of my designs. If you'd just let me take a picture once you're wearing it," she rushed on. "I wouldn't share it with anybody. Not on social media. I just... I want proof that the gorgeous, stunning Yana Reddy wore one of my designs."

Yana squeezed her hand. "Of course you can share it. Between you and me, I'm kind of getting tired of the modeling world, but I still have my foot in the door there. I know a lot of photographers and design houses. I'll get you in touch with people I trust," she added, noting Ahmed's expression.

"I'm not worried about the kind of people you will introduce her to, Ms. Reddy. If they're anything like you, my daughter is in good hands."

Yana had no idea what she'd ever done in her life to deserve such genuine affection from him but she let it drape around her like a childhood blanket. "Now..." She clapped her hands, picked Zara up and settled her on her hip. "Let's see. Zuzu baby, do you want to help me pick a dress for tonight?"

Like an octopus, Zara wound her hands and legs all around Yana, as if she never wanted to let her go. For all the hours they spent together, Yana was still dreading the goodbye that would eventually come at the end of three months. As much as she hadn't wanted to be here, under the same roof as Nasir, she'd found that she liked living at the castle.

Especially since, whatever her son had said to her, Amina had kept her distance from Yana, too.

"To turn you into a pwincess?" Zara asked.

Yana laughed. "Maybe. Although I'd like to be a princess who saves herself."

Zara nodded, as if she understood the intricacies of adulthood and wanting to be someone who saved themselves. "But I'd love Huma's help with a dress and yours with my hair so that I can be a perfect princess. Even the brave princess needs all the love she can get."

"Yay, did you hear, Gwandma? Yana Auntie said I can do her hair."

Dragged into the conversation by her granddaughter, Amina offered a tentative smile. "Are you sure you want Zara's fingers on that lovely hair of yours? She's going to mess it all up."

"Oh, I don't really care, Amina. It's not like I'm going to walk the ramp tonight and face a thousand cameras." And yet, even the wildest, longest, hardest events of her career hadn't caused this...constant flutter of butterflies.

Was she a fool to look forward to the party this much? Where were all the promises she'd made to herself that she'd treat Nasir as just another employer?

"You will look beautiful whatever Zara does to your

hair," Amina added, always wanting to have the last word, just like her son. "You're leaving modeling, then?"

Struggling to keep her shock off her face—the older woman had the hearing of a bat—she said, "Give or take a decade, Amina. It's not like I know how to do anything else."

The words left a bitter taste in her mouth.

She had to stop with the negative talk. And yet, the fact that she'd not been successful yet in placing her children's novel with an agent had left her in knots.

She wanted it so bad—this new, fluttery dream to be an author, to fill some child's life with escape and adventure and love, as Nasir's stories had done for her. But…she was terrified that she'd never make it. Never get it right. Never have what it took.

She could share the manuscript with Nasir and get his feedback and advice. And yet, the thought of him finding her talentless, or worse, laughing in her face, made bile rise up into her throat.

With Zara still on her hip, Yana moved to the huge vanity table that had been moved into the bedroom the second day of her arrival. It was the most beautiful thing she'd ever seen, and she had seen a lot of beautiful things in her life. With three different panels of mirrors, it was truly a princess's possession. She had no doubt Nasir had acquired it in some rare auction, but she wondered every time she sat in front of it why he'd had it installed in here when she was still using his bedroom. "First, I'm going to do my makeup, okay? Something soft and…"

"No, Yana Auntie. Glittery… Pwincesses have glittery makeup."

Everybody laughed and Yana groaned. "Oh, pumpkin, you don't want your papa's guests to make fun of Yana Auntie, do you?" she said, unable to keep the biggest fear that had been haunting her ever since Nasir had issued the invitation, out of her voice. More dictate than invitation, though, she thought wryly.

Whatever she heard in Yana's voice, Amina came to stand behind her. "First rule of being a woman—never let men decide if you're good enough for them."

She gave the older woman a quick nod in the mirror and wondered if she'd imagined the glint of satisfaction in her gaze. "Well, let's get started," Yana said, truly excited now at the prospect of getting ready for the night ahead. "With this many fairy godmothers, I'm sure I'll look beautiful tonight."

Yana entered the dining room and came to an awed stillness.

An otherworldly quality permeated the room with its grand sweeping ceilings and archways leading off to yet more rooms, like it belonged in an old film with its brightly lit sconces, gleaming chandeliers and the black-and-white-checkered marble floor. Through a huge archway, the room segued into an open, airy ballroom, where a couple was already slow dancing. With jazz playing on a record player and a low hum of conversation, it looked like one of those intellectual soirees she'd never felt good enough for.

The hum died as every gaze turned to her.

A huge stone fireplace blazed on one side in contrast to the French doors opening into a wide terrace with a view of the mountains. Cigar smoke drifted in from the terrace through the doors and lingered, adding to the dark, mysterious atmosphere of the room. Along with smoke, cold fluttered in, making one side of her deliciously chilly versus the warmth on the other from the fireplace. It was as magical as she'd imagined.

First impressions bombarding her, she noticed that it was an intimate group of guests. That meant less chance of losing herself. Her nervousness grew, thrashing it out with the excitement she'd been feeling all day.

It felt like an audition she was entering to find herself worthy of Nasir's highbrow group. And even if she didn't fit in, so what?

Bolstered by those thoughts, she straightened her shoulders. Her gaze moved over four couples, finally landing on Nasir, standing next to the huge hearth. His gaze swept over her, gleaming brighter than the amber liquid in the decanters on the bar cart.

The bright pink chiffon cocktail dress she and Huma had agreed on showed off her tan perfectly. It dipped low in the front with a beaded corset hugging her breasts tight, leaving her back bare all the way almost to the upper swells of her buttocks. It wasn't the most daring dress she'd ever worn and yet, maybe it was the most daring for this company.

It was cleverly held together by two straps tied at her neck, and that had reminded her of Nasir's fingers on her nape as he'd reknotted her bikini strings, and the delicious sensations that had engulfed her.

She didn't know how long they stood like that, gazing at each other across the room, quiet murmurs all around them while the jazz crooned to a soft, sinuous beat, and the sounds of the night drifted in from outside. All of it felt like an inspired, perfectly orchestrated soundtrack for this moment.

"So this is why you've been avoiding us, Nasir. You've got this beautiful creature hidden away in your castle." A deep voice quipped from her side, breaking the pulse of tension between her and Nasir. For a fanciful moment, she wondered what kind of vision she'd need to see it arc between them like a rainbow, fizzing with electricity, tugging them closer.

A second voice chimed in. "Our Mr. Hadeed is not as conservative as he'd have us believe."

Yana turned to face the two men, their arms around each other, both stunningly good-looking in completely different ways. She nodded, her mouth curving into a smile at the easy camaraderie they offered.

Nasir was moving closer. Only years of faking a snooty haughtiness helped her swallow the awed gasp that rose to her lips.

Dressed in a casual black jacket, white shirt and black trousers, he looked like one of those larger than life heroes of the silver screen. Hair slicked back, that long beak of his nose standing out, a cigar dangling from his fingers, there was a magnetic quality to him that made her greedy for every detail.

Yana let herself look to her heart's content, let herself feel the sensation of desire drench her, let her senses fill with the sheer sexual appeal of the man. She could live for a hundred years, and she knew she'd never find a man more attractive to her than he was.

Reaching her, he tucked one braid that kept falling out of its clip behind her ear. "Your hairstyle is... enchanting."

Yana laughed, trying to cover up the heat she felt at his casual touch. "Only a dad can come up with such compliments for his five-year-old's handiwork."

His brows rose. "You let Zara do your hair?"

She nodded.

"Ouch. She gives me head massages and I know how painful those can be. Somehow, I managed to talk her down to once a month." He watched her with that intense scrutiny. "I finally told her that her poor little papa will lose all his hair if she continued in that vein."

Instantly, her gaze moved to his thick, wavy hair. The gray at his temples had only added to the appeal of the blasted man. Her fingers itched to sink in and tug and stroke, until he was putty in her hands. "I see no risk of that."

"You look...delicious enough to eat." He took her hand in his. A casual touch but his fingers were rough against her soft ones, and Yana felt the contact deep in her core. "No, not just eat. Devour."

She stumbled, a helpless longing slithering through her, as if he was a sneaky snake charmer determined to wrest out all her secrets. His palm at the small of her bare back was a warm, steady weight.

He hesitated, just for a second, and then took a look at her bare back. Yana smiled. She knew she looked good most days in most outfits. Her beauty had long ago lost any personal meaning to her, if there ever had been any. It had become a tool—even a weapon to wield if Diana had had her way, a means to earn a livelihood, something to oil and feed and care for so that it ran smoothly. For a long time she'd even felt a strange dispassionate apathy toward it because she'd thought it had led her to make bad decisions, starting with this very man.

But hating oneself—one's body, one's mind, one's weaknesses—she'd learned was one of those toxic traits that hollowed one out. She'd always thought her little sister Nush was the most perfect, achingly loveliest, woman and yet Nush, she knew, thought she looked odd and weird, just because she didn't conform to some arbitrary beauty standard.

So Yana had learned to at least respect her body, her looks, her face, even if what she showed the world wasn't exactly what she felt inside. But tonight… Tonight sheer pleasure fluttered and tightened low in her belly when Nasir looked at her. She reveled in the soft grunt of his exhale, in the stunned expression that had come over his face when she'd walked in, in the way his long fingers danced tantalizingly over her bare back.

Already, she felt drunk on pleasure.

"That dress should come with a warning label." There it was again—a husky timbre to his voice that he made no effort to hide.

"It was our unanimous choice for tonight. Huma's and mine."

"No wonder she was so eager to dress you. You look sublime in it."

"All these compliments… You make me wonder what the price is going to be." Instantly, she wished she could take back the words. She wanted to enjoy tonight, didn't want to dilute it with acrimony and accusations about the past. And yet, she was the one who'd gone there.

"There is a price," he said with the smoothness that made her feel like a gauche idiot. Her temper had always gotten the better of her. And she'd never been more aware of the fact than when she was with him, enveloped in his cool control and stoic rationale. "I wish for you to simply enjoy the evening."

Shocked, she darted a look at him. Found him staring back at her. Swallowing, she nodded. Something in her responded to his offer of truce. "I'll try. Believe it or not, the last couple of years haven't left me a lot of time or energy for living in the moment, or any kind of enjoyment, for that matter."

She wanted to smack her forehead with the heel of her hand. Apparently, she couldn't do artificial banter. Either she went too far with her anger or too deep with her confidences.

His fingers tightened over hers. "Come, let me introduce you to this rowdy crowd. Stick to me, and you'll be safe."

When he patted her on the back of her hand, it made her giggle.

His gaze dipped to her mouth, an eager frenzy to it, as if he wanted to taste her smile. "What is so funny?"

"You? Rowdy crowd?" She taunted him, even as she wondered exactly how he would introduce her.

A new swarm of butterflies took flight in her tummy.

Who would he say she was? Zara's extra nanny? His ex-wife's BFF? His problematic, once-upon-a-time step-sister he couldn't wait to be rid of? His employee? Or a woman forever in his debt?

Her nerves jangled as he nudged her toward the grand table in the center of the vast room. As if he had beckoned them, his friends moved up from their various lounging positions across the room.

He didn't let go of her hand or loosen his grip around her waist. If she wasn't so nervous at the prospect of meeting his intimate friends, she'd have called his hold of her possessive.

"This is Yana, a close family friend. She's doing me an enormous favor by helping Zara settle down here after the last year."

A close family friend...

She liked the sound of that less than she should. Actually, she loathed it for how…sensible and correct it sounded. How it hovered in the space between them—a label, a barrier, the drawing of a line that shouldn't be crossed. And every inch of her rebelled at that boundary and she wondered if she'd ever be cured of this madness. Of wanting to be more to a man who'd never really seen her as a woman.

CHAPTER NINE

YANA FELT NASIR'S appraising gaze on her, as if it were a finger on her cheek. Somehow, she managed to keep her smile locked tightly in place.

His guests spoke at once, their greetings effusive enough to move the moment along. She shook their hands and couldn't help gushing when one of them was Nasir's longest standing friend and editor.

"Close family friend is so droll, Nasir. Especially the way you've been eyeing her from the moment she walked in," he said.

Before Yana could tuck his comment into a corner never to be opened again, one of the women spoke up. "This is the stepsister you're quite protective about?"

A chorus of reactions ensued, taking the whole secret stepsister idea and running with it. If it wasn't for the fact that she was tied up in knots about which one of her shenanigans Nasir had shared with the woman, she would've enjoyed the flights of fancy.

As if sensing her distress, Nasir's fingers tightened on the bare skin at her back.

The woman, sensing the current of tension pinging

back and forth between her and Nasir, said in a whisper, "Nasir just wanted to know about what kind of emergency measures one might need to take with type-one diabetes. As the castle is quite cut off from immediate medical centers."

Yana couldn't help but send a glance at Nasir, perplexed yet again by his motives.

"I have made similar inquiries about Ammi's heart condition, Ahmed's ulcers and one of the staff's recurring back pain," Nasir said calmly.

She relaxed immediately.

Another gorgeous man, dressed to the nines, grabbed her by the waist with the charming insouciance she knew well from working in the fashion industry.

"Yana Reddy!" He kissed the back of her hand with a regal flourish that made her laugh. "Now I know why Nasir demanded that I come to this party. Usually, it's my partner James that he can't do without," he mockwhispered. "He knows the rest of this crowd is too boring and fuddy-duddy for a glorious creature like you."

Yana turned to the man who wouldn't bore her if they lived together for a hundred years. "Is that true?"

Nasir raised his palms in surrender, his gaze holding hers in a silent siege. "Before you misunderstand my intentions yet again, I simply wanted you to have fun tonight."

Before she could respond, a short, squat man approached them. Recognition flared even as James introduced his famous musician partner.

"Where have we seen her before?" asked Dimitri. "Other than the fact that she's a hot supermodel?"

James quipped and then clapped. "Ilyavich's paintings. Her nudes were the best he ever did."

Comprehension dawned on Dimitri's face. But instead of the usual mockery or disdain, excitement lit his eyes. "That's it! You know, I've tried so hard to get my hands on one of those paintings. After that first private buyer got hold of them at the initial auction, they never surfaced again."

"I'm glad they didn't," Yana said. "I don't regret doing them, but the whole episode was ruined for me thanks to the dirty accusations I had to face afterward."

"It's almost like the buyer was looking out for you," said James, casting a pointed look at Nasir.

Yana's response misted away when she caught Nasir's reaction. Her skin pebbled into goose bumps. He knew who had those paintings? How? The next thought came like a torrent after the first. Strike that—he didn't just know where the paintings were.

He *had* the paintings.

Then she was being dragged away by a smug-looking James. But she couldn't help casting a look behind her.

Sure enough, the answer to her dilemma danced in Nasir's eyes. And Yana suddenly knew that she was in a lot more danger than she'd ever realized.

It was past midnight, and most of his friends had drifted off to various bedrooms when Nasir stubbed out the one cigar he'd allowed himself for tonight and sought the woman who filled him with adolescent anticipation.

His mother's warning about how necessary Yana was for Zara buzzed like background noise in his head, but made no difference as he walked toward her. Slow jazz was still drifting up from the record player and Yana was sandwiched between James and Dimitri, the three of them swaying to the soft beat.

"My turn," he said, taking her hand in his, and spinning her away from his friends. Despite her surprise, she came like a feather, light on her feet. Her delicious scent sank its tendrils into him, filling his chest.

She stiffened for a second before settling her hands on his shoulders. He wrapped his arms loosely around her waist, the bare skin there an irresistible temptation.

All evening it had been impossible to look away from her. But he also felt a kind of savage satisfaction in seeing the real, tempestuous, funny woman come out of that ice cocoon she'd spent the past few weeks wrapped in. She'd engaged in a rigorous discussion with his editor about books, given James and Dimitri a run for their money when they suddenly decided to start singing old melodies, and had generally been a warm, wonderful, passionate hostess, even if she didn't know she'd played the role so naturally.

Not even a month in, and already Nasir didn't remember what the castle was like without her. Without her and Zara's giggles and running around and playing hide-and-seek and making the staff join in and just generally filling the empty spaces in his life. But he was only an audience, as he'd wished to be for so long, instead of a participant.

Even the space and time between him and Zara was filled with how wonderful Yana Auntie was. It was as if she was a witch who'd cast a spell on all of them—

even his mother. Proving every day what Zara and he had been missing, even before Jacqueline had died.

And now she was in his arms, a perfect, soft landing at the end of a lovely day.

They danced for he didn't know how long, simply letting their bodies move to the slow beat of the music. It was a sweet exhilaration even as tension buzzed and fizzed every time her thigh brushed his or his fingers found another patch of warm, bare flesh. His heart thundered as her hands drifted from his shoulders to his neck, then back again to his chest.

When she pressed her cheek against his heart as Ella Fitzgerald crooned, Nasir felt a sweet, poignant pleasure like he hadn't known in forever. The night was perfection, one he'd needed for so long. But what had made it even sweeter was that this woman in his arms was a mysterious, interesting puzzle that he couldn't stop wanting to unravel.

Sudden laughter from behind them made them both look at Dimitri and James, who were now singing at the tops of their lungs while clutching each other.

A soft sound fell from Yana's mouth and she looked down. To hide her expression from him, he was sure.

"What?" he asked, wanting to know every thought that crossed her mind, every emotion that made her sigh. His fascination was fast turning into an obsession.

"Nothing."

"Remember our truce?"

She seemed to come to some sort of resolution because her mouth narrowed into a straight line. Bracing for either his criticism or his mockery, he realized.

"They are so...gloriously in love, aren't they? It's enough to make one..."

"Nauseous?" he asked, threading humor into his tone when he felt anything except laughing.

She slapped his arm playfully. "Why am I not surprised you find two lovers nauseous?" Her gaze dipped to his mouth, and then away. "I think it's magical. I've seen that kind of love between my grandparents. I think Thaata died so soon after her, because he couldn't bear to live in this world without her. They'd been through so much—my dad's alcoholism, bringing up three granddaughters... But their faith in each other sustained them. I see that in James and Dimitri. They're so lucky to have found each other and—"

"You think it's luck that they found each other?" he asked, genuinely curious.

"A stroke of luck, that initial meet-cute, where their eyes met across a raucous crowd, knowing James..." She laughed. "But I'm sure they work at it every day. I used to think it was magical when people just came together and stayed together. Now I know better."

"I don't think I'm interested in the formula, but I do want to know how you have learned that."

"I've seen my sisters. They're wonderful, accomplished, bright women. Caio and Aristos clearly adore them. But it hasn't been a cakewalk for either of them. There have been tears and drama and grief and pain..."

"You talk about them as if they're more deserving of love than you."

She shrugged and he thought his once petrified heart might crack open at the expression on her face.

He pulled her closer, anger and tenderness twin flames in his chest. "You know that's not how it works, right?"

"I thought you weren't interested in love."

"I'm not. But it doesn't mean I don't understand it." Fury against everyone who'd wronged her, who'd led her to believe such utter nonsense, including himself, colored his words. "There's no metric you use to measure someone's worthiness. You should get that into your pretty head."

"You're lucky I find you sexy when you're all growly and bossy."

The husky half-mutter, half-whisper dropped into the space between them, sounding like what it was. A defense mechanism, a distraction. Not that it didn't get him all hot under the collar, egging him on to act.

"Are they okay now?" he said, curious to know how she fit in between them. How she talked of them betrayed how she saw herself, and he wanted to know more. And the more he learned, the more he realized how one-dimensional he'd made her in his head. For his own purposes.

"The difficulties they faced only proved that their relationships were worth working on, I think. Worth fighting for."

"You want this…grand, glorious love, then?" A faint tremor laced his words even as he told himself her answer wouldn't make a difference to their relationship. It wasn't anything he had to offer her.

"Yes," she said, blinking. "Although it took me a while to figure it out."

"You're not out there looking for this love?"

"As you know, dearest stepbrother," she said, her breezy smile not hiding the ache, "I'm trying to fix me first. No one wants a mess in progress."

"There's nothing to fix, Yana," he said, tucking another stray braid behind her ear. A strange sort of helplessness speared him that she should think herself less than any other woman or man. "Messy and imperfect and tempestuous and volatile and stubborn is all its own kind of perfection. I'm the intellectual fool who didn't see that."

The bodice of her dress shimmered as her chest rose and fell, tension shimmering like a dark cloud around her. "*Enough*, Nasir." Her eyes flashed at him, her cheekbones jutting out. "I've let you seduce me with words and compliments all evening. But the farce ends now."

"James?" Nasir called out, knowing that the storm was about to break. He wanted no witness to their sparring or her temper. He wanted no one else to see her like this—unraveled and glorious.

His oldest friends waved goodbye and stumbled out of the room. The thud of the double doors was a loud gong in the bitter silence.

"I'm going to bed, too."

"No, you're not. Not until we have this out."

A flicker of fear flashed through her eyes before she notched her chin up in that characteristic belligerence that only aroused his baser instincts. "I'm not having anything out with you."

"I assumed a lot of things about you, Yana. Most

of them in error, to my own detriment. But I'd never thought you a coward."

That stopped her, as he knew it would.

"How dare you? I've never in my life backed away from anything."

"Then why are you so intent on running from me?"

"Because I'm tired of dancing to your demands. Because I don't trust you."

And because I still don't trust myself with you.

Yana swallowed that last bit, though.

The whole evening, Nasir dancing with her, talking with her, laughing with her, arguing with her about important topics, asking her opinion—all of it had possessed a dreamy, surreal quality. His friends welcoming her as if she was a part of them, as if they were privy to the secret but well-known knowledge that there was a *them* that was made up of Nasir and her, had gone straight to her head and heart. As if she'd inhaled a hallucinogen that provided her with a real-life version of her deepest hopes and secret fantasies.

She should've never agreed to the evening. Never dressed up for it. Never enjoyed his gaze on her. Never agreed to the truce and flirted with him all evening. Because now she was standing in a quagmire that only pulled her in deeper and deeper.

She'd never been able to resist Nasir—even when he'd misunderstood her, castigated her, loathed her— for some right and some wrong reasons. Now he had an agenda to win her over, which seemed to require her surrender, and she was definitely not ready for that.

Not again, not when this temporary fascination ended and she'd once again stand alone with her shattered heart in her hands.

"What's there to not trust?" he asked in a low, grumbly voice, and she knew that it was his truly annoyed voice. The angrier he got, the lower his tone, as if he was turning himself into a statue, determined to keep it all inside.

"Why can't you leave this alone? Leave me alone?" she said, and one of the braids done by Zara lashed against her cheek yet again. Having had enough of the charade, she gathered her hair and tied it into a messy knot on top of her head.

"I wish for things to change between us."

If he'd lobbed a grenade into her face, she'd have been less shocked. Breath didn't come to her lungs, much less words to her lips. Her entire body felt like it was seizing up on her, seizing on sensations and images she shouldn't be feeling or thinking.

She stepped back, away from him.

It didn't matter because he took a step forward, too, and Yana thought he truly looked like a beast then as he stalked her across the vast room, with the glittering sconces casting dark shadows on his saturnine features, iron-hard resolve etching itself around that luscious mouth.

"There's been too many years of misunderstandings and dislike that we've both nurtured with a lot of care. It doesn't wash off easily and I don't even want it to," she protested.

"No, you'd like to paint me as your villain for the rest of our lives."

"I don't have a different role for you. The die was cast long ago." Her words came out as shaky as she felt. "It's enough to be polite acquaintances, considering we have a child we adore in common."

He raised his palms. All evening he'd been reeling her in with his compliments and kind words but it was a false surrender on his part. Or a fake one. "What exactly is your complaint, Yana?"

"Why do you have those nude paintings of me?"

"I told you I felt responsible that I didn't warn you about Ilyavich. But when I saw them—when I saw how gloriously he'd captured all the different facets of you, that urge to protect you from all the other, greedy eyes only became stronger. Even without knowing then that this persona you carefully cultivate is all a mask, I felt an overwhelming compulsion to protect your true self."

If he'd had the words scripted to cause maximum damage to her heart, he couldn't have done it better. His reasons were why she'd felt such relief that the paintings had never surfaced again. Still, she tried to fight the spell he was weaving over her. "Why go to such lengths just so that I had a good time tonight? Why are you being so nice to me?"

If she thought he'd laugh at her irrational questions, she had him wrong once again. His frown graduated to a scowl. "That's what's sending you into a tailspin? The fact that I'm finally treating you as you've always deserved to be treated?"

"That's not an answer, Nasir."

"Fine. I want you to feel comfortable in my home. With my friends. With me. I want you to think of my home as one of your main bases in Europe."

Her heart thrashed itself in its cage. "Why?"

"Because I want you to be happy." An exasperated breath rattled out of him.

Yana knew he could be infuriatingly stubborn—a dog with a bone, really, when he got stuck on something—it was one of the qualities they shared, but she'd never expected to be at the receiving end of that resolve.

It scared her that she'd caught his passing fancy, or his sense of fairness. And where it would leave her when he'd had enough. "When you visit us, at least," he added as an afterthought.

She was shaking her head, excitement and something headier washing away the dread and fear and insecurities and the little rationality she possessed. "Don't do this. Don't trap me. Don't—"

And then he was reaching for her, and his hands clutched her arms and there was such sheer urgency, such reckless, naked desire in his eyes, that she was the one rendered a statue now. "You're the most confounding woman I've ever met. How is it trapping you if I want to do the right thing by you?"

"Because it's all pity and for God's sake, Nasir, I don't want your pity," she said, sidestepping the minefield she'd created herself.

How did she explain to him that her stupid heart had never been able to distinguish pity from liking when it came to him? That she'd take the little interest he showed her, turn it into hope and hang herself with it?

"It's not pity if I want the best for you or if I want to share your burden or if I want to tell you that I'll be here for you when you come out of rehab for your gambling addiction. I want to be the friend I should've been to you years ago."

Yana saw the trap then and it was of her own making.

Lies and half-truths and misunderstandings…she'd built them so tall and high that he didn't even see the real her. He saw the illusion she'd created, felt sorry for the mess she'd showed him, because he'd decided with that arrogant self-righteousness that he'd had a hand in it, too.

The illusion not only didn't serve her anymore but also threatened to make her worst nightmare come true. "I lied to you, Nasir. Those were not my debts. I'm not addicted to gambling and I never was."

He blinked and she braced herself for his disbelief and doubts. But he recovered fast with, "Then whose debts were they?"

"Isn't my word enough?"

"Of course it's enough. But now that we're dispensing with the smoke and mirrors, I want the whole truth. How were you in such a financial hole, then?"

"It was Diana." The words were wrenched out of her from some deep cavern, and yet immediately freed her of their dark weight. Until this moment when she'd made it real, she hadn't realized how much the secret had gouged her soul. How the pain it brought had stayed inside her, pulsing and throbbing, hollowing her out.

He sighed. "Diana took advantage of you, again."

"Yes. She…cleared out my bank accounts last year.

I took measures then. But she still managed to get hold of my credit cards, and she…maxed them out. All our assets are jointly owned since I started modeling before I was legally an adult. I'd thought I could trust her, but she forged my signature and sold the apartment in New York and the house in California. Even the few rare pieces of jewelry I owned…she completely cleaned me out."

"While you were busy looking after Jacqueline," Nasir said, finally connecting the dots. Seeing a picture emerge in which he'd been so eager to find fault with her when there was none.

"I don't regret it one bit," Yana said, memories softening her mouth. "I know she wasn't perfect, but Jacqueline showed me more love and acceptance and concern than Diana ever did."

"Your loyalty is laudable, *habibi*. Is that why you covered up her affairs?" He wasn't angry but his bitterness was clear. "You had a just reason to hate me anyway."

"That's unfair. I didn't let our past color my actions, Nasir. Even when you treated me as if…" She tugged at the neckline of her dress in a nervous gesture he was beginning to recognize. "Jacqueline was desperate to save your relationship."

"And yet, she kept cheating on me."

"You've no idea what it is to be in love, do you? And to be found wanting?" she said, vibrating with emotion.

"Love was never supposed to be a part of our relationship. She knew that."

"Don't tell me the great observer of humanity's foibles and flaws thinks relationships can work based on a chart and a few conditions?" Even now, sympathy and affection filled her words. "Jacqueline made mistakes. It doesn't mean she ever stopped loving you. She begged me to help her, to…"

"You must have known it was a sinking ship, Yana. She abandoned Zara to you to care for."

"By that time, she was drinking a lot, her modeling dropped off and her business took a dive and…then came her diagnosis. She became bitter, different from the warm woman I'd come to adore."

"You still looked after her."

"Is it friendship if we only show up for the good times?"

Hesitation flickered in her eyes before she took a deep breath. Steely resolve hiding a fragile heart—he was beginning to understand her now. And himself clearly, too, in her words. He had had all these rules and plans and conditions for his marriage and not a single one had served them well. Not with Jacqueline and definitely not with his own daughter. There was no way to shut himself out of the world without making his daughter think he didn't love her, either. Without the risk of losing her.

And here was this woman he'd thought he'd pushed to the margins, gloriously in the center of it all, lashing him with truth after truth. Instead of gentling his pain, all the rules he'd lived his life by had only alienated him from Zara and his father.

"And since we're on the topic," she said, straightening her shoulders, "I had no idea she was considering

filing for solo custody of Zara. You spent little enough
time with Zara back then. But she talked so much about
you whenever she returned from the trips you took her
on, and she sounded so happy that I knew whatever your
complaints about Jacqueline, you were trying your best
to be a good father."

Her words were a vindication to Nasir's ears.

Or maybe even a benediction and approval that he
hadn't even known he needed. From the moment he
had learned that Jacqueline had been planning to take
solo custody of his daughter, using his alleged indif-
ference to his own child, he had wondered if there was
any truth to it.

He'd never planned to be a father, something Jacqueline had been fully on board with when they'd met.
And he'd done his best to keep their marriage together
even as they'd grown apart by the time she'd conceived.

So many sleepless nights, and he'd even wondered if
he'd done such a good job of turning himself into stone
that he felt less than he should for his own child. He'd
wondered if Zara would be better off with her mother.

"I think Jacqueline never told me what she was planning because she must have known that I'd never agree
to it," Yana added.

Nasir forced himself to meet her eyes. "I should have
known that, too. My entire world felt upside down when
I realized how I'd made my own child doubt my love for
her. I was so angry and scared that I'd lose Zara that I
lashed out at you. Not that it's an excuse."

He ran a hand through his hair, marveling at how

wise she was even as she thought herself messy. But that was the magic of Yana, he was realizing.

She lived her life fully, loved so thoroughly that it was like watching a thunderstorm. Both spectacular and dangerous at the same time. And Nasir remembered when he'd lived life like that once, when he'd loved freely, lived dangerously close to the edge. And suddenly, he wanted to be there again.

There were two things he had to do. The first came easily enough.

"I'm sorry, Yana. On so many levels. For all the sins I heaped at your feet, when they were all mine. For being a beast to you."

But the second—to let her go when he knew what she wanted out of life was something he could never offer her—felt impossible to even contemplate. For the first time since Fatima died, he felt an overwhelming need to lose himself to his selfish desires. To drown himself in pleasure. To live dangerously just once more, even if that meant Yana would burn him through.

CHAPTER TEN

YANA DIPPED HER HEAD, unwilling to let him see her confusion and the little flicker of fear. Nor did she feel any vindication or relief from his apology. It was disconcerting to discover that his compliments had more than their fair share of an effect on her, though. Disconcerting to discover that all of her defenses were falling away, like the castle Zara had made out of rainbow-colored sand.

No, he was attacking her defenses, laying siege and shredding the lies and half-truths she'd surrounded herself with. To what end, though? Did he simply want to clear the air between them now that she was going to be a permanent part of Zara's life? Or was there more?

"What other secrets and half-truths are you using as ammunition against me, then?"

"Demands and more demands," she said, deploying her silken protest even as she was quivering inside. "And here I thought you were not the usual predictably powerful man who wants what he wants when he wants it."

"You've no idea what I want, Yana."

His angry tone was like a shot of adrenaline. When

he treated her as his equal, when he took her on as she was, there was no bigger high. She tilted her chin, letting him see her fighting spirit. "You have not earned the right to my secrets, Nasir. Nor to my dreams or fantasies."

"And yet, if I cover this last foot between us and touch you, I'd bet I'd find you far too willing and ready to voice at least one fantasy, *habibi*."

She watched him, every word acting like a leaping pulse within her body. Every step of his creating an ache between her thighs. "And why would you want to do that?"

"Because I have this insane urge to corner you and catch you and strip you bare until I know all of you. You're a maddening puzzle I want to unlock."

"This is about your ego, then? Because I managed to trick you—"

"You and I both know this isn't to do with my ego or pity or friendship or Zara or the past. It's about you and me." Another step and she could see the scar that bisected his upper lip and raked its finger upward toward his cheek. And she saw the naked desire in his eyes and the steely resolve of his mouth, and every cell within her reverberated.

"So will you dare let me test my theory?"

He was close now, so close that she could breathe in the heady scent of his aftershave—another weapon in an arsenal full of them. Her breath was a shallow whistle in her ears.

She should've burned, or melted, or ignited with him this close to her after all these years, and yet, the moment seemed to spring out of her deepest, wildest dreams, and suddenly, she didn't know how to be, how to act, in this reality. Did she run or did she stay and see this through? Did she dare steal this moment and live it with all she had, or did she bind herself and back away from a lifetime's temptation?

Something hard dug into the small of her back, and she pressed herself into it even more, hoping the sharp pain would be an anchor tying her to the ground when all she felt like was flying away. And then he was within touching distance, and she stared helplessly like the naive, inexperienced virgin that she was.

All the roles she'd played in her life at being a brazen seductress who lured men to make bad decisions and led them to their doom hadn't taught her any tricks or tools to get through this. She hadn't let any man get this close to her at all, because she hadn't wanted any man like she wanted Nasir.

If he'd grabbed her and kissed her to prove his point—as so many men had done before, thinking her volatile temper and confident words meant that she would welcome their crude attempts at seduction, if he'd touched her and smiled that infuriating, winning smirk of his as if this was nothing but a game they'd been playing for years, if he'd taunted her with one more word—Yana would have been able to resist him. Could have told herself that after all these years, after all the pining and longing that had become an intrinsic part of her, she was better than he was; she was better than this moment.

His palms on the dark wood on either side of her

head, he leaned closer and pinned her like a splayed butterfly with his gaze. And said the one thing that was her Achilles' heel, that shattered all of her defenses.

"I see you, Yana, the real you." His breath feathered the side of her cheek in a warm caress, his amber eyes gleaming with a feral glitter. "Finally, I see all of you. And the things I want to do to you…" A self-deprecating sigh fell from his lips. "We've come full circle, no?"

So long, for so many years, with so many people in her life, she'd longed to be seen, to be accepted, even as she'd hidden the greedy, needy parts of her away. All her struggles, all her pain, all her victories, all her defeats—had they led her to this moment with this man? Was life worth living, worth beginning at all, if she backed off now?

She braced herself as if one could brace oneself for drowning in a tsunami. Leaning closer, she pressed her mouth to the corner of his. "Test your theory, then." Then she took that lush lower lip of his between her teeth and bit down and said, "This, however, isn't surrender."

Tingles of shock and tendrils of sensation swooped when he returned her favor with a matching nip of his white teeth over her own lower lip. "Ah, *habibi*, I've finally learned my lesson. I'll never underestimate you again."

He smiled then and it was a roguish, hungry smile and it built into something more possessive and molten as his hands started moving over her willing flesh and she swallowed all of that, too, along with the heat and hunger of his lips, because he was kissing her and kiss-

ing her and kissing her. As if he, too, had been waiting
for this moment for a lifetime.

She was spinning stories yet again but even her lies
tasted sweeter when he kissed her like that. He tasted of
cigars and chocolate and like the darkest decadence she
could ever imagine. They went at each other like horny
teenagers—nipping and licking and sucking and fighting for dominance, and it was exactly like she thought
it would be. But also somehow better.

There was magic in the very air between them and
she let it seep into every pore. His jacket was discarded,
necklines were tugged aside for better access, for more.
His mouth seemed to stamp his possession all over—
her lips, her temple, her pulse, her neck, the spot below
her ear, and still, he wasn't done kissing her.

She groaned as he sucked at her pulse, arrows of sensation skittering straight down to her pelvis.

"Who knew such a prickly thing could taste so
sweet?" he groaned.

She grabbed the lapels of his collar and pulled in
opposite directions until buttons were flying and she
could palm the taut planes of his chest and then slide
down to explore the ridges of his muscled abdomen.
He was warm and hard, with a silky coating of hair
that she loved running her fingers through already. She
kept petting and stroking every inch of flesh she discovered as he buried his mouth at the crook of her neck
and shoulder.

Within seconds he already seemed to know where to
hit her the hardest. When he dragged his teeth against

the pulse fluttering already at her neck, she groaned and wrapped her leg around his hip.

They stopped then, tuned in to each other on a level that terrified her. He was so deliciously hard against her, and she instinctively rocked herself into him, the need for completion a much more primal drive than fear or sensibility.

Somehow, he'd shuffled them across the marble floor, the cold tiles on her now bare feet a welcome relief against the heat pouring through her. She wasn't laughing anymore as her back hit the plush padding of the chaise longue that was tucked against the far wall.

Nasir was on his knees on either side of her hips, gazing down at her.

It was a new angle to find herself in, a new angle from which to look at him. Except for the sizzling sparks from the fireplace and the fast, erratic whistling of their own breaths, everything was dark and still and silent.

Reaching her hand up, she clasped his cheek, rubbing the pad of her thumb over that scar. Allowing herself one, *only one*, moment of tenderness. She wasn't sure if she would get another chance like this. And she wasn't sure if she would survive another one anyway.

His nostrils flared when she dragged her thumb to the center of his lower lip and pressed. His teeth dug into the pad before he closed his lips over it and sucked, and she felt the strong pull of his lips somewhere else.

She arched her body, chasing the pleasure, and he granted it. Heavy and warm, the heel of his palm rested against the sweet center of her entire being. She writhed under that warm weight, begging him with her hips to make it more. His fingers snuck under the fabric of her dress, caressing the silky skin of her thighs, and then they were pushing away her thong and tracing the outer lips of her sex.

Sensations and need forked through her, winding her tighter and tighter. Finally, finally, his clever fingers found her most sensitive place, and slowly, softly, rubbed the bundle of nerves up and down.

Her language became gasps and groans and filthy expletives as she chased the tantalizing caress of his all-knowing fingers. "What else do you need, sweetheart? Ask me. Tell me."

His gaze pinned her in place, a dark need glittering there, when her body itself seemed to be spinning away from her. She rubbed a hand over her breasts, the tight corset covering them adding to her torment and pleasure in turns. "Touch me here, please."

Bending low, he plucked at the beaded corset and when it didn't budge, he cut it open with that damned knife he kept on himself all the time. Her entire torso arched up like a bridge rising out of stormy waters as he rubbed one taut nipple between his fingers. "Every inch of you is perfection," he said, almost to himself.

Then his mouth was at her breast and he was doing some swirly thing with his tongue. His teeth were there, too, and his thumb kept drawing those mindless circles around her nub, and suddenly, she was right there at the edge of the world.

And when she fell, splintering into so many different parts, he held her and kissed her and soothed her and he put her back together again. Yana thought she might already be addicted to those strong, knowing hands, those wicked, wanton fingers and those sweet, taunting lips. And she wondered if she might ever do this with another man, even though she already knew the answer.

But right then, tremors of aftershock still quaking through her in soft ripples, with his scent lodged deep in every pore, with his arms enveloping her in a perfect cradle as if she was precious and fragile, she didn't care. She couldn't care about the future or that she didn't have one with him.

"Come, *habibi.* Let me walk you to your bedroom."

Those long lashes fluttered as she looked around herself like a baby fawn. As if she didn't know where she was. And still, in that state of near comatose bliss, her body leaned into him, gifting him with a trust Nasir didn't deserve but was selfish enough to revel in anyway. Just watching her climax with that reckless abandon was more sensuous than any carnal act.

After several long beats, she rubbed the back of her hand over her mouth and looked up at him. For a split second, he saw a strange kind of longing for him that he'd once seen in another woman. A woman he'd failed to protect despite her absolute trust in him.

Drowning in the madness that Yana effortlessly weaved over him, it was quite possible he was imagining things he had no right to imagine, much less should, if he had any sense. He'd never meant for his dare to get this far, either.

His body was strumming with unsatisfied desire,

Yana was looking at him as if he was the answer to every dark desire she'd ever had, and he simply gave in to the sheer sensuous luxury of the moment.

"You're good," she said with a smile that stretched her lips.

He was struck by a tenderness he hadn't felt in so long, that he'd thought parts of himself had petrified out in that war zone years ago.

"I'm glad you think so," he said, tugging the sides of her sliced open dress together, but she slapped his hands away.

"The last thing I want to do right now," she said with a sudden sharp clarity to her words, "is walk through the castle like this, let everyone see you've dismissed me yet again and advertise my walk of shame."

Irritation he should have mastered colored his tone as he brusquely said, "We're two consenting adults. There is no shame here, Yana."

Her feathery brows came together in a bow. "I thought the same thing a long time ago."

"Yana—"

"If there's no shame in this, then why are you so intent on walking me back to my room?"

She was such a mix of calculation and vulnerability, a complex puzzle he'd never stop delighting in. But, he had to remind himself, she wasn't his to delight in. Come tomorrow morning, in the clarity of daylight, she might even regret this moment of madness and freeze him out.

Wasn't that the best idea, though, seeing as they could have nothing more than this one night? There was no future for them; he should make that clear to her, as he had no intention of committing to a third woman and having it go wrong again as it inevitably would. And yet, he had no taste for fracturing the satiated smile on her lips just yet. Or was he thinking with his ego again, imagining she wanted some kind of future with him? What if all Yana wanted was to get this madness out of their systems? Would one night be enough for her? With all their misunderstandings—mostly on his part—cleared up now, and with her place in Zara's life permanent, couldn't they just be two consenting adults with sizzling chemistry? Or was that him thinking with his painfully hard erection again?

"You have to know—"

She leaned up and claimed his mouth with a possessive hunger that decimated the little honor he had left that he was trying to keep. On and on, the kiss went, with her nipping at him, licking him, then running away and having him give chase.

"Why do we have to leave when we aren't finished yet?" Leaning back against the chaise, she giggled. Contrary to that light laughter, her gaze swept over him leisurely, full of desire and need and unabashed lust. She scraped a long nail over his Adam's apple, and down his chest, running down each scar on his chest as if it were a map to some long-lost treasure.

"Unless it's because you're an old man and can only 'do it—'" she used quotes as if anybody could misunderstand her right then "—missionary style on the bed?"

He arrested her fingers when they fluttered near the zip of his trousers. "You're mad," he said, bringing her hand to his mouth and placing a kiss at the center of her palm.

She shrugged it off. That thread of irritation flickered again as it dawned on him why she did that. She didn't want tenderness from him. Only sexual touch was welcomed—an arrangement that should've suited him just fine given where his thoughts had been moments ago. And yet, that thorn was under his skin again. Although he was getting used to that, too, that painful, stringent awareness, like new skin on an old wound. Like he'd never be sure of his own desires and thoughts when it came to her.

"I feel drunk. That's the first time I—"

He stilled.

She peered at him from under her lashes, something calculating flashing across that stunning gaze.

He cupped her cheek, a sudden urgency driving him. "What?"

She leaned into his touch as if his fingers weren't circling her neck with a possessiveness he could not control. "The first time I felt that kind of pleasure with a partner. Usually, I need my—" that cute little frown appeared between her brows again "—tools."

Awkwardness dawned at that strange word, and she shrugged. Something wasn't adding up. Under his continued scrutiny, color stole into her cheeks, dusting them a pretty pink.

"I meant my battery-operated devices." She rolled her eyes, as if he was being thick on purpose.

And then in a move that was clearly supposed to distract him, which it did successfully, she dragged a finger over the outside of his trousers, tracing the shape of his shaft. His erection leaped under her touch. When he went to arrest her fingers, she kissed his chin.

Eyes wide and soulful and full of longing studied him. "Now who's intent on shutting this down? Or are we still only dancing to your demands?" She pouted, to hide the very real emotion in her words. "Have you solved the puzzle that you labeled me? Is your fascination with me over now because I've thrown myself at you the moment you beckoned?"

"Shut up, *habibi*."

He closed his eyes and that was a bigger mistake because with him deprived of that sense, now all of his being was focused on her palming his erection. He grunted his assent, giving himself over to her curious fingers.

She wasn't urgent or greedy or fast now, but devastatingly thorough. The smack of her lips had him watching her again.

Pushing her hair away from her face in a gesture that was sensuality and innocence combined, she gave her full attention to the task of undoing him. The tip of her pink tongue stuck out between her teeth as she unzipped his trousers and then her fingers were sneaking under his boxers to fist his shaft with a soft, hungry growl that pinged along his length.

Breath hissed out of him in a guttural whisper, his hips automatically pumping into her hand like a schoolboy being touched for the first time. Her own mouth fell open on a soft gasp, calling his attention back to her.

Eyes drunk with passion, tongue licking her lips,

she watched him with an artless abandon that was as arousing as her slow, tentative strokes.

"You haven't done this much, have you?" he said, trying his damnedest to put brakes on a situation that had long been out of his control. From the moment he had seen her again at the nightclub, in fact. Wasn't that why he'd fought begging her for help?

Something almost like anger flashed in those gorgeous brown eyes. "Stop trying to pin me down, looking for reasons to stop," she whispered in a voice that was so husky that he felt a surge of all his possessive instincts.

Hair a mess around her face, the silky corset falling apart again to reveal small, high breasts with plump tips, and acres of smooth, golden-brown flesh...she looked like his darkest fantasy come true. He wanted no other man to hear her like this, or see her like this—messy and unraveled, and so tempting that his mouth was dry. He wanted no other man to know her like this.

A filthy curse exploded out of him when she rubbed her thumb over his sensitive tip, gathered up a droplet of liquid and brought it to her mouth. She rubbed it over her lower lip, all the while holding his gaze in a challenge that undid him.

The last of his honor evaporated. Or maybe he'd had enough of his own lies and half-truths. She was right. He'd started this, and as always, she'd risen to the challenge of his dare, proving that she was magnificent in a way he'd never previously understood.

Because now he could see the invisible scars life had left on her and how she still walked through it full of

heart. A heart that was unwillingly beginning to fasci-
nate him as much as her body did.

Holding his gaze, she licked that lower lip, even as
she cupped her own breast with her free hand. In between her fingers, the dark pink nipple peaked, beckoning for his mouth.

Hands on her hips, he lifted her and reversed their
positions until he was sitting back against the chaise
and she was straddling him, his erection pressed up
against her slick, hot sex.

Instantly, her spine moved in a sensuous ripple,
mocking all the constraints he'd use to bind her. Head
thrown back, the cut-open remnants of her dress baring her to her navel, she was the wildest thing Nasir
had ever seen.

Wrapping the fingers of one hand around the back
of her neck, he stroked his tongue into her mouth, even
as he filled his other hand with her small yet perfectly
lush breasts. She moved again until the width of his
shaft notched against her core. Sensation skewered his
spine and his body threatened to give out. He laved at
her swollen lower lip, ran his palms all over her smooth
back, the tight dip of her waist, reveling in the soft,
raspy growls that seemed to escape her mouth every
time he let her move a little. He touched her everywhere
and it only inflamed his desire further. The more he had
of her, the more he wanted.

"I have no condoms. But I swear to you I'm clean,"
he whispered against her throat.

"I'm on the pill," she said, whimpering as he bit

down on the madly fluttering pulse. "Please, Nasir. No more teasing. I need you inside me. Now."

The sheer naked need in those words was the last thing to shatter his control. Taking his shaft in his hand, holding her still with one hand on her hip, he thrust into her inviting warmth in one long stroke.

His grunt sounded euphoric to his own ears. The tight clasp of her sex made lights explode behind his eyes in a kaleidoscope of sensations.

Sweat beading over his forehead, heart pounding loudly in his ears, he reveled in the tight sheath of her body. Without even moving, he was already close. He held back, determined to wring another climax out of her. He'd leave her so boneless with pleasure that she never thought of doing this with another man.

He was so far gone, so deep inside his own head, his senses so deeply entrenched in pleasure, that it took him several grasping breaths to realize that Yana had gone awfully still.

He opened his eyes to find her looking a little shocked, one lone tear streaking down her angular cheek. He closed his eyes and cursed himself for eternity. Even then, comprehension escaped him. In his hurry to relieve her pain, he took hold of her hips and jostled her slightly, and then heard her soft gasp.

Finally, the truth dawned on him, and with it came indescribable anger.

Of course, even in this, she would make a villain out of him. He'd hurt her, unknowingly, and he needn't have. "You and your childish games," he bit out, a gravelly bitterness coating his words. "How clever you must think you are, *habibi*. Is this some kind of revenge, then? Are you winning yet, Yana?"

When she reared back to look into his face, there was pain and want and a host of things he couldn't read. She nuzzled her face into his neck, dampness seeping from her skin to his. And then she licked at the hollow of his throat and clutched him harder with her arms and below with her sex and that, too, was a pleasurable torment.

All of her was a weapon and she wielded it with such innocence.

But buried deep inside her as he was, even his anger was only an irritating hum and a tight knot in his chest that he could easily ignore beneath the unparalleled sensation streaking through him as she adjusted herself. She moved as if she meant him to burrow deep inside her and never come out.

When he clutched her hips again, this time to gently pull her off him, she seemed to come back to herself. A half-growl, half-groan fell from her lips, and she was truly the wildest thing he had ever seen then.

"No, you're not going to leave me like this. Not again. Not anymore." One hand sinking into his hair, she tugged imperiously, as if she meant to own him. "Finish this." Without waiting for his response, she took his hands and brought them to her breasts.

Questions tore through his brain, even as fresh pleasure zigzagged through him. She was warm and soft, and with her hands on his shoulders, she undulated her spine in such an instinctive ripple that he was suddenly nearly all the way out of her slick clasp. Again and again, she wriggled her hips in a sinuous dance; figuring out her own rhythm and letting her use his body to seek out her pleasure was both a delight and a torment to him, and the slip-slide of their bodies created a symphony wholly their own.

She was trembling now, and Nasir stroked her, petted her, whispering nonsensical words into her skin, even as she gained momentum and confidence. Her rhythm was crude, a little erratic rather than smooth, and yet it was still the most erotic thing he'd ever known.

"At what point is this going to be less painful and more about pleasure?" she asked with a smile, and that husky voice pinged on his nerve endings. He laughed then, and he kissed her as if she was the most fragile, precious thing that had ever come to his hand. It wasn't that hard because she was the most fragile, the most achingly lovely, thing he had ever held.

Slowly, softly, he thrummed his fingers all over her body, noting when she leaned in to the touch, and when another soft gasp escaped her mouth, feeling when she ground down. A more natural rhythm built as he started thrusting up when she brought herself down. The slap of her thighs against his, the tight tug of her fingers in his hair, the erotic slide of her breasts against his chest made his spine burn with his approaching climax.

Holding her back from him, he lifted her breast to his mouth and sucked until he could tell her own need for climax chased her. Fingers, lips, words, caresses, tongue, teeth… He used everything in his arsenal with a ruthlessness he'd long ago given up to drive her to the edge again, even as he held back his own climax by the skin of his teeth.

And then she was shattering yet again, calling out his name, as if he was the benediction, and not her, and her sex was milking him.

Nasir pushed her down onto the chaise still shuddering, and instantly, she wrapped her legs around his hips, creating the perfect cradle for him to sink into. They could have done this a hundred times before and it couldn't have been as perfect. So right. So good.

He began with slow, deep thrusts, willing himself to enjoy this moment, even as selfish desire urged him to go faster, harder, to show her how needy he could get, to somehow mark her as she was doing him with such little effort. Hair billowing around her head, pupils blown up, her lush mouth trembling with explosive breaths, and his name on her lips…she took him straight over the cliff with her.

He came inside her, and it was the most explosive release he'd ever had. All he wanted was to do this over and over again. He wanted to make her fall apart again and again. He wanted to lose himself in her. He wanted to *keep* her. And the arrogant thought released a host of other thoughts.

What a grave blunder he had committed just because his ego refused to be perceived as the man who'd done her wrong. What else could this be except a predatory urge to conquer her anger and her distrust and her wildness and *her*, in essence? Where else would this lead but to her pain and more scars at his hand when their relationship inevitably ended? What could he do to avoid that? What choices were left to him?

He'd closed himself off to feeling the very thing she

wanted out of life, because he had nothing to offer her. Especially now he knew that beneath the numerous masks she wore, she was as vulnerable as a baby bird.

Contrary to the confusion wrecking his mind, though, he gathered her soft, trembling body to him, buried his nose in her neck and whispered sweet nothings into her skin long after she fell asleep like the fragile, trusting, wonderful woman she'd always been.

CHAPTER ELEVEN

IN THE END, Nasir ended up carrying her to her bedroom, and Yana was sure a battalion of people had noticed her disheveled and thoroughly seduced state. Hiding her face in his neck, she thought she might have even heard Amina's loud, disgruntled huff at seeing her son parade about the castle with his virgin lover in his arms, like a dark sacrifice he was bringing back to his lair.

And that made her giggle uncontrollably. So much so that it skated the edge of hysteria. Nasir tapped her lightly on the cheek as he placed her on his bed.

"Care to share what's so funny?" he asked, locking her between his forearms, his torso leaning over her like a tantalizing shadow.

Yana writhed on the bed, loving the cool comfort of the sheets against her bare, overheated skin. The slick wetness between her legs coating her inner thighs and lower made itself known.

"I was trying to imagine how we must have looked to your mother."

His mouth twitched. "That's the last thing I need in

my head right now." When she continued to smile, he ran his thumb over her lower lip. "Tell me."

"Like you were a beast bringing your virgin sacrifice to your lair."

He bopped the tip of her nose even though his jaw tightened. Still sore about that secret of hers, then.

"You have quite the imagination, *habibi*."

"You don't know the half of it," she said, desperate to tease him out of the dark mood.

He straightened and watched her. A sliver of moonlight illuminated his own features for her. *Just for her.* All sharp slashes and hard contours and even with that scar ruining his lovely mouth…he'd always struck her as the epitome of sex appeal.

But she tended to forget that he'd achieved it by living a whole other life before she'd even grown to adulthood. He was always going to be out of her reach, if she thought like that. If she sought to put him on that pedestal.

But he wasn't, by his own claim. He wasn't a statue, either, however much he claimed that. And with the open sides of his shirt flapping about, his hair ruffled and made unkempt by her fingers, his chest bearing the slight scratches from her nails, he was *so utterly hers* then that her breath stuck in her throat. Possibilities fluttered through her heart, bolstered by the soreness of her muscles and the tender ache between her legs.

"No, I don't know the half of it. Or you."

And with that pointed remark, he was walking away. When every inch of her wanted to run after him like a half-naked, lovesick wraith, ready to prostrate herself to keep her with him for the rest of the night, Yana rolled away to face the other side of the bed instead, a strange kind of lethargy stealing over her.

His anger was a familiar companion she'd lived with before. Could live with again. But she did an emotional check on herself like Mira had taught her and Nush to do.

All through that long walk across his vast castle— no, even before that, when he'd roared his climax in her ears and she'd hidden away that sound in some deep part of her psyche, to be taken out in private and examined again and again—she'd been trying to muster up some kind of regret.

Or anger, or shame or guilt or any number of darker emotions that she was used to drinking up like a toxic cocktail when she made bad decisions. Because he was her darkest weakness and deepest want, and when he'd beckoned a finger, she'd gone running, hadn't she? She was a pushover if ever she knew one.

But the bitterness of regrets, the acidic taste of failure, refused to come this time. Not with the sweet, pulsing ache between her thighs or the swollen sensitivity of her lips or the soreness of her muscles to distract her... Instead, she felt alive and thoroughly debauched and gloriously loved. Maybe she should listen to her body more often and refuse to poison it with negativity, she thought.

Burying her face in the pillow, she gave in to the languid smile that fought its way through. If she put the *shoulds and shouldn'ts* aside, it felt like fate or the universe or some inevitable course she'd set herself on through the years that it should be Nasir who ultimately destroyed her fear and distrust in herself. As if all the previous wrongs had led to this one right.

But that way also lay the trap of romanticizing not just the sex they'd had but also the entire episode, the entire evening. Attaching meaning and expectations to it when there were none. The whole evening had built to this moment—no, years of attraction and dislike and even shared grief had all led to tonight. A once-in-a-lifetime thing, a self-indulgent, luxurious experience, a reward for all the bad things about her old life she was shedding, enabling her to move on into her new life. Having sex with Nasir was not a mistake, but it wasn't a new road to explore, either. There, that explanation suited her. She hoped her silly heart got on the same train.

"Turn around, Yana."

She rolled onto her back to find Nasir kneeling on the bed. Had she been so deep inside her head that she hadn't even noticed that he hadn't actually left, he'd just gone into the bathroom?

Hands on her knees, he gently opened her. A cool, wet washcloth on her sex made her hiss out a deep sigh. It felt damned good and that, perversely, made her resentful. "Have you done this a lot, then?"

"What?"

"Ministered to virgins after debauching them?"

His laugh was a booming sound—gravelly, with no hint of actual humor. "Yes. The sacrifice will come next."

Her mouth twitched. She let out a long, shuddering

exhale, so that he knew that she was merely tolerating him. The wet splash of the cloth as he chucked it back into the bathroom made her eyes pop open.

"Nasir, I can look after myself."

"Of course you can, *habibi*. I'm under no illusion about what you are capable of anymore. But indulge me, just this once."

With that terse dictate, he began to pull at the sad remains of the dress from around her tired limbs. With an efficiency that reminded her that he'd once been a journalist covering the most dangerous places in the world, he briskly gathered her hair, pulled her up and dressed her in a T-shirt of his.

"Underwear?"

"Nope," Yana answered without missing a beat.

"Better and better," he whispered at her temple and then retreated again.

Only then did she realize she hadn't felt an ounce of hesitation at giving him a straight answer. As if they were an old married couple, used to the small intimacies that made up the best parts of a relationship. She had this strange sense that this should've been awkward and sticky and messy, and yet, it had that ring of inevitability about it again.

"I think you should leave now," she said, trying to cut the strings of the parachute of her dreams before it flew away into some magical fairyland where the messy, volatile princess conquered her beast with the all-consuming power of her love.

"I think differently." He returned, dressed in loose

pajama bottoms and nothing else. All of his tautly mus-cled chest and back with its myriad scars beckoned her.

Pure, irresistible temptation.

"Scoot over."

"I don't think we need a postmortem, Nasir. It hap-pened. It was fantastic. Now we move on."

When she didn't give in to his ruthless demand, he gave her a playful shove to the middle of the bed, and by the time she'd recovered from her quick roll, he was sitting up next to her, with his fingers pushing her hair away from her face.

Under the guise of straightening herself under the rumpled sheet, Yana gave herself a moment to fight the inexorable urge to stay like that, with his fingers raking through her hair with a tenderness she'd craved for so long. She also wanted to push off the duvet, shrug off the T-shirt he'd put on her and arch up into his touch. To dig her fingers into his hair and bring that sinful mouth down to her breasts again. At the mere thought, her nipples tightened, sending tingles straight down somewhere else. It was a weird state of arousal and lan-guidness, and it took all the willpower she had to not just give in to the moment. To not just give in to him.

Shrugging his hand away, she sat up.

"Who said anything about a postmortem?" His voice was silky-smooth but with a hard undertone to it. "Maybe I'm looking for a repeat. Maybe I'm the beast who's finally got his filthy hands on the virgin princess and would be cursed for the rest of his life if I let her go."

She sent him a shocked look—his narrative was perceptively close to the one in her own head.

What was real and what was made-up fantasy between them? What was attraction and interest on his part and what was just a bunch of baggage he wanted to be rid of, in order to right his mistakes? And worst of all, why was this intimacy so easy between them? Why did the dark quiet feel like it was weaving a spell around them?

"Why all the lies, Yana? Why make yourself out to be someone you're not?"

"So I'm suddenly more valuable now because I still had my V card?" She combed her fingers through her hair, quickly braiding it to the side. "I thought you a better man than that."

"I have committed enough sins without adding that one to the list, *habibi*. It doesn't matter to me how many men you'd slept with. It does matter to me that you've created a certain image for yourself and today you've decided to reveal the real you."

"Ahh, gotcha. You're worried that I might think you're special because you're my first lover?"

He clasped her chin between his fingers, an angry frown turning his face dark. "My point is that you decided to keep lying to me, even to the last second. Maybe you thought this would all be a big laugh, proving me wrong about you. Maybe it's just a grand game to you. But I won't make the mistake of assuming that tonight meant nothing to you."

And you? Did tonight mean more than nothing to you?

"No, you'll just assume that I want more from you

than this. Isn't that why you are here now—to set the record straight? To make sure I don't see some big, bright future together?"

"Yana—"

"And people say women are the illogical ones. I won't cling to you, Nasir. How can I make that clear to you?"

"Why is even having a conversation with you a fight?" He sighed, the back of his head hitting the headboard. "This talk was coming, even if we hadn't had sex tonight. I'm not a man who bears the weight of his guilt easily, even when it's justly deserved." His tone hinted at volumes of grief and loss that shut her up instantly. "I'm here to appease my own conscience, to cater to my own ego, to make sure I don't fall off the pedestal I tell myself and the world I stand on. Pick whichever of those you feel best applies."

She laughed then and he glanced at her—her eyes, her mouth, her neck—and desire danced there, more than just a burning ember.

A whole conflagration waited there. Just that one look and everything she'd buried deep inside her heart awakened. In that moment she adored him more than she ever had, more than she'd ever thought possible again.

Here was the man who'd always been able to laugh at his own weaknesses and faults and yet had still tried to do better.

"Amina is going to hate me all over again," she said, searching for a safer topic.

"That tactic won't work."

"We have decided that it's your fragile masculine

ego that begs to be tended to. What else is there to talk about?"

"What else about you has been a lie?"

Yana looked at her tightly clasped fingers and loosened the grip.

He had no idea what he was offering her. How burdened and cut off and lost she'd felt in the past few months. How she hadn't realized that her stubbornness to do it right finally, to take charge of her life in a meaningful way, would nearly be her undoing.

She'd be even more beholden to him, but outside of the sex, she was beginning to believe that he cared a little about her. Even if only to right past wrongs.

"You know more about me than Diana knows, more than my grandfather did. More than even my sisters." It didn't even surprise her anymore that he was the one who'd ended up being the witness to all of her failures and flaws but also the one who'd see her strengths, who'd give her the validation that she shouldn't still need but longed for anyway.

"Yana—"

"If you're going to spend the rest of the night here, I propose we do something fun, at least."

When he grinned like the careless, charming rogue she'd known once, she shook her head. "Not that, you rogue."

"Ahh… What do you have in mind?"

"Since I've given you my virginity and my deepest secrets—" although there was something else she'd fight with her last breath from giving him this time "—I think a favor's fair."

* * *

Something about the naughty twinkle in her eyes, the sheer enthusiasm in her words, made Nasir want to kiss her all over again. Instead, he leaned back and gave a beleaguered sigh. "You've already robbed me blind, *habibi*. What else would you have of me? More importantly, I don't believe you've given me all your secrets." He grabbed a thick lock of hair and tugged until she arched up toward him like a bow and his mouth hovered over hers in a tempting tease. "I think you like keeping me hanging."

With a flourish that made him laugh, she pushed him away, then sat up cross-legged, shoulders straight, readying for battle. His T-shirt fell off one shoulder, baring silky-smooth skin and drowning her in it. Hair in the messy bun again, face scrubbed of makeup, she looked utterly different from the sophisticated, elegant Yana she'd been earlier at dinner.

Even more beautiful in his eyes, because this was the real version no one knew.

Maybe no man should ever see her again like that, his possessiveness crowed, joining in with the irrational crowd of voices rioting in his head.

No maybe about it, said the part of his brain glutted on endorphins.

She should be mine. Only mine, the deepest corner of his heart announced, aided by his arrogance.

And how he could bring it about danced vaguely at the back of his mind. A solution would tie a bow around two of his dilemmas.

"You can ask me whatever you want," she said, her

nose held high as if she was granting him a favor, un-aware of the scheming his libido and his brain were doing together, "and I'll do my best to give you a truth-ful answer."

"Wow, and you think you're not a hard-nosed busi-nesswoman? I don't want the most truthful answer, Yana. I just want the truth."

She frowned. "I have a pretty big thing to ask of you, so fine."

"Where do you disappear to in the evenings after Zara goes to bed? The whole damned staff knows but won't tell me. Loyalty to Ms. Reddy and all that. I should fire Ahmed because I think he's the one head-ing up that rebellious campaign."

The easy humor of two minutes ago evaporated and a heart-twisting vulnerability shone in her eyes. "Don't fire anyone on my behalf."

"Then tell me what you're doing."

Yana knew he was only joking—his staff was his family, so she should keep this particular truth close to her heart. But that reckless, defiant part of her wanted to tell him and test him and...

"You're scaring me, *habibi*. And that has happened only twice in my entire life. What secret is so dark and deep that you look like I'm asking you for a piece of your soul?"

With one perceptive sentence, he'd disarmed her all over again. "It costs a piece of my soul to tell you."

"Let's make you feel better, then. What do you want from me in return?" he asked, knowing that in that mo-ment, he'd give her anything she asked for. It was only the high of good sex, he told himself, but the claim felt hollow.

Her face glowed from within as she softly whispered, "I want to read the advanced copy of your next two novels."

His chest warmed at the childlike fascination that made her eyes glitter like priceless gems. "That's it?" he teased and then said, "Done." Pulling her to him, he kissed the tip of her nose. "Now, give it up, *habibi*."

Her chin lifted and a new kind of light shone from her. He was a writer but he had no words to describe the exquisite expression in her eyes. It was hope but brighter, shinier, more radiant.

"I'm writing a book. It's actually the second in a series and I think it's good. Like, really good. I also wrote a fantasy horror that's based on Indian mythology in the last few years. Thaata used to tell me all the scariest stories, you know? He used to say I was the only one among the three of us sisters who didn't scare easily." Pride he'd rarely seen danced in each word. She drew in a fast, shallow breath as if she couldn't stop talking now that she'd started. "I don't know if you've noticed but I had quite a rigorous discussion with your editor Samuel earlier tonight. I kinda ran the premise by him and he said he'd take a look at the book. How fantastic is that? Which reminds me that I should thank you for inviting me to today's gathering and—"

He laughed then and tackled her onto the bed until they were all tangled up in each other and the sheets, and there was nowhere she could escape to. He didn't remember the last time he had laughed so much, when listening to another person had brought him such joy, when he had felt such an overpowering rush of tenderness that he couldn't think straight.

"What's happening?" she said on a husky moan, when he covered her with his own body.

Ya, Allah, she fit so well against him—all soft curves and prickly edges and silky skin and sleek flesh and trembling thighs and tremulous moans. And those big, dazzling eyes reflecting everything she felt straight at him.

"You're so adorably sexy when you talk about your deepest dreams that I've been overcome by uncontrollable lust once again, *habibi*," he whispered at her ear and then followed it up with the filthiest words he could speak to her.

She blushed even though she didn't fully understand him and then those sleek legs converged around his back and she was lifting her hips up and Nasir ground his erection into her with no self-control.

A trail of damp kisses followed from her mouth, licking and nipping at his flesh. With one hand, she tugged up her T-shirt and through his silk pajama bottoms, he could feel the heat radiating off her sex. Pressing herself up against him, she writhed with a wanton pleasure that had his rock-hard length twitching.

"Please, Nasir. Now."

He took her mouth in a gentle kiss. "You will be sore, *habibi*. It might hurt a little."

"But after it passes, you'll make me scream with ecstasy, won't you? Twice at least."

And then without waiting for his response, she

pushed down his pajamas and freed his shaft and then he was there at the center of her sex.

Reaching for a control he wasn't sure he possessed anymore, Nasir played with her soft core. Stroked her own wetness all over her until she was moaning his name like a symphony. Taking it slow with his fingers, letting her get used to him all over again. With all the skill he had, he teased her over and over and only when she began to fall apart, calling out his name, did he slide himself into her.

Slumbering heat built and built in his spine as he went slow and deep and shifted her pelvis up until he could hit a different spot and she was moaning that she couldn't go again. But he saw the need and greed in her beautiful face and he hit that spot over and over again, dragging his abdominal muscles over her sensitive nub and it was all an erotic tango that made his muscles clench and sweat bead all over his skin. When she screamed in pleasure and went over the edge again and buried her teeth in his pectorals, he followed her and fell apart along with her in a way he hadn't allowed himself in a long, long time.

After they'd showered, despite her complaints that she wanted to sleep, and he'd fed her pieces of crisp apples and cheese and nuts, she'd wrapped herself around him like a vine. When he'd tried to give her a little space, she crawled back to him and over him, limbs akimbo, aggressive and prickly even in sleep.

When he held her against his chest, she kept throwing her legs and arms around. And when he finally got her to settle down with a long, drugging kiss, she mumbled sleepily that she'd thought it would be like this, that she'd known that it would be him. That he was worth the wait.

Nasir thought his petrified heart might have cracked open at that vulnerable admission. And he wondered if stones could be turned back into men and even if they could, if they could relearn the most human thing to do again—to love.

Or if it was all too late for him. But he knew one thing about men; that they were selfish. He was one, too, and he knew he wouldn't give her up when she fit into his life so perfectly. Not ever.

CHAPTER TWELVE

THE NEXT SIX weeks were as close to paradise as even Yana's wildest dreams could have conjured them to be. It had felt unbelievable when she'd looked at her calendar that morning and realized there were only three weeks of her stay left, as per the contract she'd signed with Nasir. Of course, the contract had no meaning left between them except as a joke Nasir used when she'd ask something of him and he'd say she'd robbed him blind already.

Time seemed to rush at an indescribable speed the more she tried to double down on it. Or was it her grasp of time as a construct that was slipping because she'd never been happier, or for the first time in her life, that she was truly thriving and flourishing on all fronts?

She'd had to finish up the last of her modeling contracts already in place, so she'd done those. She and Nush had squealed with joy at learning recently that Mira was pregnant with twins—*twins*—and the sisters had managed a weekend for a much-needed girls get-together arranged by Mira's clearly besotted husband Aristos. *And* to top it all off, she was making good progress on the second book she was working on in her series.

It was still hard for her to trust Nasir with reading her work. Or maybe it was her insecurities? But she managed to reveal theoretical scenarios to him because his mind was a maze and he was the best at brainstorming. While it rankled him a little that she refused to share more, he always indulged her outlandish inquiries and they ended up discussing craft and the industry and research so often that Yana began to fall for him all over again.

Between quick one-day or overnight jaunts to different locations for a magazine ad shoot, a perfume ad and the opening of a new night club in Amsterdam, she'd spent the past few weeks soaking in the sun, swimming in the pool and wandering the woods with Zara in tow.

Nasir, to her shock, had shown up at the same hotels as she had for almost all of her work trips. To her unending delight, he was one of those people who'd been to every damn city in the world and always knew the best places to eat, knew the real history that books seemed to forget and then there were those glorious nights of passion and tenderness and more to explore between them. The best part was that she felt as if the trips were slowly bringing out the true explorer of life Nasir was at heart.

After that first night, they didn't try to label what was between them again or set an expiration date on it, and that was perfectly fine with Yana.

Clearly, he still wanted her with the same fervor and madness she felt. In this, finally, they were equals. They were lovers and confidants and shared all the ups and downs of loving and caring for a little girl.

She was living the life she'd once dreamed of and during those glorious moments where they were playing with Zara, or reading quietly together in the evening, or talking about her book, it felt like it was more than enough. At least that was what she told herself, trying her best to not give too much thought to the future.

Not confiding in her sisters when she wanted to share the real relationship she was finally having with Nasir, hurt her heart. But they would only ask about where it was all leading, out of pure concern for her, and then Caio and Aristos would be dragged into it, and she didn't want to force the issue when it was, in the end, all a precarious house of cards.

For now their *affair*—for want of a better word—still possessed that dreamy, magical, out-of-this-world quality to it and she was loath to disrupt it with talk of reality and future and stupid, silly organs getting far too involved when they should know better.

It was the same when they were at the castle, too—as if the whole scenario and the actors had truly emerged out of a dark fairy tale into a happy romance. She didn't know if the instructions not to mention it had come from Nasir.

She was only thankful that the staff and Ahmed and even Amina acted as if they didn't notice anything. Nasir's mother had been excessively, exactingly kind to her, and Yana had cautiously returned the courtesy because Amina seemed to finally realize how much

Yana had loved her husband. How real her mourning of Izaz was.

But sometimes, Yana saw a calculating quality in the older woman's eyes and it unnerved her. She kept pointing out with a tone to her voice that Yana couldn't pin down, that Zara was flourishing, thriving, blooming, under the attention of the two adults she loved the most.

Especially since she must know that her son ended up back in his bedroom—which Yana still also occupied, every night without fail. Though Nasir left before dawn at the latest—immediately after sex sometimes—to return to the bedroom he'd used since she'd arrived.

Yana had initially found both injury and insult in his leaving right after sex until he'd explained to her, with that charmingly wicked smile of his, that inspiration for his next novel had been coming to him in waves around midnight, right after he'd made love to her. That if he didn't want to be ditched by his frustrated editor or his agent, he had to capitalize on it. And that he'd been making the trip back to her bedroom after his writing session, only to leave at dawn again because they didn't want to be caught together by his curious five-year-old.

Acting the seductress—a bad habit that Nasir demanded she'd better *not* give up because it made her say and do outrageous things just to provoke him, she'd prettily suggested to him that he'd better dedicate the book to her for her part in getting it done.

His reply had been, "I wouldn't want to shock my loyal readers with all that went into finishing the book, *habibi*. Those particular details are only for me to savor.

Especially the time you decided you wanted to be on your knees."

She'd blushed so hard that her cheeks had burned. But she'd also been secretly glad—not because she believed sex with her had some magical writer's unblocking properties, but because, for the first time in years since she'd known him, Nasir genuinely looked relaxed. Content. Happy, even.

And she wanted to think at least some of that—a tiny, little part—was to do with her.

The summer sun had already started to set, immediately bringing a cool chill that particular evening as Yana hurriedly packed up their picnic supplies. Especially since they'd ventured farther than the boundary of the woods they usually stuck to. It was her own fault for giving in to Zara's continued request for more playtime. Between keeping up with her and her own flagging energy, Yana hadn't checked the time.

Yana pushed to her knees and lugged the heavy tote bag—Zara had to bring all the rocks she'd collected today, onto her shoulder just as the little girl, in her hurry, slipped over something and fell facedown into the knee-high grass.

Dropping the bag where she stood, she rushed to Zara. The five-year-old's cry—a sudden, spiraling wail—told Yana it was more shock and fear than real pain. Fighting the worry in her head, she squatted on the floor and gently pulled Zara into her lap.

The little girl attached her arms to Yana's neck with a hiccupping cry, without letting her check her face.

Sighing, and loosening her arms so that she didn't communicate her own fear to her, Yana rocked from side to side even as she whispered that Zara was okay. When Zara finally let her look at the small cut on her cheek, Yana set about dealing with it.

She wasn't sure how long it took, when suddenly Yana noted that complete darkness had fallen. With the forested area at her back, and the castle at least a mile in the opposite way, it would be easy to get lost without light.

Pushing onto her feet, she talked Zara into wrapping her arms around her neck and her legs around her back like a little baby monkey they'd seen on a nature show not a few days ago, clinging to its mother.

Wiping her tears on Yana's T-shirt, Zara instantly cheered up.

Turning around with her lightweight baggage, Yana walked back to where she'd dropped the tote. She found her cell phone and turned on the flashlight, although there was no signal to call Nasir this far out. The sky was a dark canopy of stars she'd rarely seen and she stopped several times to show Zara this star and that constellation.

Her arms and legs hurt from all the day's exercise but soon, Yana could see the shadowed outline of the castle. She blew out a long breath, imagining herself in a hot bath with Nasir in it, too, hopefully, once they'd settled Zara into bed. It was a ritual she hadn't planned on getting involved in and yet, had been roped into when Zara had begged that they both read her a story and tuck her in for the night. As if even the little girl could sense the current of happiness between the adults who adored her.

Now, with her departure rushing at her with every day that passed, the ritual and so many more like that had gained weight and gravitas. Yana didn't want to leave. There, she'd admitted it to herself. For the first time in her life, she was happy and content and…she felt like she belonged here. Like the castle walls themselves were imbued with her very joy.

"Where the hell have you been?" Nasir's question tugged her into the present with a firm jerk.

Taken aback by his tone, Yana stared at him.

"Do you know how worried I've been? It's dark and you weren't at your usual spot."

"I didn't notice the time and then Zara—"

"You should know better than to venture out so far and for so long after sunset," he said, plucking Zara from her arms into his. "That was careless of you, Yana."

Yana froze, struck by the criticism in his voice. But whatever defense she wanted to provide was drowned out when the entire staff came toward the high entrance from all directions surrounding the courtyard, clear relief on their faces. And then she was being tugged inside, by Amina of all people, who checked her arms and legs and worried over her dirty T-shirt and shorts, and all through it Yana kept looking at him, but Nasir wouldn't meet her eyes.

Suddenly, Yana felt as if she'd been permanently pushed into a cold, dark place, shunned from all light.

All her doubts about how she'd leave when the time came turned into something else.

Finally, they were all in the full foyer illuminated by one of those blasted chandeliers with a million little lights and her gaze fell on the small cut on Zara's cheek just as everyone else's did.

"You're hurt, Zara," Nasir's voice cut through the commotion around them, like a knife slicing through. And Yana heard it then—his fear. Saw the tension carved into his face. The sweat that had gathered over his brow.

"I didn't listen to Yana Auntie, Papa," Zara said, scrunching her face up. "She told me not to go too fast but I thought I saw a dragonfly and then I fell over." Her thick curls dancing around her face, she drew in a long breath. "It doesn't hurt, Papa," Zara piped up, looking for Yana among the crowd that surrounded her. "Yana Auntie alweady cleaned it and put a gel on it. She said I get a medal because I only cwied for thwee and a half minutes. She said I was so bwave when she cleaned it that I could eat chocolate cake in the morning. Can I have chocolate cake for bweakfast, Papa?"

The tension dissipated from Nasir's face and he pressed a kiss to Zara's temple. "Yes, pumpkin. You can have anything you want for breakfast."

"Will you and Yana Auntie wead me two stories each tonight, Papa? Since I fell and hurt myself?"

Nasir laughed and hugged his daughter tight. "Manipulative little thing, aren't you?" When Zara frowned and pushed out that lower lip she deployed like a weapon, he hurriedly added, "Yes, two stories each,

Zuzu baby. After that you have to sleep, yeah? And then…" He looked up over Zara's head and met Yana's eyes. "I have a very important thing to do."

"What, Papa?"

"Eating crow, baby," he said with a sudden, heart-wrenching smile aimed straight at her heart. Zara pounded him with more questions and he went on to elaborate that her papa was a blockhead who forgot his manners when he was upset. And he had been upset, he told Zara and an arrested Yana, at the thought that his two bestest, most favorite girls in the world might have been lost and hurt in the forest in the dark.

Yana's heart swelled in her chest, overflowing with emotion. And she knew, just knew, that she was going to leave pieces of herself behind when she left.

They ended up spending more than two hours not only reading to Zara but also watching some anime with her. Even though, for the first time in his life, Nasir wanted his little energy bunny to fall asleep fast.

In the end, he left Zara and Yana cuddling in Zara's bed, both of them suddenly fast asleep together.

He went back to his own bedroom, made some quick arrangements in the bathroom, changed into pajamas and waited. He couldn't blame her if she didn't join him tonight, could he? He'd been so eager to criticize and blame her for a small hurt Zara had received.

He pushed a hand through his hair and tugged at it roughly. Of course, five-year-olds got hurt all the time. Why hadn't he controlled himself better? And now here he was, once again, wondering if he'd hurt her.

He'd worn down the carpet when the connecting door finally opened and Yana came in, locking it behind her.

They stared at each other—her expression wary as she watched him, and he...he didn't know what he looked like. Only that he wanted to make more than simple amends. Reaching for her, he took her hand in his and tugged her into the bathroom.

Her eyes widened as she saw the full bath he'd filled with her favorite lavender oil and scattered with rose petals, and the lit candles and the bottle of wine with a glass, waiting on the rim. "Nasir—"

Forestalling her argument or a justly deserved complaint, he said quietly but firmly, "Raise your arms."

He was more than surprised when she complied. Tugging her T-shirt off, he gathered her hair and gently tied it into a knot at the top of her head, like he'd seen her do. Then he stripped her of her bra and shorts and panties.

Eyes wide in her face like a gazelle, she stood there, utterly naked.

"Into the tub," he said gruffly, before his desire overtook his common sense.

She complied silently. Again.

He watched with sheer fascination that apparently refused to even simmer down into something manageable, as her limbs disappeared beneath the water and she threw her head back with a soft moan.

He swallowed when he caught sight of her tight nipples playing peekaboo under a rose petal. Needing to give himself something to do, he uncorked the wine and poured it into the glass.

She took it from him wordlessly and then took a sip. She murmured appreciatively and she wriggled her shoulders as if to dislodge a knot there. His guilt intensified. "Once you get out of the bath, I'll work those kinks out of your shoulders," he said, wriggling his fingers at her.

"No, thank you," she said, not opening her eyes. "Especially if your massage skills are no better than your daughter's."

"Try me and then pass judgment, *habibi*."

Another exhale left her. "Thank you for this. It was exactly what I needed at the end of a long day."

Seating himself at the edge, he watched the overhead lights play with the angles of her face. "I shouldn't have snapped at you when you got back. I was worried, terrified, that you both were hurt. I… I was suddenly reminded of everything I once lost…"

"It's okay, Nasir," she said, lightly tapping her fingers over the back of his hand and then retreating. "I got that from your face. But just so you know, Zara's five and she's going to get hurt sometimes. Under my supervision or someone else's."

"I know that, in here," he said, pointing toward his head. "And the amazing thing is she knows that, too, doesn't she? She's completely fearless with you. But I do worry about her, Yana. All the time. Especially since I've already messed up with her once, so badly."

Opening her eyes, Yana watched him with that silent gaze. Asking questions without asking them. Waiting for him to reveal his darkest fears.

"I never planned to be a father, Yana. And yet, ever

since I held her that first day, I've loved her. I know I can't keep her wrapped up in cotton wool, surrounded by staff who watch her twenty-four hours a day."

"You can't. And as much as you'll hate me for saying this, she'll be six in three months. She needs kids of her own age to play with, Nasir, to learn social skills, to learn boundaries. Even if you decide to homeschool her. You can't keep yourself shut out from the rest of the world and also be a good father to her. Kids need to learn about the world, and Zara's a pretty social kid."

"I don't hate you for saying it. In fact, I…" He swallowed the words, loath to unburden himself to her when he hadn't broached the topic in his head yet with her. He was aware of days dwindling at a rapid rate, of her looming departure. And yet, he held out. Told himself he and Zara would manage. Told himself that Yana would return to her normal life and yet they would still be able to resume their affair and fall into some kind of a sticking pattern, long distance.

He'd never been an indecisive man before in his entire life and he hated that he was waiting for time or something else to decide for him when he'd never done that. The certainty of time passing and the uncertainty of his own plans were eating through him.

He looked up and met her gaze. "I hope you won't ever stop saying that, Yana."

"Saying what?"

"What you think is right for Zara. Even if you're afraid that I'll get all grumpy and grouchy with you."

"I'm not afraid of you, you beast," she said teasingly, splashing water on him.

He went to his knees and then cradled her neck. Pressing his mouth to her temple, he whispered, "Even after you've left here?"

She grabbed his forearm. "I won't," she whispered earnestly and he heard the promise in it.

"Am I forgiven, then?" he said, trailing his mouth to the shell of her ear.

Her questing hands went straight to his erection. She palmed him and Nasir forgot all about the world outside. "Only if you get into the bath with me."

That was an invitation he could never resist.

CHAPTER THIRTEEN

YANA'S THREE MONTHS were up as if someone had taken the hourglass and shaken it up to make time go faster. She had an assignment in New York, then she was going to visit her mother in California and then return to be with Mira for almost a month before the twins were born. Of course, she'd promised Zara that she'd visit her, too, whenever possible in the midst of her hectic schedule. And she'd meant it. For once, everything in her life had the patina of normality and it left her feeling out of sorts.

She was at peace with herself, with where she was going in her life. She'd continue to pick up small contracts here and there until something definite came up in her literary career. Just thinking about that sent a ripple of excitement through her.

In the meantime, she had two sisters she adored and two billionaire brothers-in-law who were forever inviting her to visit and meant it. And Yana decided she would. She'd worked in one way or another since she'd been sixteen and she would take it easier now that she was already at a crossroads.

She'd kept waiting for the bubble that Nasir and she seemed to live in to break, for reality or some other ugly life thing to fracture their almost fantastical happiness. When it happened, it did so because, once again, she couldn't help herself bringing up the past.

Because the seeds of the future had already been sown somewhere in the past and, in the end, because she'd realized the truth that had never changed.

That final day, Amina and Ahmed had taken Zara to meet Amina's sister in London, leaving Yana and Nasir behind. At his dictate, she'd learned later. To make it easier on Zara when Yana left the castle, but she wondered if he thought she'd also cause a scene.

Dread and something else curled around Yana's chest. She'd miss Zara with all of her being. She'd miss the staff, Ahmed's gentle care, Huma picking at her for ideas and even Amina, who'd thawed so greatly that she'd once said Yana was the daughter she'd never had. As skeptical as she'd wanted to feel, she'd thought the older woman had actually meant it.

As if her dark fairy-tale romance had to continue the theme, a great storm darkened the skies that last evening, chasing her and Nasir indoors. As if someone had set a background score, a hum of anxiety had thrummed through her all day.

As usual, Nasir and she ate together, then worked for a little while on their respective laptops in the great big library in quiet, comfortable silence. He put the gramophone player on, and she stood up to stretch and suddenly, he was behind her, clasping his arms around her and leading her in a slow, sensuous tango around the room.

She had no idea how long they danced like that. How long they stayed silent even as their bodies communicated freely and easily and effortlessly. In her three-inch heels, she was at perfect height for the V of her thighs to feel his thick erection. She'd gone braless and her nipples felt deliciously tormented pressed up into points against his hard chest.

He tilted her chin up with insistent fingers and Yana read his raw desire as easily as she could hear the thundering pulse of her heartbeat in her ears.

She went with a willing wantonness as he pressed her upper body over a centuries-old side table full of crystal decanters and expensive candlesticks. She moaned like a brazen seductress when he pulled up the hem of the icy-blue cocktail dress she'd worn for him because he'd whispered once when he'd been deep inside her that he loved seeing her in it. She turned her head and let him see her greedy abandon with an eager push of her hips when he tested her damp readiness. She slammed her palm onto the dark wood when he thrust into her with one long, deep stroke. The decanters and the candlesticks rattled, the table hit the wall with a rhythmic thud and the entire castle felt like it was standing witness to them, and she wondered just who was seducing and who was surrendering.

And then she realized it didn't matter anymore.

Her breath came in sharp pants and shallow gulps when his thrusts began to gather speed, but suddenly *lost* that finesse. Then his fingers were at her core, and his mouth was at her neck and he was demanding she come for him and he was telling her she was the sexiest thing he'd ever beheld and he was all over her and around her. The clever, wicked man that he was, he hit the exact spot where she could see glorious stars and soon, she was climaxing so hard that she thought she might never come back together in the same way ever again.

Yana felt undone, unraveled, as if he'd wrested away parts of her. Her legs wobbled when he helped her straighten and she thought he was on shaky legs, too. She turned and smiled and then he was kissing her and telling her what a good, quiet, biddable lover she was and she was thumping him in his chest with her fist because he was deliberately provoking her all over again before he kissed her.

She had no words to describe the tender reverence with which his lips touched her. How they said so much that he couldn't or wouldn't say. She buried her face in his neck and let herself drown in the delicious scent of the man.

They stood like that, while the storm raged outside the castle, and Yana wondered at how perfectly it mirrored everything that was happening inside her.

"Come back to me, *habibi*."

"I'm here," she said and yet she felt like parts of her were going to stay behind forever with him. "I'm leaving tomorrow morning."

"I know."

"Thank you for giving me tonight. With you. With just you."

"You think it was a favor to you? It was a selfish man's selfish desire. To have you all to himself for one final night."

"Then for the first time in our lives, I think we're in agreement," she said, forcing a humor she didn't feel. "I'll return whenever I can."

"I know."

"I'll call Zara every day."

"I know."

"I'll let you know when you can drop her off with me. Mira would love to see her, too. And Aristos. And Nush and Caio. I want Zara to meet them all. I want her to think of them as her family, too."

"You're very generous, *habibi*, and Zara is lucky to have you."

"Are you mocking me?" she asked.

"Do I dare?"

She looked up and ran her fingers over the scar almost obsessively and then pulled back. "I'm sorry."

"You're welcome to touch me anywhere, Yana. Even the scar. I don't mind."

"I know," she said this time, and he smiled, and she smiled back, and it was a moment of perfect communion.

Age had only made him more handsome, more distinguished. Laugh lines crinkled out at his eyes even as grief and loss had permanently etched themselves onto those stern features.

It came to her then how much he'd changed after the

incident that had given him those scars, how a shroud of grief had hung around him. With her usual foolish na-iveté and a reckless urgency because it had pained her to see him like that, she'd not only trodden on his raw, wounded emotions but also declared shamelessly that she was in love with him and that he belonged to her.

God, had she ever read a situation so badly?

Whatever had happened on that trip had changed him—inside and out. Now she wished she'd asked him about it instead of throwing herself at him, that she'd kept a safe space for him like he'd done for her. Like he was doing for her again now.

But as much as she tried, she couldn't be mad at her-self for her grand avowal of love back then. She'd sensed something was wrong with him and with her usual all-guns-blazing attitude had desperately wanted to fix it for him. She'd thought herself enough to fix him.

But it didn't really have anything to do with whether she'd been enough or not. Something else had happened to him on that trip. Now she realized it, and like that saying, the truth did set her free.

It was life affirming to have someone who loved you by your side when you went through hard times. But in the end, one had to save oneself. One had to de-cide to live and love despite the pain and pitfalls life threw at you.

"Who did you lose on that trip when you came back with all these scars?" she asked, twisting her fingers so that they cast shadows on his white shirt when what she wanted to do was look into his eyes and see the an-swer for herself.

The atmosphere dropped to frost instantly even though he was warm around her.

She closed her eyes, cursing her impulsivity. Just because he'd found her good enough for an affair didn't mean they were going to exchange every painful secret. But to her surprise, he answered.

"A photographer I'd been training for a while. Fatima was—" a small smile painted his mouth "—young, and brash and defiant and wanted to change the world for the better. I brought her with me on an assignment I shouldn't have. She died in my arms."

"You loved her," Yana said, stating the fact rather than asking him, the final puzzle pieces that made up Nasir suddenly falling into place.

"I did. And I should've done a better job of protecting her. I was more experienced than her. I should've done a better risk analysis—"

"Weren't you yourself hurt by the blast?"

"Yes, but—"

She laughed then and it was an empty, mocking sound that rivaled the storm's fierceness. "How heavy your ego must be, Nasir. Don't your head and your shoulders and your back hurt from the weight of it?"

"You don't understand—"

"No, I understand it perfectly. I see it, finally. I see all of you, too," she said, throwing his words back at him. "I see now why you shut me down with such brutal cruelty."

Suddenly, his marriage to Jacqueline—which had had disaster written all over it from the beginning—his withdrawal from the world, from his first career, from his father, and even from her, made complete sense now. It was what Izaz had meant when he'd said his son was lost.

After that trip he'd seemed colder, harder, flatter even, with none of those soft edges that added such charm to his incisive brilliance, none of the quirks and awareness that had made him...larger than life. Her own naive stupidity had been but a cinder in the sacrificial pyre he'd already built for himself.

"You don't understand how terrible it is to have someone you love die in your arms. How utterly powerless you feel. The memory itself would haunt you forever."

His words were a death sentence to her poor heart's tentative whispers. But she was damned if she let him believe he was right. That somehow, he had to live through this punishment, forever alone. "No, I haven't lived through that exact scenario. But I know about loss and grief and...screaming at the universe for just one last chance. One do-over. I'd give anything to have one last minute with Thaata, to tell him that I was sorry, that I finally see what he'd been trying to do all along. That I loved him so much."

Nasir took her stiff hand in his and clasped their fingers tight. But still, Yana wasn't done. She was furious, actually, on behalf of herself and Jacqueline and the woman he'd lost. Not to mention Zara.

"I'm sure Fatima would have loved to know," she said, crossing all lines, venturing once again into that forbidden zone, her reckless tongue bashing out truths he'd hate to hear, "that her death has been conveniently reduced to the reason you have turned away from living a full life. And you dare call me a coward?"

"It's not cowardice if I want to leave emotions out of my decisions. Not that I succeeded with you, I admit."

"Ha! Then why hate me for so long?"

"Because you were right. I lost the battle against myself over you long ago. Don't you see how that must have driven Jacqueline crazy? My dislike for you was far more potent than anything I ever felt for her. It didn't matter that I told myself to stay well clear of you. You were always there at the periphery of my life, teasing and taunting me. I wish I'd just admitted defeat sooner. You and I both know we were heading here, one way or the other, for years now, Yana."

"Because you were so sure that I'd throw myself at you again?"

A pithy curse was his aggrieved response. "Because as much as I fought it, a few days ago, a few months ago, a few years ago, when you were Jacqueline's maid of honor, even when you were my nineteen-year-old step-sister with the body of a goddess and the innocence of a locked-up princess, I was attracted to you. I wanted you all along. You have no idea how close I came to taking what you offered all those years ago. How I wanted to use you to bury my grief, to relieve the guilt I felt about Fatima."

"And why would that have been so wrong? Why do you talk of it as if it fills you with horror to even think it? I was only nineteen, yes. But how do you measure adulthood? How dare you take away my agency? I'd been through loss and neglect and rebellion and wrong influences and bad parenting...so much already. You were a good thing in my life. Loving you was a light in a place of shadows and mistakes and I'll never ever regret it."

"Don't, *habibi*."

"I don't want to play games or fantasies, Nasir. In this, I've never been able to dupe even myself."

His forehead pressed against hers, his exhale exploding over her lips, washing away her fears all over again. His hands cupped her shoulders and held her to him, hard and tight. The contact was nonsexual, seeking and giving comfort, and yet she felt it pass down through limb after limb, vein after vein, reaching the deepest corners of her and staying there. Rooting her to the moment, to the man, to herself.

Bringing her back full circle to her own truth. That she still loved him. That she'd loved him for all the yesterdays of her life and that she'd love him for all the tomorrows yet to come.

And this time her love didn't feel wrong or bad or forbidden or immature or selfish or demanding. It simply sat in her heart, fitting in, settling into place. It felt like coming home.

"You're punishing yourself for a mistake you didn't even commit. With me and with Fatima."

"I'd have discarded you afterward. I had nothing to give you back for your declaration of love, Yana. I'd have simply used you."

"And now?" she asked, even though she'd promised herself she wouldn't go there.

"And now, I still have nothing to give you." He held

her gaze, and she saw it coming before he said, "Except marriage."

She jerked back. "What?"

"Marry me, Yana. I'll give you every happiness that I can, make every dream of yours come true. Marry me because Zara needs you and I need you. Marry me so that you never have to say goodbye to us again. Admit it. It's killing you to leave. Admit that you're happy here with us."

Tears and smiles came at her together as she gazed at him. She couldn't lie to him now, even if she wanted to. Because it was her most sacred truth. "I've been happy here. Happier than I've ever been in my life. And yes, it's killing me to leave you. The thought of coming back as just a friend into your life, of not calling this castle home, kills me. The thought of not seeing you and Zara for months on end…kills me."

"Then stay and marry me. Make a life with me." He took her mouth in a hard kiss, and she felt herself melting. Falling. Weakening. But she had to remain strong against temptation. "Stay, *habibi*, and I'll be yours in all the ways that matter."

"No, you'll be mine under conditions and caveats." Regretful tears drew paths down her cheeks. "You're still trying to pin me down. To take everything from me without giving me anything in return."

He flinched, and her chest felt like it would cave in. Because she knew he was standing there, with one foot on the precipice, ready to fall with her, but he just wouldn't take that last step.

"Only you could make me consider marriage again

after the nightmare with Jacqueline. Why can't you see that?"

"I don't want the little crumbs you can manage. I don't want anything from you," she said, trying to cover up the thundering of her thudding heart and rolling belly with a small smile. Who'd have guessed that her teen fantasy coming true would be such a horror in real life? Who knew she'd walk away when her deepest dream was finally within her reach? "Because whether you admit it or not, you're already mine. You've always been mine, by your own admission. I've owned you for a long time and I just didn't know it."

She felt free then. Free of fears and shackles and incessant demands and made-up rules. Because her love for him was a simple truth. Like the sun rose in the east. Like the storm that was raging outside but would leave the world renewed come tomorrow. Like the pain that was crashing through her right now but would settle into another scar in the months and years to come.

What she refused to do was to twist herself inside out ever again, with the foolish hope that she'd finally be loved the way she deserved to be. Not even for Zara or for him.

She clasped his cheek then and licked into his mouth. The taste of mint exploded in her mouth, fusing with her very cells. She let her hands roam the broad chest, the tapered waist, the hard planes of his back; she snuck under his shirt and traced all of his scars and…then she kissed him all over again, hoping it would last her at least until the dark dawn and the long day ahead.

"Goodbye, Nasir."

CHAPTER FOURTEEN

NASIR FOUND HER at a fashion show in Athens, Greece. He'd followed her there after learning, from his mother of all people, that she was with her sister Mira, who'd just given birth to twins.

It had been four months since she'd left.

He hadn't called her or texted her or even snuck a glance at her as she talked to Zara on a video call, stubborn and hardheaded to the end. But thoughts of her consumed his every waking and sleeping moment.

His bed felt cold and empty. His life felt colorless. His words had dried up again as had his imagination. He'd thought of a million questions he'd never asked her and wondered at her answers. That a lifetime wasn't enough for her to surprise him and delight him and annoy him and bring him to his knees again and again. And he was beginning to think it wasn't a bad idea to be on his knees for the woman he clearly adored.

And she, apparently finally wising up to what an extraordinary, incredible woman she was, didn't even steal a glance at him. Even his mother got screen time. As did Ahmed and Huma and his staff. Never a question or a comment about him or for him since she'd left them.

Not Zara. Never Zara.

Just him. She'd left him because he'd been a coward. And in one of those petty moments, Nasir found himself envious of his own six-year-old for the generous, lavish, unconditional love she got from her Yana Auntie.

All he'd wanted to do for weeks was storm through her brother-in-law Aristos Carides's lavish mansion like a bull on steroids, making claims and commitments that made him come out in a full sweat, and announce to anyone and the world and her, especially, that she was his.

He wondered yet again how long their red-hot affair would have lasted if he hadn't brought up marriage. Clever and perceptive as she was, she'd seen it for what it was—another contract he'd use to bind her to him, without opening his heart. Without actually committing to anything. Without giving her, the glorious creature she was, her due.

Now he was ashamed of how he'd attempted to manipulate her, even if he hadn't done it on purpose. Dangling the mirage of a dream as if it was some prize she would leap at.

Even though she'd made it clear that she wanted all the fireworks and passion and roller coaster of true love. Finally, it was the thought of another man giving her what he'd refused to that had spurred him into action. The thought of spending the rest of his life wondering where she was, who she was bestowing that warmth of hers on, felt scarier than the risk of opening his scarred heart to her, hoping she wouldn't deal it a death blow.

So here he was in Athens at a fashion show, the buzz that it was Yana Reddy's last show—another fact he hadn't been privy to because she wasn't talking to him, letting himself be photographed by media and paparazzi, giving rise to all kinds of speculation just so he could have one glimpse of her.

He wanted to see her shine and dazzle and sizzle. He wanted to be a part of her dreams coming gloriously true.

Whatever Nasir had imagined about how she'd look when she strutted onto the catwalk had nothing on the reality. The music, the crowd's energy and the sensual beauty of each model highlighted by carefully orchestrated lights and makeup and music…it was meant to bamboozle the audience.

Having been to a few shows in his twenties, and the couple of shows he'd been to during Yana's stay at the castle, he knew how this worked. And yet, when Yana walked onto the stage—the last of the models to do so—in the French designer's magnum opus: a glittery, rainbow-colored pantsuit, he was captivated anew.

Without a bra, the lapels of the jacket were stuck to her skin, baring most of her breasts, and she looked like a queen.

No, she was his prickly, fierce princess. And he'd been stupid to turn away from the best thing that had ever happened to him. To turn away from the incandescence of Yana's love. A coward, as she'd called him.

But there was no turning back now, because she'd brought him back to life.

He was bemoaning his habit of not drinking alcohol when the doors to the penthouse suite of the hotel opened and she stepped inside.

Smoky eyes and a pale glossy lipstick and shimmery glitter over her chest…she looked like a dark, alien goddess full of fire and passion. Her hair had been plastered to her scalp in some weird hairstyle that served to highlight the stark sharpness of her features. All angles and edges that were soothed by the promise held in that lush, wide mouth.

"I wondered if it was you I saw out there," she commented coolly, still standing there.

That explained her lack of surprise at seeing him in here now.

He nodded and swallowed and ran a hand through his hair. She watched him, and he watched her.

"Not a fan of the after-parties?"

"Not really," she replied.

He stole a glance at his watch. He hadn't expected her for hours, not until dawn. Suddenly, he felt woefully unprepared for all the words he wanted—no, needed—to say, after a lifetime of employing them. "I thought you'd be there."

"You were the one who had me upgraded to this penthouse suite?"

He shrugged, waiting for her to slam the doors in his face and run off.

Instead, she walked into the suite, grabbed a bottle

of water from the mini fridge and emptied it out. Then she opened another one, stood over the sink and poured it out over her hair and face. Her breath came in sharp, bracing spurts as the ice-cold water made goose bumps rise on her skin. "That's better. It feels as if all those lights and sounds are stuck to my skin."

He grabbed a hand towel from the bathroom and handed it to her.

She pressed her face into it and when she emerged from it, there was a resolve to her mouth that spelled his doom. "Will you tell me why you're here? Or can I go to sleep? I've been on my feet for eleven hours straight."

"Catch some rest. I'm not leaving until we've talked," he finally said, following her to the sunken living room.

"I won't catch a wink knowing you're out here." She plopped onto one of the sofas and before she could stretch her legs onto the marble coffee table, he sat down. His hands were shaking when he took her foot in his hands, pulled the lethal-looking heels off and pressed his fingers into the arch.

"God, I've forgotten how good you are at that," she said, throwing her head back.

He repeated his actions with her other foot and an electric silence built around them.

"I've brought you good news," he admitted finally.

She sat up, pulled her feet from his lap. "What?"

"Samuel loves your book. He wants exclusive rights to it. This is big, Yana. You're going to be incredibly successful."

She threw herself at him so suddenly that his heart rushed into his ears. "Oh, my God! That's...awesome.

I didn't… I can't tell you what it feels like to hear that. I…" Then she grinned, and there were tears in her eyes, but she rubbed them away quickly with the back of her hand. "Wait, of course you know how it feels. Thanks for telling me, Nasir. It means a lot. And it means even more that you came all this way to tell me."

"When Samuel told me, although I know he shouldn't have, I begged him to let me be the bearer of good news."

"Why?" she asked, her mask falling, a sudden belligerence to that one word.

"I wanted to see your happiness. Your laughter. Your victory. Your passion. I wanted to see you, Yana." And before she could probe him further, he said, "Do you have an agent yet?"

"No. I do have a pile of increasingly promising rejections from two years ago. They'd gotten more personal, came with more feedback. But after the last round a year ago, I stalled. I worked a bit more on the book and re-jigged some major plot stuff. With Diana's games and Thaata sick, my head wasn't in the right space to start querying all over again."

"Do you want me to recommend you to mine?"

"Why?"

"Why what?"

"Why would you recommend me? As a bonus for sleeping with you?" she said, half-laughing, half-mocking.

"You're never going to stop taunting me, are you?" he said, knowing he deserved it. "My agent is amazing and will do a fabulous job negotiating you the best contract with Samuel. Fair warning about Samuel as an editor, though. He's brilliant, but he might make you rip the book apart until you hate him, the book and yourself. Just stay…strong and keep your vision for the book at the forefront, okay?"

Yana nodded, feeling a rush of joy and something almost like pride well up inside her. "You believe in me, then? That I could do this author thing?"

"Of course I believe in you," he said. "I'd love to read it and get a real sense of your work but I understand that you're nervous about letting people read it."

"Only you."

"Only me what?"

"It's only you that I'm twisted up about showing it to. I've given copies to both my sisters and brothers-in-law."

His jaw tightened. "May I ask why?"

She shrugged. "Before, I was afraid that you'd mock it. Mock me."

"You really painted me as a monster in your head, huh? And at every step, I added color to your rendering by confirming your worst impressions."

"I think it helped to paint you like that."

"Helped who, Yana? Because it's been eating me up."

"Me. It helped me. Every time I wanted to give in, admit defeat, throw in the towel, give up on myself, I'd get this image of you. I'd see you looking down at me full of anger and contempt and I'd tell myself, *no way*. No way am I going to give Nasir a chance to think less of me again. No way am I giving up. You were kinda like a fire under my butt."

"I'm horrified yet again by my cruelty toward you and how it has—"

She came to him then and clasped his cheeks with that bravery that colored her every action. "It was a good thing, Nasir."

"From which damned perspective, *habibi*?" he retorted, with an angry flush.

His fingers moved over her cheeks, soft and slow and reverent, as if he worried that he might mar her.

Yana leaned into his touch. "Even when I loathed you, you were a positive force in my life. I loved you. I wanted to be worthy of you. I—"

"You're worth a million versions of me, Yana. You're fiery and beautiful and worthier than a thousand sunrises and a thousand sunsets. Your heart is beauty and joy and life itself, *habibi*."

"You're making me cry."

"Par for the course, then," he said with a twinkle, and then he was kissing her, and every nip and lick was lust and reverence—two such opposing shades of the same sentiment. "I wanted to be the bearer of good news. Even that was selfish. Shall I tell you why I'm here, truly?"

"Yes. Now, Nasir. You've stripped me of all my roles and defenses. I can't be strong for too long. Tell me now. Please."

"The second piece of good news first. I had three pieces."

"There's more?" she said, wiping the back of her hand over her cheek with a vulnerability that squeezed his heart.

"I'd fill your days and nights with all the good news I can muster, *habibi*. But these are small in the scheme of things."

"Tell me, please."

"I have finally convinced Diana to enter rehab."

"What? How?" Yana pressed her hands to her mouth, disbelief a giant balloon in her chest. In all the months since she'd agreed terms with Nasir, she hadn't been able to make any progress with her mother, who had broken down and admitted that she had a problem but wanted no part of the solution. Yana had seen shades of a woman she'd once adored, and her resolve to help her had only intensified. But her efforts hadn't borne fruit yet.

He shrugged, as if it was indeed a small thing. "I tried to persuade her. Offered her incentives. Then I…" He rubbed a hand over his mouth, as if unsure of her reaction. "I sort of threatened her with being completely cut off from the rest of her family. I think it was a culmination of all three that finally brought success."

Yana laughed and then cried, feeling as if gravity had been stolen from under her. She knew how much he disliked her mother, how many bad memories were associated with her. How much he'd have hated even talking to her. And yet, he'd done it. For her peace of mind. For her happiness. She took his hands in hers. "I can't thank you enough."

"Now for the third piece," he announced, as if her gratitude made him uncomfortable.

"I'm ready," Yana said, her words a mere whisper compared to the loud thundering of her heart.

He placed a sheaf of papers on the coffee table in front of him. "These are custody papers. If you sign them, we'll share custody of Zara. You can have her for more than just a month. You can course correct me when I get it wrong. You and she can have each other without me in between."

Whatever high she'd been riding deflated and she crashed with a hard thud back into reality. "Why are you doing that?"

"Because I know how much you love her and I want you to have everything you want, Yana. I never want you to doubt your place in her life."

"Everything I want, Nasir?" she said, throwing his words back at him.

"Yes, everything. Including my heart, if you still want it."

Yana stared wordlessly.

"I'm in love with you, *habibi*." His gaze searched hers, studied her, seemed to devour her. Even now, confusion danced in his eyes and she wondered if he felt as untethered without her as she felt without him. "You're a sorceress, like in the dark magic tales of the old. Only instead of cursing me to a wretched existence, you brought me back to life. And if you'd let me, Yana—" now he was on his knees in front of her, his large hands on her thighs, his amber eyes glittering with such pride and devotion and love "—I'll show you how much I love you for the rest of our lives. Life without you is like words without emotions. You are my heart and soul, Yana. And I'm sorry it took me forever to realize that you were already and always mine. I was the one who had to grow worthy of you. Do you see?"

Tears filled and overflowed down her cheeks and he still couldn't stop talking. "And I'm so glad that you came to me, *habibi*. That you found me all over again. That you gave me another chance because now, finally, I see you and I'm so ready for the exquisite, fragile, prickly and precious thing that you are, love. I'm ready for all of you, sweetheart."

And then she was crying in earnest then, falling into his open, waiting arms, her shoulders shaking with these great, heaving sobs that seemed to rush out of her in a torrent, and Nasir just held her, feeling his own heart break and tear and come back together again, in some kind of loop, as if it could be made and unmade by her tears and her laughter and her joy and her promises.

It was a long while before she raised her head and looked at him. Her eyes and nose were all pink and splotchy and she was so achingly beautiful that a flicker of fear flashed through him. "Do you want to marry me?" she asked.

"Yes. Now. Tomorrow. I... I've wasted enough time as it is."

Then she hid her face in his chest and held him so tight that he was reminded of his daughter's hugs. "Zara's already your child as much as she's mine. Just give me a chance, too, Yana," he said with growing alarm that she hadn't really given him an answer. "Give me a chance to do this right."

"And if I have lots of demands and conditions and negotiations?"

"Only if you agree to all of mine."

She was kissing him now and laughing at the arrogance creeping back into his words and she thought she loved him most like this. "And what are they?"

"You'll hire a wedding planner so you don't get stressed out. You'll sleep in my bed even before then. And if you want babies, *habibi*, then we'll have babies, even if it means I turn old and decrepit by the time they go to college. But the wedding will be in two weeks, Yana. No more. I won't wait, not even for your sisters. And it will happen on the castle grounds."

Yana couldn't help smiling at how he'd tried to make it sound like a request and utterly failed.

"The castle? The whole world will know where you live, then. Because I don't want a hush-hush affair, Nasir. I want a big bang of a wedding. I want the whole world to see you're mine. At least a thousand people."

His eyes widened and he flinched and then recovered fast. "Fine. It will be gloriously extravagant and beautiful and loud, just like you are. And afterward, we'll move to a different castle then and we'll have two different ceremonies and you can invite the whole damned world if you want."

He picked her up and carried her to the bedroom and Yana buried her face in his neck, her heart full of joy. "I'm all sweaty," she said, offering a token protest, but Nasir was already unbuttoning his shirt and she pushed his hands away because that was her job.

And then he was inside her and they were laughing and she was still crying a little and she wondered if one could explode out of sheer happiness.

Hours later, in the dark of the night, Yana sat up and looked at the man next to her, deep in sleep. She'd tired him out with her incessant demands, she thought with a smile. Switching on the night lamp, she pulled her clutch open and took out the letter she'd been keeping for just such a moment.

Her heart was full of love and happiness and courage and she wanted to greet her Thaata like this. Settled in her own skin. Finally, accepting all of herself. It was all he'd ever wanted of her.

To my wonderful Yana,
    You're funny and brave and loyal and contrary and argumentative and reckless and messy and I know you keep stealing my cigars. But my darling girl, did I ever tell you that you're perfect just as you are?
    You're loved so much, Yana, I promise you. Try to love yourself a little, too.
    Thaata

Tears filled her eyes and fell down her cheeks, the world blurring and reforming and blurring all over again. Yana pressed the note to her chest, laughing and crying and wishing she could hug her grandfather just one more time.

"Yana?" Alarm crossing his face, Nasir gathered her to him until she was drowning in the familiar scent of him. His mouth was at her temple, tension vibrating through him. "What's wrong, *habibi*? What happened?"

Yana showed him the letter and buried her face in his bare chest. "He loved me all along, Nasir. I gave him such a hard time, and still, he loved me."

"Of course, he did, my love. As I keep telling you,

you're perfection indeed and your grandfather was a wise man to see it. As am I," he added with that exaggerated pride in his voice that he knew got her back up. "But if you still don't believe it, I'll tell you every hour. And show you every hour." His hands on her shoulders, he flipped them until she was straddling him and she could see those sparkling amber eyes fill with such tender reverence that she fell onto his chest.

"I love you, Nasir. And you're right. Let's get married. But I need at least a month, okay? Mira and Nush and Amina will kill me if I don't give us all enough time to look spectacular. Huma could design the dresses. Would you be mad if I wore black?"

And then while he grumbled about being thrown over for her sisters, she sat up, pressed her back to his chest and decided to call her sisters and share her good news.

When they arrived at Mira and Aristos's home a few weeks later with Zara in tow, Nasir made good on his promise to put up with her shenanigans whatever they comprised. He greeted Mira and Nush with that solemn look in his eyes, withstood Aristos's and Caio's inappropriately territorial questions about his feelings for Yana and then picked up her niece and nephew Eira and Eros in the cradle of both arms with a reverent care that only confirmed her own wishes to make their family bigger.

When he looked up and their eyes met and he showed that he understood her most urgent and fervent wish with a raised brow and a hungry look, Yana knew that her life couldn't possibly get any better.

* * * * *

#4177 CINDERELLA'S ONE-NIGHT BABY
by Michelle Smart

A glamorous evening at the palace with Spanish tycoon Andrés? Irresistible! Even if Gabrielle knows this one encounter is all the guarded Spaniard will allow himself. Yet, when the chemistry simmering between them erupts into mind-blowing passion, the nine-month consequence will tie her and Andrés together forever...

#4178 HIDDEN HEIR WITH HIS HOUSEKEEPER
A Diamond in the Rough
by Heidi Rice

Self-made billionaire Mason Foxx would never forget the sizzling encounter he had with society princess Bea Medford. But his empire comes first, always. Until months later, he gets the ultimate shock: Bea isn't just the housekeeper at the hotel he's staying at—she's also carrying his child!

#4179 THE SICILIAN'S DEAL FOR "I DO"
Brooding Billionaire Brothers
by Clare Connelly

Marriage offered Mia Marini distance from her oppressive family, so Luca Cavallaro's desertion of their convenient wedding devastated her, especially after their mind-blowing kiss! Then Luca returns with a scandalous proposition: risk it all for a no-strings week together...and claim the wedding night they never had!

#4180 PREGNANCY CLAUSE IN THEIR PAPER MARRIAGE
by Kate Hewitt

Honoring the strict rules of his on-paper marriage, Christos Diakis has fought hard to ignore the electricity simmering between him and his wife, Lana. Her request that they have a baby rocks the very foundations of their union. And Christos has neither the power—nor wish—to decline...

#4181 THE FORBIDDEN BRIDE HE STOLE
by Millie Adams
Hannah will do *anything* to avoid the magnetic pull of her guardian, Apollo, including marry another. Then Apollo shockingly steals her from the altar, and a dangerous flame is ignited. Hannah must decide—is their passion a firestorm she can survive unscathed, or will it burn everything down?

#4182 AWAKENED IN HER ENEMY'S PALAZZO
by Kim Lawrence
Grace Stewart never expected to inherit a palazzo from her beloved late employer. Or that his ruthless tech mogul son, Theo Ranieri, would move in until she agrees to sell! Sleeping under the same roof fuels their agonizing attraction. There's just one place their standoff can end—in Theo's bed!

#4183 THE KING SHE SHOULDN'T CRAVE
by Lela May Wight
Promoted from spare to heir after tragedy struck, Angelo can't be distracted from his duty. Being married to the woman he has always craved—his brother's intended queen—has him on the precipice of self-destruction. The last thing he needs is for Natalia to recognize their dangerous attraction. If she does, there's nothing to stop it from becoming all-consuming...

#4184 UNTOUCHED UNTIL THE GREEK'S RETURN
by Susan Stephens
Innocent Rosy Bloom came to Greece looking for peace. But there's nothing peaceful about the storm of desire tycoon Xander Tsakis unleashes in her upon his return to his island home! Anything they share would be temporary, but Xander's dangerously thrilling proximity has cautious Rosy abandoning all reason!

YOU CAN FIND MORE INFORMATION ON UPCOMING HARLEQUIN TITLES, FREE EXCERPTS AND MORE AT HARLEQUIN.COM.

HPCNMRB0124

Get 3 FREE REWARDS!

We'll send you 2 FREE Books plus a FREE Mystery Gift.

FREE Value Over $20

Both the **Harlequin® Desire** and **Harlequin Presents®** series feature compelling novels filled with passion, sensuality and intriguing scandals.

YES! Please send me 2 FREE novels from the Harlequin Desire or Harlequin Presents series and my FREE gift (gift is worth about $10 retail). After receiving them, if I don't wish to receive any more books, I can return the shipping statement marked "cancel." If I don't cancel, I will receive 6 brand-new Harlequin Presents Larger-Print books every month and be billed just $6.30 each in the U.S. or $6.49 each in Canada, a savings of at least 10% off the cover price, or 3 Harlequin Desire books (2-in-1 story editions) every month and be billed just $7.83 each in the U.S. or $8.43 each in Canada, a savings of at least 12% off the cover price. It's quite a bargain! Shipping and handling is just 50¢ per book in the U.S. and $1.25 per book in Canada.* I understand that accepting the 2 free books and gift places me under no obligation to buy anything. I can always return a shipment and cancel at any time by calling the number below. The free books and gift are mine to keep no matter what I decide.

Choose one: ☐ **Harlequin Desire**
(225/326 BPA GRNA)

☐ **Harlequin Presents Larger-Print**
(176/376 BPA GRNA)

☐ **Or Try Both!**
(225/326 & 176/376 BPA GRQP)

Name (please print)

Address   Apt. #

City   State/Province   Zip/Postal Code

Email: Please check this box ☐ if you would like to receive newsletters and promotional emails from Harlequin Enterprises ULC and its affiliates. You can unsubscribe anytime.

Mail to the **Harlequin Reader Service:**
IN U.S.A.: P.O. Box 1341, Buffalo, NY 14240-8531
IN CANADA: P.O. Box 603, Fort Erie, Ontario L2A 5X3

Want to try 2 free books from another series! Call 1-800-873-8635 or visit www.ReaderService.com.

*Terms and prices subject to change without notice. Prices do not include sales taxes, which will be charged (if applicable) based on your state or country of residence. Canadian residents will be charged applicable taxes. Offer not valid in Quebec. This offer is limited to one order per household. Books received may not be as shown. Not valid for current subscribers to the Harlequin Presents or Harlequin Desire series. All orders subject to approval. Credit or debit balances in a customer's account(s) may be offset by any other outstanding balance owed by or to the customer. Please allow 4 to 6 weeks for delivery. Offer available while quantities last.

Your Privacy—Your information is being collected by Harlequin Enterprises ULC, operating as Harlequin Reader Service. For a complete summary of the information we collect, how we use this information and to whom it is disclosed, please visit our privacy notice located at corporate.harlequin.com/privacy-notice. From time to time we may also exchange your personal information with reputable third parties. If you wish to opt out of this sharing of your personal information, please visit readerservice.com/consumerschoice or call 1-800-873-8635. **Notice to California Residents**—Under California law, you have specific rights to control and access your data. For more information on these rights and how to exercise them, visit corporate.harlequin.com/california-privacy.

HDHP23